UNDER A JUNGLE MOON

Byzantium Sky Press
Ellendale, DE, 19941

Under A Jungle Moon is a work of fiction. Any reference to historical events, real people, or real places are used fictitiously. Other names, characters, places, and events are products of the author's imagination, and any resemblance or similarity to actual events or places or persons, living or dead, is entirely coincidental and not intended by the author.

ISBN 978-1-955872-14-0 (paperback)
ISBN 978-1-955872-15-7 (eBook)

Library of Congress Control Number: 2022916534

First Byzantium Sky Press paperback edition: October, 2022

Cover & Interior design by Crystal Heidel, Byzantium Sky Press

Manufactured in the United States of America

Body of book is typeset in Garamond Premiere Pro
Decorative fonts in typeset Mrs Eaves Petite Caps and Timberline
Cover Design: Crystal Heidel

Cover Photographs:
Woman on Left: Jessica Felicio
Woman on Right: Shutterstock, Metamorworks
Rocks and Cliff face, Roberto Reposo, Unsplash.com
Waterfall & Leaves/Trees created in illustrator by Crystal Heidel
Various Star, Milky Way, & Moon images blended in background, Unsplash.com

UNDER A JUNGLE MOON

A NOVEL

KATHLEEN L. MARTENS

ACKNOWLEDGMENTS

Maribeth Fischer, irreplaceable, patient editor, superb writer, and novel class teacher who guided and inspired me to complete this novel.

Judy Catterton, story editor, who dedicated endless hours sharing her incisive insights, logic, and uncanny ability to understand a character's inner drive.

Nancy Powichroski Sherman, eagle-eyed copyeditor, for her invaluable feedback, patience, and guidance through the editing process.

Kristen J. Solleé, talented daughter and author, with the skillsets of writing and editing that enabled her to confidently guide me through my writing process for both *Really Enough, Wanderlust, Rising Women, Rising Tides,* and now, *Under a Jungle Moon.* Her creativity abounds and her wisdom and insights into people and life are invaluable. Thank you—you are cherished.

Jean Kempshall Aziz, brilliant, life-long, trusted friend who tirelessly read my chapters in the early years, giving me such solid, honest, on-target advice to shape the storyline in my pursuit of authenticity. Her decades as an educator, wise woman, and book clubber, and her sisterly love have proved priceless to me.

Sarah Barnett, talented writer and generous friend, who contributed her editing skills to the final draft of this book.

Christy Briedis, dear friend and reader, for her time and wisdom in helping me shape the characters. Her insights helped me to refine the storyline, to capture my intent, and the motivation and inner drive of each character.

Jane Klein, patient reader who took a fresh look at my many iterations. Her support and insights gave me confidence as I approached the final draft.

My friends and readers, who tirelessly read my chapters and iterations, giving me honest, on-target feedback and advice:

Jean Aziz
Christy Briedis
Jane Klein
Fran Mossberg
Kristen Janine Sollée
Judy Wood

Rehoboth Beach Writers Guild, for providing unparalleled support, encouragement, and writing opportunities to those fortunate enough to be members.

Novel Class Colleagues, talented writers who provided excellent feedback through the many iterations of this novel.

Seaside Scribes, the sisterhood of women writers and friends who have been so generous and loving as I pursued my later-in-life venture into writing. They keep it fun!

Crystal Heidel, owner of Byzantium Sky Press, for her faith in my work and outstanding creativity in designing the dramatic cover and interior for *Under a Jungle Moon*. Being in the hands of a dedicated publisher who is also a gifted designer and writer is a blessing to an author. She gets it! And to Byzantium Sky Press for providing professional services with a personal touch.

Steuart Martens, my loving husband—immeasurable gratitude for cheering me on in my passion for writing, and for his endless support throughout my pandemic publishing pursuits and beyond.

DEDICATION

I dedicate this book to people everywhere who have risen above gender-based oppression and endemic injustice. May this story encourage acceptance of others who are different from us as the path to a more loving world.

In memory of my mother who enjoyed a good suspenseful story, my father who taught me that I could, and to my loving husband, children, grandchildren, siblings, and women friends who are a powerful and gratifying foundation of safety and love in my life.

Dear Reader,

IN THE 1970S, DURING a fearless and spirited time in my young life, I was dropped by helicopter, along with my adventurous business partner, deep in the mountainous jungles of Irian Jaya, the Indonesian island now called Papua. Leaping onto a page right out of National Geographic, our assignment was to help bridge the extreme culture gap and promote cultural understanding between the indigenous populations and the American miners and their families at a copper mine project. As intercultural consultants, we worked among one of the few remaining societies in the world still living a "Stone Age" existence.

Nothing in my educational background in sociology, psychology, languages, or cultural studies, could have prepared my uninitiated young self for that assignment. The issues that arise when cultures clash and modern capitalism and technology impact previously isolated tribal peoples are complex. The challenges that face people from diverse cultures as they learn to live together in our shrinking world have captivated me ever since.

While living between Jakarta and Bangkok for several years, our company continued this line of work in other dramatic Indonesian islands where natural resources abound—from the Sumatran jungles to the equatorial island of Kalimantan (Borneo.) The fascinating peoples, exotic environments, and my experiences were shockingly eye-opening for a young untraveled post-graduate school woman who hailed from New England and grew up in New Jersey. This complex, ever-evolving world of intercultural challenges that persists today formed the backdrop for this book. That is where the truth ends, and the story begins.

Under a Jungle Moon is a work of fiction, informed by my experiences, but with a fictitious mining company, characters, tribes, cultural norms, and storyline spawned in my imagination. Culture clashes, acceptance, forgiveness, and the redemptive power of a mother's love are the messages that drive the outer life of the storyline and the inner life of the characters.

This novel had remained in utero for three decades since I wrote the first draft while waiting for my life to be quiet enough to give birth to it. Again, the book was delayed for the release of my first book, award-winning memoir, *Really Enough*, written with Margaret Zhao. Stricken with late stage, Lyme disease, I was blessed with the window to finally have the time to give life to my passion for writing and cultures. Herein lies the potential hidden beauty of the challenges of a chronic illness. I learned that opportunities could arise unexpectedly out of the ashes of life's trials when you ask yourself, "What can I do?" while ignoring the "Now look what I can't do."

With the Covid pandemic and our recent forced downtime, I published the novel, *Wanderlust* and a book of short stories, *Rising Women, Rising Tides*. And finally, three decades after I had begun the first draft, it was time to complete *Under a Jungle Moon*.

I'm wishing you the wisdom to find the unexpected opportunities to be bold or fulfill dreams in the seemingly stagnant or challenging times of your life.

With gratitude,
Kathleen L. Martens

UNDER
A
JUNGLE
MOON

CHAPTER 1

HIDDEN OBSESSION

Vanessa

STANDING AT THE WALL of windows, Vanessa watched the city of Los Angeles come alive. The gray mist lifted as the traffic thickened below like an infestation of ants. She flipped the wall switch, and the darkening blinds lowered, squeezing out the searing morning sun. Just how she liked it—dark, quiet, and alone.

Her *Turning Prism* television studio office was Vanessa's haven where she came to think, review segments for her TV show, and watch documentary footage before Tony and the film crew arrived. Taking the yellowed *Daily News* from the safe, Vanessa slipped it out of its plastic cover. The shocking headlines on a passenger's newspaper on her flight to Berkeley twenty years before were scorched into her memory. April 30, 1970.

No one could possibly connect her to the decades-old crime now, she thought. She'd long ago changed her natural self from a scarlet redhead into a brunette. That naïve co-ed had matured to become the world-renowned woman she was today.

Under the gaze of the ancient bronze Buddha that her life partner Tony had brought back from Thailand, Vanessa retrieved an 8mm movie projector from a lacquered wooden trunk. Before closing the lid, she dared to touch the cold metal grip of her old Bell and

Howell Zoomatic Camcorder she'd bought for her filmmaking class. The salesman had said the same model camera had filmed President Kennedy's murder. Could Vanessa have ever imagined the tragedy the camera would capture in her own life?

Regret churned inside her.

The Buddha's eyes seemed to follow her. If only you could bring *me* peace, she thought. Watching the aged two-and-a-half-minute film was her annual ritual, a necessary self-torture. With trembling hands, she threaded the narrow strip through the tracks in the projector and poured the first of her many cups of strong Kona coffee she'd traditionally consumed each morning.

Vanessa flipped the page on her desk calendar. How could it be April 30, 1990? Two decades, she thought, as the terror of that day swept through her body again. Endless efforts to identify the boy in the film had led Vanessa to a dead end. She would make another pitch for an eyewitness on her *What Did You See?* live segment at the wrap-up of today's TV show, *Exposé*—just like she'd done for years.

Curling into her white leather swivel chair, Vanessa nudged her stilettos off one-by-one onto the sea blue carpet and tucked her legs under her. Not bothering to lower the theater screen, Vanessa let the decades-old film cast a small dust-flecked rectangle onto the stucco wall. The images spread over the pocked, wavy surface turning the silent footage into an underwater nightmare.

Burning acid rose in Vanessa's throat as the old projector ticked on. Being an investigative reporter was not what she'd dreamed of for her life's career. With her usual disbelief and shame, she pictured her college-self capturing the footage.

After visiting the cloistered convent in Brooklyn where she'd grown up, Vanessa had taken the subway to the Marcy Avenue stop. She'd hoped to film some unique scenes in one of the nearby ethnic neighborhoods before her flight back to her California campus. The pressure was on to bring back the winning film footage to her college teammates Tony and Canyon. Was it pathetic to have craved their acceptance so much? She'd wanted to impress her friends—the only real friends she'd ever had. Perhaps, Tony would be her first romantic connection.

A sun-filled day in the old Brooklyn neighborhood came to life as twenty-year-old Vanessa filmed the streets of her father's former home where she'd been forbidden to go. Vanessa's father's words rose in her memory as she filmed. *You are not to go back to the old neighborhood! Understand me? They reject their own son; they can't have the joy of their only grandchild!*

With her movie camera running, Vanessa studied the streets of her father's Hasidic past. The trees were beginning to lose their white blossoms in the spring breeze. A sea of bushy-bearded men filled the busy avenue. With swaying curled tassels of hair at each ear, they wore long, black frock coats and large brimmed hats.

Two young scholars wearing yarmulkes sat on a nearby bench flipping through the pages of their books, fervently arguing about passages.

As Vanessa walked past them on the sidewalk, she recognized the holy volume from her childhood as the Talmud. The devout men appeared immune to the early morning cacophony of city noises that assaulted them—the beeps, whooshing air brakes, and rumbling of delivery carts. As she approached, they tucked in closer to each other and held hands up to halt the intrusion, clearly annoyed by her camera.

Across the street, a teenage boy jumped off a bus onto the curb and into the center of her lens. His red plaid flannel shirt, tattered jeans, and wool ski hat stood out in the Hasidic Jewish community, flagging that he was foreign to the neighborhood.

Vanessa's jeans and hooded sweatshirt with her *Turning Prism* college filmmaking team logo on the sleeves drew attention too. Wouldn't the footage of such contrasts work well for her Berkeley film school competition? Perfect for the theme—Culture. The scene of the aging religious man's slow, almost holy pace contrasted with the upbeat, bobbing body of the gangly teen would be unique.

She studied the extreme disparities in their garb through her lens—the elderly man wearing a black, formal, flowing coat. The Jewish prayer shawl with its knotted fringes on men walking along the street and their flat-brimmed fedoras added to the fascinating scene. She remembered the shawl's name—a *tallit*. Round skullcaps topped the heads of the young men on the bench reading, while the boy from the bus from another neighborhood wore a blue and white wool ski cap. Could the cultures be any different or more fascinating?

The excitement increased as Vanessa scanned the streets that were coming alive with cross-cultural comparisons. How did all these traditions evolve? What did they symbolize? She would do more research when she returned to school. These were thoughts she'd never had before; they intrigued her. All the dramatic differences were woven together into the fabric of the Brooklyn ethnic neighborhood. Multi-colored and monochrome threads entwined with the New York City backdrop of benches and buses, taxis and tree-lined streets, shops and subway stops with deep staircases that led to the bowels of the frenetic city. The script she would write to accompany the film began to weave together in her mind.

Vanessa drew into a tighter ball on the sleek leather cushion of her office chair and viewed the moment in the film that had changed everything.

Sweeping the lens across the narrow street, she had focused on an old man carrying a book. His dense beard masked his face, leaving only a pair of deep-set, dark eyes below his hat's brim and a touch of pink where his mouth was buried deep in a silver nest. His every movement rode the edge of slow motion. He had a gentleness about him.

The boy followed him with bouncing steps and one hand in his jeans back pocket.

Turning in the boy's direction, the older man hesitated while searching through his book.

Approaching the aged gentleman, the young teen stopped, and then moved swiftly as the man dropped his book.

It appeared the boy would help the gentleman retrieve it from the gutter. A smile of thanks passed over the elderly stranger's face. There was a familiarity in his warm smile.

Her shoulders dropped as Vanessa's guilt over being in the forbidden neighborhood settled into relief. The scene of the old Hasidic Jew and the kind teenage boy from another community touched her. This could be the winning film clip that would launch her career behind a camera.

The excitement at finding something she loved to do after her sequestered life, homeschooled in the cloistered convent, rushed through her. Vanessa thought she could create a new life as a photographer or videographer.

Then it all changed.

Swallowing through her dry throat, Vanessa grasped the camera handle tighter and kept the boy in her sights.

The young teen in the film pulled something from his pocket.

Alarm gripped Vanessa. Was it a weapon? Could the boy's intent have changed so rapidly? Focused on the glint of the metal item, she vacillated. Was she witnessing a crime or an act of kindness? Should she capture whatever was happening on film, or should she run?

Using the book to lure him, the boy grasped the aged man's earlock and wrenched him off balance.

The gentleman stood suspended, held upright only by the lock of hair. He called out in pain.

Then *snip*.

Vanessa zoomed in with her camcorder and captured the attack on film as the boy cut the lock of hair beside the stunned man's ear with a long pair of sewing scissors. The victim toppled back onto the curb along the grassy strip that edged the sidewalk, bringing the boy with him. They were lost in the blast of a bus horn and a momentary blur of fumes.

She ran across the narrow street to help.

The old man was sprawled out flat on the ground next to a tree with the scissors embedded in his shoulder. Red was oozing over his white shirt, his silver beard absorbing the crime. Beside him, the flee-ing boy's bloody wool ski hat lay in the gutter.

The injured man attempted to speak. "Are . . . you?"

Vanessa lowered her eyes. She couldn't look at him. Her father's words were always there, warning her, *You are not to go back to the old neighborhood!* She should call for help. She was torn. Tend to the man, or follow the boy? Unable to face the old man, she ran after the teen, calling, "Wait!"

The images in the film moved up and down with her youthful hurried steps as she followed the teen. Then he stopped. Their eyes met. They froze and shared a moment of confused connection. Then he ran again.

In the shaking footage, Vanessa filmed the escaping boy with a swas-tika etched skin-deep into the hair on the back of his head.

Young Vanessa stood in the street, remembering her father as he'd torn up the photo of her grandparents and burned it in the fireplace. The old man's pleas for help were overshadowed by her father's words: *They disown me for marrying your beautiful mother? I disown them. I burn their memory. You are forbidden to go there, you understand?*

Still, she returned to the old man.

"Please, help me, miss?" He reached out his hand to Vanessa.

She withdrew, stunned.

The old gentleman's voice was rusty and weak. He tried to get up. His pleading eyes, red around the edges, were magnified through his rimless, crooked glasses. His look of agony pulled at her heart, but she detested the Hasidic community on her father's behalf. She knew their rejection had caused his misery. Because of them, her father had taken his own life.

"Please!" The old man looked at her as though he knew her. His eyes widened.

Fear and anger battled inside her, reminding her of the car crash outside her parents' apartment window. Images of her father's head against the steering wheel and his twisted neck still haunted her. It was no accident, they'd said. He'd left a note.

The old man tried to speak again. His lips released an utterance, almost a word, a whisper that Vanessa strained to understand.

A woman came out of her door onto the stoop with a trash bag and spotted the victim. She screamed—the scream that should have been Vanessa's. Trembling, as a crowd of passersby gathered, she flipped her hood up to hide her distinctive scarlet hair and pushed up her college sweatshirt sleeves that read *Turning Prism*.

Stumbling back, Vanessa disengaged from the old man's eyes. Sirens whined close by, and policemen's voices cut through the gathering crowd that surrounded the victim. "Step back, folks. Step back."

Hidden behind an ancient oak tree, Vanessa stared through the lens with waves of nausea and regret that she hadn't tried to stop the crime. Her hands shook under the weight of the camera and her realization. She'd read in the news about the Brooklyn gang's hateful rite of passage—cutting the earlock from a Hasidic man as a requirement for membership.

At first, Vanessa had no clue that she was witnessing the hateful hazing. The film footage she thought would show a kind gesture between people of different cultures had become a nightmare of hatred and cultural divide.

Images in the film showed flashes of sidewalk, sky, and row houses as she'd fled the dreadful scene with the camera still running.

Reliving that long-ago morning through the flickering scenes on her office wall, the chilling sensations returned. Vanessa now knew her grandparents' rejection wasn't the only cause of her father's misery. His note had made it clear. Her mother's repeated absences had betrayed her father's sacrifice to leave all he'd known to be with her. Because of his heartbreak, he'd taken his life. Why wasn't his own child enough for him to stay? That thought had disturbed Vanessa since childhood.

Wiser now, with years of experience in intercultural research, Vanessa understood her grandparents' disapproval of her parents' improbable marriage—the son of an honored Hasidic Rabbi and a young Irish Catholic, free-spirited musician. Her grandparents believed they were protecting their way of life, their son's legacy, and all they knew. And didn't it turn out they were right about Vanessa's mother and father's fateful match?

Peeling away her perspiring leg stuck to the leather chair, Vanessa tugged at her short black dress and watched the final scene she'd filmed.

She'd stepped out onto the street again. From her oblique angle, young Vanessa filmed the scene of the Hasidic man's worn-out, black shoes, rocking back and forth as a sympathetic passerby comforted the victim in his arms. A thick cluster of black-coated Hasidic men stood vigil as two police officers interviewed witnesses. The injured man was taken away in an ambulance. She'd hoped the prank of prejudice hadn't caused the old gentleman serious injury.

Vanessa clinked her coffee cup down onto the glass side table and replayed the cop's voice in her mind. "Hey! Hey! Redhead! You with the camera!"

As the familiar scene unfolded on her office wall, she checked her watch. It was getting late. Tony would be there soon to line up the sequence for today's exposés. She dialed her baby-blue, retro Princess phone. "Tony, what's your ETA, honey?"

"Hey, babe. Depending on our lovely LA traffic, be there in thirty. Plenty of time to review the clips for today's main segment."

"OK, see you soon. Drive safely." Well-practiced in controlling the tone of her voice, Vanessa surprisingly heard it crack.

"You OK, honey?"

She sighed. "Oh, it's nothing, just that day again. I'm retrieving the usual script for today's *What Did You See?* segment."

"April *already*? I get it. Wish *that one* would let you go. See you in half an hour. I have a leftover hug from last night if it'll help."

"Oh, Tony, always." She hung up. Could the man be any sweeter or more understanding? Could Vanessa love him any more than she did? Ironic. His affection often caused her guilt to surge. Could she have been a bigger fraud when it came to what had really happened twenty years ago on that April day?

Reverse, forward, reverse, forward—Vanessa obsessively clicked the metal rod on the side of the old green projector, reviewing the frames that had changed everything. The story's horror unfolded in stuttering clicks—the boy's lithe teen body, the scissors poised. Then the bus and the blur of the boy and the man falling out of sight.

Advancing the footage, Vanessa found the second scene she sought. Click, click, forward, reverse, forward, reverse—she watched the boy turn his head over his shoulder, meeting her camera's eye as he ran away.

Flipping the projector switch, Vanessa watched him turn toward her, turn away, toward her, away. The swastika appeared and disappeared as the culprit fled.

Flecks and threads flickered in dancing patterns on the wall as she let the tail end of the film finish—slap, slap, slap. It punished the old projector, as she suffered her usual remorse.

In the chaos of the crowd, no one had seen Vanessa's personal crime. It was not punishable by law, only punishable by her shame and deep regrets.

The moment she'd seen those newspaper headlines on the flight back to UC Berkeley, Vanessa's life had changed.

"HASIDIC RABBI MOSHE COHEN SLAIN: Redheaded Witness Sought For Questioning."

Vanessa could recite the article from memory. Perched with a perfect view from her front porch, a neighbor described seeing the old man grasp the boy to prevent his fall. Toppling back, the man brought his unsteady young assailant with him. The woman on the porch couldn't identify the face of the perpetrator. She saw only the flash of the scissors that the police found embedded in the old man's shoulder. Not the cause of death. The ragged remnant of a broken street stop sign was sticking up menacingly through the thin grass along the curb, the witness had reported. As the aged man hit the ground, it had its revenge, taking the feeble man as its own innocent victim.

The witness had only seen one brief glimpse of the boy's profile as he'd fled the scene. Flailing his head doglike into one flannel shoulder and then into the other, he'd tried to wipe the bright red evidence from his face. The witness reported seeing a young woman in the crowd with a movie camera, wearing a hooded sweatshirt, who'd tried to chase down the offender.

It was a mere instant, yet Vanessa's eternity.

From that day forward, she'd never once put her eye to the camera lens. Vanessa passed that role on to Tony, her classmate, film-team member, and her first and only romantic interest. Driven by her passion for unveiling clashes of culture and crimes of hate and discrimination, Vanessa had taken on scriptwriting, interviewing, and film directing. Her roommate Canyon, a social anthropology major, was the perfect consultant for their documentarian film team.

Walking to the wall mirror behind her office desk, Vanessa ran her fingers through her dark brown dyed hair. Along with her name change, Vanessa's new hair color had provided the cover-up she'd needed for her life on the other side of the country. Still, she'd felt forever suspended on a fragile wire crimped with lie after lie since that day, so profoundly against her religious upbringing, her true self in constant conflict with her actions as a young college student. Could she ever make amends without destroying who she was today and everyone she loved?

Yes, she would make yet another pitch for information on the antisemitic homicide, as she had in previous years. If she shared the actual film evidence, she would risk unraveling her entire life's façade. Still, she would use her popular segment, *What Did You See?*, to again attempt to find the boy who would now be a man.

Can one incident change the direction of a person's life? That one incident had. Vanessa understood that ever since that day, she'd pursued the flaws and lies of others to compensate for her own.

She'd watched. She'd stood there and watched as her estranged grandfather was killed on a Brooklyn sidewalk.

CHAPTER 2

RETURNING SPIRITS

Lukeem

FREEING HER GRASS skirt from the grasp of thorns, Lukeem cleared her way through the rocky, overgrown thicket. With no path to follow, she pushed the dripping broad leaves aside and tore at the gnarled vines. As she ran, insect-infested logs crumbled into dust under her weight. Branches stung her bare breasts, but she ignored the pain. Above her, Lukeem tracked the enormous flying creature she'd seen once before with the faces of the sky spirits inside.

She had to follow.

Lukeem might finally prove to her mate, Kralu, that she hadn't lied—she'd been honored by the appearance of the sky spirits in the past, and now they'd returned.

Her woven head sack, heavy with her gatherings, was fastened around her forehead and hung down Lukeem's back as she tilted her eyes skyward. Losing sight of the creature as it vanished in the dense canopy of trees above, Lukeem focused on its powerful fluttering sound until it reappeared. It had the body of a peculiar being with odd-shaped legs and no wings, yet with top feathers that whirled and a small spinning feather on its pointed tail. A giant bird? A huge insect? The markings on its side made Lukeem's eyes go wide. It was the same sharp-edged pattern she'd painted on her cave wall from memory after she'd first spotted the flying creature five rainy seasons ago—a patch of blue sky splattered with shining stars beside many red and white flowing fronds.

Running beyond her familiar tribal area, Lukeem's rapid breath and thundering heart blended with the whizzing noise overhead. She'd tracked the flying creature from dawn to near exhaustion until the sun shone through the greenery overhead. The swishing sound led her to a wall of twisted vines.

Lukeem peered through the thick vegetation, straining to see into the curious clearing, a perfectly-round, barren area mysteriously shaved out of the undergrowth. No vegetation, no vines, no trees. An openness strange to her, allowing her to see across the exposed space. Lukeem tried to imagine the distance to the other side of the open area. Having no experience with *emptiness* in her jungle world, she nodded her head, taking imaginary steps. It seemed more than fifty strides wide. The space gave a freedom to her eyes she'd never known living in the impenetrable jungle.

As though stung by the poisonous green wasp, Lukeem's muscles lost their power to move. The flying creature hovered above. On the ground, encircling the edge of the clear space, the hollow eyes of many skulls peered back at her. She'd once overheard the men describe this revered space. It was clear, empty, welcoming, edged only with the remains of her honored ancestors. The drumming in her chest wouldn't calm. She'd found the men's secret ceremonial circle, its location forbidden to be whispered into a woman's ear, its soil forbidden to be crossed by a woman's footstep.

Halfway across the clearing, the enormous bird with its constant whooshing sound floated to earth and landed. Small openings appeared on each side, and two mystical beings jumped down to the spongy earth. They appeared to be human, but Lukeem knew they were beyond mortal. They were the sky spirits with powers to command the magnificent bird. They were the sky spirits from above who had brought the gifts of food that had saved her people in the old days of hunger.

Lukeem was awed by the pale faces of the spirits—one with pieces of the sky for eyes. Towering tall, as legend had said, only their heads and hands were bare. Their body coverings were the light color of the tubers she'd daily dug from the ground to sustain her and her son Abruce before he'd disappeared. The loss of her only child invaded her thoughts, but Lukeem pushed the boy's memory aside as she'd learned to do.

The two sky spirits spotted her.

Lukeem pressed the palms of her hands to her bare chest to keep the thundering inside her. Five rainy seasons ago, when she'd shared the news of her first sighting of the sky spirits' flying creature with her mate Kralu, he'd shunned her for her lies. "No sky spirit would appear to a *woman*. You are wicked to lie that way," he'd said.

Now Lukeem gazed at the long-awaited sky spirits up close, remembering her tribal stories. In her grandfather's times, when asked by the tribal honored one if they would return, the sky spirits' leader had nodded and awkwardly repeated the tribal words. "We will return."

They had kept their promise.

Just as her grandfather had told her as a child, the sky spirits standing before her glowed with skin the color of smooth, white river stones. One had shiny hair like the morning sun, the other, dark, like her people's hair, but shimmering and straight. Did the spirits cover all but their hands and faces to protect us, so we are not blinded by their full light?

"Hello, beautiful!" The sky spirit with hair the color of the night spoke with a gentle rhythm, different from her tribal men. The first sound of the sky spirits' words was also unlike her own, not one she knew how to form. Lukeem searched her mind for a common sound and found it—the noise of the striped lizard as someone comes upon it suddenly—*hhhheh.*

Heh-lo. Was that the spirits' special greeting? Bee-u-tee-ful. The utterance carried no meaning for her. Drawn by the delight in the sky spirits' eyes and the beckoning of their arms, Lukeem desired to greet them in the sky spirits' way. She shared their greeting, copying the tone, suspending the second beat. "Heh-looooo bee-u-tee-ful."

Watching the sky spirits bend in half with joyous laughter, Lukeem drew in a deep breath and threw her arms to the sky. "Heh-looooo bee-u-tee-ful!" She stepped closer. The stories of their kindness heard as a child from the elders encouraged Lukeem. She watched them smile and move their arms in the air, pleading her to advance in their direction. Still, Lukeem couldn't leave the safety of the entwined thicket at the edge of the clearing.

Could it be wrong? She'd only wanted to delight in the precious gifts they might bring her, as they had in the time of her father before Lukeem was born. They'd given her tribe food for their thinning children, sweet brown treats, strange tools, and hope for her suffering tribe in the times of failing hunts when animals had become scarce. Maybe sharing the sky spirits' gifts with her tribe would make them accepting of her again.

As if there were a mighty wind at her back, Lukeem entered the men's ceremonial space. Could she lessen her wickedness with a gentler step? She kept her footfall light, dancing with her elated feet flying under her. She danced as her tribesmen did after a successful hunt or when pleading for the sky spirits to return.

They had returned!

Lukeem's eyes ran over the bird's body with no feathers, its smooth skin glinting in the daylight. A shiver of happiness passed through her. Lukeem's feet became heavy again as though her mate's pleading hands held them to the ground. The hollow eyes of the ancestors' skulls encircling her sent a warning, but the sky spirits smiled and called to her.

"Hello! Come see the helicopter."

The sky spirit spoke with more sounds she'd never heard—sky spirits' words. The taller one with hair like the morning sun waved, nodded his head, and pointed. Lukeem thought she understood. He beckoned her to come closer to their flying creature. The enormous bird waited only twenty paces away. Or was it an insect as tall as two sky spirits? Its peculiar top-feather mesmerized her, slowly spinning, *whoop, whoop, whoop.*

Like the mammoth blue moth's wings, a fluttering whispered down Lukeem's arms. She lifted her chin to look into the eyes of the dark-haired sky spirit.

The sky spirits said more friendly words that she couldn't fathom. The sun-haired spirit pointed at the massive bird. "Helicopter." His smile, sky eyes, and extended arms with palms up invited her, compelled her.

She tried to repeat the strange word. "Heh-li-cop-ter." As a woman, Lukeem felt honored yet ashamed to speak so boldly to a sky spirit, thus breaking tribal tradition. Still, it seemed to please them.

Mere paces would bring her to them. Her feet urged her and she moved closer to the magical spirit bird. She was in their protection, and weren't they commanding her?

Moving her tongue, Lukeem mimicked the lizard's sound to shape the words. "Heh-loooo. Bee-u-tee-ful."

As she approached, the sky spirits again broke into friendly laughter like women. They did not have the usual quiet nature of the men of her tribe. They didn't scowl and turn their heads away at her boldness. She'd pleased them. If only Kralu were here to see them. He would understand she hadn't lied. He would see the sky spirits had welcomed *her*, a woman.

Lukeem succumbed, stepping closer to the dark-haired sky spirit.

"OK. I feel a little strange, Brad, you know, her being bare-breasted and all. I mean, I know it's natural here . . . and she's beautiful. And she did call *me* beautiful."

The sky spirits laughed.

"Help me out here, buddy."

"Traditional greeting is a western-style handshake. Then they place their right hands over their own hearts to add sincerity to the greeting. I don't know about the traditions of these more remote tribes," the light-haired spirit spoke. "Pretty awkward. Start with the handshake and follow her lead, Jim. You don't want to make a mistake and send the wrong signal."

"Yikes. OK. I'm game. Don't want to be rude." The dark-haired sky spirit shook Lukeem's hand, then hesitated. It was her honor to be greeted by the sky spirit. She released his grip and placed her hand on his chest, waiting for him to respond. His heart fluttered faster under Lukeem's palm. No one had ever looked at her in such a way before. Holding his gaze, she sensed his fear but felt no danger, so she smiled.

"Holy shit, Brad. She wants me to . . . this is so weird. If I did this at home . . . well."

Would he complete the traditional greeting?

He did, placing his hand over her heart. Lukeem was honored.

"What's the glow on her skin and the smoky-bacon scent, Brad?"

"Rendered wild pig fat keeps them warm in the mountain air," the light-haired one answered.

"Seems she's not the least bit self-conscious. But I sure am." The dark-haired one laughed. He pointed to himself. "Jim." Then he pointed at Lukeem and lifted his shoulders.

She understood. He wanted to know her name. She lowered her head. "Lukeem."

"Hey, her name's Lukeem. This is amazing. A naked woman in a grass skirt standing right in front of me, just cool as can be. It was enough to see the naked tribesmen, wearing those long, twisted gourds over their you-know-whats. And the tribal women at the mine site are required to wear those white bras. They run away when any westerner approaches."

"You're new, Jim. You'll get used to it . . . maybe. This tribe, being so isolated, and her reaction to us, clearly says they've had little if any, contact with the outside world since the incident during World War Two." The light-haired sky spirit shrugged. "And I doubt there were many Allied troops in this remote area back then. This had to be an isolated accident, a miscalculation of the supplies drop point. That's what the missionary, Father Carey, said."

"Can you imagine? Let's see how she likes our chopper."

The sky spirit Jim encouraged her once more. "Want to sit in the helicopter? Don't be afraid."

Lukeem listened with fascination, aching to understand his words. "Hel-li-cop-ter."

"Amazing you spotted this place, Brad."

"We never had any reason to come up this high until we decided to build a second tram. Well, not true. The former pilot scanned the area on the other side of the waterfall five years ago when the mine was first built. It's still easy to miss this clearing under the denseness of trees. It's the only bare land on the entire mountain range."

"Brad, is it true the new copper and gold discovery is massive on this side of the mountain?"

"Yeah. They think maybe the world's largest."

Lukeem watched as the sky spirit Jim bent over and picked up one of the gifts sent to her people so long ago.

"Damn, look at this, Brad, an empty K-ration. Canned chopped eggs and ham. From World War Two. So this was a cargo cult?"

"Yup. Planes must have dropped supplies here for our soldiers." The spirit with hair like sunlight spoke. "The indigenous peoples assumed the food and supplies were gifts from the sky spirits."

Lukeem watched the light-haired spirit sweep his arm across the open space.

"Tribal peoples all over the South Pacific thought they could lure the planes back by keeping the circles clear. They even created more circles exactly like the soldiers had cleared for their supply drops. Fascinating. Anthropologists have a field day with these cultural phenomena."

"So they kept carving out this circle, expecting the sky spirits to return? Lucky for us. Now we don't have a clearing job to do."

Ready to move closer to the magnificent bird, Lukeem lifted one foot and listened to the senseless utterances.

"Wait, Brad, then she must think *we're* gods. Like supermen?"

"I think that's why our present company has that glow on her face."

"But I'm concerned she's thin compared to the native women working in the garden at the mine site." Sky spirit Jim spoke.

"Father Carey says they're having a period of food scarcity. The wildlife scattered. He believes that all the mining commotion caused their hunts to fail these past five years. I imagine the original piling pounding shook this entire area to its roots."

"Damn. And ongoing explosions can't help. Does the company know about this, Brad?"

"Sorry to say, Jim, they're not particularly known for cultural sensitivity. I hope the new security director, Scott, will have a different attitude. The last guy was prejudiced and culturally ignorant to the max."

Lukeem could listen to them all day. She moved closer to hear the light-haired leader's words and attempted to say his name. "Br-ad."

"Lukeem said your name, Brad. She looks at us with such awe. I hate to disillusion her. We're just a couple of American guys. It's like how we would feel if a Martian landed in Texas, right? Except we wouldn't assume they were gods. And what if you'd never seen a plane or a helicopter or anything modern—even people in clothes?"

Lowering her head, Lukeem humbled herself again as the dark-haired spirit Jim turned to her. He gazed at Lukeem and fanned his fingers back and forth. "Don't be afraid, sweetheart. Come see the helicopter. We won't hurt you."

"I love seeing her face all lit up." The light-haired sky spirit, Brad, smiled at her in a way that gave her courage. She would do it.

"Imagine if she saw the copper mine and the town. Does she speak the same dialect as our native workers? We have to take her down for a ride, Brad. Like a little anthropological study."

"Not sure, as the company's pilot, I'd do that, Jim. A young native hid out in the chopper some years ago. When I heard about it, I was concerned about how he would ever return to his tribe again. We need to be more sensitive to their cultural norms. We've disturbed their lives enough already. Probably in ways we don't even know."

Spirit Jim extended his pale hand to Lukeem. "But we could bring her right back, Brad."

CHAPTER 3

FACING FORTY

Vanessa

"VANESSA?"

At the sound of Tony's voice in the hallway, Vanessa returned the projector to the lacquered chest. Tony knew the story of that day two decades ago—the truth but not the whole truth. He knew about the crime on that Brooklyn street, and he knew about Vanessa's search for the perpetrator. But he knew nothing about the victim. He had no idea that the old man wasn't just a rabbi from the Hasidic neighborhood. There was more to the story.

Tony knew only the illusion of the woman he loved, she thought. The most authentic thing about Vanessa was her love for him. "Just a sec, honey." Lowering the massive screen with shaky hands, Vanessa teed up the video for the day's main segment and unlocked her office door.

"Ten minutes, guys," the director, Freddie, called down the hallway.

Tony entered the office and kissed Vanessa. "Good morning, sweetheart. OK, let's get the exposé ready for prime time. What else do we have today?" He sat down at the editing console at the far end of her office. "You were up early, babe."

"Yes, the *What Did You See?* segment is ready." She kissed his neck from behind. "I reviewed the script. Well, it hasn't changed."

Lingering with her arms wrapped around his shoulders, she took a deep breath and released it. He was her rock. That made her nearly laugh. No one would guess that from the outside. Her public image loomed large over her reality.

Vanessa imagined sitting in the spotlight on stage in her famous leather chair, reading the details of a crime each week. She'd ask for any eyewitnesses to come forward, and then field the dozens of quack calls and good witnesses on her private line afterward. But this spring day always resurrected that familiar twist in her stomach. It ripped back the scab on the painful memory and had produced no clues for years.

"Crazy, it's another year already. I don't know why that case is so important to you. But I get it. After all the good work you've done, it's hard to have one left on the books. It pulls at you, right?"

Vanessa ignored the remark. She felt Tony's back tense as he edited the new film footage for the main story. He focused on the little girl's trembling mouth as she related the details of being stolen from her tribal reservation. The child's voice was so fragile that the words crawled inside Vanessa. She squeezed Tony's shoulders. Only the judge and jury would see the child's testimony, but these excerpts had left them both deep in thought.

"Cut. That's a tough one to take." Tony deleted the scene. "Well, it won't happen to another child. This kidnapping ring is busted."

Vanessa understood what Tony was feeling while watching the film footage he'd taken. The young Native American girl, Kima, would resurrect his thoughts of having children. She saw the familiar look as he searched the child's face. It had happened off and on in their years together.

Witnessing the ten-year-old in the interview reminded Vanessa of being taken from her own home after her father died. She would have been just a little older than the Native American girl.

What would a child of theirs look like? Tony's dark Italian good looks or Vanessa's childhood soft red hair, a spray of freckles across her high cheekbones, and her green eyes? Vanessa's chest constricted. She ran her fingers through her hair and tried to focus.

Early in their careers, they'd agreed that investigating crime, corruption, and culture clashes around the world made their lives too hectic, unstable, and plain dangerous to have children. And marriage? Too traditional. Children? They were too young, too poor, too busy building our careers—and now, maybe too late?

Abstaining from motherhood also served a second purpose for Vanessa—she would never risk being like her own estranged mother.

"She's adorable, isn't she?" Tony turned.

"A darling." Vanessa closed her eyes and sighed. Amid the noise of Vanessa's hectic work, her lies had silently burrowed into her very cells. Now they were resurrecting while working on this case with the kids. So many of their investigations came with heartbreak. The ones that involved children were the worst.

"Do you think we've made a mistake, Van?" Tony said. "No marriage, no kids? Looking back, it's hard to remember making those decisions."

She put her hand to his cheek. "Oh, honey, I don't know. We did what we did, but we have each other and meaningful work now. And think of how many kids we've helped." Vanessa moved behind him again. Avoiding his eyes, she massaged his tense shoulders. It wasn't just their lifestyle that precluded her wanting children, Vanessa thought. She owed Tony long-overdue honesty about the well-kept secrets from her past, but the reveal would come with too high a price tag. She wasn't ready to share her confessions.

"Maybe you're right. I guess it's just me pushing forty and second-guessing my life."

Vanessa had never wanted her personal life in the spotlight, in the hands of the dogged press. Too late. Winning an Oscar at nineteen for their documentary with scenes of the Kent State Massacre prevented them having a discreet life. Being at the right place and time had launched their filmmaking into the limelight.

Vanessa had been terrified when she'd slipped yesterday in an interview with *The New York Times*. It had just come out when asked about her family history. It wasn't like Vanessa to blurt. In her interviews, she was "controlled, cautious, and considered," as the *Newsweek* magazine article had said last month. "I don't have a moth—" It was clear that the word she'd tried to swallow was *mother*. What had been the question anyway? Vanessa couldn't remember. She only remembered the shield she'd thrown up to prevent the questioning from going further.

The thought of the carefully constructed dead-end the press would find if they dug into her childhood made her shudder. She wouldn't let herself think about her mother's tabloid life. It threatened Vanessa more than any of her treacherous investigations.

And then the awards. That kind of attention made Vanessa worry. It wasn't her embarrassment or humiliation; it was the pain she would cause Tony, his career, and his reputation should the truth be revealed. Her entire team would be tainted too.

The interviewer had continued his questions. "Would you like to tell us more about your mother? I'm not sure I know anything about your childhood."

Vanessa imagined the words laid out before her on the newspaper, above the fold. She knew firsthand from her relentless pursuit of others when an investigator hit that proverbial wall, they would endlessly search until they found that one loose stone they'd missed. One pull and her life would collapse—too much to hide, too much at stake. She'd quickly redirected the interview, a skill at which Vanessa excelled. The strategy ensured that the facts of her past would be lost in the importance of their latest exposé, her recent nomination for Woman of the Year, or her upcoming ceremony for The World Truth in News Award.

Vanessa had steeled herself against her tender childhood realities and sudden abandonment through a lifetime of dedicated practice. The memories of feeling socially awkward, the first time she'd left her cloistered convent home to go to Berkeley, rushed in. Maybe her innocence had attracted the young handsome Italian boy in their freshman year. She panicked that Tony, the only man who'd ever loved her, even admired her, would discover she'd concealed her truth. Her scandalous mother's reputation would certainly overshadow *Turning Prism's* good work.

"Two minutes," the director warned, and Vanessa took her position on the white leather chair on stage. She furtively pulled her sleek, fitted, black dress down to keep the shoulders from rising up on camera and in an attempt to cover some measure of her thighs. Yes, the "little black dress," indeed. Vanessa was not quite used to the audacity of wearing the new short dress style on the set, but secretly she enjoyed defying the norm. Tony always said she had the legs for it. So sweet. As the "face in front," she worked to wear it well. It was simply part of their job, part of their allure. Vanessa despised the industry pressures and the "show" required to get the spotlight to shine on their documentaries and exposés. It was a price she had to pay, her assistant, Edward, had constantly reminded her.

A familiar moment of self-consciousness returned as the camera zoomed in on her. A tacky touch of moisture formed on her upper lip from the heat of the lights. Was everything in place?

Her hair and make-up guy, Clark, swept up behind her, patted her lip dry, and touched up her lipstick. "There you go, Vanessa."

"Thank you, Clark." She inhaled and exhaled as if blowing out a candle. Any nervousness passed quickly. Vanessa was in her element. Lovely irony, she thought, that I make my living from excavating the truth, yet spend my life eluding it.

Freddie pointed to Vanessa and mouthed, "And three, two, one."

She was on. "Good evening, and welcome to tonight's *Exposé.* I'm your host, Vanessa Gold, and tonight we are taking a raw and intimate look at a story of Native American children."

She went on autopilot. Following the teleprompter until the segment wound down, the unused footage of the young girl's escape and testimony ran in the background of Vanessa's mind. She had painfully learned the skill of detachment, the only way to cope with the kinds of issues she dealt with every day.

"Cut!" Freddie yelled. The light flashed for their commercial break. The studio broke open with familiar sounds of clinking spoons in coffee cups and murmurs about angles and lights.

"Nice job, hon. Really tough." Tony blew her a kiss.

Nodding, Vanessa smiled at Tony, who studied her with moist eyes from his perch on the stool in front of her.

Why was it pressing on her *now* to tell him her truths? How could it make things anything but worse?

He winked and sent her one of his familiar crooked smiles, one side of his mouth pulled back, accenting a dimple no grown man should still have. Pushing his dark hair back, he flashed her a thumbs-up close to his chest and launched an air kiss. Tony hadn't lost that disarming charm he'd been known for when she'd first met him in their first year at Berkeley.

Vanessa felt a twinge of conscience. She smiled back with a churning stomach, still working to move past her emerging apprehension. Glancing at her watch, the date instantly struck a chord again. She drew in a quick breath. If only she'd screamed at the sight of the scissors. How could she have known? Among all the men on the street that day, the victim was the grandfather Vanessa hadn't seen since she was a little girl—an old, bearded man she wouldn't recognize after so many years. But hadn't her grandfather recognized her? Hadn't he tried to whisper her name, *Colleen*?

In hindsight she realized she was watching the last moments of her grandfather's life. If it had been anywhere else, her instincts would have been different, she thought. But standing in that forbidden neighborhood with her beloved father's voice in her mind, running was the only instinct she'd had.

Oh God, Vanessa, stop! Quit spinning that haunt over and over, she chastised herself. Why are we doomed to have dates from the past burrow so deep into our memories, hiding out, holding us hostage, waiting to attack us when the clock strikes? Why do our sins go so deep, and become our hidden enemy?

Tony stepped onto the stage and whispered, "I love you."

She pulled at his lapel and lowered him to press her cheek against his, her effort to avoid staining him with her lipstick.

"Let's do a run-through on the last segment." Freddie repositioned Camera One.

Vanessa scanned the blue walls of the studio. The crew knew what color Vanessa liked—blue walls, rugs, coffee cups. Her signature sky color was in honor of the Madonna's robes on the old statue of the Virgin Mary in the entryway to the cloistered convent that had been her childhood home.

Freddie pointed at Vanessa and again mouthed the countdown, "And three, two, one."

"What did you see? Place: Williamsburg, Brooklyn, New York, nine thirty-two a.m., April thirtieth, nineteen seventy, at the Marcy Avenue stops of the J, M, and Z trains." Vanessa felt a line of sweat roll down between her breasts into her push-up bra. "Crime: the murder of Hasidic Rabbi Moshe Cohen. Weapon: sewing shears. Description of perpetrator: fourteen-to-sixteen-year-old white male, approximately five-foot-eight, wearing plaid flannel shirt, blue jeans, and a blue knit cap left behind at the murder scene. Distinguishing mark—" Vanessa cringed inside. What if the policemen involved watched her segment and remembered the fleeing redhead? Silly, she was no longer that redhead. Vanessa continued, "Distinguishing mark: a swastika shaved into the hair on the back of the perpetrator's head. What did you see?

Call me on my private line: one, eight hundred, five, five, five, six, six, six, six. Reward offered, and, as always, privacy ensured."

"OK, that's a wrap." Freddie saluted and smiled. "Good work, Vanessa. See you at the award ceremony."

"Good night, Freddie." Vanessa headed to the door where Tony stood. The World Truth in News Award. How ironic. She knew what conversation she would face when they got home—the one about children. She could see it in Tony's eyes when he'd rolled the film of Kima's story in today's exposé. At times, Vanessa had yearned for a child too, but she refused to repeat the sins of her mother. She refused to have a child with a grandmother like Fiona. She couldn't bear to bring a child into a world of danger and lies.

Strangely there were no urgent assignments in sight, nothing that would give Vanessa the distraction she needed. Was it selfish? She needed a project to dive into—something compelling for the public, someone's life to save, a wrong to right—to take the focus off her own life.

CHAPTER 4

MORPHING INTO MAN

Lukeem

LUKEEM GRASPED THE sky spirit's warm hand. Her heart couldn't be contained. Would it escape her body with its thunder? Supporting her arm, the dark-haired spirit led Lukeem up the three steps and onto the sky spirits' bird. Legs shaking, she scanned the magical circles with their black lines and strange images inside, repeating the word slowly, "heh-li-cop-ter."

The sky spirit Jim smiled. "That's it, *helicopter*. Brad, did you hear that? She said it. So cool."

"You know what I love? Her sincere big brown eyes." Brad stepped closer, looked up at Lukeem, and introduced himself.

The light-haired spirit, Brr-ad was certainly the supreme leader, the honored one, Lukeem thought. She sensed his strength, and he was the commander of the bird. Her fascination with the light-haired sky spirit who stood on the ground beside the helicopter was endless. Lukeem wanted to touch his hair. Was it warm like the sun? And the dark-haired one had a joyful nature like sunlight breaking through after days of rain.

"Oh, here, I bet you haven't had one of these." Spirit Jim handed her a packet and signaled her to eat, lifting his hand to his moving mouth.

Copying the sky spirit, Lukeem peeled back the brown outer

leaf and broke off a piece. The sweet scent made her swoon. Pulsing her tongue, she savored the delicious brown food as it melted in her mouth, smooth and pleasurable. She lowered her head in thanks, remembering her grandfather's legends about the irresistible food the color of the soil, from a plant unknown to her tribe.

The sky spirit nodded. "That's chocolate. Good, huh?"

He pointed to the shiny black circles in front of her, speaking with a soft tone. "See, this is the altimeter, airspeed indicator, turn coordinator. Here's the throttle."

"No flying lessons, Jim. Let's get things done and get back before the weather changes."

Lukeem ran her hands over the cool, shiny insides of the bird. This was no ordinary bird—no heartbeat, no feathers. Where did it take the sky spirits? Where do they come from? A splatter of questions washed over her like a downpour in the rainy season. Were her tribesmen's whispers about the *others* who lived on the far side of the mountains also true? Did they look like her tribe but were nothing like them? Her breath quickened as Lukeem watched the sky spirits take many strange things from the belly of the bird. They stacked them in the center of the circle.

"Let's finish up our reconnaissance. This looks like the perfect place for the helipad. Most of our work's done. After we unload the supplies, I'll get some photos."

"Yeah, Brad, no clearing work needed, and we're not far from the upper tram platform. Convenient spot. And we'll fly over that spectacular waterfall across the way every trip up here." Spirit Jim pointed into the distance. "Too bad you can't see that from the mine site's basecamp."

"Right? It must be a thousand-foot drop, spectacular. Only one of many. You'll see them when we fly back to the valley."

Lukeem loved seeing spirit Brad's face illuminate like the full moon with his words. She wanted to understand.

"Come on, see what we have inside." Spirit Jim invited her.

Lukeem descended the helicopter stairs and watched them unload long slices and large, hard, round pieces of trees, and many containers of things unknown to her. A shiny object in the pile caught her attention. She put it in her head sack.

"Hey, I wouldn't have taken her for a kleptomaniac. She snatched the prism for the telescope."

"I have another one. Let her have it. And no, Jim, it's not considered stealing. These tribes have no individual possessions except their weapons and a few essentials for cooking. They have no concept of ownership. If they're finished using something, they leave it against a tree, and the next tribesman to come along who needs it, takes it."

"So hasn't this kind of *innocence* caused trouble at the site?"

"Definitely. There have been lots of misunderstandings about the tribal people stealing things, Jim. More than a few local natives have been locked up in the holding tank. As if that would teach them a lesson."

Lukeem watched the serious look on spirit Brr-ad's face. She ran her hand along the side of a wooden object he'd unloaded. It was marked with the sky spirits familiar image with colors of the sky, blood, and the small, white vine flower that hides its face in the night. Lukeem pointed to it.

"That's a flag, an American flag." Spirit Jim ran his hand over the image.

"Ffff-lag." She bit her bottom lip, pushed air out between her lips, pressed her tongue against her teeth, and mimicked the sound of the sky spirit.

"She's getting good at English."

Another small design on each of the blades that opened to the inside of the helicopter caught her eye. It was round, the color of the sun with a green spiked tree and small marks that were new to her. Lukeem wished she understood the images of the sky spirits.

"Look, Brad, she's fascinated by the Zell Baxter Mining logo."

"Yes, everything is new and exciting for her just like it is for you coming here. OK, these materials will get them started building the storage shed we'll need."

"The skulls really give me the creeps." Dark-haired Jim closed his arms around himself for protection.

Fear from what? Lukeem wondered.

"Those are their ancestors' skulls." Spirit Brad spoke.

Lukeem knew she was no longer like the other women now. A secret was hidden inside her. She'd felt her feet touch the soil in the open place as if they belonged to a man. Could the power of a man spirit be pressing inside her? Her womanly fear and weakness wanted to leave her as she insulted the men's sacred circle with her female feet. Had the power of an ancestor entered her? Hadn't she danced like her tribesmen when she'd first entered the men's circle?

While watching the sky spirits finish unloading the strange objects from the creature's belly, Lukeem remembered the day her mate, Kralu, had tracked her to her hidden cave, its entrance obscured by the thick vines she'd planted. Studying the painting of the flying crea-ture on her cave wall with its top and tail feathers and the design of the sky spirits on its side, Kralu had become fearful for her. "Do not tell anyone of this vision," he'd said. "It can't be true. The sky spirits would not appear to a woman. These are just your imaginings."

Lukeem had insisted they were real—the flying sky creature and the *A-mer-i-can ff-lag*.

Kralu's words pierced through her thoughts. "Our people will call you wicked! They'll accuse you of sorcery." Kralu had stepped back as if Lukeem could contaminate him with her evilness. "Our fathers and grandfathers have forbidden women to speak of these nature spirits from the sky whom we've offended. There will be no chance of their returning with their gifts if we continue to displease them. Come back with me to our tribal area and never speak of this. It's best."

Lukeem didn't tell Kralu she'd already spoken of her sighting to a few of the women. Discovering her hidden side had changed him. She was saddened by the loss of the attention of her mate. Before she'd told the women of her sighting, before she'd failed to give him more sons, before he'd been shamed by the men, before her son Abruce had disappeared, her mate Kralu had been proud to be with Lukeem.

Spirit Jim returned with her to the helicopter, and Lukeem's thoughts returned to her fascination with the sky bird. And yet, the sky spirits have shown themselves to me, a woman, Lukeem thought, as she shifted in the helicopter seat and fingered the black hide from an animal she'd never seen. Lukeem tried to push away thoughts of Kralu's warnings. Would he never look at her with kind brown eyes or share the meat from his hunt with her again?

Beyond her will, the faces of the sky spirits' summoning made her want to celebrate like the men. Still, the memory of Kralu's words made Lukeem slip down from the helicopter seat. Shuttling down the three small steps to the ground, Lukeem turned and ran with the sky spirits' kind voices calling her. She would barely have time to visit her cave and return to the tribal encampment before the tribe's meetings by the evening fires.

"Wait, don't be afraid. We won't hurt you!"

Their allure was like a vine wrapped around her ankles, pulling at her, drawing her to turn around again. But no, her fear of tribal punishment overtook her joy. Leaving the echo of their sweet laughter behind, Lukeem knew she would return. She knew she would see them again. "Heh-looooo, bee-u-tee-ful," she called out the sky spirits' greeting over her shoulder.

MEMORIZING THE PATH of broken branches and crushed plants she'd created, Lukeem reversed her route until her legs gave way and she had to crawl from fatigue. Painful red lines crisscrossed her body from the clawing of the undergrowth on her moist skin.

As the sun angled and disappeared into the canopy above, she reached her cave where she'd hidden from her tribe to paint her images on the rocky wall. She dropped to the ground. Removing her woven head bag, she took out a small package of green paste pounded from special healing leaves. Lines of the cure followed by handfuls of cool water from the cave's weeping walls soothed the scratches, and the raging stings subsided.

Twisting new grasses onto the broken strands, Lukeem repaired her damaged grass skirt. Her breath was still rapid like the wings of a split-tail swift. The familiar gurgling sounds of the streams of water that snaked down the craggy walls of the cave comforted her, calmed her, as she built a fire. There, alone in her cave, Lukeem had no tightness in her chest. She had no desire to be with the women and their many children since her only son Abruce had disappeared.

When Lukeem first sighted the spirits' sky creature five rainy seasons ago, she'd searched the maze of many caves that tunneled through her tribal area. She'd needed a hideaway where she could capture her memories of the flying creature on the wall.

Scraping a rare berry along a stone, she'd mashed it into rodent fat left over from her meal—the first dark sky-color smear she'd ever made. The red and white colors were plentiful in the flowers, berries and plants around her, but the sky color had been so hard to find. Spreading the ooze with a brush made of dry weeds, Lukeem had finished painting the sharp-sided symbol she'd memorized from the sky spirit's flying creature. Flipping the tips of the weeds, she'd created the splatter of many speckled stars. The red and white flows of color finished the painted image on the gray stone walls of her secret cave. She stepped back and admired her work.

Lukeem ran her fingers over the outline of her creation. Closing her eyes, she remembered her body's tingles upon first seeing the unknown pattern on the side of the sky spirits' magical flying creature—the *A-mer-i-can ff-lag*. Now she'd seen the flying creature once more. Now she knew its word. She'd sat inside the wonderful mystery—the heh-li-cop-ter.

THE FIRE LUKEEM made in her cave had dwindled down to small fingers of light that waved up from a blanket of red embers—too little for warmth, too little for light. She'd been gone since dawn. The women of her tribe would wonder. Her mate would be shamed by her absence from the night meal. It was time to return.

Would she appear different to her tribe since she'd entered the ancestors' place forbidden to women? Touched the hand of a sky spirit? Looked into his striking blue eyes? The joy she saw in the men's faces after a successful hunt was now her joy, Lukeem thought as she rushed back down the path to her tribe's encampment. Hadn't she held her chest out, her spine straight, and chin high with that same pride when the sky spirits had chosen her and had beckoned her into the men's ceremonial space?

Now Lukeem had no desire and no option to live normally among the tribal women who'd shunned her. She'd changed—like a long thick vine had taken root in another earth so deep it couldn't be torn from its new soil. Lukeem wanted to believe Abruce was with the sky spirits. Hadn't he yearned to see them after Lukeem had shared her sighting with him? Perhaps they had returned for him, as they'd returned for her. She wanted to ride their helicopter to the sky spirits' home to find her only son, touch the hand of a sky spirit again, his skin smooth like white river stones, see their faces with pieces of the sky for eyes, and explore the alluring world of the *others* that the tribesmen had whispered about on their return from long hunts.

She wanted to greet the sky spirits in their words—Heh-looo,

Bee-u-tee-ful. To see again the sharp-edged marking on their sky bird—blue sky, splattered with many shining stars, the red and white flowing fronds—the American flag.

Checking her body, Lukeem searched to see if she'd morphed, changed into the man she'd felt herself to be from her boldness. Yes, she had the spirit of a man now—unafraid.

There was no change to see but much to feel.

CHAPTER 5

NOW AND THEN

Vanessa

THE 1960 PRINCESS phone sat silently on the table next to Vanessa's chair. She had time before the taping of the next episode. Last week's *What Did You See?* segment haunted her. Still no calls.

Vanessa slipped her favorite Billie Holiday album and turned up the volume. However, in her mind, she could still hear the Princess phone slogan from her childhood: "It's little. It's lovely. It lights." Her mother had splurged for Colleen's tenth birthday. For months she'd gathered up the wrinkled dollars from her piano students' sweaty hands into a big glass jar, saving to buy the phone. On her birthday, the jar had sat empty on the edge of the piano that filled their apartment's tiny living room. A pretty package sat beside it.

Vanessa remembered her excitement as she opened the ribbons and tore at the paper. Her mother had instantly composed a lighthearted, bouncing jingle on her piano. Then they'd laughed together, singing, "It's little. It's lovely." Her mother had paused. With her hands suspended over the keys, she'd stopped, smiled, turned back, and finished the jingle. "It lights. Just like you, Colleen, my dear one."

Now, nearly thirty years later, her mother's words stung. Vanessa's thoughts ticked back in time. *Back then*, Vanessa was named Colleen. *Now*, she and her mother were estranged, no trace of their connection.

Then, there were no friends to call Colleen on her beautiful new phone—all of the neighbors were bent and gray in the dilapidated apartment that smelled of their fear of dying. *Then*, her father was alive and too worried to let her go to the nearby gang-ridden school. "Da will teach you, Colleen. I was going to be a rabbi, you know." Her father's words held a tender memory for her.

She couldn't picture her Da as a Hasidic rabbi, which had been his dream to follow in his father's and grandfather's footsteps. *Then*, in his anger toward his parents and his love for his wife, he'd embraced her mother's Irish Catholic traditions with his whole heart, even to call himself the Irish nickname for father, *Da*. *Then*, Vanessa had seen no beard, no lengths of braid along each ear, no head covering or shawl with tassels. Back *then*, there was family and connection.

Now, there was none.

Vanessa ran her fingers over the shiny blue plastic handset. It was exactly like the one left behind in her parents' apartment after her father had taken his life. In her grief and rush to move to the convent with her mother's best friend, Sister Anne Marie, young Colleen had forgotten all about the phone.

Two weeks later, her mother still hadn't returned from her concert tour. She'd always had time for endless worldwide concerts every year, but she wasn't there for her husband's death and to comfort her daughter. So out of character for her loving mother to not return for her husband's funeral. Forgiveness just wasn't an option, Vanessa thought. *Now*, Vanessa had learned that hurt could be more powerful than love.

The story of the sentimental phone once shared in a rare moment of openness with Tony had resulted in him finding Vanessa the same retro phone for her 30th birthday present. Princess baby blue, with lights. How could he have known how painful a memory that would be when he was only working from carefully constructed half-truths and illusions about her childhood? Tony's thoughtfulness was touching, but the daily reminder of her mother was painful. No excuse to remove the beloved phone from her room would ever make sense to Tony, except the truth, and the truth was not an option.

The lighted blue phone was silent, and the hotline hadn't rung since Vanessa's plea for a witness to come forward the week before. Normally, she would be non-stop on the phone for hours after a *What Did You See?* segment, fielding calls from both worthwhile witnesses and crackpot callers. But there were no responses the previous years on the anniversary of the Rabbi's death when she'd aired the call for clues.

Again, just silence. Right now this gave her too much open space in her mind to think about her past.

A soft triple knock, short pause, then triple knock resonated in the room, giving her the distraction she craved.

"Come in, Edward." Vanessa pushed away her taunting thoughts and watched the door open slowly, nudged by one familiar size 13, black patent Prada men's shoe. She turned down the Billie Holiday song, its lyrics, "Good mornin' heartache, sit down," aching in the background.

"You're wearing the shoes I bought you in Florence. Nice." Vanessa admired her personal assistant Edward's sense of style. Only two years younger than she, he looked less than his thirty-eight years by at least a decade. Edward entered in a silver-gray, raw silk sport coat and pink dress shirt with a perfectly coordinated raspberry pocket scarf and bow tie. He walked in stiffly with a full glass of red wine and today's mail tucked under his arm.

As Edward made his way across the room, he flashed his eyes between the waving movements of the scarlet liquid in the glass and the immaculate blue carpet. "Special delivery. As they say, the sun's over the yardarm somewhere in the world, right? OK, so this is a twenty-year-old, 100-point Barolo, a gift from the Italian Ambassador. Just arrived. Oh, and I sipped it and wiped the glass."

Vanessa jerked her head up to look at him.

"But with my rose silk pocket scarf if that helps. Better to be honest since we all know you have a nose for lies. And I'll end up drinking it anyway since you don't drink much. But I had to tell him you enjoyed it, right?" He laughed. "Try?"

"Thank you for covering for me *since* we all know *you* have the nose for *wine*." Vanessa took a larger sip than she felt was acceptable at midday.

"Whoa . . . easy girl."

Straightening her hair and pulling at her short dress, she waited for her assistant's daily schedule he'd prepared for her. "Go ahead, Edward, what is it? By the way, love your new tan."

"Yeah, thanks. I live in LA, but I have to use a tanning booth. What's wrong with that picture?"

"Sounds like some cruel woman is overworking you."

"True, a cruel but loveable woman." He poured Vanessa a sparkling water and squeezed a lemon slice into the bubbly beverage. "Oh, here's your mail, madame. Let me get some coffee, too, while you peruse."

Sorting through the thick stack of correspondence and magazines, one by one, Vanessa tossed them on her desk. The last piece was a shock. It was her mother's first correspondence since Vanessa had left for Berkeley over two decades ago. Vanessa knew it was a birthday card from the shape, size, and timing. She ran her thumb over her mother's name on the return address—an unfamiliar one in Southern California. Too close for comfort. What was going on? She tossed the card like it was burning hot into her open briefcase on top of the desk.

She couldn't open it. She couldn't destroy it. A twisted sentimental addiction. The contents are predictable, Vanessa thought. Would she offer a long list of explanations and excuses—her mother's pleas about the pressures of her own fame, her loneliness that spurred international scandal? And wouldn't that list include her mother's love affairs, the broadcasted partying, her drinking, and drug abuse that had publicly taken down so many lovers' lives?

Vanessa didn't want to hear it. What could the letter say that would change anything? All Vanessa had to do was open the tabloids to find out what her mother was up to.

Yes, you should rest, Fiona. Too much philandering and partying can wear a sixty-year-old woman out.

She should throw the correspondence away. No, impossible! Vanessa would read it at home tonight when she was alone.

Edward returned, sipping his coffee. He glanced at the letter on top of the scripts in Vanessa's briefcase. "Fiona O'Farrell? Fan mail? Do tell."

Vanessa feigned disinterest as she flipped through magazines with her mother's face featured among the Who's Who of the music world. Articles with headlines caught Vanessa's attention.

"Fiona O'Farrell's Secret Respite. Where is Fiona O'Farrell?"

Her mother had taken a three-month hiatus from concert touring—apparently a much-needed respite.

Tilting his head at her, Edward launched into the schedule. "So, Vanessa, this week is packed right up until Saturday's award ceremony. OK, we have Tony at eleven a.m. on ABC tomorrow. Of course, they wanted *you*, but they finally settled for him—as always, had to save you for the big ones. The car comes for you at eight-fifteen a.m., and you have an hour and thirty minutes to get across town and . . ."

Edward's rapid-fire words faded. Vanessa disappeared deep into her inner hideaway with the memory of her mother's Princess phone jingle and the unexpected card haunting her.

"Oh, I know that look, Vanessa. Whenever you go there, I know the party's over. What are you on to now? I know there must be something."

Shifting on the leather sofa, she didn't answer.

"Please, Vanessa. At least take a week or two, can't you? What's the point of just one do-good documentary after another if you don't turn on the afterburners. Take advantage of your being in the limelight—just give a few interviews. Let them see who you are a bit."

She glanced toward him, conscious of not wanting to make the gesture—her "tell." She'd always reach up to stroke her earlobe whenever she was about to stretch the truth. Vanessa tucked her hands under her thighs.

Edward was right. She needed to promote herself, their work. But, oh, that spotlight burned. Oddly, there hadn't been a request for help in days. Typically, she'd be bombarded with pleas to intercede in some human rights fiasco, some international culture clash. It repulsed her to think she was praying for something terrible to happen in the world, something that would entice Tony, something to buy her another diversion. Well, her wishing wouldn't cause it to happen, she consoled herself.

With a finger inserted in his starched collar, Edward rocked his neck.

She knew her loyal assistant could always read her moods.

"God, Vanessa, you deserve personal time with Tony too. It's always life or death, all or nothing with you."

Vanessa held up her hand. "Eddie, please, honey?"

"But, you have *commitments*. Oprah wants you on Friday. Larry slotted you for, oh, God, do you know who they bumped you for?" He tossed his clipboard down on her office sofa.

"I will need these next four days to prepare for this new documentary, Eddie. And I'm sorry, but I can't share my new assignment with you." Since there isn't one, she thought. Another link in her chain of lies.

"Yeah, I know. Puts me in danger, right? Better I know nothing. And calling me *Eddie* won't endear me."

She slipped back into her emotionless and distant retreat where she could steel herself from her troubled mind. The recent *Time Magazine* quote came to mind, "Vanessa Gold—nearly four decades of tightly woven Irish linen." She'd laughed when asked about it by the press, not because she *wasn't* affected by the taunt about her uptight, impermeable, public persona, but because she was.

It hurt.

Vanessa was used to the public's misperception of her. She'd always told herself it didn't bother her. It went with the territory. After all, she understood it was all she'd given them to go on.

Vanessa played a well-practiced role—the "queen of exposé," as Edward called her. But the constant posturing and the relentlessness of the press had become exhausting. The more she was in the spotlight, the better chance her past would be exposed. The more she personalized her interviews, the more likely she would be the victim of her own exposé. She understood that the impression of *perfect* came with a price tag. She was perfectly alone behind the façade. Fortunately, they can't see the frayed threads in that tight Irish linen, she thought.

"It's a trade-off, Van. You know that." Edward paced in front of the office windows with his hands clasped behind him and spoke with his back to her. "If you're gonna do news-breaking things, you've got to share yourself, do the circuit."

She shook her head and surfaced, bringing her attention back into the room. "I despise that trade-off, Edward. You know that. This work we do isn't about me."

"You can't just ride the merry-go-round, spinning your career faster and faster, hiding in the blur. Eventually, something's gotta give."

CHAPTER 6

DARK DISCOVERY

Lukeem

LUKEEM'S EYES WERE fixed on the glowing orbit of tribesmen huddled around the men's communal fire. Her face blazed red hot with fear as she studied Kralu's squatting, naked body. The subtle flinch of his muscled back, the deep rumble of the men's voices, and their side glances at her mate worried her.

Wilting down to the ground, she tried to blend in with the women by weaving a bracelet from threads of the plants and roots she'd collected. She thought of her sky spirits and the suspicions of the tribe. The women had pushed her aside, but Lukeem was not a sorceress. She'd cast no spell to cause the hunts to fail, but she *had* broken tribal rule entering the men's circle, she thought. Silently, she left the women's gathering place to observe the men's meeting up close from behind a nearby tree.

Lukeem knew each man by his unique tubular penis ornament, his koteka, jutting out proudly between his legs. Their penis gourds with distinguishing twists at the end nearly reached their chins as they crouched. With its three spirals winding upward like a wild climbing vine, the old honored one's distinctive koteka commanded respect. His lifted chin spoke of his pride as the tribal leader.

Her mate, Kralu, had hung stones with twine around his gourd as it grew, patiently waiting, shaping the perfect koteka that finished with two twists at the end. Lukeem remembered his happy spirit as he carefully preserved the length of the unique gourd root that he'd hollowed out and dried in the sun. She knew he'd wanted her admiration. On the day of the mating ceremony, Kralu had tied the gourd onto his seed shaft with root twine to protect his manly pride.

It was a woman's right to choose her mate by tradition—she'd chosen Kralu. He was strong and skilled at the hunt. She'd thought his strength would mean protection for her and their many children. And the kindness in his smile had drawn her to him.

But now, the days of his kind eyes were over. Lukeem sighed with deep regret. Their mating was rare since he'd seen her cave painting and she'd first told him of the sky spirits. She couldn't find him in his eyes when he finished their ritual and came to sit before her by the fire. She'd no longer felt the great spirit rush inside her. Something had changed. Attached, yet separate from him, she felt like the moss that thrives only at the tree's base with little notice. It saddened Lukeem that Kralu's spirit was distant now—hidden deep within him, separate, like the sap in the core of a thick tree.

Why did Lukeem not blossom with more children as the other women had, season after season? Lukeem was always looked upon as different long before she'd first seen the sky spirits. Hadn't she taken her own mother's life to enter this world? Wasn't that proof enough of her wickedness, of being a sorceress? Was that the reason no child would dare grow within her since Abruce was born, she wondered.

It had left Lukeem hollow inside, an emptiness she'd filled with the warmth and nurturing of her only offspring. Other women who'd given birth more times than they'd desired had offered to give her a baby of their own. Lukeem refused and was shunned for her defiance of tribal tradition. She would not pass on her curse to the child.

With deep sadness, Lukeem watched the women sitting around the fire, holding their children. Had it been five changes of the seasons since Abruce had left the tribe and disappeared? It was not long after she'd first caught sight of the sky spirits' bird. Abruce's desire to stay close to his mother, long after it was time to undergo his manhood ceremony, delaying his move to sleep in the men's area, had insulted his father. Now she had driven her son away, Lukeem thought.

Wrapping her arms around herself, Lukeem endured the familiar shiver. Her son had become enraptured with the news of the sky spirits and disappeared for days in search of them. Lukeem knew he was desperate to prove himself to the men. She understood her strangeness had caused him to be pushed aside by his father and the tribesmen on their hunts. Had he left the tribe to escape his shame brought on by his own mother?

Perhaps Abruce was taken by the sky spirits to punish Lukeem for her strangeness and lies about the sighting of the sky spirits, as Kralu had said. No! She couldn't believe that. Not the sky spirits. Their happy smiles, beckoning hands, luscious, sweet brown gifts, and their heh-li-copter were fresh in her mind. She imagined Abruce living among them, happy and safe.

Lukeem's peculiarities and the disappearance of their only son had also shamed her mate in the presence of his fellow tribesmen, he'd said. She knew Kralu feared the tribe's rejection, yet he feared the revenge of the sky spirits more. He wanted to honor them. Kralu's scowling face revealed his displeasure daily. As if the sun had drifted behind a storm cloud, his deep affection for Lukeem had left his dark eyes.

Her dreams of life beyond the small area where her tribe wandered had also angered him. Lukeem's curiosity about the rarely-talked-about *others* who were rumored to be living on the other side of the mountains was beyond her right to know as a woman, Kralu had said.

Kralu's accurate eye and his sense of the prey were admired. Wasn't he often the first to find the target—his arrow the first to strike its flesh? Lukeem had heard the men talk of his skills in prideful ways around the fire at night. Yet she knew he was shamed by his flawed mate when she'd begun to spend time painting her visions in her cave away from the other women. How much longer would he be tolerated only because of his hunting skills now that the hunts were failing?

Lukeem's loneliness pressed in on her. She turned her eyes to the women. Preening and purring over their children, they sat twenty paces away by their dying fire. As they shared meager bits of dried rodent flesh, mothers forced smiles onto their faces to keep their thinning children from sensing their pending plight.

The lack of food was beginning to show in a reversal of bellies; sunken on barren women, swollen on babies. There were no pigs to render the fat that kept them warm on the cool mountain nights. The tribe believed there had to be a sorceress among them. The curse of a sorceress's spell was inescapable. They knew the men's seeds would not take, and their hunts would fail until the spell-caster was sacrificed to the river spirit, Ranu Lolo.

With her eyes still on the men around the fire, Lukeem observed their leaning bodies as they followed the honored one's pacing by the fire. Questioning heads shifted like a swarm of angry bees, jerking back and forth as they followed their leader's final nod toward the unfortunate guilty one. The indecisive glances of the tribesmen turned into glares as their eyes riveted on the rigid man seated with his back to her, the accused, her mate, Kralu.

From behind, Kralu's tense squatting torso with wide-splayed knees formed the shape of a downward arrow—a symbol of the arrow she knew could soon rip through her heart. Yes, the tension in Kralu's back told Lukeem that she would be the one to be sacrificed. The message was clear—they believed she was a sorceress. She trembled.

The men's words were just beyond her hearing, but their bodies spoke of her pending fate. They shifted and tilted, and one by one turned their heads and angled their feet in her mate's direction. Lukeem's name rose up in a low growl amid the spits and crackles of the fire, but she couldn't pick out the condemning voice that had started the chant.

"Lukeem, Lukeem, Lukeem."

The men sat on haunches, knees apart, young and old, with fists tight around their weapons planted in the soft earth. A pulsing rhythm of beams and shadows from the blaze raging before them flashed on their intense dark faces. Some fidgeted with their nose bones, flipping them or sliding them through a well-worn hole. Others shifted their bows and arrows in anticipation or adjusted the rough twine around their hips that secured their hollowed-out penis gourds.

Taking in a sudden breath, Lukeem shivered as her mate's powerful shoulders drew back in response to their claims. Her swallow came with difficulty as the fearsome, guttural chants arose. Her name again emerged from the men's mouths. Their murmurs gathered in strength and melded into a single powerful voice calling out, "Lukeem! Lukeem!"

She moved around to the other side of the tree to watch. Her squatting husband gripped his bow and tucked his elbows inside his taut thighs. Lukeem heard the honored one blame Kralu for choosing a sorceress for his mate. Quickly releasing his knees, Kralu spread them wide again to compensate for his gesture of fear. Even the slightest sign of weakness meant he would lose position among his fellow tribesmen.

The intensifying sound of the hunters' growling voices finally drew their mates' delayed attention. It reached the ears of the women in their nearby gathering. "Sorceress, Sorceress, Lukeem, Lukeem, Lukeem!" With the chant of her name, the women finally knew Lukeem was to blame for their hunger and suffering. Condemning stares from the men sent a contagious ripple of fear through the group of women, causing an instant clutching of children.

Lukeem's strangeness had insulted the sky spirits. She alone was to blame. She alone must be sacrificed.

In unison, the women scuttled away spider-like to avoid contamination from association with the proclaimed sorceress, leaving Lukeem isolated, squatting by the tree on the edge of their gathering.

Absorbing their disdain, the choice screamed at Lukeem—her own death to save the life of her tribespeople who despised her, or the chance for a life with her mysterious sky spirits who might help her find her son?

Why was it wrong?

Lukeem had felt a deep honor upon first seeing the long-lost sky spirits from her ancestors' stories. Only the fate of her tribe's fading children caused her conflicted, aching heart. Had her own actions and desires been the source of the curse that carried with it their suffering? She felt no clenching of her chest for the women who'd shunned her, nor for the men who'd condemned her, and certainly not for her mate who carried such contempt for her. No, it was only the children's faces that pulled at Lukeem inside.

She nearly stood to surrender to the claims of the honored one—to confess her act far beyond the crime that the tribe had imagined. Should she meet her fate willingly for the good of all?

But Lukeem had cast no spell. She'd not only imagined the sky spirits in her mind for many years, not only drawn her visions of them on her cave walls, but she'd felt her feet step on the sacred ground of the ancestors. She'd entered the sky spirits' magical bird. How could Lukeem have resisted the call of the sky spirits with their strange and exciting words?

Why did the clawing creature still reside in her? She tensed her arms around her legs to keep herself from rising to accept the honored one's blame. Hadn't the sky spirits called to her, smiled, even laughed with joy when she'd entered the men's ceremonial circle? She had managed to say their strange greeting, "Heh-loooo bee-u-ti-ful." A glow spread through her at the thought of those sky spirit words and their laughter.

Lukeem cast her eyes to the glowing moon floating amidst the trees in the patch of dark sky above her. The sky spirits hadn't chosen the honored one or the elders. They'd chosen her, Lukeem, a *woman*.

She was meant to live.

She chose her own life.

She chose the sky spirits.

Lifted as if by a power greater than himself, the honored one raised his arms, thrusting his bow and arrows above him. The thundering voices instantly stopped. He stood solid on his aging bowed legs. His distinctive, twisted penis gourd bobbed up and down in the heavy silence, hypnotizing the tribe with its power. He adjusted his broad nose bone. Its smile-like upward bend on his fierce face caused no softening of his intense and serious stare.

Holding his frightening weapons in one hand, drawing all eyes, the honored one stood by the fire's edge and began to speak. "We have not had a sorceress among us since the coming of the sky spirits when the hunts also failed for many rains." The honored one stared in the direction of Kralu and passed his eyes over the tribesmen. "I have led you in the sky spirits' ways. Still, they have not honored us with their return. I understand now. There must be a sorceress among us. Surely a woman here is the cause of our troubles. She is the reason the sky spirits have not returned. They are displeased. Ranu Lolo, the river spirit, is also angry, raging over his banks."

The honored one glared at Kralu. "The sorceress's death is required to make the apology. The ritual must be done by the pregnant moon. Only then will the sky spirits return with many gifts, and we will be in their favor again."

A roar of men's voices responded, and they sprang to their feet.

"It is not the weakness of my power, but the strength of Lukeem's evil spell that keeps them away!"

Lukeem stared at the honored one through the thicket near the women's fire. He took out the sky spirit's foot protections left to him by the past honored one. The tribesmen were silent as he fastened the heavy, cracked, brown skins on his feet with twine that crisscrossed through holes securing them above his ankles. Proudly, he stomped around the edge of the fire.

The men circled the flames, lifting their legs stiffly with their arms straight at their sides. Then with elbows bent, they alternated their legs and arms—left, right, left, right, as the sky spirits had done so many years before.

"The message is clear. A sorceress has surely displeased the spirits. Her name is Lukeem, mate of Kralu," the honored one said.

Convinced of the truth and fearful of the sorceress's spell, the tribesmen resumed their ferocious chants.

Lukeem understood their thundering sounds were designed to replace their fear with bravery. The tumult of angry voices swelled behind her, and she imagined all eyes intensely on her mate.

The honored one kept his eyes on Kralu. He would never directly address Lukeem, a woman and a sorceress. They would never think she'd have the boldness to refuse the chance to save her tribe. Her people had not sacrificed a woman since the sky spirits left in the days of her father and grandfather.

The tribespeople are peace-loving, she thought. Would they carry out the sacrifice? Yes, the honored one had much pride, but Kralu would be expected to complete her punishment.

The sudden rumble could be seen in the dense vibrating greenery around them. It could be heard in the spattering of heavy raindrops delivered from the canopy above. The water slapped its way down from one level of foliage to the next in a smacking, hollow stick upon hollow stick rhythm, creating a waterfall from the broad leaves above. The rain doused the intense fire.

Gasping at the unexpected downpour in the middle of the dry season, the tribesmen bolted to their feet and scattered. Their attention was riveted on the honored one as he disappeared behind the spiraling tower of smoke. The sizzling sounds of the fire signaled its last efforts to survive the deluge.

Lukeem looked skyward and thanked the sky spirits. Was it not their doing—this downpour so long after the rainy season had ended? The impossible torrent spoke to her. Taking advantage of the distraction, Lukeem turned her back to the echoes of the accusing voices that doomed her and slipped into the dark shadow of a twisted banyan tree.

Kralu's choking voice calling after her was swallowed by the chaos.

Wrapped in the shroud of blackening clouds, Lukeem escaped into the jungle.

CHAPTER 7

TARNISHED GOLD

Vanessa

EDWARD WAS RIGHT, Vanessa thought. Something's gotta give. Being in constant motion in the heat of a shocking story was her smokescreen. She could redirect attention, get lost in the chaos. She could forget the past and live in the better part of herself. Whenever the smoke cleared, she most feared the attention would turn to her. Someone would investigate her past and her scandalous mother who'd abandoned her. Such a juicy story. Worse yet, her failure to act when the boy committed the crime. If she'd screamed a warning, wouldn't her grandfather be alive today? And wouldn't her fleeing the scene scream out *antisemitic*? Destroying her career was one thing but bringing Tony and Canyon and their film team down with her was another.

"This is useless, isn't it, Vanessa?" Edward handed her a magazine. "You know you're up for Woman of the Year. But, um, you didn't make the cover of *Global Limelight*. They needed a fresh face, and yours, gorgeous gal, needed a rest. In the meantime, I will have to go begging and groveling for sponsors and underwriters again, won't I? One of these days, they won't forgive me for not delivering you."

The cover photo stunned her. She didn't answer. Twisting her glass around on her desk, Vanessa created a vortex of sparkling water.

She swallowed the irony at the sight of her mother's face.

"Do you know how hard it is to be me in this town?" Edward sighed, straightened his jacket, and poked his bow tie into place. "You know I love you, sweetie, but sometimes you're your own worst enemy."

Vanessa gathered her cool. "Edward, you should know by now that is what I do. I don't really care about awards. My work is my reward." For a moment, her attention was captured by Billie Holliday's longing voice in the background, "You're the one who knew me when." *Who did know me when?* A pang of sadness shot through her. Vanessa pushed the magazine out of sight to the other end of the sofa.

Focusing again, she covered his hand with hers. "Eddie, the press wants the story. They don't care about me. They can flash my photo. I can do a remote feed."

"You lose friends in this industry playing this way. Eventually, Vanessa, they will cease to cover your stories when you're not on their set charming them. Then what good will they be, these exposés?"

"Having friends in this business? No hope. How could I? I have no time, no personality for it."

"So sacrificial. What about *you*? You know sometimes I could almost feel a pang of sympathy for you, but . . . uh, not quite." He indulged in a short laugh. "Seriously, they never get to see the *you* that I see—helping the kids, the secret scholarships, your tenderness with Tony, and what you did for *me* in salvaging my life. Oh, never mind, having a baby will fix all that. So exciting. I bet it will be a girl and look like you as a kid. You're gonna succumb, right? Big forty coming. *Who* will you honor with the exclusive? Or will you make the rounds?" Edward continued, "Tony said—"

"Edward! You overheard Tony's and my private conversation? Please, promise me you won't . . . no leaks. Eddie, please, let's just focus on the show, OK? There are no set plans for a child. We're just reassessing. Turning forty does that. What exactly did you hear?"

"Just a tiny snippet, but I figured . . . Well, I've seen you with kids.

Remember Maureen? You both lit up when you were together out of the spotlight. It was the only time I saw you act silly. But I won't tell."

"Eddie, please."

"OK, sorry, you're right, but I'm still your best girlfriend, right?" Edward shrugged his shoulder, smiling. "See you out there, sweetheart. And you know it's just because I want you to be happy, right?"

Vanessa caught his wink. He could be so infuriating and, at the same time, lovable. "Bye, Eddie."

Edward's words twisted in her stomach as the break ended and the two-minute call for another episode taping echoed from the studio. She walked up the hallway whispering laments. What bedtime stories could she tell a child? Murders, hatred, culture clashes, political prisoners? Female victims of cults? Pictures flashed through Vanessa's mind of her childhood—her small bed in the convent with her tan wool blanket, the rustic heavy mahogany dresser that stood in the corner on the gray stone floor, the wrought iron decorative bars on her window that protected her from the outside world, and her only friends—her books, her wonderful books.

A memory of her mother, her back turned, leaving with her travel bag in hand, invaded Vanessa's thoughts. Over and over, the door had closed—always that sound of the door shutting. She could *not* become that mother. Vanessa's constant and dangerous travel, the late nights at the studio, the hate mail. No world for a child, she thought. No world for herself. Not a career she'd chosen—it had chosen her. How could she? She loved children too much for that. Yet how could she not give Tony the family he wanted?

Vanessa knew one thing; she could have no more closed doors, especially from the only man who'd ever loved her.

She had to give Tony something hopeful, a half-promise that would buy her time to think of a way of becoming a mother without abandoning a child, without devastating her own career, or exposing her past, or a way to avoid motherhood altogether without losing him.

A mission that felt impossible.

Pausing outside the studio door, Vanessa stared out at the teeming city scene. She thought of her mother, beginning to truly understand the powerful allure of her booming career. Still, the abandonment, not showing up for her own husband's funeral or to comfort and care for her own daughter? Unjustifiable, unforgivable. Why was Vanessa's mind obsessed with the same torturous thoughts from her youth, lately? Hadn't she put those haunts to rest?

The discussions with Tony about having children were forcing her to remember, to look back at who she really was, where she'd come from. Vanessa hadn't stood outside her reconstructed self in many years. Her facade had become so real.

The Vanessa Gold she'd created had been fantasized, learned, memorized, and perfected down to the smallest detail. Colleen had bought herself a new name and changed her life with forged documents. Vanessa wanted no connection to her famous mother. One more reason to be scrutinized. It wasn't too hard to fake a past, as a homeschooler from a cloistered convent. It was Brooklyn. Back then, money could buy anything; corruption could be your ally. She would have done anything to separate herself from the mother who was never there, whose absence had caused her father's suicide.

Vanessa thought back and shook her head, amazed in hindsight at how easy it had been in the end to become Vanessa Gold. In the back alley with the forger, she'd randomly taken her name from a pawn shop window—*We Buy Gold*. Later, she liked that her surname, Gold, had roots in Ireland and had become a common Jewish surname, as well, that honored her father. Perfect.

Her story had become so convincing over time, even to herself, and certainly to Tony, the first and only boy in her life.

Entering the green room, Vanessa spotted something new on the side table beside the tray of frosty sparkling water that awaited her. She examined the photo and stared at Tony, his arm around his mother with his seven sisters and their ten children surrounding them. No spouses. So telling. She knew Tony well. His look of belonging, his happiness surrounded by family, crushed her. Familial love. And who could blame him? It tugged at Vanessa's heart too. Painfully.

She'd been so thrilled when Tony had fallen in love with her illusion freshman year, and she'd fed it. There was guilt. She remembered the tenseness in her stomach that made it impossible to eat in his presence when she was first trying on her new identity. Where did you go to high school? Have you ever been in love before? What were your parents like? The natural barrage of questions from a new love posed a threat, not excitement. The story was simple—homeschooled in a cloistered convent away from the world. There was always fear back then that Tony would somehow see through to her truth, like walking around the other side of her Hollywood set and discovering the angled rotted posts that held her illusion in place. A liar raised in the holy womb of a convent. Too ironic.

Any fear, any awkwardness, had quickly dissipated with their first kiss. Tony made her feel safe, cherished, and special like her father had always done. Her love for Tony had become something real, very real. In time, she'd forgotten how despicable her lies had been. He had no idea who she really was in the past, yet he knew her depths in the present. Over time, Vanessa believed she was the woman whom he adored.

The press and the world fed her illusion, making it easier to maintain. They'd painted her as a powerful, successful woman with a passion for honesty and truth. Inserting herself as a heroine in every possible international horror story had powerfully defined her sense of self.

Vanessa's eyes passed over the wall of photos in the dimmed light of the room—grateful looks on soldiers and refugees in rubble, cheering crowds, and tearing parents with rescued children. She realized that the same horrifying things that people did to one another that they'd seen in their work had tenderized Tony but had hardened her. They were polarized—him living in the hope of their successes, her driven by the hopelessness of the endless cruelty in the world.

Vanessa rushed back down the hallway to retrieve her script she'd left behind. She was a mess since the birthday card from her mother had arrived. As she entered the office, the blue phone rang. Vanessa dove to answer it before the first ring finished. "This is Vanessa Gold. *What did you see?* Please feel free to speak openly. I can promise you anonymity." Her heart was slamming in her chest. She couldn't breathe. She hadn't really considered what she would do once she'd found him. Vanessa folded in half on the chair, her head in one hand and the old phone in the other. She'd given up on the possibility of a call.

The man's low voice and breathing on the crackling line made her shudder. "Do you remember a boy with a swastika shaved into the back of his head?"

Vanessa went on high alert. "Were you there at the scene?"

He hung up.

CHAPTER 8

SACRIFICING THE SORCERESS

Lukeem

PUSHING BEYOND THE peril in her heart, Lukeem focused on yearning for her son. The familiar feeling overcame her—the parting of the clouds within her mind, the clarity of the vision that resonated beyond her thoughts, the pulsing of her racing heart. She saw the faces of the sky spirits, heard their kind voices in her mind, and yearned to be in their protection. They would surely know where her son had gone, she thought. He was all she had.

It was she, herself, who'd caused her own pain. She was her own betrayer, Lukeem thought. She'd broken tribal rule, hadn't she?

The rhythm of the heavy droplets from the umbrella of treetops above led the way as she pushed through the lush jungle, intuiting the direction of the cave.

Safe inside her cave, she took out a strong stick and a strip of rattan. Skillfully, she planted one end of the stick into a small nest of dried twigs and shaved roots she had protected from the misty night. Rubbing the string back and forth against a reliable twig, the friction built as Lukeem enlisted her feet to keep the stick in place. The fear that drove her gave rise to a smolder and a series of small sparks that ignited a fragile fire. She carefully fed the tiny glow with more shreds and long breaths until it began to glow. Squatting with knees jutting out like a frog's and her arms crossed with cold hands tucked under, she sought to preserve what little heat her body still held while waiting for the fire to grow.

Lukeem looked down at the only things she would have to remind her of her life with the tribe—a woven head bag, a crude necklace, and a skirt that hung to her knees, made of shreds of plants and dried grass, tied with a cord at her waist. Her chest was squeezed as if a thick snake had wrapped around her, hungry to steal her breath. I will have no gift for the sky spirits, she thought. She began to draw more visions on the cave wall to calm herself.

Engaging her focus, she rehearsed the path to the clearing—the sunbeams, sounds, textures, angles of the trees—every detail that would bring her to the circle where she'd first met the sky spirits. Thumping exposed gnarled roots of the banyan tree to assess the distance, Lukeem listened as the sound echoed through the jungle. She promised herself she could once again find the sacred place where the sky spirits had alighted.

FOLLOWING IN THE direction of her memories, Lukeem burst through her dense world to take in a perspective she'd never known—a depth so deep, a vision so far. She knew she'd found the magnificent Long View.

If she'd taken one more step, there would be no more earth beneath her feet. The strangeness spread her eyes wide. She'd heard the men sing of the privilege of seeing the Long View, but Lukeem could never have imagined its splendor. She wouldn't be able to translate it clearly enough to draw it on her cave walls.

How do you draw *forever*?

Her heartbeat was rapid at the sight of the valley where the Ranu Lolo River spirit raged. Dipping her foot over the sheer cliff's edge, she felt a puff of air. Lukeem pulled back as her eyes adjusted to the newness of the forever view.

The tall and magnificent trees appeared smaller and smaller as her eyes scanned the scenery down to the river far below. Standing at the precipice, Lukeem realized she was not far from the men's ceremonial circle. No woman's eyes had been honored with the glorious sight of the legendary Long View. She smiled with delight as she again reached out to touch the river's white foam, but it was an untouchable distance below her.

With her hand shading her eyes, she traced the waterfall across the way. It fell from an even higher limitless ledge that reached from the sky above down to the valleys' heart where the river Ranu Lolo presided over all. There were no broad leaves or palm fronds to block her sight, no maze of tall rattan to dodge, no woven thickness above to impair her view of the swelling moon and the burning sun. The space was deep—deep and open and free. Her eyes were free to blossom, free to reach out to embrace the scene's glory. She felt released, and her heart began its special dance inside her.

Gripping the waist cord of her frazzled skirt, she dropped belly-down to the safety of the ground and cautiously nudged her head over the edge. She watched intently with staring eyes and mouth agape. The leaves and vines of her closed and small dense world had spread open to magically reveal the expansive sky and the deep gorge. It was filled with angled rocks and trees that changed from massive to miniature as she scanned the open space to the valley's floor again. The wind spirit sent a push of warning into Lukeem's face, and she pulled back.

Craggy tops of lush mountains tucked into one another as far as she could see. She sat in reverent silence, watching a large midnight blue moth flutter over the chasm. The tension shivered through her body. Lukeem closed her eyes to calm herself and enticed the tingling to begin. It passed over her skull and flowed sap-slow down her shoulders and along her arms. When the feeling reached her hands, she slowly turned her palms up, and with a pleading gesture, she beckoned the creature to come.

Closing her eyes, Lukeem let the corners of her mouth turn up and gently rocked her head. She lifted her hand, drawing her pointing finger upward. Then she opened her eyes, and as though in a trance, the brilliant blue moth spiraled down, swirl after swirl. It softly landed and clasped onto Lukeem's welcoming finger with its angled, saw-toothed, spindly legs. The wings of the enraptured beauty opened slowly, then closed, opened, and closed again for a suspended moment. Two long iridescent antennae reached toward her and twitched in a happy dance. She lowered her shoulders, and her tension melted as she let go of her fear. She whispered, "Heh-lo bee-u-ti-ful," as the creature's colorful fans with intricate blue designs stretched open wide before elevating into the new daylight.

Breaking the moment's spell, a golden blade flashed up the mountain, and lit up the white rapids of the powerful Ranu Lolo. As the light moved toward Lukeem, she rose, sensing no fear of the rising blaze as it reached its illuminated arms up to embrace the waterfall. It was the first beam of the morning sun. She'd never seen its source before, rising from below. She'd only seen its glowing beams above her through the trees that blocked the view of the sky.

With the explosion of light that split into shoots of color, the valley came alive with a concert of day sounds and welcomed light, silencing the night's noises. Only then, did Lukeem understand that her life had been lived up high, that her world was closer to the sky than the river far below. She'd only then realized that the sun came up each day from the sky spirits' home below.

With her finger in the air, Lukeem traced the snakelike curves of the white water that writhed in and out of the rocks, and down the side of the mountain. Her heart roared in concert with the falling water's voice, the sound filling her ears, calling to her.

Now she understood the thundering, falling water and its snaking white foam below was the mighty spirit, Ranu Lolo. She shivered. This was the place the tribe had planned to complete her sacrifice.

CHAPTER 9

TRUE CONFESSIONS

Vanessa

CLENCHING HER JAW against the silence, Vanessa lifted the heavy satin quilt without any risk of disturbing her peaceful lover. Tony had been blessed with the sleep of the innocent. The bright moon cut a beam across their bedroom through a crack in the raw silk curtains, lighting her way. Vanessa slipped into the hallway with her mother's unopened card in her silk robe pocket and a glass of sparkling water in hand. She passed the glass cabinets filled with a lineup of silver and crystal awards, including three prominent Oscars. As she walked, she read the dates in sequence from 1970 to 1990.

In the lighted mirror, she glanced at her red roots illuminated like a narrow runway down the part in her hair. Combing it back with her fingers, she moved down the hallway, stopping before turning out the light in the music room. The walls read like a history of their travels with dozens of stringed instruments from every corner of the world. Her father's violin was featured in a place of honor on the fireplace mantel. Vanessa felt the familiar ache, imagining the sweet purring notes of his playing.

Vanessa ran her hand over the smooth python skin that covered one end of a Dahu. The large, vertical, bowed instrument with its two slack strings brought Tiananmen Square painfully to mind.

Tightening the strings, she adjusted her favorite antique on the wall—a silk-stringed fiddle with its coconut body covered in animal skin. She could hear the Saw Sam Sai being played at the Palace in Bangkok. When she'd smiled at its haunting sounds, the King had stopped the concert and given it to her as a gift—a *thank you* for her work on his behalf. She still felt touched by that unexpected gesture. On her way out of her music room, she plucked a string on a crude Spanish mandolin, and the note echoed in the cathedral ceiling.

Walking barefoot down the hallway on the cool tiles, she was guided by the blue glow of the swimming pool that lit her way along the glass wall. Slipping into their home theater, she sat in a fetal position on the chair in the front row. Vanessa pulled the sheer nightgown over her painted toes and took the letter from her silk robe pocket. As she slipped her fingernail under the flap, her hands began to shake. She sensed the card could be the door to her demise.

The front of the card had a hand-painted cluster of shamrocks on it. Good luck, Mother? Really? Peeling open the card, a letter dropped onto Vanessa's lap. She began to read the familiar handwriting. The first two words made Vanessa tense, *Dear Colleen*. Fiona knew damn well that her daughter's name was now Vanessa.

Dear Colleen:

Happy Birthday. I hope you're well, my darling daughter.

Vanessa snapped the letter to her lap. She was tempted to throw it out with that first line alone. "Darling, indeed. And happy?"

How do I begin to apologize or explain my behavior to you when I don't understand it myself? Contrary to the news, I have spent the past three months in California in residential rehab and counseling, getting sober, analyzing my actions, regretting, and trying to forgive myself—hoping I could find some way to get you to do the same some-day—to forgive me. It began with your grandmother. She never called me to tell me about your father, or I would have returned to take you in my arms, my darling child. I confess, I fell apart when the news reached me. Indulging in the temptations that seemed to accompany my career of touring and fame, I did anything to numb myself from the truth of my life without your father and you. I promised Mother Anne Marie I would not sully your life, and I couldn't find you while you were in college. Once I discovered who you were, I didn't have the heart to taint you.

If my actions had been secretive or private, that would have been one thing. Still, the public disgrace I made of myself, hitting the front page of every tabloid with my scandals, affairs, and addictions over the years, is beyond mortifying. I'm sure it was for you too—even if only you knew the truth about our relationship. I know I promised you, through Sister Anne Marie, that I wouldn't be in touch. I owed you that. But things have changed. I keep feeling I should star in one of your exposés—confessing all, to get it all out in the open, and make a public and private apology.

Vanessa bit her lip at her mother's mention of publicly exposing her sins. She read on.

Maybe you would let me back into your life someday after I've restored my reputation, made amends? And I will.

"Oh, God." Vanessa put her hand to her forehead as a flush raged in her face.

I'm writing on your fortieth birthday to ask you to consider just that. Forgive me? I have decided to stop all touring. I know that lifestyle, the egotistical aspects, adulations, and being rootless is not the answer to straightening out my sinful existence. How many years can one float in mid-air? I need to ground myself. You've inspired me. I plan to start an international music foundation for children—schools that engender understanding across cultural barriers to help stop the hatred. Misunderstandings are at the core of all hatred. I know that from what happened with your sweet father, his suffering, and mine, and yours.

I will be announcing the World Peace Music Foundation soon. I'm sure you'll read about it. It's my apology to the world, and to you. I've had an epiphany over these past three months. And beyond hope, I wish you would consider forgiving me. I can't take my life any longer the way it is right now. For you, my darling daughter, if not for myself.

Love,

Mother

Vanessa gathered her things and went next door to her home office. She sat at her desk, rotating in her chair, the anger and hurt surging through her. The threat of her mother exposing their truth was quaking through every part of her. But she couldn't deny there was some satisfaction in her mother owning her sins, regretting, and sharing some of the same sufferings Vanessa had endured. She couldn't deny that a part of her was seething with fury and regret. A part of her ached to reconnect with her mother. But the hurt won out.

In the end, the birthday card from her mother was a threat. Now that she'd been in rehab for her addictions and redesigned her entire life, there was bound to be a public reveal. Fiona's card would force Vanessa's hand. The weight of more than two decades of deceit pressed in on her. It would soon be time to unwind her own twisted lies—for Tony, for herself. If there were any chance of their relationship surviving, Vanessa had to tell him the truth. Didn't she? Or would the truth cause her to lose everything that mattered to her?

Fiona O'Farrell, one of the world's most celebrated pianists, could no longer be trusted to keep her secrets, she thought.

Vanessa picked up the pen and took three pieces of her letterhead from her desk drawer. It was a long story.

April 30, 1990

Darling Tony,

I owe you the truth. I know sharing it will change everything between us and your memories of me. I'm not who you think I am. God, that sounds like such a hackneyed or overly-dramatic thing to say, darling, but I'm not. Should something happen to me, I would rather you find out from me rather than the press. I know how we both feel about being caught off guard by the media—learning things about ourselves before we even know it. We've been swimming on display in this aquarium for so long, with so many faces staring in with magnified eyes, just waiting for one of us to devour the other for their entertainment. I just couldn't bear to give them the bait to turn us into a famous couple of Siamese Fighting Fish. I wanted to tell you the truth, my real name, my past, from the first time you kissed me outside my dorm at Berkeley when I was eighteen. Can you imagine that those first weeks on campus using my fictitious name, my concocted façade were the first days I'd spent outside the convent since I was ten? But my words stuck, the fear set in, and the longer I held back the truth, the more I had to lose—you, us.

I often weigh which will hurt you more, me telling you at this point in our life after more than twenty years together, or you learning it in the future from some news source. No win.

I know you've always said that you and I have no "personal story." The only stories we have belong to other people from our work. This is my story, and now it's yours. We have a story, Tony—just not the one you thought we had. Forgive me.

Where should I start?

When I turned seven, my mother won a Grammy for one of her piano pieces, "Rise to Be You". We all know that song well. I then learned the meaning of the word "tour." Tour meant lonely. Tour meant loss.

I knew my mother loved me. "More than life itself," she'd said, despite her constant leaving on her worldwide concert tours. But I hated the sound of the door closing, the wave of her perfume sweeping out behind her. My parents didn't die in a car accident, Tony. There was no wealthy Aunt Angela who hosted me on college breaks on the Upper Eastside. I told you one truth—after my father died, I was raised in a cloistered convent by a nun, my mother's best friend, Sister Anne Marie. She later became Mother Anne Marie. Ironic, because she became like a mother to me. And, no, my father didn't just die. I should just use the right word, suicide. He took his own life, and my mother didn't die in the car accident with my father—she's alive.

Do you remember how I failed to bring back a film clip for our college competition, Culture? I want to explain. I went to my father's old neighborhood. He was—

Scratching a deep X through the last paragraph, Vanessa clicked her pen in a continual stutter. She wedged her partially written confession to Tony under her arm and crossed the room. Such irony, she thought. *The mother who'd stolen my childhood would devastate my adult life too.*

Vanessa had often feared her most scandalous exposé could be her own. It was no longer only the facts themselves that held the threat, but the fact that she'd withheld them from Tony.

The priceless, hand-painted reproduction of the bold 1918 *Blue Flowers* by Georgia O'Keefe pulled back easily on its hinge. Vanessa spun the dial combination and opened the wall safe. To the left of the film boxes she sought, she saw the black box that contained a bracelet Tony had given her for their anniversary the year before. It reminded her of the twin velvet boxes that held the matching silver shamrock necklaces her father had given to Vanessa and her mother the Christmas before he'd died—the year before her mother had abandoned them for her music career. Vanessa had left them behind at the convent. Too painful a memory. They'd never worn them as her father had intended, she thought. A sentimental bond that had broken before it had a chance to form.

Vanessa tossed the card inside the safe, and transferred a pile of Kodak films into her briefcase. She clicked the safe shut and pushed the painting flush to the wall.

Slumping into the loveseat by the window, Vanessa thought of the date—May fourth, Kent State Massacre and the beginning of her career, the documentary on the timely protests that had thrust her and *Turning Prism* into the spotlight. As a child, Vanessa loved that she shared the same birthday as Fiona. Not anymore. Forgiveness could never reach as deep inside Vanessa as the pain of being abandoned.

The wall of photos across from her felt like an uninvited audience—Ronald Reagan, Nelson Mandela, Lady Di, and a dozen other world leaders. The grateful faces and cheering crowds from Vanessa's high-profile human rights documentaries seemed to be watching and smiling out at her from her wall of truth, as Tony had once called it. She turned the art lights off.

Rubbing the disfigured fingers of her right hand, Vanessa was thrust back into her past, memories of the old home movies. The wiggly shot of her mother and father dressed up, waving goodbye as they left her childhood apartment. Vanessa's little girl self had twirled with joy, blowing kisses to the camera. She hated thinking about her mother, but she couldn't stop imagining her father again. What would she do with the few old family films that Mother Anne Marie had salvaged for Vanessa from her parents' apartment? I should edit Fiona out, she thought.

The memories returned—finding her Da slumped in his rocker, repeatedly with the empty pill bottle on the floor. Had those images ever left? Weren't they always lurking in the shadows?

The car crash that had been his final demise flashed in her mind. How could she have fabricated the story that her mother had also shared her father's tragic ending on the street outside their apartment? Vanessa dueled with the dark memories.

She wanted to stay with her father's smile.

SLIPPING UNDER THE covers next to Tony, Vanessa prayed her connection with her mother wouldn't be revealed. Splashing Vanessa's face on the tabloid side of the news would destroy the focus she and Tony had so carefully cultivated to support their good work.

Would her mind forever spin with that fear?

Pressing up against Tony's back, she wrapped her arm around him. He didn't rouse. He slept peacefully, like a baby.

It had been so long since she'd left her safe home with Mother Anne Marie in the cloistered convent to leave for college. No one would have hurt her there had she stayed. But then her mother would have found her, and Vanessa wouldn't have Tony or her dear friend Canyon, or all those years of making a difference in the lives of others, she thought. No, staying was never a good choice.

Her entire career, *Vanessa* had generated headlines, but one day soon *she* could be the victim of a reveal. She imagined the headlines, "World Famous Truth-Teller, World Famous Liar." Vanessa tried it on for size, envisioned how it felt to be on the other end of the firing line, the bull's-eye on *her*.

CHAPTER 10

FEARFUL REVERENCE

Lukeem

AS LUKEEM ARRIVED at the ceremonial circle, it was quiet. She heard no spirit bird. She saw no sky spirits. She would wait for days if she must. Nervously, Lukeem kept vigil with her flat feet planted in the chilled mud, feet that had sunk deeper and deeper while waiting for the sun to wisp away the last murky gray of the night. With head cocked, she listened for any unfamiliar sounds through the resounding chirps and croaks as the nighttime noises were again silenced with the insistence of the sun.

A new sound began in the distance, a sound she knew well—the chants of a hunt. Lukeem bolted up as a group of her tribesmen, with arrows set to kill, surrounded her in the sacred men's circle. They thumped their weapons on the ground and chanted for her death. Under the eyes of the honored one, her mate adjusted the bone that hung from his flared nostrils and pulled the arrow back taut on his bow. Although Kralu stood motionless, his elongated gourd suspended from his waist echoed his hurried anger, rising and falling.

"It is forbidden for a woman to enter here! You have cursed the ceremonial circle and now the Long View." The honored one raged. "Ranu Lolo commands the punishment—the sorceress's life to appease him." He signaled with a flick of his bow to one of his tribesmen.

Lukeem flashed her eyes to find a path to her escape. Pointing, she screamed. The group of her tribesmen looked in the direction of her finger. She scrambled past them.

Kralu lunged at her and stopped her flight, pushing his bow and arrow across her chest. His betrayal was more painful than the thrust of his weapon, though his eyes spoke of his regret.

Two men dropped their bows, grabbed her, and struggled to drag her the long distance from the clearing to the edge of the thousand-foot drop. The chanting tribesmen followed. Lukeem glanced down, then closed her eyes to the distant Ranu Lolo that gathered a massive waterfall from above into its commanding arms and tumbled it down into the valley far below.

Her breathing came with difficulty.

Stepping forward, Kralu took the privilege of the bow and arrow from the honored one to complete the ceremony.

The deepest sorrow she'd ever known crushed her chest. Lukeem would never see her son again. As the men surrounded Kralu with looks of admiration, Lukeem howled like an injured animal.

"Shameful! You should accept your sacrifice for us all." Kralu's voice was filled with anger. He pushed closer to her and engaged Lukeem's eyes with a pleading look. "Please," Kralu whispered.

She noticed his sad eyes as her mate stood proud and ready with his bow in hand.

The honored one gave his unspoken permission to proceed.

Lukeem was no longer Kralu's mate. She was a sorceress.

Her foot slipped over the crumbling edge.

Two fellow tribesmen tried to lift her high above the sheer precipice. Sending an arrow through her heart would complete the ritual, delivering their sacrifice of apology to the river spirit.

Struggling and writhing, her hands slid over their greased, dense muscles, gripping, digging in. She pushed desperately at their faces and clawed at their eyes. Her piercing screams cut through the violent chants that rose from the choir of men, releasing their power, energizing their intent.

Looking down into the deep gorge, suffering in her last moments suspended over the beautiful Long View, Lukeem screamed. "The sky spirits called to *me*, a woman! I am not a sorceress!" She would never see her son again. She would never know the sky spirits' home. "*My sky spirits!*" she screamed looking skyward with desperation as Kralu set the arrow and pulled back the string.

Rising within feet of Lukeem, the bird with the alluring colorful American flag on its tail burst through the bank of morning fog and suspended in front of them. The thrust of its spinning feathers and the blast of sudden wind, drove the group back from the edge of the precipice.

The sky spirits' flying creature swooped down again and swept up the rock wall within feet of the men holding Lukeem.

Falling to their trembling knees, the tribesmen cowered at the sight, releasing her to the ground.

Lukeem and the frightened men looked up at the light-haired spirit who held a strange black object to his eye. He pointed it threateningly toward each of their shocked faces—one, then another.

The sight of the sky spirits flattened the entire group to the ground in terror, except for Lukeem. With adoration, she pleadingly reached up to her saviors in the sky.

The honored one and the group of tribesmen remained with their unworthy faces to the earth. They quivered with fearful reverence as the strange bird tilted and dropped down the razorback mountain.

The truth screamed out for all to see. Unfamiliar courage overcame her at the sight of her sky spirits. "*You see!*" Lukeem turned to face the honored one.

He rose unsteadily from the ground, the fear still riding shamefully on the leader's face.

"I did not lie." Lukeem welcomed her bravery. "The sky spirits have returned. They showed their faces to me, *a woman*, in the men's ceremonial circle! And they saved *me*—Lukeem."

"*Sorceress!*" Her husband sprung to his feet and thrust his bow up to the sky. He did not dare to touch her or even glance her way.

She understood Kralu's display of courage. Lukeem knew about his long-held desire to displace the aging honored one to become the leader of their tribe. With one last look at her mate's cold face, Lukeem scrambled away and melted into the brush.

CHAPTER 11

DUBIOUS SECURITY

Scott

FROM HIS DESK, SCOTT spotted Brad through the window of the security department trailer and waved him in. "Good to see you, Brad. Come in. Have a seat."

The metal folding chair scraped on the linoleum tile floor as Brad sat and pulled it closer to the desk. "How did your first week on the job go?"

"Well, I've had harder security director jobs, but I admit not as exotic."

"I have to agree with that. I've piloted for projects all over the world but well . . . you'll see. This place is beyond exotic." Brad pulled an envelope from his jacket. "Thanks for meeting me so early, Scott."

"No problem. I'm an up-at-dawn guy. Military habit." Scott settled into the padded office chair behind the desk. The heat of the morning sun was already blasting through the window, threatening to overwhelm the rattling air conditioner in the Quonset hut. It reflected off the rippled roof of the trailer on the mountainside below Scott's office. He stood and closed the Venetian blinds. "Crazy weather up here, huh? Cold nights, sweltering days. So, Brad, I hear you had quite a trip up into the mountains."

"Word travels fast. I guess my new co-pilot, Jim, likes to share. I asked him to keep it quiet." Brad slid the envelope across the dusty desk toward Scott. "I have some photos you won't believe. Just got back from a quick turnaround to the coast to develop them."

"I was looking forward to seeing them. Jim's report about what you found up there was wild. You were right to come to me first."

"Yeah, sure. We happened onto some kind of ritual, a human sacrifice, I guess you'd call it. The tribal woman was innocent. Honestly, we called her into that clearing we'd discovered." Shuffling his chair closer to the desk, Brad tapped on the barren circle in the photo. "We lured her, actually. She was so fascinated. Apparently, by tribal rule, women are forbidden to enter that space. I feel pretty bad about that. Not to point fingers, but Jim being new and . . . well, look at these. They could cause serious trouble. It may have been our fault. Better to handle it sooner rather than later."

"For sure, we need to protect the company." Scott lit a cigarette, lifted his chin, and blew the smoke toward the metal roof. "I suggest you don't repeat that line about our culpability to anyone else. Could be severe consequences—I mean for Zell Baxter, and maybe you and Jim too."

"Got it."

Scott could tell by Brad's face that he'd understood the veiled threat. Opening the envelope, he shuffled through the photos. One good thing about being the new head of security—all the news came your way first, he thought. "What exactly is going on here?"

"The bottom line is, we landed on the clearing where we're building the new helipad, and a local tribal woman saw us. I know you're new here, Scott, so I don't know how much you know about the local cultures. But that remote area had a fluke exposure to World War Two troops, and they've been waiting for the so-called 'sky spirits' to return ever since."

"And tag, you're it—you're a god or some nature spirit. Some kind of cargo cult, right?" Scott enjoyed being in the know when it came to guys like Brad—intelligent, polished, and obviously educated with those preppie good looks.

"Right. Oh, so you know about that cultural phenomenon?"

"The missionary, what's-his-name, Father . . ." Scott purposely let Brad fill in the blank.

"Father Carey."

"Yes, I had a meeting with him when I arrived. He gave me the skinny on the various mountain cultures, but go on, Brad." It was better to listen to Brad's version, even though Scott already knew what had happened from Jim. Inconsistencies. Always listen for those differences in an accounting, he'd learned. Paying careful attention to Brad's report and reviewing the photos told the tale. "So I see she escaped the sacrifice." Scott held up the photos of the tribeswoman fleeing away from the tribesmen as they lay on the ground. "Looks like you scared the hell out of them." Scott laughed.

"I mean, this tribe is remote, apparently untouched by the outside world except for that one World War Two incident in the forties. Father Carey says that it was a tribal no-no for her to enter that clearing, some men's ceremonial space, so that's why the sacrifice." Brad shifted in his seat. "They released the woman, I should say they dropped her, when they saw our helicopter. She took off along the edge of the cliff."

"So you don't know where she went?" Scott knew what he was facing. When it came to the locals or any company he'd worked for, profits came first over doing right by any indigenous peoples. The company would do anything to keep the workers moving—anything, Scott thought. And any information on the native's whereabouts would be to his advantage.

"We tried looking for her, but she'd disappeared into the jungle. Impossible to see anything through that canopy up there."

"So the consequence is?"

"She's to be sacrificed to the river spirit. In other words, thrown off the cliff into the Ranu Lolo River by the next full moon. The belief is that the curse on the entire tribe won't lift until she's killed."

"What curse?"

"Food scarcity. Well, animal scarcity in the remote mountain tops where these tribes wander. You may not know, but there's been a change in the wildlife these past five years. Fewer animals—the tribe's primary source of food. Seemed to coincide with the construction of the first mine."

"Sacrifice. Heavy punishment for the woman just for meeting you two. And I imagine some of our employees and miners recruited from the other mountain tribes might hold the same beliefs?" Scott dealt the photos out on his desk and studied them.

"Traditionally, it's always a woman they blame, like witches. Happened two years ago, different tribe, but they tortured and killed a woman when a man fell from the tram. Yes, the word will spread fast, I'm afraid. Even if they don't hold to the belief or participate in the practice, they wouldn't want to take a chance with the nature spirits. I hate picturing that sweet woman being sacrificed. There will be pressure for the ritual to take place. I'll talk to Father Carey. He may know more. But that's how he explained it to me, Scott."

"Big financial loss for Zell Baxter if this isn't resolved. We've just invested a lot in transporting and training locals for the new expansion. And without those laborers, we're screwed."

"True. And I hate to think I contributed to that."

Scott ran his hand down the back of his head to smooth his dark hair. "So, what do you suppose we should do?"

"I would think . . . get some intercultural expert."

"Like, who?"

"Vanessa Gold's *Turning Prism* group if you can get her attention. Right up her ally. She knows how to get to the bottom of these kinds of things. You've seen her documentaries, right? She can help the company figure out how to build a bridge."

"Wait, Brad. I thought she only did exposés. We've got to protect the company. I've read about some of her investigations, and they can be wicked."

"No, I don't mean her TV show. Her cross-cultural communications team does documentaries—helping American companies and even foreign governments handle these kinds of misunderstandings with indigenous peoples. And she's plugged into every anthropologist and sociologist worth their salt. You know Professor Canyon Swenson, the anthropologist, was on her original team until she went into teaching. Read an article about them in *National Geographic*."

"OK, that's impressive. I've been out of touch. It's not exactly TV land where I've been these past decades. Thanks, Brad. I'll talk to the Mining Director and see what he thinks." Scott patted Brad on the back and opened the door for him. "Nice work."

Unbelievable, Scott thought as he closed the door. Vanessa Gold is popping up everywhere. Gathering up the photos, Scott slid them into a DHL express package. They had the quickest international courier service from Jakarta, he thought. And it had to be fast. He checked his calendar—the full moon would be May 20th, only weeks away.

Scott ran down a list of potential local people who could help before this whole thing got out of hand. He'd seen it before at other South Pacific sites he'd worked on. Superstitions, mumbo jumbo, damn cultural crap causes so much trouble, he thought. And all the hatred and bigotry. A familiar thing for him. That kind of thing had screwed up his whole life. Just what he needed to start his new job.

He folded his arms and tilted his head. Hey, this could work out, he thought.

He knew Brad was right about Vanessa Gold. She knew how to get to the bottom of these kinds of things. Too perfect. Damn. He almost had to laugh when Brad suggested her. Well, she would never recognize Scott's voice from the call he'd made over that crackling phone line. How the hell had she ever gotten hold of that old footage the redhead took? All these years later? He could have fallen over. The first time he'd ever seen her TV show, and twenty years later, he hears about his own haunt. Talk about an exposé.

Scott smoothed the back of his hair and adjusted his balance against his desk. Yes, Ms. Gold, he thought. Please come to the other side of the planet to help us with this little intercultural issue. Be my guest.

Scott sealed the DHL package and addressed it to the *Turning Prism* Studio in LA. He would kill two birds.

CHAPTER 12

SHOWERED WITH LOVE

Tony

TONY DESCENDED THE fifty steep steps that led down the cliff-side from their house to the beach. He needed a good run before the day began. Hands-to-his-knees at the bottom of the wooden staircase, he bent over to catch his breath. Scanning the hazy, crashing waves he breathed in the misty sea air. In its usual abracadabra way, the LA sun drew up the fog, and the light broke through.

Lately, Tony's desire to have a family and move on to the next phase of their lives together was palpable. His disappointment churned like gravel in his stomach. He ran the two miles to his favorite spot and sat down on the bench for his daily ritual, a call to his mother. They'd become close since his father had died. As the only male, he was now the head of the family, and it came with responsibilities.

This was not the conversation he'd ever expected to have with her. But he needed advice. After he'd told his family that he and Vanessa felt their life was unsuitable to having children and having heard all the arguments and disappointments from his seven sisters and his mother, he'd never mentioned the subject again. They'd never really given Vanessa a chance after that. Not that they'd been unkind but his mother and sisters hadn't gone out of their way to welcome her into his close-knit Italian family.

And wasn't part of her *no-kids* decision due to Vanessa's fear that she couldn't be a good mother, having spent most of her childhood without one? Tony continued his run. He would call his mother later.

As his running shoes thumped on the hard wet sand, Tony struggled to figure out how to meet his needs and yet respect Vanessa's feelings. She was right about the danger in their lives and the obligations of their chosen career, but couldn't they lessen their workload? Couldn't they focus on meaningful cases and subjects that weren't so serious or contentious? They could stop doing the international documentaries and concentrate on her TV show to limit travel. He didn't really like the endless traveling anyway. Although seemingly fearless, Vanessa could also do without the danger, he thought.

These nagging desires had all started the first time he'd seen the young girl, Maureen. Through the lens of his camera in the documentary about foster children, he'd imagined Vanessa in her childhood. In the girl's pure green eyes, he'd faced his personal loneliness without a family of his own. He was tired of not being true to himself, and he desperately wanted to be a father.

Tony's family had been so hard on Vanessa, blaming her for cheating him out of having a family. Talking to anyone other than Vanessa about it felt like a betrayal. He thought about her life in the cloistered convent without other children around. He'd been raised in an intimate, Italian pile of puppies, seven sisters, and Tony, the only boy and youngest child. Tony's birth was like the second coming of Christ, his father had joked.

Alone? He couldn't even remember being alone, except when Tony was older and had moved to college, and then he'd found Vanessa.

Maybe it was hard to imagine being a mother when you hadn't really had one yourself, he thought. It was tragic that her parents had been killed in a car accident. It made sense that Vanessa had such extreme fear of repeating that possibility with her own child with her dangerous work.

That must weigh heavily on her, he thought. It was beyond what he could fathom.

Tony finished two miles of his run and turned around. Vanessa had always put up a good front, but he knew she was vulnerable as tough as she pretended to be. He didn't blame Vanessa for being afraid after so much damage, loss, and isolation in her young life at the convent.

A seagull soared overhead. Tony shaded his eyes to watch it drift, floating free, white, and gray against the vast blue. Vanessa's favorite color. When was the last time they'd sat and watched the sky, the ocean, or a gull?

Running back along the shore, Tony tried to burn off his disappointment. Shouldn't his relationship with Vanessa be enough? She was everything he wanted in a woman. He just didn't have enough access to his woman. Their lives had been so hectic since they'd started filming together, barely out of their teens in college. Winning that Oscar for their Kent State massacre and Berkeley protest documentary so young had started their careers off with a boom. They weren't even legal age to celebrate with champagne afterward. Maybe now that they didn't have a project in sight, they should take a little vacation together. Wouldn't time together help fill the void?

Taking a slower pace, Tony climbed the stairs to the top of the cliff and headed back to the house. He needed Vanessa in his arms. While standing by the pool behind the house, wiping the sweat from his forehead with a tennis towel, he spotted Vanessa up in their bedroom wearing her blue silk robe. Through the floor-to-ceiling glass windows, she looked like a miniature doll in an oversized dollhouse.

Their beachfront mansion, with its massive redwood panels and glass walls, suddenly looked absurd—so big for two people. It had been his choice. Ironic, now, those see-through walls seemed like a metaphor for one more exposé. It seemed to call out for a big, bustling family celebrating a birthday or a wedding. Why else have it? Maybe their lives would feel less empty if they downsized. They were never at home much to use it anyway—all those bedrooms, the pool, a guest house, and the tennis court. It was a beautiful place to live, on the cliffs, with that all-glass view overlooking the water—if they'd ever spent time there, if their work hadn't always devoured any leisure time.

He couldn't think of the last time they'd taken a vacation. Why was he feeling so cheated out of life lately?

"Hey, Tony." Edward jolted him out of his thoughts.

"Hey, what are you up to so early?"

Leaving the door open to his Mercedes convertible, Edward held up a magazine and a DHL package. "Forgot to give Van the mail yesterday when she shooed me out. Good news and some not-so-great news, and a DHL rush package arrived late last night—intriguing. Maybe that new project she'd been praying for."

I hope not, Tony thought. "Let's start with the bad news." Tony took the package and mail. "Come in for a coffee?"

"I'll have to pass. I've got some appointments to reschedule. So, check out who beat Vanessa for Woman of the Year—*Fiona O'Farrell*. Can't believe a pianist could beat out Vanessa. But read the article, then you'll get why she was nominated."

"Edward, you know she doesn't care about that stuff. But the DHL package, that's another thing. I sense another project coming our way." Tony shrugged. "Just when I was going to take her away for vacation for a change." Tony patted Edward on his shoulder. "Cross your fingers. Maybe you'll get a well-deserved break too."

"Your mouth to God's ears. But you gotta love her, right?"

"Right." Tony turned to go into the house. "Wait a minute. What's the good news?"

"Oh, a Native American couple saw their daughter Kima's interview on the show. They were the parents. Pretty emotional." Edward sighed with his usual empathy that Tony recognized was such a part of why her assistant and Vanessa were so tight.

The thought of the child's reunion with her family after her terrifying kidnapping stirred up Tony's inner desire to have children again, along with the memory of Maureen, the orphan from the foster care exposé. "That's fantastic."

"OK. Gotta go." Edward slipped into his convertible and tore out of the driveway.

TONY WENT UP THE staircase two stairs at a time and followed the sound to the shower.

With her face in her hands, Vanessa stood with her back to him. All four showerheads were riveted on her.

Global Limelight magazine, with the face of Fiona O' Farrell on the cover, sat on Vanessa's vanity. The stereo filled the misty room with the Grammy-winning woman's familiar piano music. Was Vanessa celebrating the famous pianist's win or lamenting her own possible loss? It wasn't like her to care about these awards and titles. Still, they seemed to come her way despite her lack of interest.

Tony undressed and slipped into the spacious glass enclosure. "Hey, honey."

She flinched at his arrival.

He rubbed her shoulders. "One of your little downturns?" Turning Vanessa to face him, Tony held Vanessa's face and looked deep into her eyes. What was she thinking? He kissed her and watched two rivulets of warm water roll down her chest like tears.

She put her hand on his cheek.

Stepping back behind her, he poured shampoo into his hand. In hopes of lulling her into a conversation, Tony washed her long hair patiently in silence, rinsing it with the handheld showerhead.

"We're both overworked," he said in her ear from behind. "You'll be OK. You know this always happens to you when a project ends."

"I'm fine, just tired. But you always know what I need, Tony." She reached behind, pulled his face into the crook of her neck, and turned to kiss his wet forehead. "And maybe it's this turning forty thing. Silly, huh?"

"What do you think of a nice vacation? We'll celebrate alone. Remember those things where you go away and have fun and no work?"

"Maybe that's what I need, something completely exotic and foreign to me."

"Funny, Van." His clipped laugh echoed in the tiled shower. Tony knew her well. When her lows hit, it was no time to bring up sensitive subjects. The discussion about having children pressed hard on his lips, but he swallowed it. He knew the window of time for that had regretfully closed once again. And not on her birthday. "Happy Birthday, babe." Tony couldn't bear it when Vanessa was without her usual passion and upbeat spirit that came with a new adventure, especially on her birthday. He couldn't hold back. Vanessa had to come first. Even though it was good news, any talk of Kima and her reunion with her parents might also trigger a conversation they shouldn't have right now. He quickly soaped up, rinsed himself off, drew a heart in the steamed glass with the initials *VG* inside, kissed her, and left the shower. He turned around and saw Vanessa correct the initials with her finger to read: "CAC".

She hastily smeared away the foggy letters.

What was *that*? Tony wondered.

TONY LOOKED UP from his chair in the bedroom, where he sat, reading the article about the Woman of the Year Award. He couldn't read the painful look on Vanessa's face as she towel-dried her hair. "You need to talk, hon?"

"I'm good. I just didn't sleep."

Tony stepped forward, kissed her, and held her tight. "The World Truth in News Award banquet will be fun tomorrow night. What a serious honor for you, not like those other awards." He tossed the magazine with Fiona O' Farrell's face on the cover in the trash beside his chair.

Taking a deep breath, Tony embraced Vanessa and squeezed her harder, as though he could physically press his desire into her heart. Staring over her shoulder, the DHL package called to him to be the man she thought he was, the man he wanted to be. "Van, I think we might have a new inquiry. Edward dropped off a DHL package. Let's see what the magnificent Vanessa Gold and her dedicated film team are doing next."

CHAPTER 13

THUNDERING APPLAUSE

Vanessa

THE DIN OF THE thundering applause subsided as dinner was served. Vanessa scanned the elegant room filled with couture, haute cuisine, famous faces, and tables dressed as stylishly as the formal guests. As she targeted the people in the audience who could most help her cause, Vanessa swished an empty crystal glass casting colorful lights on the white tablecloth. The signal was picked-up immediately by a passing waiter.

"More water, Ms. Gold?" The young waiter approached her at the head table that stretched endlessly across the front of the enormous ballroom. "Congratulations on your Truth Award. This should be an interesting night." His words and his tone caught her attention, activating her fine-tuned intuition. There was a flicker of a thought, but her mind was preoccupied with the evidential photographs in the DHL package. Marked *personal*, the photographs were sent from the director of security for an unfamiliar mining company in Indonesia. The opportunity had come just in time, her new and much-needed distraction delivered like a gift.

Closing her eyes, Vanessa sighed with relief, then chastised herself for finding comfort in the treacherous situation. Most importantly, she could do something meaningful for a woman in grave danger. A cross-cultural challenge. And Canyon would be perfect for the job. Could Vanessa lure her off campus for just one more adventurous assignment? A woman's life was at stake, and that was something she knew both Canyon and Tony would understand. There was a ticking clock on this one, with the full moon only eight days away. They would have to leave in two days, she thought. It would give her another delay to any discussion about having a child, and would take her mind off her mother.

Vanessa didn't look up from her stack of note cards and photographs. Her slight gesture to the young waiter seemed to be enough. He dramatically poured an icy waterfall from above, carefully avoiding the exotic flowers perched on the edge of the abundantly plated table.

Sensing his eyes were on her, Vanessa drew the evidence into her lap below the table and adjusted her signature, tinted glasses. Selecting two of the photographs, she was struck by the indigenous woman's contrasting looks—the same face—one expression hopeless and tortured, the next hopeful and euphoric. The pleading face looked upward at what Vanessa assumed was the helicopter and the anonymous pilot who had taken the photos from above.

Vanessa smiled at Tony, who stood mid-room with his eye to a movie camera. He changed his angle upward to take in the three-foot letters behind her, "WORLD TRUTH IN NEWS AWARD 1990."

"Excuse me. Excuse me."

Glancing up, Vanessa watched Edward, in a perfectly tailored, blue Armani couture suit, bee-lining toward the head table. He stepped behind the waiter and positioned himself beside her.

"Vanessa, I'm so excited to hear about the new project. Knock 'em dead, girlfriend. I got things set up with the sound guys, and they have the new slides for one unforgettable acceptance speech."

"What would I do without you, Eddie? Were you able to contact the phone number the letter provided?"

"Yes, I spoke to the mining director's head of security, a guy named Scott. He says they're grateful that you've agreed to take on the project. Although that's what they always say."

"You realize this changes everything." She calmly tapped her finger on a photo of the native woman. Raking her hair back again, Vanessa examined the tortured look on the indigenous woman's face and then stood.

Edward flinched.

"Relax, Eddie." Vanessa nodded at the guests around her. Expecting a tense, heated evening, she removed her swingy satin jacket.

Sweeping in for the interception, Edward hung it neatly on the back of her chair with one swift gesture while pulling her seat back to give her more privacy.

"You always get my signals." Vanessa released a quick puff of a laugh and sat down. Tapping Edward's shoulder, she re-focused on a photo of the woman being held overhead by two threatening men.

"Oh my God," Edward whispered hoarsely. "This next case is over-the-top! Forget the interviews next week. I'll postpone everything. Now tell me more, just a few details."

"Human sacrifice in nineteen-ninety! Edward, a woman is about to be sacrificed. Thrown over a cliff. And it's an American mining company's fault. Cultural insensitivity." Vanessa pulled a letter from her purse. "I received this too. Some very important information from the company pilot, who took these photos. Apparently he doesn't totally trust the security director who sent the evidence. The mining company did no intercultural reconnaissance before invading the lands of these untouched societies."

"Where is this exactly?" Edward squatted next to her chair.

"Irian Jaya, an Indonesian jungle island." Vanessa pulled at the hem of her dress. Mumbling, she stared at the woman in the photo. "Why do I have to be white and American? It's so stereotypical to be the great white savior, rescuing her stone-age sister."

"Boss, if you were not from the privileged side of society, you wouldn't likely know about—let alone be saving—an aboriginal woman from a cliff on the other side of the world. At least you're using your privilege for good." Edward bent to straighten the silverware in front of her. "And no one cares about the color of the activist who exposes a wrong to right a situation. After everything you've done, no one would ever think that way about you. Seriously, you're the most inclusive . . . sometimes you think the craziest things. But I admire your cultural sensitivity." Edward flashed a paper in front of her face. "OK, let's review tomorrow's schedule."

She ignored his rapid-fire litany of obligations. "Edward, unless it's about prepping for the trip or finding an anthropologist we can trust at the last minute, we can't afford to waste time. There's a deadline here. Before the full moon."

"Whoa, so when's that?"

"Moon in eight days, leave in two."

"Here goes Wonder Woman."

"Well, Wonder Woman will need a sidekick. I'm calling Canyon tonight."

"Perfect. Love her. You think she'll come back, especially for this one? Remember when you were in the Amazon and—"

"Two minutes." The Emcee walked behind Vanessa, hesitated, and bent over her shoulder. He lingered a second too long. She glanced back and nodded at him.

Vanessa saw Edward flash a look of disdain at the Emcee's departing back.

The other illustrious guests took their seats beside her along the head table, exchanging brief greetings. The music began to play softly.

"They chose 'I Am Woman' to intro you? Really?" Edward laughed.

Looking out over the room, Vanessa watched the guests who had switched tables ending their visits. With cheek kisses, touches to shoulders, and smiling departures, they returned to their places.

"What did you say, Eddie?"

"I said, 'You'd certainly never run out of exposé material in this world.' Seems everyone has something to hide, except you, maybe." The music swelled, indicating the ceremony would resume. "Break a leg, darling. This will be one incredible acceptance speech—front page for sure. And by the way, that supposed classy Emcee was ogling your cleavage as he passed. What a creep." Edward swept away half-bent to lend a clear shot to the flashing cameras.

Turning her attention to her role as the honoree, she smiled at Tony, who studied her from his camera position. He'd insisted that he film her special night. Or was he avoiding a long evening at his mother's table with his sisters? He launched a small wave, and Vanessa felt a twinge of sadness.

He winked and smiled.

God she loved him. Maybe they should take that vacation right after this project. Sliding the photos into the shipping envelope, Vanessa glanced at her watch, and again the date struck a chord— the day her father had died. She drew in a quick breath and forced a smile as a photographer flashed a photo of the head table.

Men in black suits, fingers to ears, twitched nervously throughout the electrified room, failing in their attempt to blend in. With all the people of fame and fortune in that audience, they were on high alert.

The silver-haired Emcee's baritone voice cut through the hum of the room, and the waves of conversation turned to mumbles and then ceased. "Good evening, esteemed members of the press, Ladies and Gentlemen, honored guests." The Emcee adjusted his cummerbund over his expanded middle, cleared his throat, and the rustling of starch and silk, the clinking of glasses, and the scraping of chairs settled down.

Adjusting the DHL envelope beneath the table, Vanessa flipped her hair in front of her shoulders. Looking out over the audience, she gathered her expected composure.

The Emcee continued, "And now, for her unprecedented body of award-winning and compelling documentaries by a single investigative journalist—let alone one of such beauty and youth," he added, turning to Vanessa, obviously impressed with his own charm.

A ripple of soft chuckles passed over the audience in response to the Emcee's histrionics.

"Sexist," Edward mouthed to her from his nearby seat.

"It is my distinct honor to introduce to you, yet once again, and deservedly so . . ." The Emcee turned again to smile at Vanessa and continued, "Former Woman of the Year, and a nominee again this year, an advocate of the oppressed and defender of human rights, three-time Oscar-winning documentarian, and host of the Emmy-winning television program, *Exposé*. Shall I go on?" He feigned a loss of breath, panting.

The audience laughed.

Edward rolled his eyes.

Vanessa nodded, shifting her eyes toward Edward in agreement.

"And now, the nineteen-ninety recipient of The World Truth in News Award." He said each word with just the perfect pause, then added, "Ms. Vanessa Gold!"

The room of luminaries delivered a roar of applause and an extended standing ovation.

Vanessa stood humbly, moving to the dais to accept the coveted heavy crystal bowl with the familiar globe-shaped base. She passed behind the editors of the *LA* and *New York Times*, and overheard their exchange. Her ability to laser-in on a single conversation, deftly plucking it out of a room full of chatter, was uncanny, she'd been told. It was a valuable skill in her line of work. Vanessa was well aware of that fact, having accessed many vital clues through that singular talent in researching her stories for *Exposé*. It was her secret weapon that no one could explain.

One editor, a W.C. Fields sound-alike, talked out of the side of his mouth, mimicking a carnival barker. "Step right up folks and win a prize! Once again, gorgeous Ms. Vanessa Gold snags the coveted award." He flicked his fantasy cigar at the corner of his mouth and laughed at his own cleverness.

"Stop, you're just jealous." The woman next to him snapped his arm and released a controlled snort.

Was it any wonder she resisted being in the limelight? She blew a kiss to Tony, stood before the microphone, and made a sweeping gesture toward him. "My life partner, cameraman, and co-producer, Tony Amorino, who shares this award with me, Ladies and Gentlemen." Hundreds of eyes followed the path of the kiss she sent to Tony, and the clapping rose again.

Leaving the camera in the hands of his assistant, Tony wove in and out of the crowded tables to reach a handsome older woman. Leaning over, he kissed both her cheeks and followed suit with the seven younger women seated at one of the forty ten-tops. Tony picked up a little girl from the lap of one of the women. The child snuggled affectionately into his shoulder, and he kissed her and returned her to her mother's arms.

Vanessa tensed and then announced, "Tony's mother and sisters, Ladies and Gentlemen. Thank you for being here for us." She sent them a similar but unreturned air kiss.

Vanessa heard a female guest shout through the applause to the guest next to her at the nearest table. "Now, *he* is gorgeous." It took some of the intensity down inside her. Vanessa still loved his strong face, his easygoing, solid ways—the other half of the "perfect couple," as she'd heard them described—her loyal rock.

The room began to quiet as they all took their assigned seats. Vanessa didn't expect a return kiss from Tony's sisters. She'd overheard them speaking around the corner from her as she'd prepared her notes for her speech just before the ceremony. It was the same old thing.

"Tony is definitely the man behind the woman," one sister had said.

"Or is he the man cleaning up behind the elephant," another one whispered.

A third followed with, "I guess we'll never see a niece or nephew out of Ms. Exposé?"

Now, the room went silent, but Vanessa could see the sisters with covered mouths, their eyes gesturing back and forth between Tony and her. Their mother sent a look of disapproval. Avoiding Vanessa's gaze, all seven look-alikes adjusted themselves properly in their chairs, returning their attention to the front of the room.

She turned to see her shapely shadow cast on the widescreen that began to fill with a collage of her accomplishments. Vanessa stepped aside to view the video.

Music accompanied the tribute with historic images of her TV interviews for *Exposé* and her documentaries: a group of robed women revealing only furtive eyes, two young men enduring the removal of swastika tattoos, a seated, smiling man behind bars holding a cross, young girls fleeing from a brothel in India, a Chinese student dissident in Tiananmen Square.

Her documentary accolades went on for nearly ten minutes from the Berkeley riots to the Berlin wall, to the Jonestown massacre, and to the Cambodian Genocide. With each unforgettable event, the audience responded with waves of applause, colored by gasps and mixed looks of both admiration and jealousy.

She could read faces, and she could read lips. The skill was both a liability and an asset. Vanessa removed her tinted glasses and set them next to the mic. She welcomed the glaring lights that blocked out the faces of the audience—the only comforting thing she'd found about being on stage. Lowering her head slightly to the renewed applause, Vanessa put her right hand over her heart and began to speak.

"Your Excellences, esteemed colleagues, and most honored guests and friends. To receive The World Truth in News Award is—"

"Here's the real 'truth in news,' *bitch*!" The same young male waiter who had poured her water yelled from the back of the room. His words were met with a shockwave of audience murmurs. The entire room swiveled around to find the young man who'd confronted her. "She don't care about other people's lives. She's a *phony*!"

CHAPTER 14

APPLAUDING THUNDER

Lukeem

LUKEEM PUSHED through the thick greenery for long hours, toward the unfamiliar valley in her mind. The image guided her onward—to near exhaustion, to her pain's limits. She arrived at the edge of a cliff as the sun gave up the day.

From her perch at the top of the frightening drop-off, Lukeem overlooked the strange cluster of huts with twinkling rippled tops nestled between three massive mountains. Far below, she saw a tiny perfect replica of the sky spirits' bird, humming and hovering amid a grouping of reflecting shapes. Was it the home of the sky spirits?

Heat rushed to her face. It was confusing how the flying creatures could grow and shrink like that when they left the cliff. What would make the loud, whooshing helicopter appear, at first, like an enormous bird, and then, with its sound fading, transform into the size of a tiny flying insect?

With a pleading look, Lukeem reached out over the abyss, attempting to capture the helicopter in her hand. She called out to it, just as she'd summoned the blue moth. Disappearing, it landed among the shiny, sunlit objects far below.

What must the sky spirits' world be like?

How would she ever descend such a distance?

Would she also become smaller if she flew with the sky spirits?

Would she ever return to herself again?

Following the sound of a distant roar, Lukeem ran on in a daze. When she reached an awesome drape of water, and her exhaustion finally took her legs, she made one last effort. Lukeem pushed through the narrow space beside its chilling wall onto the safety of a hidden rock shelf. She'd run far beyond the ancestral area that had been her home before she'd felt safe enough to take refuge, to rest, and to take in her plight.

The anger of the Ranu Lolo churned inside Lukeem. Her deep losses—her son, her tribe, her sky spirits—made her sorrow erupt, and she wept. Trembling with raw fear and exhaustion, with heaving shoulders, she rested behind the massive curtain of crystal water that crashed before her with applauding thunder. She had escaped the sacrifice. She was alive. But where and how would she live now? Behind the thundering waters, she found a hollowed-out area, and she tucked into the corner of the dry space and slept.

In the morning, Lukeem moved out from behind the splashing water to sit on a jagged rock softened by thick green moss. A small rat scurried past her, but she had no weapon to capture it and no will to make the fire to cook it. Her hunger gave her a new understanding of the power of bow and arrows denied to her tribal women.

Lukeem recalled the many times she'd seen the men crafting their own weapons of survival. She'd never thought to need or use one. Her whole life she'd seen the men use them, yet she'd never closely watched the technique—the details of pulling back the string, aiming, and letting go. Without them, she would have to sustain herself on roots, berries, beetles, insects, and spiders. There would be no fullness from the meat of a roasted wild pig or even a small rat. Without the fat of the animals, how would she tolerate the cold of the jungle nights?

When she felt stronger, she would create her own weapon, she decided. No one would see.

AFTER DAYS ALONE staring at the pounding flow of the water, distraught and desperate for sustenance, Lukeem left the protection of the waterfall. Still driven by her vision of the sky spirits, she ached to be in their village she'd seen from the grand precipice.

Her son filled her mind. She could still feel his unique vibrations when her hand pressed over his heart in greeting. The other women spoke of no such instincts. They'd looked at her strangely the first and only time she'd shared her belief with them. She was different. Simply through her touch, Lukeem could always sense her boy's fears like a small quivering bird, his sadness like the heaviness of a stone, his confusion like the entanglements of disrupted spider webs.

She thought of Abruce when he was a child, his skittering notes tripping like dragonflies across a stream's surface. He seldom paused to rest except to send sweet glances into her eyes by the fire at night. When she held his warm body, she'd instantly felt some familiar part of herself in him. He had a freedom inside. Something she did not sense in her mate, Kralu.

Despite the many seasons Abruce had been gone, the pain was fresh and hot inside her. Would she ever feel his warmth again? Had she known, she would have held him so much tighter, touched every nub of hair on his tiny head, brought every butterfly from the sky down to make him smile. Had she only known.

As a young man, Abruce was also like her—molten inside, flowing freely, quick to embrace her visions as truth, with a smile that spread easily on his open face.

She'd always had pictures racing in her mind as a small girl, but when Abruce was born, the clarity began like glimpses of the blue sky through the dense canopy that covered her world. Without under-standing it, Lukeem saw a place in her mind each time she looked into Abruce's black eyes. She began to draw pictures of that place on her cave wall in her hideaway, where she'd sat with her only son for hours trying to understand.

In her mind, she saw strange people who glowed with pale faces. She saw her place up high and theirs down below. From her grandfather's whispers, she imagined an angular image. Its long broad lines the color of blood, waved side by side with other long lines the light color of the small flower that appeared in the morning and slept at night. She pictured the blue of the clear sky after thunderous rain with many sharp white stars cutting through.

Trying to make it clear, Lukeem had drawn the image many times. She'd searched for days to find the right stain to make the rarely found sky color on her image. She wanted it to be a perfect match to the picture in her mind. Now it was complete, and the sky spirits had taught her the word *American flag*, and it was time to leave her cave and her paintings forever.

As her connection to the other women was severed, Lukeem had suffered inside. She'd distanced herself from them, captivated by her constant need to understand her thoughts that grew stronger as rainy seasons folded in, one upon the other. The women pulled at her to return to their ways—to spend her time gathering seeds and roots with them, to sleep in the women's area far from her cave, but she could not. After meeting the sky spirits, she could never be like her fellow tribeswomen again.

Feeling a drive that began in her gut and traveled to her arms, Lukeem stood from the rock. Chills passed down them in pulsing waves as she blindly ran a full day with a powerful intuition. As the sun went into hiding and Lukeem broke through the brush, she saw the shocking image. She held her breath.

Tucked behind the nearby metal shack, Lukeem saw a man with a dark face, very much like her tribesmen but dressed in the coverings of the sky spirits. He made a bird-like call with his lips tightened into a circle and lifted his chin toward her. Smiling, he sent a sky spirit's greeting to her, quickly waving his open stiff hand left and right, three times.

Lukeem carefully repeated the gesture and added the greeting. "Heh-lo Bee-u-tee-ful."

A look of confusion and a smile passed over his face. Stepping out of the hut, he called to Lukeem, "Hati, hati! Careful, tram's coming!" He pointed down the mountain and nodded again.

The sight took her breath away as a screeching sound announced the approach of an enormous angular beetle shell, or a nest the color of the sun with the sky spirits' special symbol on its side—red, white, and sky.

"Tram," she whispered to herself. She'd never considered the *others* would have different sounds to speak to each other. The man did not seem to understand the sky spirits' greeting, Hello Bee-u-tee-ful. The idea unfolded so many new thoughts that she couldn't capture them. They scattered and stung her mind like a disturbed hill of red ants.

CHAPTER 15

COLLATERAL DAMAGE

Vanessa

THE YOUNG MAN could not have chosen a more threatening word—*phony*. Vanessa thought she was about to be exposed, revealed for the fraud she was—false name, false history, false image. A poser, a phony. She'd almost forgotten over time. She'd even believed her own façade. Her face went flush. Images flashed: her mother walking out the door, her father rocking violently in the dark, her last glimpse of her grandfather's kind face, her little-girl-self staring through the grates of the convent window waiting for her famous mother to return.

Within seconds, she'd gathered her composure. Staying calm in a crisis was her strength, she counseled herself.

The familiar drill unfolded quickly as index fingers went to earphones, voices whispered into cuffs, and the security men in black suits converged on the young male.

Vanessa could see that the Emcee was flustered. He lifted his shoulders, and spread his hands palms up, looking to her for guidance from his place at the end of the head table. His gesture instantly transferred the stares of the audience to her.

Launching into autopilot, Vanessa sent him a nod and a reassuring smile, signaling she would handle this herself. It took all she had to remain in her well-practiced character. With a slight lift of her chin and an almost imperceptible flicker of her eyes, Vanessa signaled to the sound director in the booth to play the short trailer of her most recent documentary—an exposé of the kidnapping ring. She needed sound and a diversion.

Flagging his assistant to take over the camera, Tony intercepted the young waiter first and waved off the suits who were anxious to intercede. Seeing that the boy calmed down visibly with Tony's hand on his shoulder, they hesitantly let him take control.

A sputter of scattered, repressed laughter erupted from a small cluster of competitive colleagues in the audience. Vanessa cleared her throat into the mic to refocus the crowd's attention. Shaken inside, Vanessa controlled her body, feigning composure. As was her habit, she twisted her water glass on the tablecloth next to the podium, rolling the etched stem between her fingers to absorb her tension. She assessed the crowd's reactions.

Vanessa desperately wanted to redirect their attention—the one room full of people who could shine the world's spotlight on the native woman's plight—the press. Their powers could cut both ways. Her plan was to engage their sympathy. How could this have happened? Who was the young man?

Vanessa knew that nearly every person in the room had likely been the target of public criticism or disdain. "Being in the spotlight has its price tag, as everyone in this room knows." She battled to keep fear from affecting her voice. Working to steady her lips, she managed a warm smile. It drew tilted nods and smiles in return, defusing the tension in the crowd. "I want to share a sneak preview of the *Turning Prism* documentary to be released next week. You'll please excuse my cameraman and partner while he speaks with this young man to see why he feels I deserve the 'B' word."

It all happened seamlessly within seconds, and the audience visibly relaxed while watching the film clip. In the darkened room, Vanessa negotiated around the head table. Taking a short cut along the empty wall, she tried to catch up with Tony who was exiting into the foyer.

"I know the boy. It's OK." Tony reassured the guards.

Vanessa followed close behind Tony with a roar in her ears. What could this young man know? She prayed for his silence until they left the earshot of the crowd.

The teen torqued his head back, engaging Vanessa's eyes as he continued his harangue. Then he walked cooperatively with his head down, hosted by Tony and a cadre of security guards.

Edward caught up with Vanessa, folding in behind her. "Name's Jason. He's the son of the man you nailed in last month's foster care story." His words were for her ears only, then he disappeared.

Vanessa's knees nearly gave out from under her with relief.

"You *are* a phony." The boy twisted around again and spit the words at her. "You pretend you want to help people, but now my dad's going to be in prison, and my mom's sick. He never did anything but work hard. He told me the real truth. It was a setup. That girl, Maureen, was a liar."

Vanessa wasn't surprised at the lie the man had told his son. "Oh, Jason, I'm so sorry, but those children were being—"

What could she do to prevent the collateral damage that came with justice? Vanessa's chest was tight with regret that the boy had to be impacted by his father's despicable crimes. She imagined Tony's eyes as he'd watched young Maureen's testimony on the video screen—that longing stare that resurrected the discussion about marriage and children between them.

Music swelled in the ballroom.

"Van, I've got this." Tony tossed the reassuring words over his shoulder.

The boy slumped down to the ground sobbing.

Vanessa hesitated, stepped closer, wanting to comfort the teen.

Tony sent her that rare look, the one that said there would be no negotiating. "Really, honey, go ahead. They're starting." Tony squatted next to the distressed boy.

Nodding in agreement, Vanessa sighed, shimmied her dress down, straightened her hair, and pushed through the heavy ballroom door. Still unnerved by the boy's suffering, Vanessa returned to the front of the ballroom and gathered her composure. She was relieved Jason's words were not what she'd feared, revealing one of her lies about her past. Yet Vanessa felt an aching sadness for all the children caught in the crossfire of their parents' crimes.

Drawing in a deep breath, she released it slowly, regained her composure, and waited for the video to end and the lights to come back on. Adjusting the mic, Vanessa launched forward as though nothing had happened. "In deference to the minor, I will maintain his privacy, but I'm told an apology is forthcoming."

There was a ripple of light applause and a few titters from the audience as she began to speak.

"Collateral damage is often the price we pay for the truth." The boy's anguished face invaded her calm again. Vanessa watched Edward as he scurried around the glass sound booth in the back of the ballroom, ensuring the photos for her new keynote speech were in the order she'd requested.

Despite her sudden wooziness, she continued, "Tonight, I want to tell you a story of collateral damage—the devastating impact of modern technology on one of the few remaining aboriginal societies on Earth who still live a Stone Age existence. These shocking photographs were recently delivered to me."

The series of slides flashed across the screen. Guests audibly gasped in shock. Two tribesmen holding a near-naked woman aloft by the edge of a sheer cliff; a close-up of her tortured face; shocked tribesman, outfitted with bows and arrows and strange tubular objects jutting up from between their legs; two men with terrified, wide eyes, dropping the woman to the ground; the woman reaching up, pleadingly; the same woman scrambling away, and the group of perpetrators sinking to their knees in fear.

She watched Edward whisper into the ear of the director behind the glass at the back of the room. The director nodded as Edward flashed a thumbs-up to Vanessa. They had adapted nicely to the surprise change in her plans. She was grateful for the loyal few.

Like sharks going for blood, her colleagues in the audience reached for their ever-ready pens and notepads to capture the scoop. Vanessa watched the assistant cameraman panic, waving to Tony for guidance. He whispered into his mic to the director behind the glass at the back of the room.

The screen went blank, then a high-impact close-up of the native woman's tormented face appeared. The photo remained on the huge screen, leaving the guests to grasp their neighbors' arms.

Vanessa paused, then spoke, emphasizing each word, leaning in closer to the mic. "This is the result of the unpredictable evolution of culture when insensitively contaminated by modern society and technology—misinterpretations, confusions, a morphing of traditions, and in this case, the potential death of an innocent woman," Vanessa spoke softly with a deliberate, intimate delivery. "Why is it?" Her voice cracked unexpectedly and she paused. Vanessa turned away to loosen the tensed muscles in her throat with a soft breath in and out, and she let the question hang in the air seconds longer. "Why is it that the male of our species puts a woman on a pedestal, pursues her nurturing with a passion, has a protective instinct for her, depends on her to have his children to carry on his line, writes songs and poems about her, conducts wars over her, would even *die* for her . . ." Vanessa engaged the Emcee's eyes for a moment and returned her gaze to the room. "And yet he can commit such atrocities against her?"

Vanessa noticed the forward lean of the audience and felt more encouraged. "We have seen it all in our careers as investigative reporters. It isn't reserved for the isolated societies or the extreme few. It's pandemic. A worldwide story of abuse, rape, acid burnings, sex trafficking little girls, and unthinkable atrocities against the very persons men adulate and desire in their own lives, the very females they fight over, who give them life, intimacy, nurse them, hold them in their arms."

A weighty silence filled the room.

Emotion coated Vanessa's voice. "I, for one, will never, ever, *ever* comprehend that."

Reversing through the slides, she showed the photo of the woman suspended awkwardly above two men, with her pleading, contorted face in focus and a man pointing an arrow at her from a few paces away. Vanessa allowed the poignant moment to breathe. She scanned the solemn looks on the faces in the crowd.

"This ritual of sacrificing women to the nature spirits, the murdering of so-called sorceresses had not been carried out for generations by this tribe until an American mining company built a modern copper and gold mine on their tribal lands, high in the mountains of Irian Jaya, a remote island of Indonesia. A local missionary in the area described this tribe as 'rarely seen, non-violent, and affable.' So remote, they'd had no known previous contact with the miners, let alone the outside world—unlike some of the other tribes who live nearer to the mine site and had been recruited as workers." The pilot's letter, which had arrived the same day as the photos, ran through Vanessa's mind. She went on, deciding what to reveal, knowing she only had pieces of the story in hand. "Recently, a helicopter from an American mining company landed in a clearing in the thick jungle of the remote island. It attracted this fascinated and innocent indigenous woman into that same clearing. By tradition, this ancestoral burial ground and ceremonial circle forbids entry to women."

Vanessa showed the photo of the woman reaching up to the sky with pleading outstretched arms. "A co-pilot who worked for the mine lured her closer to the helicopter with gifts, chocolate among them.

Seems stereotypic, doesn't it? A World War Two mimic? 'Just for the fun of it,' he was overheard saying, according to my sources. His bragging started the news. It rapidly spread among the local tribes who followed the widely held tradition of 'no women allowed' in men's ceremonial spaces."

Flashing another photo, she continued. "This circle was different. It was originally cleared out of the dense foliage and ultimately abandoned by the US military during World War Two. It was a remote place where supplies were once dropped for troops: K-rations, cigarettes, canned goods, instant coffee, chocolate, gum, jungle combat boots, and the like." Vanessa paused and looked around the room for Tony, but he'd not yet returned from dealing with the young man. "The local inhabitants who'd found the strange treasures believed these sky spirits had sent the exotic supplies as gifts. In a place where food is sometimes scarce, and there is no concept of possessions, this was a welcome miracle from the sky spirits."

The audience was entranced—leaning forward, propping their chins on clenched fists with elbows on tables, or placing their hands over their mouths.

"Naturally, after World War Two ended, these generous spirits never returned, but the barren circle became a hopeful and sacred place for the tribe, reserved for men."

The only sound in the room was the scratching of pens as press members took notes.

"It was an innocent and practical action on the part of the Allies back in war times. They had no understanding of what they did to impact the indigenous people's culture." Vanessa cleared her throat and took a drink of water. "There is much more to this story. These cultural phenomena are sometimes referred to as cargo cults. After waiting for the 'sky spirits' to return, the tribe had suffered profound guilt, assuming they had offended them. These are animistic people who worshiped spirits of nature, not gods per se. The indigenous people thought if they repeated the behaviors of the sky spirits, in this case, marching, smoking cigarettes, and saluting, they would forgive them, return, embrace them, and bring more gifts." Vanessa read the audience; they were spellbound. She went on.

"Of course, history tells us, the sky spirits never returned after World War Two. Missionaries in the area tell us that the honored one, and the tribal leader before him, had lost face. Eventually, he had to find a scapegoat."

Vanessa watched several reporters rush from the room. She understood they couldn't wait any longer to give their editors a heads up to hold space for the breaking story. She continued, "In many cases, when things go wrong in societies, a woman is accused of being a sorceress or a witch. In America's past, the Salem witch-hunts are an example. Tribal beliefs in sorceresses' spells are so powerful that their hunts for food began to fail, and their women were rendered barren. The sky spirits sightings reported by the accused woman were even more threatening to the honored one. He called her a liar, a lowly woman whose spells had prevented the gifts from flowing from above. Audaciously, she'd claimed to have seen and spoken to the sky spirits."

Pushing the words out of her tightening throat, Vanessa remembered the pilot's firsthand intel. The letter that arrived after the DHL package had revealed the facts. "Much to the honored one's chagrin, as we might imagine, the woman did see the sky spirits, the pilot and co-pilot. They'd even talked to her and had given her chocolate." Vanessa glanced at the clock. It was nearing time to wrap up her speech.

"In the tribe's view, she must be sacrificed to appease the river spirit for the woman's desecration of the men's ceremonial space. If the Americans hadn't invaded the tribe's simple, so-called *primitive* Stone Age society with their helicopter and tram construction that attracted her into the ancestoral burial ground, this woman would not be in danger today. The fiasco could have been avoided if some research and consideration for their culture had been conducted. The pilot and co-pilot were innocent victims of a culture clash between the aborigines and the mining company. We should know better at this juncture in history." Vanessa continued to scroll through the slides again.

There wasn't a sound in the room.

"Savage and uncivilized primitive rituals, you might say? I remind you again of Salem, Massachusetts, not so long ago in our own culture." She returned to the first photo of the accused woman. "As such an accused sorceress, the tribe plans to sacrifice this woman according to an ancient tribal tradition. When found, she will be thrown over a massive cliff into the jagged rocks and the rushing waters of the Ranu Lolo River a thousand feet below."

Vanessa's voice broke. "Imagine your entire society turning on you in such a way. As is customary, these cultures mark events by the moon. They have until the next full moon to make the sacrifice. That means eight days from tonight."

Vanessa moved to wrap-up. Returning to the photo of the woman being held overhead by two angry native males, Vanessa said, "There is surely more to the situation than I am privy to. We are gathering our team and leaving for Indonesia. I promise all of you in this room, and oppressed women everywhere, that my *Turning Prism* team will make this a passionate priority."

Tony was behind the camera again, nodding his head, sending that support she depended on. His hand over his heart sent a message that put her further at ease.

Leaning forward, she paused, then spoke, accenting each word. "Ladies and Gentlemen, if one exposure to modern technology can tilt a cultural norm, change a cultural belief, move a group to act in a new way, I believe another can do the same. If one action, one misunderstanding, one change, can cause a cross-cultural tragedy, can't another change cause a new cultural norm? One of peace? Mutual understanding?" Vanessa paused. "We need to creatively and sensitively intervene for all of our sakes and for the sake of one innocent woman. My team will work cooperatively with Zell Baxter Mining to seek that change. Good night, and thank you." Vanessa's words were met with supportive applause.

The clapping, raised voices, and the press running from their seats to get the scoop told her she had accomplished her goal. Despite the interruption by the boy, the strategy was in place. It was the only way she'd ever succeeded in her long string of successful missions—conducting the dangerous assignment in front of the entire world.

CHAPTER 16

SPIDER'S THREAD

Lukeem

SUSPENDED IN MIDAIR, the tram crawled up along a thick cord toward her. It was attached like a spider's thread to the valley below. Lukeem drew in her breath. In the deep crevice between three mountains was the place that had inhabited her mind for years. The home of the sky spirits shimmered in the sunlight. Lukeem quivered and felt the wings of a hundred startled birds flutter up inside her.

The openings in the sides of the tram were filled with so many eyes. The eyes of men—men with the familiar dark skin and faces of her tribe, yet strangers speaking strange sounds.

The *others!*

The hunters had sometimes told tales of the rare *others*, but her questions about them were not for women to ask. A few times, the men had brought back symbols of the *others*—rare body decorations, beads, and feathers unknown to her tribe. Still, Lukeem had no imaginings about their looks or sounds. Kralu would not share any details about their world or ways; it was the men's realm, not hers.

Lukeem stepped forward from beside the shack and waved her hand at the light-skinned spirit in charge. Or was he a mere man?

"*Hati, hati, Ibu.* Careful, ma'am." His words did not convey, but his arm and concerned smile did.

The men in the tram were dressed like sky spirits—their bodies covered in earth-colored tops and tan bottoms and foot coverings made of skins. Their hands and faces were bare, but they were dark-skinned like her people.

"OK, let's go, guys. We have work to do." She heard the *other* at the top, standing next to the leader, greet them as he slid open a blade on the tram to free the men. "Hard hats, hard hats, let's go." He handed one to each man.

Grabbing the yellow hollowed-out shells, the men strapped them on. The strange head shells were certainly an honor bestowed, she thought, as Lukeem watched them leave the tram that swung gently on the thick spider's thread.

"Hard hats." She tried out the sounds for the head coverings. The breathy 'h' was no challenge. "Hahr." She mimicked the lizard's sound again and tried out the words. "Hahrd hats."

One after another, she heard the dark-skinned men say the strange words to their leader as each received the honored headdress. Lukeem listened intently, concentrating, seeking to magically force some meaning from their rhythmic utterances.

"*Terima kasih, kasih, kasih,*" each dark one said.

"*You're welcome,*" the light-skinned leader said.

All the words were unlike those of her own tribe.

Standing beside the small tin hut, she watched the long line of men with weary faces and unfamiliar weapons in hand as they entered the dark opening in the mountainside.

A wave of energy passed through Lukeem as her son's face emerged like a sunburst through the shadows in her mind. She moved closer to the tram. The ache from his disappearance had not subsided. She'd held her breath through all five changes of the seasons since Abruce had vanished—wet and dry, wet and dry, on and on, living with the crushing pressure of a fallen tree upon her chest. The thick splinter of sadness still festered there with a blazing pain from the loss. A faded memory of his smile was the meager salve she had for a wound that would not heal. She could not let go of him and the sight of the Long View. The sky spirits' home below awakened her hope. The memory of Abruce and the visions of her sky spirits pulsed back and forth in her mind as she watched the dark men step down from the tram.

Lukeem had sensed some connection between her missing son and the sky spirits. The pull that attracted her to the valley below grew stronger. Like a tendril erupting from the jungle floor, it wrapped around her heart, insisting she follow.

The growling and whining of the empty tram began as it passed by her to start its descent. Abruce's presence became clearer. She could sense him.

He was below.

He was alive.

Leaping into the opening on the empty tram's side, Lukeem huddled on the floor in the corner, unseen. It rocked her like a baby, went still, then hummed down the mountain. She was stunned by her own bravery.

Soon the swishing sounds and her curiosity brought her to her knees. She gripped the cold edge of the wall. With her eyes just above the clear opening, Lukeem watched the cluster of sparkling shapes below grow larger and larger, coming closer, becoming clearer as her long-held dream of the sky spirits' village manifested before her.

It was astounding to move through the air, drifting over the magnificent abyss. Lukeem's breathing stopped, choked by the overwhelming view. She wrapped her arms around herself and closed her eyes for just a moment, gently rubbing her arms to calm herself. Soon she was able to breathe once more.

Looking back at the mountain, Lukeem watched the only life she'd known fading, shrinking, disappearing behind her.

Her swallow came with difficulty. Tears pushed hard at the edges of her eyes as the uncertainty of her future with the sky spirits overcame her. How would she live? As a woman, would she be allowed to make her own weapon to survive? It struck her—she'd never seen a woman of the sky spirits' tribe. Did they also wear the coverings? Would she sleep in the women's area? She was sure she would have food—the sky spirits always had magical gifts and food. Memories of their voices and laughter told Lukeem she would have kindness.

Questions buzzed inside her as the reality of her new life came into view. How would she speak with them? Could she learn their strange sounds? Yes, she'd learned "tram" already, she thought, and "hard hats," and "helicopter," and "hello beautiful." She was sure the whispers of her visions would be understood by the wisdom of the sky spirits, and her strangeness would be embraced. Perhaps, she was an *other*, like the men she had seen on the way up the mountain, so much like her people, yet not. Perhaps that is why the sky spirits chose her. Yes, perhaps she and Abruce were *others*. That would explain why they had never matched with their tribespeople, she thought. The idea lifted her.

The whoosh of the cool air caressed Lukeem's face, and she dared to extend her arms out of the opening, smiling as her hands floated, rising, and dropping with the pulsing currents of the wind. Turning and dipping her hands, Lukeem tested the boundaries of the fascinating wind spirits. Her fear began to fade. Waves of chills started at her skull and passed down her spine as her anxiety and rejection by her tribe melted into rapturous joy.

She turned away from the peak and faced downward. To her left side, Lukeem examined a steep cliff, a wall of earth with roots and holes where a portion had surely broken off from some powerful force beyond her imagining. The gnarled exposed roots beckoned to her. She had much to discover.

As she was lowered closer to the village, Lukeem saw a bright blue space that marked the center of a circle of huts below. It was the familiar shape of the sky spirits' symbol on their helicopter. She could see many miniature sky spirits standing by its edge. Children? Lukeem had never considered there would be sky spirit children. They had removed all but a small part of their coverings. She was shocked to see their pale bodies for the first time.

Some adults were readying themselves for a ceremony unknown to her. The men were stretched out prone on long colorful slabs wearing small clothes covering only their manhood. Some women wore large colorful covers from breast to thighs, while other females wore two separate cloths, top and bottom. These sky spirit women must be honored ones to wear such colors. So many thoughts filled Lukeem's mind.

Women were unthinkably sleeping beside the men out in the open air. Lukeem searched her memories to add meaning to the scene as the sky spirits grew magically in size the closer she drew to the earth. She inspected herself to see if she was also becoming a larger version of herself. But no.

Young sky spirits jumped over the special space disappearing for a time into the blue and reappearing on the other side. When white splashes rose up as each child went head first, Lukeem understood it was a bright blue pool of water. Children squealed and screamed as they descended into the water or approached the edge in fear and slipped in cautiously. Some adults clapped their hands and made howling sounds with prideful looks as each young one made their ceremonial jump. There was so much to learn about the home and ways of the sky spirits, but she was not afraid.

Approaching the end of the thick silver spider's thread, Lukeem witnessed many thinner black threads connected to tall bare trees. They were spun in a web linking all the sparkling huts of the sky spirits. Mystical golden glows came from the openings in some of the beautiful dwellings. Tiny suns trapped inside? What kind of enormous spider must have spun these threads? Lukeem shuddered. Yet, if the sky spirits lived among them, she must have nothing to fear.

A strange whistle sounded. Lukeem focused on it. Waiting at the bottom of her mesmerizing ride down to the ground was a gathering of natives honored with the dress of the sky spirits. With the shrill sound, they stood taller and quickly moved into a rigid straight line, man behind man. Where were they going?

When she found no more space inside her to contain her happiness, Lukeem dared to throw her arms in the air and released a long sound, "Aaaaaahhhh!" Her call bounced off the cliffs surrounding her and echoed back. It was a vibration in her body she'd only known since the coming of the sky spirits.

CHAPTER 17

FRESH FACE

Vanessa

VANESSA WRAPPED HER arms around herself and stared down through the glass wall at the ripples of light on the pool below their bedroom suite. The word *phony*, coming from the teen waiter's mouth, had its effect.

Hadn't Vanessa finally pushed her childhood pain far enough into the background buzz of her mind? After the boy's outburst at the banquet, her conversation with Tony about marriage and children, and her mother's card, Vanessa knew that even her stash of lifelong sleep aids couldn't quiet the noise of her secrets. Vanessa removed her glasses, dropped them on the chaise lounge, touched the wall switch, and the heavy blue silk curtains drew closed with a hum.

In the low light, Tony sat in lotus position with his eyes closed wearing a faded, UC Berkeley T-shirt. The wall of startled grins and gruesome frowns on the exotic, grotesque mask collection behind him brought a comedic counterpoint to his peaceful pose. She'd watched him meditate every night before bed for over twenty years, and it never failed to make Vanessa feel deep tenderness toward him. He was her unwavering support through all the crazy assignments they'd faced—calm, loyal, taking her lead, trusting her instincts. She'd never thought to meditate.

Could she ever clear her mind?

Silence her taunting memories?

Slipping under the covers, Vanessa propped herself up with two Thai silk pillows and pulled her work file from the side table. Within seconds, she was intent on researching and taking notes on the moon phases in Indonesia while absentmindedly eating Japanese rice crackers from The World Truth in News Award crystal bowl. Her tension eased at the absurdity of junk food snacks consumed from a Lalique Champs-Elysees Bowl.

Glancing up from her notes, Vanessa saw Tony open one eye then the other. His intense gaze was on her. "Oh, God, sorry, honey. I'm so wired." She stopped her noisy snacking.

He gave up on his meditation and came to stand beside the bed.

Vanessa stayed focused on her notebook until Tony turned her face up toward him and engaged her eyes. A look passed over his face that Vanessa recognized. She slipped into a feeling of discomfort, clearly sensing the not-so-subtle distancing that always came after spending time with his family. He was pressured to be what they wanted him to be—married with children to carry on the family line. She could almost read his mind. "Tony, I know you want to talk about getting married and having kids again."

"Will we? Get married? Have a family?" Tony sat on the edge of the bed.

"It petrifies me to think of bringing a child into our crazy lives. We've always agreed on that." She was no longer afraid of commitment. Maybe just getting married would help ease the tension, she thought. She would never want anyone else. Living together was a decision they'd made with the mindset of the 1970s. Now that she trusted their commitment to each other, Vanessa realized she had no objection to marriage.

But Tony saw marriage and family as one.

"Things change, Van. We agreed that right after the kidnapping story aired, we would talk about it. We can't take on the whole world forever, right?"

"No, but we can save one person who represents an injustice in *front* of the whole world." Vanessa grew more nervous and drew into her avoidance place inside.

"Life *is* short, Van. Why is this adventure with me any more threatening than the crazy things we've done for others?"

"Please try to understand. I know nothing about motherhood."

"Look how Kima opened up to you in the interview. And so did Maureen. I can't imagine you would doubt your ability to be a good mother. You're so compassionate." Tony stood and paced by the side of the bed, rubbing, and stretching his neck. "You were the one who set the rules for no holds barred when it came to taking care of kids who were collateral damage to our exposés."

Vanessa remained in the safety of their bed. The sweetness and emotional interviews with the children, especially with young Maureen, were fresh. Still, Vanessa filed her feelings off into that overstuffed place inside where she stored anything that touched her.

"Forget some woman on the other side of the world. How about us? *We're* right here." His voice sounded strained.

"Tony, I never actually . . . agreed to have a child," she spoke slowly. "I said 'it sounded like something we should *discuss*.'"

"Sweetheart, I assumed that *discuss* meant *timing*." His voice raised an octave. "There's no handbook for parenting. You just love hard and muddle through." He paused, sighed, and lowered his voice to barely audible. "The danger in our work could change, you know. It's a choice. We could stop the travel part, the documentaries. And we can choose to cover more positive subjects."

Vanessa watched him hesitate as he considered his next words.

"You could just do your TV show, Van. Maybe shift the emphasis a bit—about culture without the clash. Don't you think you've brought enough justice to the world?"

She focused on Tony. Her keen understanding of body language kicked in. His eyes widened, then squinted. And from his backward lean, Vanessa knew she was losing him.

That was a first. She'd always taken her self-definition from the news, from the press, from her heroic stories, but mainly from the reflection of herself in Tony's eyes. She felt that illusion unraveling with the change in his gaze.

"I'll always be a target, and you know that. I can't let a child be in the line of fire because of me." Vanessa persisted in stacking the arguments in her wavering tower of Jenga.

"I just don't get it. Wait—" Tony paused as if a proverbial lightbulb switched on in his mind. "Is this your way of balancing out one mistake you made twenty years ago? Punishing yourself? Driving yourself to do more? You said you couldn't have done anything to stop that boy from murdering the rabbi. It was a hate crime—so let it go, for God's sake!" he said. "So you didn't turn in some evidence on a kid you couldn't even ID. You were a kid yourself."

The headline about her grandfather's death was never shared with Tony, the final scene that played in her mind incessantly. "Tony, that is not why I do this." She ignored the sensitive topic that she'd colored with so many fabrications and moved on. "You leave in two days for Irian Jaya, and I have a ton of research to do—full moon, human sacrifice, remember? What are we supposed to do?"

The threat of the discussion pushed her into lockdown once more. Her love for him, her fear of motherhood, and the unraveling of her whole world wrestled behind her wall. "And you haven't even . . ."

She looked down at her papers, searching for a distraction.

"What? I haven't been fitted for my penis gourd?"

Neither of them could resist a laugh. "Funny. Tony, seriously, we're talking human sacrifice in the twentieth century. A woman's life is at stake. We have a *story* to do," she pleaded.

Tony paused and scanned the room. "Van, sadly, *we* have no story.

Look around. Notice there isn't a single personal or family photo in this house? I've been thinking about that a lot lately."

"But our story is—"

"Sweetheart, we *have* no story." Tony put his hand to his forehead. "We have everyone else's stories and a boatload of money that we pay other people, a boatload of money to watch since we never have time to spend it."

She tightened her shoulders as his voice rose in frustration and she watched the vein in his neck protrude—a raging-red vein with a sharp detour that she'd never noticed before. "We have a purpose, Tony. That's what inspired us to do this work."

He paced in front of the dresser and pointed. "I fantasize walking past that dresser and seeing a family photo—you, me, and a child."

Vanessa said nothing, searching desperately for a way to redirect. She felt her control slipping fast. The discussion was always the same, but this time, something was different.

"Or maybe we can frame some of our magazine covers." He lifted a copy of *Global Limelight* with Fiona O'Farrell on the cover that sat in a pile next to Vanessa's white chaise lounge, then tossed it down.

His sarcasm didn't sound like the man she'd known and loved for two decades. Vanessa cast a quick glance across the room at the magazine. She drew back into her pillow at the sight of her mother's face on the cover. Ironically, that *would* be a family photo, she realized. A chill sizzled down her arms. Vanessa composed herself. He couldn't have known it was her mother.

She took in a deep breath and sighed. "Please, Tony." What point could she make that would turn the argument around? It was gone, her well-honed skill for winning a point that was always easily at her fingertips in an interview, with even her toughest adversary, failed her. She had no weapons against the threat of his sudden changes and no truthful answers to his questions.

An unfamiliar vulnerability overcame her; it felt as if she were standing stiff on the receiving end of a firing squad. With Tony, she had no well-practiced-signature-Vanessa Gold *slam dunk*, as the press called it. She heard a rushing hum in her head. Her cool was unreachable, her face red-hot.

Vanessa saw him waiting. She too waited—waited for her brain to engage, waited to hear her own words. Nothing.

"You're addicted, Van. It's the adrenalin rush of these relentless exposés. You never stop to take a breath. There are no exits and no stops with you. It's like a . . . a high-speed LA freeway gridlock."

For the first time, her carefully constructed world was crumbling, and an unfamiliar panic took hold. "Tony, that doesn't make sense."

"Exactly my point."

A long silence hung around them. Vanessa looked down at her documents. "I didn't know your feelings had reached this point, Tony."

"Because I never have time with you to tell you." He ran his fingers through his hair. "Oh, honey, I didn't know either until I saw the foster child Maureen's face in that taped interview. And with us turning forty and seeing my sisters and their kids tonight, it all resurrected."

Silence.

"I never actually knew the phases of the moon. We're going into a waxing gibbous moon phase in Irian Jaya when we arrive. That's just a few days shy of full." Vanessa was instantly aware of the absurdity of her words, the foolishness of their timing. Still, her heart was pounding too loud for her to think.

"Are you *serious*, Van?"

"I'm sorry. I don't know why I did that . . . more avoidance. It's just when your family gets involved, I feel so marginalized and afraid."

"Afraid of what?" Tony moved and sat angled away from her on the chaise lounge and angrily shuffled through the magazines. She could almost hear his threatening decision rumbling in his mind.

"Losing you. Losing *us*. Please try to understand. I refuse to be another absentee mother. What about the threats to my life? How can we keep a child safe? How would we feel if we were never here for our child, Tony? That's the honest truth." Her stomach twisted at her own use of the words, *honest* and *truth*.

For twenty years, nothing had ever threatened their tight relationship except this discussion. "I know nothing about being a mother. I lost mine so young." The lie stuck on her tongue for the first time, but she forced it out. It was a half-truth. Vanessa's mother hadn't been there for her once she'd begun touring. She dropped her file on the nightstand and reached her arm out to Tony, beckoning him.

He returned and sat on the edge of the bed again.

She could read the hurt in his eyes. "I'll cut back when we get home from Indonesia. I promise, darling. Maybe if we had more time together. But children? I'm also turning forty." The tender, pleading edge that wrapped around her words was sincere. She wanted it for him, and impossibly she wanted it for herself. Vanessa avoided his eyes. Without looking up, she offered the bowl of rice crackers to him.

He stared down at the few, pathetic, remaining cracker crumbs.

"The way to a man's heart, they say."

Smiling, she flirtatiously shook the bowl.

"I would like to find the trail of crumbs that leads to *your* heart right now." His sigh told her he was relenting a tiny bit.

"We'll try, Tony. We'll talk about it, I promise." Picking up on his Hansel and Gretel fairy tale thread, she was grateful to return to their usual banter. "But the trail of breadcrumbs—wrong story, honey, that trail of crumbs led to the witch's hot oven." Vanessa stroked his hand that was splayed out on the bed, supporting him.

"Now that's another trail I'd like to follow if we ever find the time." He gave a little ground.

"Don't you leave for the woods early tomorrow, Hansel?" Vanessa looked up and smiled. She counted on his love and pushed to regain his warmth.

"Come on, Gretel." He ran his hands down her shoulder.

"You better brush up on your fairy tales, mister—seconds ago, I was the witch's hot oven, and now I'm your sister."

His one-sided smile crept across his face, and he laughed.

A small element of normalcy returned with their fantasy exchange.

Tony sighed and got into bed beside her. "You're trembling. You, OK? Getting sick?"

"I'm fine, just had a chill. It's a little cold in here tonight."

He embraced Vanessa and rubbed her arms up and down.

She could feel him coming back to her.

After minutes of quiet, he sighed and acquiesced. "I don't know how you keep up this pace. OK, babe, you're right—it is what it is for now. We're already publicly committed to the trip. I know what that means. I'll leave in the morning for the studio and get the *Turning Prism* team organized. My flight's at eight tomorrow night."

"And I'll talk to Canyon. See if she'll join in. Wouldn't it be great with the three of us together again?" Vanessa knew having their best friend back on the team could help their threatened connection.

"I can't believe she'll agree, but I know how convincing you can be." He narrowed his eyes and shook his head.

"Maybe she'd be willing to be my maid of honor . . . maybe we could—"

"Really?"

She saw hope in his eyes and a begrudging half-smile on his face.

"Look, we'll talk when we come back, OK. It's worth it to wait two weeks to consider our new life." Tony brushed her hair from her face. "I know better than to try to corral my skittish partner when a woman's life is hanging in the balance."

With the dread dissipating inside, Vanessa curved her hand around his face. God, she loved him. She would think of a solution, later. She was relieved to have a delay. *Stop playing that cursed song of hers. Your mother's not coming back. If she loved you, she wouldn't have left you here where nobody wants you!* Lately, her grandmother's words were never far from Vanessa's daily life.

Vanessa held Tony's gaze. She had to give him something soon. "Thank you." She kissed him, held him by the back of his neck, and pulled his forehead to hers. "I love you."

"Me too." He pulled away, punched his pillow, and slipped under the Egyptian cotton sheets.

Vanessa leaned over and kissed him on his turned shoulder in a continued effort to reconnect their fraying bond. "Tony, I have one last question for you."

"What's that?"

"Which college am I calling tomorrow, for Jason?" Vanessa turned off the light.

"Think green. I told him he wouldn't be using that kind of language where he was going. Kind of cruel, I let him think he was headed for jail. But just for a minute. Then I told him the Notre Dame coaches wouldn't tolerate words like 'bitch' in training camp. He was incredulous. I made sure he knew college was a gift from you."

"Let's be sure our team checks up on him. He has no one now."

"The team knows your rules, babe. Damage control for all children in the line of fire—he's on the A-list. He'll be OK once he gets involved in his dream at Notre Dame." Tony adjusted the covers, and Vanessa smoothed back his hair.

"Van?" He spoke softly with his back to her, "We *will* figure this out, right?"

She knew he needed hope. So did she. "It'll all work out. I love you." She chose her words carefully and rubbed the soft skin of his earlobe between her fingers to soothe herself.

Their entire adult life together, she knew she could count precisely to ten, and her partner would capture that elusive blessing reserved only for the Tony's of the world—deep uninterrupted sleep.

"The sleep of the innocent," Vanessa whispered with an envious edge. From her twentieth year on, she had never enjoyed the sleep of the undamaged because she had watched—she'd just stood there with her eye to the camera lens and watched.

CHAPTER 18

DESCENDING INTO HEAVEN

Lukeem

WHEN THE TRAM'S movement stopped with a jolt, Lukeem scurried out through the legs of a group of helmeted dark-skinned men. They stood ready to be lifted to the top of the mountain with their tools—or were they weapons—over their shoulders?

Tools, Lukeem decided. The clumps of dirt and vines still clinging to the flat end of the objects told her they were strong digging implements.

Lukeem folded in with a few dark-skinned tribal people like her who stood by in fascination. The women wore only thin grass skirts and beads around their necks. The men wore kotekas of all different shapes and lengths, but none were twisted at the ends like her tribesmen's tradition. A few men were decorated with honors—face paint, feathers or shells on strands around their necks, or woven pig skin bands accenting their arm muscles. These were the *others* who'd come to see the camp of the sky spirits, she thought.

Stealthily, she ran down a path to the safety of a flat area where she blended in with a flock of tribal women wearing strange white covers over their chests as they labored. They tended greens and root vegetables, food that grew obediently in rows. Lukeem marveled at them. There would be no searching and gathering required through the day to feed their children. The wisdom of the sky spirits was everywhere, she thought.

What could the purpose of the white coverings be? Lukeem stared at the workers and then at her natural self. Their breasts were held high by the coverings. Her breasts had dropped from the years of giving nourishment to her son.

Was this a sign of status? Perhaps women are not worthy of the full body covers? Colors must be a blessing only for men, Lukeem thought, seeing that only white was worn by the women. Perhaps like birds, only the male deserves the beauty of colors, she concluded.

Reaching back with both hands, one woman awkwardly disconnected her white breast covering from behind. Packing sweet potatoes in each of its twin round sacks, she held the sling to easily transport her burden to the fire, revealing its true purpose to Lukeem.

"Hello, bee-u-tee-ful." Lukeem tried out her words. Did the dark ones also speak the words of the sky spirits?

The woman waved her hand in greeting. "You like garden?" She pointed to the rows of plants.

Not knowing the words but understanding the meaning, Lukeem waved and smiled. Yes, she understood.

When the field worker had nestled the ruddy gems down inside the ashes to the depths and warmth of the roasting pit, she waved her hand again at Lukeem and returned to her labor.

Keeping her eyes down, Lukeem moved closer and followed the alluring aroma of the sweet potatoes roasting in the fire pit. There were so many that the women would want her to have one, wouldn't they? Tickling one near the top with a stick, she felt its tender skin give way, and she smiled. Gingerly, Lukeem rolled one sweet treasure into the opening of her head bag, then she ran to another garden away from the women.

Following a path, in a low squatting run, Lukeem kept watch over her shoulder until she reached a hut with a rippled roof that reflected the setting sun into her eyes. This was the sparkling light she'd seen from above, the twinkling shacks of the sky spirits.

Inside on the floor by the door was a bound bundle of bright leaves with an array of colors she'd rarely seen. Lukeem bit through the twine that trapped them, freeing them into her arms. Slipping a few of them into her head bag, she left.

From the hut, a path led her to a field where many kinds of vibrant flowers grew. A nearby cleverly-made, wooden shelter was the perfect place to rest and eat, she thought. Inside she marveled at the implements like the men carried up on the tram with dirt clinging to the sharp bottom edges. Smaller tools also fascinated her. Through an opening on the side of the hut, Lukeem let her eyes enjoy the vibrant colors of the flowers, the shapes so unlike any she had seen. Some reached up to her with open palms and long antennae like butterflies. Some raised their blooms high like tribesmen thrusting their bows high in victory, and some shaped like long spears had nubs along their edge, reminding her of her son's sweet head. The memory saddened her.

A young man patiently tended the flowers in the distance. His sinewy muscled back reminded her of her husband. How strange to see a man doing the gathering work of a woman, she thought. Dropping to the dirt floor of the shed, weak with hunger, Lukeem reached for her head bag and opened it to rescue the steaming sweet potato.

Lukeem spotted a bow and arrows leaning against the wall. It was so like the ones Kralu had made for Abruce's manhood ceremony. The sight of it made her chest ache. Would she find her son?

The door hesitantly dragged along the uneven soil and opened. Lukeem scurried into the corner, but when she turned, she saw the face of her beloved man-child, her son, Abruce. Is it possible? She stared in disbelief.

He dropped the flowers he held in his hand.

A renewed strength brought Lukeem to her feet.

"Ma?" His word erupted rusty from his throat.

Ma. Was it a sky spirit word?

He was real. Her boy stood before her. "Abruce." She reached out to feel him, to see if he was real, but he pulled his head back to avoid her caress and slumped into a shameful pose as though unworthy of her touch.

"Why do you feel shame?" Lukeem examined her son's face.

Abruce stepped backfrom her penetrating gaze, and extended his hand, offering a sky spirits' greeting.

Staring down at his hand with momentary confusion, she quickly suspended her hand in midair to honor his new ways. Why would a son not press his forehead against his own mother's? Lukeem waited in pain, needing his touch, craving their physical connection.

Looking at his hand as if it were a stranger, Abruced raised his face to hers and dropped his arm to his side. Then like a wounded warrior, he stepped forward, placed his forehead against Lukeem's, and positioned his hand over her heart.

She returned the gesture, feeling her thundering love for him. "Abruce, my son." Lukeem's words squeezed through her tightened throat. She pulled his forehead closer to hers, pressed her hand over his heart, and felt a strange density that resided within him. She was shocked to feel the unfamiliarity of her boy's essence.

She knew his vibration.

She knew his flow.

Abruce has changed, she thought. Some unknown spirit has inhabited him. Lukeem couldn't resurrect his former softness. She was unable to draw the matching sympathetic rhythm of his heart. "Your father said the sky spirits punished me by taking you away, but now they give me this gift. Nothing could be more painful than the loss of you. Nothing could bring me more joy than finding you again."

"I am sorry I left you, Ma . . . I was ashamed. Your visions on the cave wall made the other men reject me in the hunt." He paused and shuffled his foot into the soft dirt floor. "Father and the men always spoke evil about you, pushing me aside during the hunt. Their eyes sent unkind messages to mine when I told them I believed you about the sky spirits. Under the stares of the men, I could never hit the mark in the hunt like father, even though I could see it in my sights and my hand and eye were set. How would I ever provide the food for a mate and children without the skill to hunt?"

Lukeem nodded her forgiveness, pushing it firmly into his eyes.

Tears dammed by his nose bone gathered force and streamed down the edges of his mouth when he cocked his head and reluctantly smiled at her. Staring into her eyes, he breathed in and exhaled with one word. "Ma."

Perhaps "Ma" was a sky spirit word, Lukeem thought, but his meaning was clear.

"I am sorry I left you." Abruce gazed at the ground.

Still, Lukeem couldn't find his trueness. He sighed and his eyes squeezed out more sorrow. "I saw them—the sky spirits from your vision and the beautiful bird in the sacred circle. I hid inside the bird's belly and rode the creature with the sky spirits. My heart grew beyond my body when I was set down here in the sky spirits' village you had seen in your mind."

"I did the same." She pointed out the tiny opening in the hut at the tram that was strung from the mountain peak.

They stood suspended together until Lukeem felt their hearts quiet in matching rhythms. She sensed a slight return to his familiar ways, but his new density still permeated the aura around him.

Lukeem's head rolled slowly in a circle. She was faint from hunger.

"Sit." He gently pushed some steaming sweet potato into her mouth. Opening his head bag, Abruce carefully removed a package and handed her an unfamiliar bright red berry. "Here, share my strawberries, Ma."

She tore the leaves off the top and ate them gratefully. It gave her little pleasure. He held the berry to her mouth, and excitedly she bit into the red flesh. Her lips drew together, her eyes popped, she giggled and made a sweet humming sound as her teeth pierced each morsel to release its pleasure.

Abruce opened a vessel filled with a warm, sweet-smelling liquid. "Ma, it's called 'tea.' Drink it."

The bite of the scent watered her eyes, and the taste of sweetness made her smile.

"Cinnamon," he said. "From the bark of a tree unknown to us."

Lukeem could see Abruce was proud of his expanding knowledge. He picked up the flowers he'd dropped on the floor and set them in her lap.

She sat beside him with the momentary unfamiliar feeling of contentment. Lukeem rested her eyes on the curled petals of the yellow blossoms. "You live among the sky spirits." She didn't want to ask him about his shameful women's plant gathering work. He didn't even have the honor to work in a garden growing plants that sustained the sky spirits, she thought. Instead, he planted flowers. Perhaps they were the kind of flowers that would heal or cure. "You are a healer, a grower of powerful plants?"

He said nothing.

"You have not yet been honored by their coverings, like the men I saw being lifted to the sky on the spider's thread?"

"Our people's spirits are weakened when they wear the coverings of the Americans. Our power comes from the sun upon our skin, the wash of a waterfall, and the protection of the blackened pig fat." Abruce glanced over his shoulder.

His gesture and his words troubled Lukeem. Americans? This word was used by the sky spirits. She remembered the American flag. So much to learn.

"You can speak like the sky spirits?"

Abruce nodded. "I'm learning every day. I don't let them know I understand their words. I refuse to wear the coverings of the white people. This is why I tend plants. I have learned much listening to the leader of this place and his mate."

She saw he was holding back more words. Why did he call the sky spirits white people? This was not the time to ask the many questions that rumbled in her mind. Still, it was good to hear her native tongue again. She could relax into his words and understand him.

"Ma, I'm sorry. They're not what you think. They are searching for you. The leader of this place, he searches for you. He wishes to give you as a gift to our tribe so they can make the necessary sacrifice. You need to hide, Ma!"

CHAPTER 19

SOLICITING SUPPORT

Vanessa

ESCAPING INTO THE FRESH evening air, Vanessa caught a low-heeled slipper on each foot on her way out the door. The hard soles clicked across the patio as she swayed past the chameleon rainbow lights that warmed the lava rocks at the deep end of the pool. From the circular overlook that cantilevered out over the Pacific, the powerful outdoor spotlight beam drew her eyes to the crashing foam below. Vanessa breathed in the strong salty air and listened to the thunderous waves.

A cloud passed over the moon, drawing Vanessa's attention to the sky and her thoughts flashed to the aboriginal Indonesian woman who was to be sacrificed. With the night fog in wisps around her, thighs pressed against the cold metal rail, Vanessa thrust her arms high and wide above her. She imagined the woman's despair as the helicopter departed. The terror that darkened the face of the native woman suspended over the cliff by her accusers crawled inside Vanessa. Intuition told her that the final phases of the moon held more than the fate of a woman on the other side of the Earth—it held hers, as well.

Once again, Vanessa changed her focus, replacing her pain with the plight of the Indonesian woman. It was a magic trick she'd practiced for years—silencing her mind with the crimes and crises of others, burying herself in her relentless life's work.

Passing the pool, Vanessa entered the house through the sliding glass doors and walked down the long hallway. The line of hand-blown glass sconces dimly lit a history of photos of Tony and her with a host of world leaders and international celebrities. The echo of Vanessa's heels on the stone tile floor kept time with the grandfather clock she loved, with the sun, moon, and stars emblazoned in gold on its face. Someone else's grandfather, not hers, she thought.

Vanessa stopped in front of a picture of their old original *Turning Prism* crew the year they'd won their first Oscar. Ronald and Nancy Regan stood smiling in the center flanked by her best friends Canyon and Tony on the right and Vanessa on his left with the lighted White House Christmas tree towering above them. Tony was correct—there wasn't a single personal photo in their home. The picture of Canyon was as close as it got.

They'd never displayed the photos of his family that they'd received every Christmas. They were buried deep in the drawer of her desk. Vanessa pulled them out on the rare occasion when Tony's relatives came to visit. She liked things clean and neat, and she liked surfaces clear. It calmed her; she'd told Tony. How much of it was jealousy, or resentment over their judgments about her, or not wanting a reminder of the loss of her own loving family?

What would it mean to have a child? She imagined a festive holiday season, dragging out the decorations she'd never used, wrapping presents like a real family to put under the tree for their daughter or son. It drew her back to her childhood. She let in a warm memory of her father filming her and her mother at the piano next to their Christmas tree the year before her mother left for her endless cycle of concert tours—when everything was still so sweet.

In their past, she and Tony were always gone for the holidays. She'd made sure they exchanged gifts in some exotic place alone or as guests in some prominent person's home. They never lacked for invitations, always having a choice from a long list for any occasion, so it was easy to do. Tony was the one who shopped each year for the crew and their friends and his family. Vanessa loved to buy gifts for all the children who were collateral damage to her work, the ones who had parents in prison from their crimes she'd exposed.

A new thought struck her—the work she did often left children abandoned too.

Leaning against the cool stucco, Vanessa ran her hand over the taupe, pebbled wall. She was numb, void of emotion, out of touch with her true self, a self she was happy to leave in the past. She felt like an empty paper bag that she held in her fist, a bag she'd filled full of illusions. She was terrified if Tony stomped his foot down to explode it, he would discover nothing but her deceits and deceptions inside.

Vanessa entered her library holding her breath. She let it out slowly, and dialed the phone. A sleepy voice answered. "Canyon?"

"Van? What's wrong? Is everything OK?"

"Yes, fine. I'm sorry it's late." Vanessa pulled herself together. "Did you see the news?"

"I know. I'm so mad I missed your award ceremony, sweetie. Someday I'll get there. You know—finals, grades, faculty meetings I just can't miss. Sorry. You guys are on to quite a story."

"Right up your alley. Primitive cultures. Intercultural clashes." Vanessa tried to sound lighthearted.

"Only *my* restless natives are in Social Anthropology one-oh-one, slouching in chairs with paper airplanes as their only weapons."

"I doubt it. They're on the edge of their seats, if I know you, Kit Kat Swenson. And not at Reed College, they aren't. I thought it was an intellectual, notch-above school."

"Van, you're out of practice with my sense of humor. You're the only one who still call me that. I confess I haven't given up the Kit Kat bars." Canyon laughed.

Vanessa pulled the chain twice on the antique Tiffany lamp to give more light to the room. She checked for dust on the milky-colored glass panels, and instantly her finger found the chipped spot. She liked the thought that it had a history in someone else's hands, and she imagined the gasp they made when the precious lamp had been damaged. "I'm looking at the picture in the campus newsletter you sent. Seems now you've moved on to pigs. 'Professor Canyon Swenson Has New Following.'" Vanessa read the headline as she perused the cover photo of her friend. Walking along, her blonde dreadlocks and outdated long, flowing, tie-dyed skirt dancing in the wind, Canyon was followed closely behind by a dedicated gray and black, sagging-belly piglet and a gaggle of grinning coeds.

"Is he adorable or what? And *loyal*, I might add. Follows me all over campus. Even waits outside my classroom for me. He's a potbelly. Someone abandoned him by my office, poor thing. I named him 'Cheater' after Ernesto. Now, if I could get him to carry my books."

"Cheater? Ernesto? When did this happen?"

"Oh, two days ago. I didn't want to tell you. You know, the award ceremony. I caught them in *our* bedroom, and she's not even tenured faculty."

"I don't know how you can joke."

"It's either joke or cry all over you," Canyon said. "Oh, let's not talk about that Neanderthal—another day, another dull professor."

Vanessa could hear that Canyon was on the verge of breaking down. "Seriously, are you OK? I hate that you're so far away."

"I'm fine. Today I went out and bought old-fashioned Campbell's alphabet soup. You know my comfort food. I was eating it, and suddenly I realized—that's been my love life. Albert, Boris, Chad, Dominic, and now Ernesto. That makes it easy. The next guy's name must start with an *F*, which is also my grade for failed relationships with pompous professors. Someday I'll find a sweet guy like Tony. Listen, I watched the ceremony. If ever there was a time I needed to 'get out of Dodge,' it's now, and I know that's why you're calling, but Van, I just don't think—"

"That's the idea. Just don't think. Come on, what can I say to get you to come write and consult for us again, just this once?" Vanessa removed one shoe, then the other, to silence her pacing on the hard tumbled stone tiles. She set them on the desk. The nighttime floor was cold despite the warm Southern California May days.

"After almost being killed a half dozen times back in the day and nearly getting you two killed, I am not sure there's anything you can say."

"Well, that's overstating a bit, and I know how you feel Canyon, but this is—"

"Yes, I know it's *different*. There won't be *any* danger, right? In the Irian Jaya jungle?"

"Canyon, no one writes like you, and you are the anthropologist of the century."

"I know what's next . . . and I'm a professor who did her thesis on Southeast Asian Island cultures?"

"Thank you, Canyon, you just added to my arguments." Vanessa knew the timing was terrible, but she had to enlist Canyon's help. Maybe Tony would listen to her. Canyon understood the choice between kids and career.

Sitting on her leather desk chair with her feet tucked under her, Vanessa shuffled through the photographs of the tribal woman again. Canyon didn't understand as much about Vanessa as she thought. Even her best friend from college didn't really know her. Vanessa's ongoing charade had made her feel as foreign as the native from Irian Jaya.

"Something's wrong. What's going on? You always have a silver tongue, and I know something's up whenever you pause with me. Tell me, sweetie."

"I feel we're coming apart, Canyon."

"Sweetheart, not a chance. I know we don't see each other very often, but—"

"No, Canyon, not us. Tony and me. Oh God, this is such bad timing to lay this on you just after you and Ernesto."

"Van, I can handle it. This breakup thing is old hat for me, remember? Come on, you're scaring me. What is it?"

"You know we decided not to have kids, right?" Vanessa's voice cracked.

"Yes, of course."

"Right, our whole life hits the eleven o'clock news before I even know about it. I'll be honest, it's one thing if it were only me, but putting a child in the spotlight?" Vanessa paused, measuring the level of honesty she could share on the phone. "I feel like we're unraveling. Seriously, we need you. Somehow, when you are with us, it's like the old days. Maybe it will remind him, you know?"

"Remind him? What do you mean you're unraveling? You two are so tight."

"I'm panicking. He wants to change our lives, back off our careers, and have a child." Vanessa blurted. "And Tony can't take any more of this life constantly suspended in midair. He says I'm like a beautiful helium balloon rising, and the string is slipping from his grasp."

"Balloon? What?"

"Someone overheard us discussing children and marriage in the studio. Now, it's on the news. Edward swears it wasn't him."

"Van, I know you're private, but these things blow over when the next news story comes in."

"Tony's been . . . I don't know. This time I think he really wants this."

"Well, the new assignment in Indonesia will be a distraction."

"Canyon, I know, and there's a woman's life at stake."

"Actually, I'm more worried about you guys. I am so sorry, Van. We knew he was a family kind of guy. You're both forty this year. So, I guess maybe he figures it's time."

"I can't believe you said that. You're right. Forty is a factor. And can you imagine me getting pregnant at forty? Canyon, would you consider helping these two crazy friends of yours? Our writer can't make it, and this is a big one—human sacrifice—right up your alley. I need you, Canyon."

"Oh Van, honey. This is a first."

"I know. Right? 'Vanessa Gold Finally Turns to her Old Friend for Help,' the next *Global Limelight* headline. Why does everyone talk about my life in headlines?"

"Because you are newsworthy, Van. Look, I don't have kids. I am not exactly someone to turn to for marital advice, but you know I'll always be there for you."

"Canyon, we'll keep you safe, and we can prevent a woman's death." For the first time, Vanessa felt herself wanting to let it out, to tell Canyon everything. She trembled at the thought of the fallout, the possible loss of her only true friend. If you can call a person you've lied to since you'd met, a true friend.

"Maybe I'll find my prince charming in the jungle since I found all of my cavemen on campus—a lovely piece of irony for my next anthropological study. So is that all of it? Seems like you're holding back."

"What do you mean?" Vanessa felt the crack opening wider.

"You are hiding something, overcompensating. I know you. Am I going to pee my camouflage again on this one?"

"The whole world is watching. You'll be safe, and I won't put you on the front lines. I promise. I can have a ticket waiting at the Portland airport in the morning. I know I am being selfish, but I need you to come." Vanessa swallowed hard. "OK, I admit it. This is a first. I am saying it. Please, I really need you . . . for more than your insights and writing. Canyon, will you do it for us?"

"Oh God, how can I refuse you? You've never pleaded before. I owe you, and like I said, I need an adventure away from here. What about Cheater? Who will take care of my little piggy?"

"Isn't there a gorgeous hopeful professor who owes you a favor?"

"I'll come if you promise to honestly tell me what's going on when I get there. Promise? This sounds like more than the children issue, right?"

Vanessa was silent.

"I thought so, Van. How will I get to your house from LAX?"

Vanessa could feel the impervious world she had so carefully created disintegrating. She pulled at her weighty gold earring, removed it, and tossed it onto the leather blotter. The truth was building up pressure inside her, like the familiar tension when a story was about to break. "I'll send my cute Jimo-with-the-limo, as you call him." Vanessa was happy to move on to practical subjects. She took out the second earring, rubbed the soft skin of her earlobes to soothe her tension, and scooped both earrings into her robe pocket.

Canyon broke the silence. "Now I'm smiling for the first time in hours."

"Hours?" Vanessa laughed. "Well, you're getting good at your romantic recoveries."

"I miss you, Van. Wait! You have my passport, remember? I FedEx'd it out to you when we thought we were going to China for your birthday last year—although that never happened like nearly every other plan we've made. Which country blew up that week?"

"Sorry, Canyon, I know. Now you sound like Tony. I didn't forget. I've got your documents. Edward can work miracles. He'll get the visa done tomorrow."

"Love that guy. He's too much. Honestly, I could use a real-life experience away from this bubble world filled with cerebral poppycock."

"You know you love that world, Canyon."

"Yes, my cocoon. I wonder about that. I gave up everything for this life? Why was that again?" Canyon released her signature cackle. "You just made me realize I can't stand here teaching something I've never experienced in the field for nearly ten years. I miss our team, Van."

"OK, be ready with a week's worth of jungle regalia. See you tomorrow, and we're leaving the day after," Vanessa said.

"Wait, I don't know if I have the right *regalia*. I'm wearing exactly what I always wear—my school uniform. A long skirt and leather Birkenstocks. I've kept this style so long, I've gone retro, and now I'm cool again."

"Clothes are no problem. Edward can take care of that and have them ready when you get here. He'll love that diversion. You still a voluptuous eight?" Vanessa asked. "Oh, and boots, size eight too?"

"Yes. And I wish I were a size four in jungle clothes. Your closet is nirvana! I think it's bigger than our house, or I should say, 'Ernesto's house' now. So, Van, why do I feel this is going to be a mistake?"

"Because you're mistaken!" Vanessa laughed. "Oh, and Canyon?"

"What?"

"Thank you . . . I love you for this."

"Did you just say that, Vanessa? Now I know I need to come."

CHAPTER 20

BRIDGE TO PEACE

Vanessa

"BABE, I'M GOING OUT for my run. I'll be a while," Tony called from the hallway.

"OK. And honey?" Vanessa sat looking at the calendar with the moon phases she'd printed the night before. She nervously pushed her hair behind her ears. "Are we OK? I mean, for now?"

Tony entered the room in his running shorts and familiar UC Berkeley T-shirt. "I'm counting on it."

Vanessa had always admired Tony's dedication to staying in shape. She did so effortlessly through her own activity level and self-denial. "Oh, and who's the new pilot? Are we sure of him?"

"You mean, her, not him. Our new pilot's name is Crysti Walker. She is expediting the paperwork and filing flight plans for both of us. I'll fly commercial with the crew and equipment. She'll take you and Canyon, on a private jet."

"Tony, I'm impressed! A woman pilot." Vanessa smiled.

"She's got great credentials—former Navy pilot, and she's a believer in Vanessa Gold's quest for justice."

Vanessa's head spun around at his remark that fell perfectly on the fence between sarcastic and good-natured.

"Edward can handle your side of things." Tony smiled. "Lots to do, but I'm on it. We're good. You just get Canyon squared away. You two leave in forty-eight hours."

"OK, you're right. I already spoke with her and was about to call Edward to arrange visas, then I'll start packing."

"Gotcha! You really worked your magic on Canyon." Tony kissed her as he passed by, and Vanessa watched his dark wavy hair bob, left and right, as he took the front stairs down toward the beach.

There was no trace of anger left from their 'marriage and children' discussion the night before and no hint of her pain showing on a well-disguised face. Her mention of marriage was timely. She was ready, but as for children—she hadn't quite said yes, but she hadn't said no. It was easier to just put it off—her modus operandi. *Motherhood* was not a word she had much faith in. She would figure out what to do later. They had their new project in hand, and Vanessa had an excuse for another delay. She was in her element.

Vanessa looked at the grandfather clock in the hallway outside her office and dialed her cell.

Edward answered before the phone could ring.

"Eddie? How is it you always answer before the phone rings?"

"My split-second timing, Ms. Truth in News. And by the way, you are Woman of the Year in my book, no matter the outcome."

"Eddie, you know that isn't what matters."

"And *you* know I've adored that about you since day one. Well, maybe day two, and maybe not adored. What's up, Vanessa? I take it you saw the cover of *Global Limelight* magazine? *Time*, maybe? Or *People*, or *Cosmo*, for that matter? Happy?"

"Cosmo! Oh dear God! No, I haven't had a Cosmo. I just got up."

"What? The world-famous passionate fighter of evil slept past six a.m.? So do I call you Countess Dracula now?"

"I had a restless night. Don't hold me in suspense. What's on the cover?" Vanessa enjoyed her dark banter with Edward, a no-risk, feisty openness she didn't share with anyone else.

"'Exposé Is Her Forté' for one—that's the *Global Limelight* header. It gets even better from there. You are the heroine of America for busting the kidnapping ring, and the world is awaiting the fate of the Indonesian woman. Oh, and sorry about the boy's 'bitch' comment last night. Is that what kept you up? You, a *phony*? Imagine. What shall I arrange to do for the kid?"

"Tony says Jason's dream is Notre Dame, football. The usual, Eddie, scholarship to cover room, board, tuition, and pocket money, OK?"

"Fighting Irish, huh? Lucky leprechaun. I'm on it. Hey, so where are Tony and you with the family plans?"

"Edward, stop." Vanessa sat at her desk and randomly shuffled through the mail.

"OK, I'm stopping. But I'd babysit, you know."

"Edward, sweetheart, can we please move ahead with Indonesia. Human sacrifice? Remember? I have no time to chat."

"OK, Boss, what do you need?"

"First, please get in touch with a missionary named Father Carey, and then contact the Zell Baxter pilot—the information's in his letter. I left you a copy in the secure file in your desk. Tony needs to meet with the missionary when he arrives in Indonesia. We have to get more info on what's happening from someone we can trust. Background check first, and then make a donation. That priest deserves it, working out in the middle of the jungle."

"How much?"

"Eddie, you decide. But no strings."

"Now we're talking. A little well-deserved power. Thanks for the vote of confidence."

"Next, I have an old eight millimeter film that needs converting to media I can use in Indonesia."

"VHS is your best bet. Need a player with you?"

"Definitely." Vanessa ticked through the things on her list. "Oh, and please line up security for Tony's team. Canyon and I are good alone."

"Are you serious, Jungle Jane?"

"Yes, the company pilot will bring us in by helicopter from the coast."

"Oh boy, here we go. I got your message about Canyon's jungle clothes, and I'll hop over and pick up the eight millimeter film right after I finish this film cut Tony gave me. Just leave your Kodak in the lockbox in the front hall, and I'll bring the tape and articles back with a player. Two, three hours tops."

"Perfect, just come on in. I'll be up in the third-floor closet dragging out jungle-appropriate fashions. Marianna's day off, so I am on packing patrol, and Tony's out on a long run. He leaves at noon for the office to meet up with the advance team before going to the airport tonight."

"Got it!"

"Oh, and Edward, this eight millimeter film is for my eyes only—not even Tony's. You know the drill—I don't want you exposed. No watching while you copy it. Promise?"

"I get it! It's one of those 'for my own protection' deals. Do it blindfolded with my brain in neutral."

"Remember what happens to nice young men who know too much when we are doing an investigation?" She warned.

"Don't worry. I learned my lesson on that underworld story—although that big brute from the mob was cute in an *'Oh, my god, I'm gonna die'* kind of way."

"Funny boy. But not my fondest memory. If anything had ever happened to you because of me . . . Now I really need to wrap this up. Are we good?"

"Aw, you do care, don't you?"

"Don't push it, Eddie." Vanessa laughed.

"Want to give me a hint about this little film?"

Not more than one second of silence passed on the other end of the phone. After a decade as Vanessa's loyal right-hand man, she loved that Edward knew when to shift gears. "OK, OK. You got it! I'll read it in the news just like all the other commoners. I won't peek when I do the transfer. Consider me blind, but I'm not colorblind—go for the camouflage green with that gorgeous Irish skin of yours. You'll be a regular Tarz-Anne woman of the jungle, fit for the front pages again."

"Do you still have that 'contact' at the Indonesian Embassy, Eddie? Do not tell me how you do it, but Canyon and I need visas, so can you get our passports from the safe and take care of our visas?"

"That I can do, no problem."

She didn't want to know how he got in the fast lane for things like visas. "Nothing shady, right, Eddie?"

"No, I wouldn't risk sullying your reputation, my dear. Just honest favors."

"Gotta go, Eddie. You are truly my best girlfriend! Good-bye, take care, and wish us luck." Vanessa was ready to hang up.

"My pleasure. Oh, wait! Wait! I forgot! Guess who eclipsed you for this year's Woman of the Year? Have you seen the news yet? No, of course not. Only because you say it doesn't matter to you, it's Dr. Fiona O'Farrell!"

He got Vanessa's attention.

"She gave up her career!" He prattled on. "Can you imagine, the most celebrated pianist and composer in the world, and she quit to personally underwrite an amazing children's music foundation?"

"Actually, I can't imagine." Vanessa gripped the phone and felt her nail break under the pressure. The leak about her mother's plans shocked her. Really, so soon, Fiona?

"She says it's the bridge to world peace for the next generation. Don't you just *love* her?"

"Yes, doesn't *everyone*?"

"OK, true, I mean, she's a hot tamale, even at sixty—always in the heat of a scandal, but she can really play—piano, I mean."

Vanessa shook her head at his familiar sputtering laugh.

"Have you two met? I don't think so. Come to think of it, I am surprised you haven't met. You two should meet." Edward delivered the words in a non-stop, electrified, long string.

"Edward, human sacrifice, remember? Honey, we are in a time crunch!" Vanessa pushed away from her desk, and hesitating, she thought of the card from Fiona.

Vanessa heard papers fluttering and imagined Edward's dramatic face.

"Sorry, sorry. Love you, girl. See you soon. Oh, and the little secret eight millimeter film—my lips are sealed to a frozen pole in winter."

"Edward, this is LA. There are no frozen poles in winter."

"Oh, right."

CHAPTER 21

SPECIAL DELIVERY

Vanessa

VANESSA SORTED THE stack of mail, reviewing the magazine covers Edward had delivered. She groaned at the various airbrush jobs that had wreaked havoc on her natural face. For every cover she graced, Fiona's face smiled back on two. Vanessa stared at the cover of *Global Limelight* that showcased the current Woman of the Year—Dr. Fiona Anne O'Farrell.

With a nervous finger, Vanessa scanned the first article: "World Famous Concert Pianist and Composer Fiona O'Farrell Gives up Career to Form Children's Music Foundation."

A children's foundation? That will always hurt, she thought, skimming the story.

Vanessa murmured snippets of the article out loud, "Shocking the world of music, the twenty-time Grammy-winning pianist and composer left a decades-long, stellar career to establish her personally funded . . . students, hand-selected from villages to capitals, from peasants to private school students, from forty countries . . . meeting with heads of state."

Vanessa snaked her finger down the page to read her mother's quote: "Whether your parents are government officials, farmers, factory workers, or teachers, and no matter what faith they follow, the goal is to encourage friendship across cultures through the love of music. World Peace Music Foundation will help to equip the next generation of leaders and workers from all socio-economic strata with understanding and compassion for each other through studying music and living together for ten years."

Her mother seemed so poised and prepared as she explained. "It's my passionate belief that bringing these children together in equality in these special non-sectarian, apolitical, worldwide music schools is our only hope to stem the violence and hatred in our future world. The residential schools are free, and everything is provided to ensure a quality education from age seven to seventeen."

The interviewer continued to paint the picture of the Woman of the Year as a compassionate person with a big heart. "Tell us about how you got started?"

"After I won the World Piano Prize, I came from Ireland to the US to perform my song at Carnegie. While in New York, I met and married my now deceased husband and became an American. Gaining citizenship was the proudest day of my life. We struggled. I taught piano lessons to little ones for six years while we raised our young daughter and barely scraped by in Brooklyn."

"That's when you composed your second and biggest hit, 'Rise to Be You'?"

"Yes, I submitted it to a competition, and miraculously, thank God, our days of struggling were over. With my daughter and husband gone now, well . . . I have toured ever since."

Gone, indeed! Vanessa flipped pages to read more about her birthday concert to launch her worldwide network of schools.

"Whatever made you decide to leave your amazing career to take on this project?" The interviewer had pressed on.

"It is my sixtieth birthday present to myself, and I have always, always loved the little ones and believed in the power of music to transcend our differences."

The interviewer went on to describe "the poised, charming woman whose lovely Irish brogue had suffered the influences of a half dozen languages."

"What made you change the date and location of your opening concert so suddenly, Dr. O'Farrell?" the interviewer continued.

Vanessa took in a sharp breath as she read on. It was to be held in Jakarta, Indonesia, the same weekend *Turning Prism* would be there investigating.

"I had a compelling offer from the government."

The interviewer pushed. "Dr. O'Farrell, I did promise I wouldn't probe into the loss of your husband and the disappearance of your daughter, Colleen, but is there anything you wish to say?"

"God rest their souls."

Thank God, Vanessa thought, we'll be in the most remote part of the country. She scrolled down to the accompanying photo, recognizing the beautiful auburn-haired Fiona with her perfect aquiline nose, who sat smiling, playing the piano. A petite, cocoa-skinned little girl sat at her side with one finger poised over a single note.

Vanessa hypnotized herself with the clink-clink-clink of her spoon as she swirled her coffee, her inner child's jealousy raging. Breaking her decades-long rule, Vanessa read through several articles. Like a voyeur, she nervously studied her mother's life in detail, experiencing the familiar wrenching in her stomach as she locked her jaw against a flood of tears. She touched the face of the woman on the glossy page and steeled herself to accept her abandonment.

Now with her mother's voice in her mind, Vanessa wept, rubbing the dented fingers of her right hand. She hated her, yet ached for her—her perfect mother.

Fiona had never used her married name. She'd kept her maiden surname for her professional persona. One brief paragraph in the article had hinted of a long-lost daughter named Colleen. Gratefully there was no link to Vanessa. The father who raised her and adored her was simply a footnote about a young husband who was killed in a car accident. Fiona O'Farrell was living her life suspended from the truth, just as Vanessa was living her own contrived lie, she thought—her fictitious life and name purchased in a back alley in Brooklyn.

Vanessa closed the magazine and turned it face down. It was too much to see her mother's face after twenty years dedicated to avoiding the constant tabloid photos, articles, interviews, and TV concerts. It had been almost impossible to avoid her at one Presidential Inauguration. Vanessa had managed a last minute, high-profile interview during the special performance. Feeling an aching need, Vanessa picked up the phone to call Canyon. The line rang a half dozen times. No answer. Must not be off the plane yet. Vanessa left a message.

The ringing of the gate bell jolted Vanessa.

"Delivery, ma'am," her guard announced on her intercom.

"I'm not expecting anything."

"It's from Brooklyn, from some convent. A piano. I checked. It's OK."

"Thank you, Stewart, let them in," she answered, picturing the contents of the dreaded delivery. Through the glass wall of the front of the house, she saw two burly men wheeling a massive, blanketed object toward her—clearly her *mother's* piano—its bench stacked on top, along with a large cardboard box.

"Excuse me," the delivery man said. "Where do you want it?"

Vanessa shrugged. "Oh, there, on the left in the music room, I guess."

He wheeled it in, eyeing the priceless antique instruments that surrounded him.

"Wow, this is like a musical museum in here. Do you play all these, whatever all these wild-stringed things are? Your first piano in your collection, huh?"

"Yes, it was my mother's." Her words had the desired effect. She wanted to end the conversation.

"Oh, I'm sorry. My condolences, ma'am." He handed her the clipboard. "And there are these too." He placed the old mahogany metronome, a box marked *home movies*, and an unlabeled cassette on the covered piano, and lowered the bench into place.

"Thank you." Vanessa signed the paperwork, saw him to the door, and returned to the shrouded delivery.

Pacing back and forth, she eyed the covered piano nervously. When she lifted the drape, the instrument opened a path of pain that resided in a place she'd forbidden herself passage for years. Her wound felt fresh all over again. Dropping the edge of the fabric, Vanessa left the room to the safety of her coffee and computer in her office across the hall, but she had a driving need to see *it*.

She returned to the piano in anguish and stripped off the cover that protected the century-old keys. Vanessa positioned her fingers to play the first chords, but the song wouldn't come.

Memories of her mother's glowing face from a happier time pushed open a small space in her heart, but just for a moment. Her fingers shrunk back from the chord position as the loss vibrated through her, remembering her joy sitting next to her mother, her little-girl-self waiting for the moment, waiting to play the one note that finished her mother's beautiful composition. The award-winning piano piece, "Rise to Be You", that had opened the door to her mother's departure.

For a moment, Vanessa suspended her one finger over the final key. Instead of playing the note, she opened a small box on the mantle, took out her spare cell phone, and dialed the only stored number.

Finally, an unexpected voice answered.

"Sister Mary Joseph? Hello. I'm surprised. Are you answering because Mother Superior is busy?"

Silence.

"Is she alright?" Vanessa's heart started to race.

"Colleen, how are you, my dear? Did you receive the piano and your things, alright?"

"Yes, yes, but why the piano? Why now?" Vanessa ran her fingers over the yellowed ivory keys. "May I speak to Mother Anne Marie, please?" An unfamiliar panic began to build inside Vanessa.

"Mother Superior thought it was time you should have your mother's piano. Better than having it sit silent in the convent, dear."

Vanessa picked up on the nun's subtle hesitation.

"Colleen, we had no idea you were Vanessa Gold until Mother Anne Marie told us to ship it to you last week. She kept your secret all these years."

So that is why she begged my name and address from me for a possible emergency in the future, Vanessa thought. "What do you mean it's *time*? Is Mother not well, Sister?"

"She will be fine. The doctor has been here. She's resting. When you return from Indonesia, Mother says she will see you to hear all your trip details."

Something didn't seem right. Maybe it was her own guilt, Vanessa thought. "Sister, promise me you'll call me if she needs me. I'll call later when she's awake. Do you promise me she's OK?"

"Yes, dear, she says she looks forward to your visit after your trip. We miss you."

"Thank you, Sister. I think of you all frequently. I need to hang up now. I'll call you back. You understand my absence, don't you?"

"Yes, of course, but one more thing, dear." She hesitated.

"Yes, of course, anything, Sister. What does the convent need?"

"Oh no, my dear, we have everything we need with thanks to you. Mother Anne Marie asked me to request that you play her favorite of your mother's songs for her when the piano arrived—the one you always played with our dear Mother Superior. You played it so beautifully. I will pray for you, my child. Please come and visit when you can. It has been so many years, but your room is always here waiting." Sister Mary Joseph hesitated and then stammered on, "Colleen, will you . . . forgive me?"

"What is there to forgive, Sister?" There was a silent moment and a muffled covering of the phone.

"Colleen?" The familiar voice was hesitant.

Vanessa went rigid. "It's Vanessa. My name is Vanessa." Mother Superior knew I would call when I received the piano. The importance of the timing of the piano delivery dawned on Vanessa. Mother Anne Marie was playing intermediary.

"Hello? Colleen?"

Vanessa couldn't bring herself to say anything.

"Oh, I am sorry, but I can't get used to calling you, Vanessa. Please, say something."

"You're at the *convent*?"

"I came as soon as Anne Marie called. She had a bit of a spell, but she's fine."

"I don't know what to say to you," Vanessa responded flatly, realizing she had been ambushed by the holy woman who had been like a mother to her.

"Say that someday you might forgive me."

There was a long silence.

"*She* is my mother now," Vanessa said.

Vanessa threw the phone across the room, knocking a precious antique mandolin to the floor. Opening the heavy wooden fallboard that protected the century-old piano keys, she positioned her fingers to play the first chords, but the song wouldn't come. She saw her mother's face, felt Fiona's soft hand on her cheek, heard her comforting words whenever she was upset as a child. "Colleen, you mustn't keep your angry thoughts locked up inside your heart. Give them to *me*, darlin'."

Mother Superior asks that you play your mother's song for her. Vanessa thought about the loving nun's request. Out of habit, she touched the empty place on her chest where she'd worn her childhood shamrock necklace. Hesitating, she suspended one finger over the final key. Flipping the old worn metronome upright, she tested it to see if it still worked. Vanessa let the brass finger go, and it swayed back and forth, accentuating the time that had passed since she'd been without her mother. Nodding her head to the timing of the familiar song, with the loving nun's face in her mind, she trembled and placed her finger over the last note as she had as a child, waiting to fulfill her role.

"Where did your new acquisition come from?"

Vanessa jumped at the sound of Tony's voice as he entered the music room.

"Oh, I didn't hear you come back. The piano? A gift from an old family friend," she answered from the bench with her back to him.

"Some friend. That has to be turn-of-the-century Europe." Tony walked around her and the piano, shaking his head. "So, I get it—another gift from an admirer? I swear, the things people give you."

"Yes, the things they give me," she said.

"We should have someone come and play—bring some live music into our home, huh?" He started to leave, but then Tony's face told Vanessa he'd sensed something was wrong. "You OK?"

"I'm fine. One of the nuns from the convent in New York who helped raise me is ill. I'm so sad."

"Shall we send something?"

"No, Tony, I've already given so much. I may make a quick stop on my way to Jakarta with Canyon."

"Everything else all set?" Tony probed.

"Everything is set except I'm not packed and a million other little things."

"Can't wait to see Canyon. We need a supreme anthropologist on this one. Maybe it will be good for her too—inject some realism into her career, like you said, honey. Anyway, it will be great for the three of us to be together again."

Tony came up behind Vanessa, wrapped his fingers into her long hair, and buried his face into the crook of her neck. He breathed deeply. "I love it here. Maybe I'll stay. But seriously, I've got to go."

Vanessa quickly kissed him goodbye, fearful that the connection would unleash her tears.

"I'll see you both on Friday, OK? Oh, yeah, Edward met me at the gate when I got home. He's sending the equipment you need to the crew, and he gave me a little eight millimeter and a VHS videotape for you. I left them on your desk. Red, are you alright?"

She tried to avert his eyes. "Can you please not call me that, Tony?"

"What? *Red*? Honey, I've called you that ever since we met. I only use it in private." He pulled on his jacket.

"But I've been a brunette since senior year in college. You know I hate how that scarlet draws attention."

"Honey, I never thought . . . your wish is my command." He kissed her like he always did whenever they parted—deep and long.

"You always kiss me like it will be our last time."

"No, I kiss you like I want it to *last* until the *next* time." Tony winked and cupped her face with his free hand. "See ya, babe. We're on again."

CHAPTER 22

MOTHER CONFESSOR

Vanessa

THE DOORBELL startled Vanessa. She stopped playing the piano, opened the door, and hugged Canyon, holding on for an uncharacteristically long time. Her guards already knew Canyon and had let her through.

"I can't believe I agreed to this." Canyon pulled away and looked at Vanessa. "What's wrong, sweetie? Are you alright?"

"Now that *you're* here."

"OK. Who are you, and what did you do with my never let them see you sweat friend?" Vanessa knew Canyon was examining her red puffy eyes. She distracted her by looking behind her friend to help her with her luggage, but there was nothing there.

"No jungle-appropriate clothes, remember?" Canyon shrugged.

"Right. No worries, I'll get some wine. You grab the piece of luggage I set out for you. Eddie brought over some things that will fit. He left them in my closet. You hungry?" Vanessa closed the door.

"Starving!"

"I had to order-in. Marianna's visiting her sister. It should be here shortly."

"Yes, heaven forbid the great Ms. Truth in News makes her own dinner." Canyon flipped her blonde dreadlocks over her shoulder.

Vanessa smiled at the signature gesture, then laughed. "It's so good to have your smartass back."

UPSTAIRS, CANYON rolled the empty piece of luggage into Vanessa's walk-in closet. "Just like our dorm days, you always had the clothes."

"Nothing like an inheritance to help the fashion sense," Vanessa said, flatly, having returned without the wine.

"Oh, Vanessa, I am so sorry. I wasn't thinking of your parents and your loss." Canyon opened the suitcase and set it on the stand.

"Not to worry. I didn't take it that way." Her lies that had come so automatically for years had begun to twist and grow inside Vanessa, burning her stomach. She pushed it down once more. "Only one bottle of white left. Take out is on the way."

"I'll drink the red, any color, just lots of it." Canyon dragged an armful of outfits to the closet island. "Oh, Vanessa, I forgot how huge this closet is. It's like the entire Rodeo Drive." She fingered the evening gown section, a long row of couture labels organized by color.

"OK, Canyon, think jungle."

"Vanessa, I haven't felt like *me* in such a long time. Thank you."

The doorbell rang.

Vanessa went downstairs and returned with two wine glasses, one bottle of white wine, two bottles of red, and a large bag of take-out. "I still can't understand how you could give it all up for classrooms and Neanderthals—your words, not mine."

"I don't know. I needed to belong somewhere." Canyon tried on an outfit in front of the mirrored wall.

"You belong here in LA with us. That's where you belong." Vanessa poured their first glass of wine.

"Van, LA is out of my league. I am just a plain Midwestern girl. Oh, my Lord!" Canyon gasped. "The sweatshirts, the Berkeley *Turning Prism* sweatshirts! Where did you get these?" She reached back into the far corner of the closet.

"Don't look at *me*. That had to be Tony's doing. I never saved those things." Vanessa felt a rush of sudden nausea.

"I'm surprised they survived the Berkeley riots. I'm surprised *we* survived, sticking our camera in those demonstrators' angry faces. If Governor Reagan hadn't shut the campus down, we wouldn't have even received a grade for it instead of winning that Oscar." Canyon tried on a pair of black jeans. "Van, do you ever stop to think about that brilliant idea of yours—submitting our documentary to the Academy? And what about that amazing hunch you had when I heard from my cousin at Kent State. Those were the scenes that haunt me to this day. Vanessa, that was the footage that won it. I can see you sticking your thumb out on the highway with those very short, shredded jean shorts of yours, which left very little to the imagination, as Tony used to say. Oh, and the Mediterranean blue Greek fisherman's T-shirt with no bra was a hit. Every single trucker screeched his brakes when we put you out there for bait." Canyon changed the subject, laughing. "You know how they always accuse women of getting ahead with their looks? I rebel against that, but without your looks and that body of yours, we wouldn't have made it in time for that horror, that 'historic footage,' as the press called it. I don't know whether to thank you or smack you. God, it was so horrific, wasn't it?"

"It still seems so surreal." Vanessa looked off into space.

They moved to Vanessa's bedroom suite. Drinking wine and lounging on her luxurious bed, Vanessa directed the conversation into the past to escape the present until the containers of the gourmet delivery were empty and scattered around them.

"That was soooo good." Canyon groaned. "How can you survive on just those veggies and rice?"

"You know us vegans. We can't eat anything with a face." Vanessa filled their glasses again, trying to sound lighthearted. She nudged a take out box away with her foot, and stretched out on the bed.

Canyon took a pen from her purse and drew a face on a banana from the fruit basket. She turned it toward Vanessa. With a ventriloquist's voice, Canyon asked, "How 'bout me? I have a face!" Canyon coaxed a smile from pensive Vanessa. "That just brought me back to when I lost my meat-gorging friend forever. Remember, right after you got back from seeing good old Auntie Angela in New York when the campus closed senior year. Suddenly you had dyed hair, tinted glasses, and went vegan? What *was* that really about anyway? You've always skirted that conversation."

Vanessa knew Canyon would expect a quip, a comeback. Would she see the telling look of pain on Vanessa's face? Her grandfather's bloody accident always flashed in her mind at the thought of eating meat.

"Hold on a minute." Canyon ran back to the closet and returned with the hooded sweatshirts. "Come on, Van. Put this on like the old days, and you can tell me what's going on in that head of yours."

"I'm *not* wearing that," Vanessa protested.

"Oh, come on, Ms. Fancy Pants, put it on." Canyon laughed. "Those were great times—pretend that it's Berkeley couture. That first game of truth or dare we played in the freshman dorm was the only way you would open up to me. Remember, that's when you told me about your parents' accident?"

Vanessa didn't respond.

Canyon changed topics. "Seriously, Vanessa, am I crazy to join you on this assignment? The last time we worked together, I nearly got you both killed. That has never left me, you know."

"Canyon Swenson, that was not your fault."

"Well, I felt like the girl in the Sound of Music when they hid in the church from the Nazi's."

"And just like that scene, we weren't caught either." Vanessa took a swig of her wine. "Castro never knew the difference. We were in. We were out. We've been through this, Canyon. We were all petrified."

"Yeah, but you're made of something else, Van."

Seeing that the white wine was empty, Canyon poured red wine for Vanessa, spilling a few drops on her hand. Vanessa stared at it and quickly wiped it down her black linen slacks.

"I was living a lie trying to be a part of *Turning Prism*. I was never like you. I don't do real things anymore. I just teach about them. What a fraud, huh? I'm just a chicken." Canyon slurred a bit. "I owe so much to you, Vanessa. It was your brainstorm. How did we have the nerve to do that second film when we were twenty-three years old? I will never forget how close that was—the interview of the Cuban Anti-Castro rebels? The film footage you secreted out of Cuba in your bra? I haven't felt that intensity ever since. I feel like an amnesia patient finally having flashes of who I really am." Canyon took another swallow of her wine. "I've never really lived one single adventure, not one, except when I was with you two."

"Well, you're making up for lost time now, Canyon."

"I am a little out of practice, but I get the feeling this one is going to stretch me right back into shape. Without a doubt this is the most unique project I have ever been a part of, and I dread the potential ending. Do you think we can stop the sacrifice?"

"Canyon, have you ever stuffed something down for so long you don't know if you can hold it in anymore?"

"Ha! I am the proverbial jack-in-the-box. Remember? Until the pressure built so high, I exploded out of the lid."

"You're still the queen of imagery. Look at it this way—maybe you're springing back to life." Vanessa winked.

"Wait a minute, Van." Canyon froze, her arms, in the sweatshirt sleeves dropped to her sides. "What do you mean? What do you have to stuff down? What's going on?"

Vanessa was silent.

"God, Vanessa, how many decades before you feel safe with me?" Canyon slipped into the sweatshirt.

"It's nothing, Canyon. I'm just tired."

Canyon threw the other sweatshirt at Vanessa.

She looked at it with horror. "I cannot wear that. Canyon, we're not college kids. We're forty years old!"

"You promised to tell me what was going on, remember?"

"It's nothing. I'm sorry I brought it up." She tilted her glass for the last drops.

"You know you'll feel better if you tell me the truth," Canyon said.

"How do you know that?" Vanessa realized her tone had an edge of cynicism.

"Because truth is the soul's never-ending desire to be free."

"What have you been reading lately, Canyon?"

"We humans do evolve, Van." Canyon kept up her relentless eye contact. "Come on, you know me. I will sit here all night until I get the truth out of you." Canyon wriggled the too-tight sweatshirt to fit better. "You were always so generous to us paupers. I will never forget when you gave these to Tony and me before we left campus."

"Really, I don't want to wear this." Vanessa was shaken and tossed it aside.

"OK, OK, sweatshirt or not, start talking, Van."

Vanessa was silent.

"Come on. I told you about Boris verbally abusing me our entire relationship—emotional black and blue, and how I took it because I thought I deserved to be punished. You know, the whole state senator, love affair thing. Who dates someone named 'Boris', anyway? What deep dark secret could possibly be haunting the most celebrated teller of truth?" Canyon rambled on, clearly spurred by the wine.

"It always killed me that you stayed. How many times did I beg you to leave him?" Vanessa poured herself another glass of red, trying to steer the conversation away from herself.

"I know, and how many times did you intercede for me, and did I thank you enough for extricating me from his grip? You had him running so he would never come back to hurt me. What was I thinking?"

"You were young, Canyon."

"OK, let's get back to you, my friend. You're on." Canyon sat up straight as though waiting for Vanessa's big reveal.

Vanessa remained still, unable to begin.

"Van, after all these years, if you can't . . . *come on*! This is your best friend and confidant here who is going with you to someplace where my chances of dating are nil unless I want to dance around a penis gourd!"

"OK, you're right, Canyon. I owe you at least that." Vanessa downed the full glass of the red wine. "I am not who you think I am." Vanessa made no eye contact.

"I know you like I know myself," Canyon answered. "I will give you one minute while you gather your honesty, but then you are *on*. You *promised*."

Vanessa vacillated but finally shared. "I . . . never had an inheritance."

"What do you mean?" Canyon leaned forward. "Then, where did you get all the money, the clothes?"

Vanessa poured and sipped more wine.

"Van, why do you look like you lost your best friend when I'm right here?"

Taking a deep breath, Vanessa slowly exhaled. "Canyon, you and Tony always had the sleep of the innocent," she tried to begin.

"Van, what's wrong?"

"My mother . . . is ill." Tears filled Vanessa's eyes.

"Wow! You get your fourth Oscar. Come on, how can you even joke about that?"

Vanessa drew back, never intending to tell all—just enough to let the air out of her proverbial balloon to prevent an explosion. She felt if she let go of the end she'd held so tightly between her fingers, if she let go of all the lies at once, like a balloon, Vanessa would insanely fly about the room losing all control until she was completely empty and deflated on the floor. "It's true." Vanessa stared out through the glass wall at the pounding Pacific.

"I can't wait to hear how you explain this one since your mother died when you were ten." Canyon replenished both glasses.

"I'm half Hasidic Jew." Vanessa's tone was low. "My real name is Colleen Anne Cohen,"

"Very funny, and I am half Hindu Egyptian priestess, and my name is Cleopatra Singh." Canyon began to get giddy. "Come on, Vanessa. You're an Irish colleen if I ever saw one—with that gorgeous red hair. I still don't get why you suddenly dyed it dark brown in senior year. We didn't even recognize you when you got back from New York—the make-up, and those signature, tinted glasses of yours. That cool factor—you're like Jack Nicholson wearing those all the time." Canyon threw her head back laughing. "OK, sorry, but where does the Hasidic Jewish part come in? I have seen your parents' picture. And what about all the money?"

Vanessa downed another full glass. "The only truth I've ever told you was that my father was killed in a car accident. We were poor. There was no inheritance."

"What in heaven's name are you talking about?" Canyon gawked.

Vanessa drifted away into thoughts of her grandparents—her grandfather's sweet, kind face and her grandmother's venomous tongue screaming, *she is a mix, and a mix is always a mix.* She pictured her grandfather waving from the sidewalk up to the grated window of her room in the convent on the day she left to live with Mother Superior. And then she saw him, reaching out to her from the ground. It all came rushing back; the boy with the swastika in his hair, the blood, the scissors. Vanessa inhaled and slowly continued. "My father was the son of a rabbi—a Hasidic rabbi, in Williamsburg."

"Virginia?"

"No, a neighborhood in Brooklyn."

"You're talking black hat, long beard, and long sideburns kind of rabbi? How could he marry your mother? Wasn't that against their religion?"

"He was beaten up once. A bus driver brought him to a clinic outside of his community. Walking home, he heard my mother playing in a café. Once he crossed the threshold, that was it. They fell in love." Vanessa was at a threshold too. The truth about her mother wanted to erupt from her mouth.

"So, your mom played the piano?"

"She was . . . *is* amazing. She won her passage to New York as a prize for her music composition. She was alone, no family, barely surviving on her music. She emigrated from Ireland with her best friend, Anne Marie, who went into the convent after they arrived."

Canyon sat on the edge of the bed listening.

Vanessa hugged a silk pillow.

"So, wait, your dad became a rabbi, but you were raised Catholic?"

"No, he gave it all up for her, married my mom, then was disowned by his parents. We lived in another part of Brooklyn. I was born a year later. My mother tried to bring me to see my grandparents, but my father's mother slammed the door in her face. My father refused to ever see them again. We were forbidden."

"This is unreal." Canyon moved closer, pressuring Vanessa to share more of her truth.

"You know what they say about truth and fiction." Vanessa wanted to stop there, shut the door on her confession.

"OK, so she composed beautiful piano music and gave lessons, but you never learned to play the piano? So wait, what happened to you when your father died? I thought you said she died too, right? I'm confused." Canyon squeezed Vanessa's arm, pleading for clarity.

"No, Canyon, I lied. My mom abandoned us." Vanessa bent the truth enough to avoid disclosing her mother's identity. "My father took care of me. It was just him and me for months while she toured. After my dad died, I went to live with my mother's best friend in the convent . . . cloistered, no contact with the outside world. She became the Mother Superior. I called her, *Mother*. She is my mother." Vanessa put her face in her hands. "She's ill, but we have to leave for Indonesia tomorrow, and she wouldn't hear of me coming to see her. But I have to."

"I'm so sorry, Van." Putting her arm around Vanessa, Canyon continued her questions. "Why didn't you go live with your Hasidic grandparents?"

"I nearly did." Vanessa took a long swallow of wine and ran her fingers over the knuckles of her right hand. "I'd never met them before. My father forbade it, but my grandparents came to get me at the apartment after my father died. My grandmother couldn't stand the sight of me—the daughter of the woman who took her only son. That's how I got these scars. She slammed the piano cover down when I played my mother's hit song. She was in a rage. I'm sure she didn't mean to catch my fingers because she seemed so shocked and remorseful."

"God, I'm so sorry. So it wasn't a car door that made those ridges?" Canyon wiped the tears from Vanessa's cheeks with her napkin and hugged her. "All these years, I've never seen you upset, let alone *cry*. To be honest, Van, you're scaring me." Canyon kissed Vanessa's cheek and held her.

Dismissing Canyon's sympathies with a wave of her hand, Vanessa pulled away. "My grandfather was the only person who ever came to see me at the convent—every Sunday for eight years until I went to college. I refused to see him. After all those years of hearing my father's angry words, I think I believed I had to hate them *for him* after he was gone."

"I get that," Canyon said. "They saw your mom as some Irish Catholic siren who lured him with her music into the café, a place he would probably never have dared to go."

"With the loss of my father, his only son, the old rabbi lost his dreams of continuing the family legacy. I was too young to understand that, but my father obviously fell into a deep depression during my mother's long absences for her concert tours."

"I'm sure he never dreamed that the same mesmerizing music that had stolen his heart would ultimately steal her from him."

Vanessa listened to Canyon weave the dramatic story together.

"It's like a sad movie, Van."

"Sad, yes."

"She really didn't come back to get her own daughter when her husband died? And how could they disown their own flesh and blood—an innocent child?" Canyon probed. "You never saw your grandparents again?"

"No. I went to their old neighborhood senior year when the campus shut down. Remember our assignment, focused on cultures?"

"Sure, I remember." Canyon shuffled closer.

"There was no Auntie Angela on the Upper West Side. The only angel was Mother Superior. I didn't leave the convent to live at an aunt's penthouse. I never left the convent. Anyway, I wanted to see if things in my father's old neighborhood had changed. But once I got there, I had to leave. I just couldn't." Vanessa colored the truth again.

"Wait, where did you get all the money?"

"Special delivery—an envelope full of cash delivered every Sunday until I graduated Berkeley, from my grandfather's weekly visits. My grandfather must have felt differently. I'm sure his wife didn't know he was helping me. And I figured they owed me."

"So, wait, what about your name?"

"Canyon, that was Brooklyn where money could buy anything." Vanessa told Canyon the story of acquiring her new name. "Colleen Anne Cohen became Vanessa Gold, homeschooled with straight A's according to my transcripts. Vanessa was my Irish grandmother's middle name."

"You did that alone at seventeen?" Canyon held Vanessa's hand.

"No, the convent maintenance man brought me to some shady guy he knew. A stack of cash later and a falsified application, and I was Vanessa Gold on my way to freshman year at Berkeley. Anyway, my grandparents died a long time ago. Canyon, all that I told you—everything you thought—it was all just a sham. I'm just a sham." Vanessa raised her glass in a toast. "Or as a wise young man named Jason recently said at my World Truth in News Award ceremony, I'm a *phony*." Vanessa splashed her glass full again.

"I don't know what to say. I'm stunned. God, why didn't you feel you could tell me this? I've been your best friend since we were teenagers. I wouldn't have cared."

"I'm sorry. I'm just afraid after all the lies. You and Tony were the first two, no, the *only* friends I'd ever had . . . *have*, actually. Well, except for Eddie. All those years alone, homeschooled in the convent, imagining who I wished to be, buried in books, fantasizing. I created a new self when I left for college. The admiration in your eyes, the inheritance—after a time, the lies became *me*. I didn't want you to try to make me reconnect with my past, either—too painful, too pathetic."

"No wonder you always had that quiet strength. God, you're a rock and so generous and compassionate. Look what you have dedicated your life to . . . you're selfless. You kept this in for this long? I still don't get why it was such a big deal to hide your past? So why tell me now?"

"Comes from playing the little Dutch girl. It just started to get too close—you know, Tony wanting kids, interviewing Maureen and Kima. Holding up the dike got a little stressful, especially with Tony. God, it would devastate him. And damage everyone's reputations around me."

"Wait. So *Tony* doesn't know? Now I don't feel so bad." Canyon refilled her wine glass as she took in all of Vanessa's truths. "Wait, the exotic travel and the stuff you brought back from your travels with your Auntie Angela?"

"Lies—all bought in good ole New York City. Every vacation, I went home to stay at the convent in a ten by ten stone room. Aunt Angela and the blue-blood relatives were all figments of my imagination."

"You must have hated those people who rejected your mom and then you." Canyon commiserated.

"Not now. They were just trying to protect their own way of life, their family legacy. They'd lost their only son. Canyon, I'm so deeply sorry I lied to you."

Canyon was stone still.

Vanessa was ready to face the consequences. What friend would stay? With a deep sigh, she waited in the suspended silence.

"You know, honey, maybe if you hadn't been the rock, we wouldn't have been friends." Canyon gazed down at her wine glass.

Vanessa was confused.

"It wasn't your money I loved, Van. You wanted to expose corruption, fight for human rights, protect children, track-down murderers. God, I didn't even know what socks to wear. You were my hero. You opened my eyes to life, to seeing things differently, and finding my career."

"But you had the idyllic childhood, a sister, mom, and dad. No secrets. I envied that. I wanted that."

"This isn't about me, Vanessa."

Exhausted from her confession, Vanessa needed to redirect the conversation. "Mother Superior shipped my mother's old piano and a box of my things. They arrived today."

"Oh my God! Where's the box that got delivered? Have you opened it?" Canyon asked.

Vanessa shook her head.

"And you're supposedly one of the world's most renowned investigative reporters? Get the box! We might as well go all the way here."

VANESSA AND CANYON sat on the floor in the music room, opening the box. She pulled out the childhood photo of her mother and her at the piano, her one finger poised over an ivory key. Wrapped in a shawl were a photo of her father at his bar mitzvah, a yarmulke, a photo of her grandfather captured through window grids, her birth certificate, and dozens of little 8mm films.

Canyon picked up one of the old Kodak boxes. "What are these? Home movies?"

"My mother's old camera. She captured everything," Vanessa explained.

"Like mother, like daughter."

Vanessa stiffened at Canyon's innocent comment.

"Oh my God, we have to see these, or would it be too hard? Oh, let's see what's in these jewelry boxes." Canyon took a silver shamrock necklace from one of the boxes, held it to Vanessa's chest, then fastened it on her. "Sham, rock. God, I'm sorry, things come out of my mouth before my brain engages, but you say you're a sham, and I say you're a rock. Like you always preach, there are two sides to every story, the turning prism."

"You're drunk, my friend." Vanessa slurred. "And I said *many* sides, not just two."

"True. Remember trying to come up with that name for the company? We stayed up all night. Then you did it, our brilliant one."

Vanesssa touched the necklace at her throat. It felt wrong to wear it because it was part of a gift meant to be shared with her mother, with someone she loved. And she *had* loved her mother at the time. Not now. But Vanessa didn't want to take it off either. It was as if sharing her truth with Canyon was sharing the gift. Vanessa stared at Canyon through bleary, tired eyes. "You wear the other one."

"What?" Canyon tilted her head. "I can't."

"You can and will. You know me now . . . the real me."

Canyon's eyes glassed with tears. "Are you sure?"

Vanessa took the second velvet box and handed it to Canyon, who put the second necklace on.

"Sisters-in-arms." She saluted Vanessa.

Vanessa felt herself smile for a moment.

Canyon picked up one of the 8mm films. "Van, I want to see these, please? I want to understand. I can't get my head around this."

Vanessa and Canyon stood by the projector in the home theatre and threaded the film. They watched the wiggly shot of her parents dressed up, waving goodbye as they left the simple apartment. The face of a smiling nun appeared with her arm around a child amid birthday decorations. The young girl twirled with joy in the tiny apartment, blowing kisses to the camera.

"That was Sister Anne Marie before she joined the Cloister."

Canyon set up the second movie. They watched as young Vanessa sat playing the piano in the flickering film with her mother beside her. "*You* really do play the *piano*? Wait, was that was you playing when I came to the door today? It wasn't a recording, was it?"

"Yes, I used to play. Could never find the stomach for it after my father died." Vanessa felt a pang of guilt remembering the hours of Mother Anne Marie's years of dedicated piano lessons.

The camera came in closer as the father surprised the woman and the child. While holding the camera awkwardly, his arm appeared in the frame, placing two little black jewelry boxes on the edge of the piano. The next scene showed the mother-daughter duo smiling and holding out the matching shamrock necklaces for the camera. The final frames focused in on the woman's beautiful face.

Canyon stared at Vanessa. "Your *mother* is Fiona O'Farrell?"

"The one and only." Vanessa could barely hold her head up from drinking the third bottle of wine in her hand.

"Oh—my—God! Oh my God, oh my God! How did you keep that secret for all these years?"

"Wouldn't you?" Vanessa fell back onto one of the theatre chairs, slurring. "Promise you won't tell Tony." She dropped the wine bottle over the arm, and a red stain oozed onto the carpet.

Canyon struggled to remove the too-tight *Turning Prism* sweatshirt and tried to absorb the evidence.

"Wait, there's more, Canyon, there's more," Vanessa pleaded, wanting to finally release the remaining lies that clawed at her inside.

"Sweetie, we do *not* need more wine. Enough drink for one night." Canyon touched the shamrock necklace around Vanessa's neck and Vanessa reached unsteady fingers to the one now at Canyon's.

Canyon tucked a blanket around her on the theatre cushion with the throw from the back of the chair and kissed her forehead.

Through a blur, Vanessa watched Canyon clean up the rest of the wine from the carpet. As Canyon closed the door, Vanessa heard her whisper, "Van, you are no phony."

Surfacing momentarily from her wine stupor, Vanessa murmured, "And you are no chicken."

CHAPTER 23

NIGHT AND DAY

Lukeem

SHE KNEW HER SON was wrong. The sky spirits would not harm her. Lukeem took off her head sack and showed Abruce her colorful treasures. She needed to understand them.

"Magazine. These are called mag-a-zines," Abruce explained. "Made from thin slivers of trees. They carry news in the spirit god's special language for the eyes."

Language for the eyes? Lukeem was amazed as she flipped through the colorful leaves, cherishing the images of two smiling sky spirits on the top of each magazine—one with surprising ruddy-colored hair, one dark-haired, both wearing the most beautiful things she'd ever seen. Their light green eyes, looked back at Lukeem with kindness. Like no eyes she'd ever seen. Their warm smiles sent a knowing into her heart. She ran her finger over the shiniest, thinnest of leaves she had ever beheld. The newness of the many shades and tints were so unlike the simple blue of sky, green of leaves, or orange and brown of the earth—the only color shades for which she had any need of words. Lukeem was entranced by the sight of the vibrant colors that decorated the sky spirits. It was the same joy she'd felt when a colorful Cassowary bird landed in the green canopy above her tribe's sleeping area. She loved color.

"I was amazed when I first saw these colors too, Ma. I wanted to keep them in my eyes, to never look away," Abruce said. "The Americans have more words for color than there are trees in the jungle. The leader's mate tries to teach them to me in the garden."

Lukeem wondered at the magic that had captured the women's spirits, their exotic, unmoving, happy faces living in the flattened surface of the waving pages. These women sky spirits are special ones, she thought, holding them to her chest. "How can they live in this shiny place?" She pointed to the faces on the pages.

"They live in two places, Ma. Here on these flat slices of trees and walking alive like us. I don't know how their spirits are kept in here." Abruce ran his hand over them. "In their language, this image is called 'foto.' It pleases them. Only the most powerful ones are honored in this way. These fotos bring happiness when the person gazes at the images."

Lukeem kept her eyes riveted on the faces of the women on the magazine covers.

"Ma, I heard my boss talk of this woman." Abruce tapped on the dark-haired sky spirit's face. "She is an honored one, but I do not understand where she lives. She will fly on a sky spirits' bird to come here to find you. She wants to stop the sacrifice."

"On the heh-li-cop-ter. She is the special one." Lukeem touched the woman's face. "Now, I see her here." Lukeem touched a finger to her chest. "Don't worry, son. I will not be sacrificed. The sky spirits will not allow it." Lukeem dropped her head. "My son, are you ashamed of your mother who defies tribal tradition—a mother who refuses to be sacrificed?"

"Ma, no. This is not something your sky spirits wish to do. Only some of the *others* wish to see you die. And the white boss." He held the magazine. "I believe she will come. When she comes, I'll bring her to you, Ma, but we need to hide you now. You can't stay here. Soon the woman of this house will return. My job is to protect her."

Lukeem knew Abruce was lying about his work from the lean of his torso and the direction of his gaze. She knew he was ashamed.

Abruce led Lukeem to the far end of the mine site. They silently walked along the deserted edge of the mountain, looking down at the activity below. People with and without the coverings of the sky spirits moved with intent like a line of determined ants, in and out of the large huts, and entering and exiting the tram.

Skirting the line of workers who were beginning to line up for food, Abruce guided Lukeem behind a patch of thick brush and left his bow with her.

A line of men and women snaked alongside a ripple-roofed hut and entered an opening. Abruce followed them.

Through a clear opening on the side of the long shed, Lukeem watched Abruce from the bushes. She could see a gathering of people inside devouring food.

Lifting a thin wooden slab, Abruce slid it down two shiny supports, choosing foods piece-by-piece. Lukeem imagined tasting more foods of the sky spirits for the first time, just as she had the strawberry.

As he emerged from the food hut, he signaled Lukeem to follow him. He picked up his bow. Abruce walked along a narrow, twisted path toward the sheer rock wall. Pulling back vines, he searched for the opening to a cave. "There is an opening near here." He shuffled the vines back and forth.

Lukeem closed her eyes. She felt the familiar energy flow through her. Following her knowing as she'd learned to do long ago, she pointed to the twist of dense vines that hid the opening to a cavern.

Once inside, Abruce put the food down beside her. After eating a piece of roasted pork, she wiped the excess fat on her arms. "You have food like this often?"

"Three times each day. As much as I want. I have no need for a weapon for hunting. When I work, I leave my bow and arrows in the garden shed where we first met, Ma."

The idea was beyond her imaginings. But what would men do to find their power if not from the hunt, she wondered. Lukeem touched the familiar red berry, tore the leaves off the top, and ate the fruit gratefully. She bit into the red flesh and caught the escaping droplet of the sweet juice with one finger from her chin, savoring each indescribable bit of the glorious food of her sky spirits. She reveled in one delight after another, trying to repeat their names after Abruce. Rice, chicken saté, and many delicious colored plants. Closing her eyes, overcome with emotion, Lukeem was unable to contain her joy. Exploring the new tastes and practicing the new words flooded her with shivers.

"Your face glows, Ma."

"I know now, my son. I know how glorious the sky spirits' home is." Her eyes misted.

"I am so happy to bring you so much happiness, having brought you so much pain." Abruce hesitated, then he told Lukeem more of the truth than she wished to know. "When you put your hand on my heart, I could not find myself," Abruce said. He explained that he was caught between the familiarity of his tribal life and the confusion of his new life with the sky spirits and the *others*. He was disillusioned with them and yet still in awe. Abruce ached with the uncertainty of his future. Suspended between cultures, two worlds, fitting neither one nor the other, he was accepted nowhere. He told Lukeem he could never cease his floating, since fluttering down from his tribal land to the white men's home on the sky bird.

"Why is it you call sky spirits *white men*?"

Abruce hesitated. "They are not spirits. They are human. Some come from a tribe of kindness, and some can have an evil heart. The cloths they wear are no honor. They feel ashamed of their bodies, so they hide them." Abruce hesitated again.

What was he afraid to tell his own mother, Lukeem wondered?

"Their leaders care only for the shiny treasures they dig from the mountains to take far away to their lands. It brings them power." Abruce held out his hand to her. "We need to go, Ma."

Lukeem did not believe her son, but his words troubled her. Why had he become so heavy in his heart?

When Lukeem was rested, Abruce brought her to the bottom of the steep wall at the edge of the mine site. They passed the field of women gathering sweet potatoes from the garden. "What about these women? Won't they be at a nearby engagement ceremony at the next full moon where one might choose you? You need a mate. It is long past your time, son."

"What kind of woman would have me? I am not a hunter. What kind of woman would understand my rhythms, my language, and my density inside?"

"But these garden women have the power to command plants to grow in rows. There is no need to hunt through the dense greenery for food to eat."

"The women working in the garden are similar to our tribe, as familiar as you, mother. But they don't speak in a way I can understand. Their smiles draw me, but their words and ways are no match. Ma, they are not like us, although they have our look."

Lukeem admired her son for his wisdom. "Son, do you still carry anger toward me for the pain I caused you?"

Abruce stood silent for many beats of Lukeem's heart.

"For five rainy seasons I did, but at the sight of you, the rock lifted from my chest. You told the truth about the sky spirits, Ma. There is so much for me to tell you, but we must go." Lying on the ground, Abruce reached out with his bow to lift the designated section of growth. It parted, revealing another entrance he'd sought. The narrow opening, just wide enough for their bodies to slip through, led them to a cave like the one where Lukeem had hidden to paint her images. These walls were untouched and empty of her thoughts. She would fill them.

"You will be safe here. I will come when I can." He set down the bag of food. "When the white woman, I mean the *sky spirit*, arrives, I will bring her to you, Ma."

"My son." Lukeem touched the face she thought she had lost forever.

"Ma, there are many caves under the mountain connected to this one. You will be safe here. I will come every day. I'll bring food for you." He left a sack on the ground beside her. "The food comes to us here, Ma. We don't need to go on a hunt to find it."

She would blossom in her new life, painting in the endless caves with her son nearby, and no need to hunt for food, she thought. The sky spirits' powers sent a dance of celebration through her.

Abruce took an object from his remaining head bag. "You see? Touch this spot one time to bring light, and touch it again to make it dark. It's called *flashlight*."

Its magic startled Lukeem.

Abruce placed it in her hands. "Ma, there is a man here making fotos. He is the mate of the woman on the magazine. She is coming soon. I will bring her to you."

Barely hearing his words, Lukeem could not stop staring at the glowing light, wondering at the sky spirits' creation. She touched Abruce's face. "It brings me hope to have you in my eyes again." She shined the flashlight in his direction, relieved to have a brief respite from her grief. Lukeem had her son again.

His smile lingered, then she watched it turn to concern as he left.

Flicking the switch off, Lukeem practiced its name. "Fl-ash-light," she whispered, refusing to let her mind drift to her confusion about the *others*. She loved the joy of her new words of the sky spirits stacking one upon the other in her mind. She ran her hand in front of the light. It's a fire with no burn, she thought. Lukeem couldn't stop staring at the glow it brought—touching it on and off, on and off, wondering at the magical black stick that had captured the sun and moon, the day and night.

CHAPTER 24

AMBUSHED FROM ABOVE

Vanessa

VANESSA STEPPED OUT of the Brooklyn taxicab, followed by Canyon. Arm in arm, they walked up to the old stone building. The familiar crumbling sign read "Sisters of the Holy Spirit Convent."

They entered the massive carved side door and were enveloped in the heavy scent of incense from a recent Mass. Vanessa's head ached from her hangover and the scent. Morning sun splashed through the stained-glass windows surrounding the chapel and lit up a white dove holding an olive branch in the circular frame above the altar.

The statue of Mary stretched her arms out with a beckoning smile. Curls of blue revealed the raw plaster where the old paint had failed along the folds of her robe. The Madonna's familiar, kind gaze followed Vanessa as she walked under the stone arch into the chapel, evoking a tender childhood memory.

"Van, why don't I wait here? It's been so long, you know?" Canyon squeezed Vanessa's hand, then slipped down into the last of a dozen pews that lined each side of the chapel.

Vanessa mouthed "Thank you" to Canyon.

"I'll be here if you need me."

Vanessa touched Canyon's shoulder, pointed with her chin, and stared ahead.

A nun in flowing black and white was busy clearing the altar. The Sister genuflected, and steadied by a wrought iron handrail, she cautiously descended the large stone steps and walked toward them.

Vanessa stepped out into the aisle. *Mea culpa, mea culpa, mea máxima culpa—through my fault, through my fault, through my most grievous fault*, she recited the Latin prayer of contrition in her mind, feeling the weight of her guilt.

The echoing clicks of the string of the nun's large wooden beads and cross that hung around her waist reminded Vanessa of daily Mass with the three dozen nuns who had become her family after her father's death. There was no other sound that was as connected with her past as the rhythmic beat of the Sisters flowing down that aisle. She counted. The sound of eighteen footsteps, eighteen clicks that rebounded off the hard surfaces of the chapel, and the Sister stood before her.

They embraced.

"Sister Mary Joseph, I've missed you."

The Sister's face was framed in crisp white cotton. Her eyes edged with a spray of deep creases at each corner, and her wrinkled hands were the only clues to the woman's age.

Vanessa realized she'd always thought of the caring nuns as ageless angels, not mortal women. She prepared herself to see the decades of aging in Mother Anne Marie's face. The cathedral ceiling and the stone walls stole the privacy from her words, and she lowered her voice. "Is Mother Anne Marie . . . oh, I am sorry. Sister, may you speak?"

"We're not in silence for your visit. A special dispensation was allowed. And yes, Mother Superior is still with us. Come, Colleen, I'll take you to her."

An archway led from the chapel into the living area of the ancient convent, and the incense followed them. The alcove, where the old piano had stood since Vanessa had first arrived as a distraught ten-year-old, was eerily empty. They stopped.

"I was thinking back. It's been over twenty years since you left for college." The nun looked up into Vanessa's eyes. "You look so much like your mother, Colleen, with your green eyes, except that your hair is no longer red."

Self-consciously, Vanessa ran her hand over her hair. The hard gray stone walls accentuated their words again. "Being here makes me suddenly feel not so grown up, Sister. I feel more like a child who should never have left." Vanessa hated hearing that her resemblance to her mother was so obvious to Sister Mary Joseph.

"Jesus forgives, my dear. You are here now." She opened the heavy, dark-stained, wooden door to the sparse room. A dozen lit candles cast pulsing shadows on the wall from the draft of the open door. A group of nuns kneeled around the bed, praying.

Sister Mary Joseph urged Vanessa to sit on the bare wooden chair next to the bed, and the other Sisters nodded, smiled, and graciously stood. Silently, they moved in unison to the other side of the room and resumed their prayers in a low, soft chant.

"Mother Superior?" Vanessa took the nun's limp hand. She ran her thumb over her thickened veins like gnarled roots that had risen on her beautiful hands over the years. She knew every inch of those hands that had moved gracefully over the piano keys when they played together. "I always love calling you 'Mother Superior.' You deserve it." Vanessa searched for the right words to say.

A smile emerged on the nun's face as she opened her eyes.

On instinct, Vanessa sat up straight.

Mother Anne Marie drew Vanessa's scarred hand to her lips. Her voice was weak. "My child, you needn't have come, darlin' Colleen. You have such important things to do."

Vanessa smiled to hear her Irish brogue that had faded with time. "You are my *mother*. What else is more important?" Her voice caught as she kissed the nun's hand in return and tucked it into the crook of her neck.

"I was your mother for Fiona. It was her love you felt through me. She so loves you," she said. "I wanted you to have your mother's piano. It's time, darlin'."

Vanessa wanted to avoid any talk about Fiona. It was too precious a moment to waste on her. Instead, she focused on the gentle face of the woman who had loved her through everything she'd done, kept her secrets, forgave her every flaw, her every sin. Vanessa fought to memorize Mother Anne Marie's features, her smile, and the flecks of gray in her pale blue eyes, to capture every detail of her confessor and supporter, knowing time would steal the loving woman's image from her.

During the decades in her absence, Vanessa had often lost it, felt Mother Anne Marie's visage evaporate, grasped at it desperately, until she had to pull Mother's picture from its hiding place to find her. The memory of her face with its porcelain pure skin had faded in subtle stages—the shape, fine features, and even her smile had dissipated with the years. Only the softness of her forgiving eyes remained. Vanessa was terrified of losing her comforting demeanor—the compassionate face and tender voice she'd conjured during her most difficult times and many sleepless nights.

"Seeing you today puts me back, Colleen. You look so much like her. Fiona and I pushed that piano from her house to the docks. Have I told you that? Well, we had the help of a few strapping Irish brothers." Mother Anne Marie laughed softly. "Yes, of course, I suppose I've told you that story many times, haven't I?" She smiled. "At my age, there are only so many leaves left dangling on the tree of memories."

"You have kept all the precious leaves, Mother, but I never tire of hearing that story. Tell me again." Vanessa anticipated the sweetness that the memory would inevitably bring to Mother Anne Marie's countenance.

"'America Imagined' brought me to this wonderful country. It was Fiona who took me as her companion with the prize money. She has such a big heart, your mother. Can you imagine two poor Irish innocents from Dublin off to America? It was I who submitted her song to the competition behind her back. There is my confession." The color momentarily returned to the nun's pale face.

"If that was your only sin, you're a saint." Vanessa tried to lighten the conversation, avoiding any further mention of Fiona. The small laugh Vanessa released, laced with pain, sat like a guilty sinner in the room filled with the earnest murmurs of the nuns' prayers.

"It was not my only sin. I lied to you."

"What lie?" Vanessa stiffened.

"The money for your education, all of the money, it was not a trust, my child. It was from Fiona. I knew you would never take it from her. I wanted you to have what you deserved. Forgive me?"

Vanessa didn't hesitate. "Of course, Mother, I forgive *you*." How many lies did she ask of Mother Anne Marie? I'll pay back every penny, Vanessa thought, gripping the edge of the blanket to control her anger.

"Colleen, you always played Fiona's song so much better than I ever could. I always smile at the apt meaning, dear. 'Rise to Be You'. I'm so proud of what you do, my child, what you've become."

Vanessa hadn't thought of the meaning of the song title before. Was it a message from Fiona to Vanessa or to herself?

"Promise me you will play your mother's exquisite piece for me when you get home. I will hear it from my place in heaven, God willing."

Vanessa looked at her hands. "I always played it for Daddy when he was depressed, and we missed her." Vanessa gazed through the grates of the windows, remembering the creaking sounds in the darkened room in their small apartment as her father rocked in his chair, staring vacantly.

Mother Anne Marie drifted away for a moment. The pause in her breathing brought the group of Sisters to her side, and their voices raised in prayer as their dangling, matching black rosary beads swayed from their hands in rhythm.

The nun opened her eyes again. "Anger can transform you, you know, dear." She stroked Vanessa's hair.

"Mother, you shouldn't talk. Rest."

Vanessa picked up the Murano glass rosary from the blanket—a gift she had bought for Mother Anne Marie at the Vatican on one of her trips to Rome. She draped the string of blue glass beads over Mother's hands and held on to one side, nervously rolling a bead between her fingers. *Holy Mary, mother of God, pray for us sinners now and at the hour of our death, Amen.* Vanessa suddenly found meaning in the rote prayer she had recited a thousand times. "Ave Maria." Vanessa pictured her mother's hands playing. Her childhood-self emerged.

Mother Anne Marie took Vanessa's scarred hand in her own, rubbing it gently to soothe the memory. She tenderly hummed Fiona's song, "Rise to Be You", pulling Vanessa into her arms with unexpected strength.

"If you hadn't come to get me that day, I would have been left with a woman who hated the sight of me, my own grandmother. And you had to break your vows of the cloister to come for me. Can you forgive me?" Vanessa sighed into the nun's arms and listened to her weakening heart beats.

"I've made my peace with God in that matter," Mother Anne Marie said. "And we were once women in a cloistered convent who were never meant to have a child. What would we have missed without the joy of you? I am afraid for you, Colleen, that you will be consumed by the same anger that destroyed your father. He never forgave his parents. Forgive your grandparents and your mother, darlin,' not for anyone else, but for *your* sake." Her breathing was labored.

Through the wrought iron grids of the massive window, Vanessa stared at the old tree that had lost so many branches in the years she'd been away. She was as far from forgiveness for Fiona as she'd ever been. With such limited connection to the outside world, Mother Anne Marie had no way of knowing the current Fiona. She would be shocked at what had become of her best friend.

"What is it, Colleen, dear?"

"Just thinking about the day I came here to live with you, Mother. I've missed you. I'm so sorry I never came home after I left for college. I just couldn't risk her finding me." The emotion spilled down her cheeks. "It all seems so foolish now. I've missed so much. I should have *come*." Vanessa's words bounced back at her off the room's hard surfaces.

"You had a life to lead. *I* chose this cloistered life, not you. Your letters and calls were enough." Mother Anne Marie slowed. "Our bond survived the distance, my dear. You and my service to God were beyond my dreams, the joys of my life." There was a sudden lift in her voice.

Vanessa could sense Mother Anne Marie fading as a quiet aura surrounded her.

"Colleen, don't delay because of me. Help the Indonesian woman after I go."

"Mother, no! I can't leave this time as though nothing happened. I need to honor you."

"Do your good work in my name. You are my legacy. Your work will honor me, my love." Her grip weakened. She put her hands together, pointing them heavenward. "Now pray with me, my only one." Her voice was barely audible, and Vanessa could feel her pulse slowing.

Pressing her hands together as Vanessa hadn't done for many years, from habit, her knees slipped down to the cold, rough floor beside her precious mentor's bed. A sudden breeze cast shadows of dancing leaves on the foot of the bed from the tree outside the window. Vanessa wanted to reverse time, rewind, re-write her script.

"Our Father, Who art in Heaven, hallowed be Thy name." Her voice chanted on, in concert, joining with the angelic sounds of each imploring Sister. The choir of voices gathered in the high rafters and returned to Vanessa's ears as one celestial sound.

Mother's lips moved silently. She managed only the final word of the prayer, "Amen."

Vanessa leaned down to hear her words.

"Forgive her. I love you, child."

Moving closer, Vanessa kissed the lips of her departing mother and devotedly took in her final loving gaze. Lifting Mother Anne Marie's weak hand, Vanessa rested her head on her mentor's chest and listened.

The nuns' prayers created a hum around her, and she lost all sense of time. Mother Anne Marie's heartbeat slowed, then stopped. Vanessa gasped. Her heavy grief immobilized her as she kept her ear on Mother Anne Marie's chest with foolish hope.

Sister Mary Joseph helped her to her feet. "Come, Colleen, we have prepared your old room for you. It was unoccupied—our numbers have dwindled these past years. The Sisters have settled your friend into the room next to yours. She was tired. Father O'Connor is on his way. We will take care of everything. It is what we do, my dear. You should go to Indonesia, as planned, and do your good work."

Sister Mary Joseph led Vanessa to her own rustic childhood room. The memories met her at the door. Vanessa could almost feel the divots in her knees, like craters on the moon from praying on the rough stone floor. She scanned the sparse room. The stripes of light broke through the window's iron bars and flashed across her squinting eyes, just as it had, when as a child, she'd sat up in her bed with the rising sun. She could hear the sweet silence that surrounded her as she walked down the cold hallway with a small, white, rough towel over her arm.

The large window crisscrossed with wrought iron lattice grids and the window shelf still held her dozens of childhood books. "Everything looks the same, Sister."

"Yes, no one has touched a thing since you left, dear."

Vanessa's eyes caught something new. She glanced back at Sister Mary Joseph. "Except for this." Vanessa crossed the room and picked up the photo of Fiona and Vanessa, age seven, sitting at the piano. *Even from the beyond, Mother Anne Marie does her work,* she thought. On the same handmade lace doily on the dresser was the familiar photo of a young man with a black-edged funeral card tucked into the corner of the frame. *In Memoriam, Daniel Cohen,* it read. Vanessa picked up the photo of her father and turned the image of Fiona facedown.

"Perhaps you could take them both with you?" Sister Mary Joseph left quietly to join the double line of Sisters floating in their black habits, moving silently like angels through the stone archway, the ever-present sounds of three dozen pair of heavy black rosary beads clicking in harmony, as they walked toward the chapel to pray Vespers, the evening prayers.

Vanessa closed the door and sat on her bed.

Nothing makes sense, she thought. *Why didn't I come to visit? How could I have not seen her for all those years, cloistered or not?* The logic of her choices eluded her.

"Van?" Canyon cracked opened the weighty door, let herself in, and sat on the edge of Vanessa's bed. "I'm so sorry."

Vanessa felt Canyon's arms around her. She tried not to stiffen, her instinct. She felt raw from her profound loss. Still, she pulled away.

"I know you." Canyon held Vanessa's shoulders at arm's length and squeezed slightly too hard. "You'll want to tough it out, not accept my sympathy and comfort, but this is one of those times, Van, that I won't let you. This is your true mother who has just died."

Vanessa let Canyon pull her closer. She shuddered and rivulets of tears ran down her cheeks.

A heavy silence surrounded them.

LUNAR LANDING

Scott

SCOTT RUSHED DOWN the path to Jeff's house, perched on the elevated outskirts of the makeshift mining town. He took in the dramatic landscape. Stretched out to the horizon, floating in the azure sky, the striking green expanse of a dozen mountain tops made him sigh. Large swooping birds scanned the tops of the trees as the fog rose up from the valleys, encroaching on the mine site.

Boy, Jeff, you picked the spot, he thought. What a view. Maybe my Quonset hut near the helipad a half-mile away isn't as impressive, but it gives me better access to the comings and goings, he consoled himself.

They needed to revisit their strategy. Scott wanted to review Jeff's thoughts before they met with Brad and the team. Vanessa Gold's impending arrival, the company's sponsorship for Fiona O'Farrell's concert, employee protests, and the damn full moon fiasco were too much.

On the side of the house, the bedroom window was ajar. Jeff and Delilah's voices carried out into the yard. Scott couldn't resist eavesdropping. He was the director of security after all. He laughed to himself. Slipping closer to the house, he pressed his back against the wooden siding and spied inside at an angle out of sight.

Delilah's southern-belle voice was unmistakable. "I am so nervous about the next few days, Jeffrey."

Scott could see her adjusting her hair in the mirror.

"If I were home in Savannah, I would know what to do. Hosting a dinner party here is another thing—and for Vanessa Gold, no less." She lilted her words in her distinctive accent, then carefully stroked red lipstick across her pouting lips. Blotting them on a tissue, she looked behind her. "Jeffrey, you haven't heard a word I've said, have you?"

"My mind is on that damn Yankee woman, Delilah."

Stepping back a few feet, Scott continued his espionage. True, he and Jeff were on the same page, but it never hurt to hear the perspective from the inner sanctum.

"Delilah, wherever she goes, trouble follows. We can't afford for Ms. Exposé to be sticking her nose into this situation. Now the whole damn world is watching."

Flashing his head in front of the edge of the window, Scott watched Jeff button his white dress shirt, while admiring himself in the full-length mirror on the back of the closet door. "And, yes, I heard everything you said, Delilah. Do you really want to go there? We are not back in Savannah because you couldn't keep your hands off every young guy I ever hired. Well, I finally have a guy who knows something about loyalty."

Pulling back at Jeff's words, Scott flattened himself against the wall.

"Your lackey, Scott? Delicious, but no thanks."

Scott nearly gave away his secret eavesdropping location with his sputtering laugh at Delilah's back-handed compliment.

"Jeffrey, it's been five years. Isn't that punishment enough? You needn't have taken me to the other end of the Earth. It might have been different if you'd just paid a little attention to me. All you ever do is work. It's so uncivilized here with this bizarre koteka thing, and no proper household staff. At least, the servants at home spoke

English. These caveman people are so savage, and they smell. And all this obscene nakedness."

"I would have thought that would be right up your alley, my dear."

"I'm a Christian woman, Jeffrey."

Scott could almost feel the sting of Jeff's retort.

Delilah prattled on, "I just want to get this whole sacrifice thing over with. Everyone's so out of sorts. For Pete's sake, one black woman in trade for the fate of the whole project and every employee's job seems like a no-brainer. And it's what the tribal people want, Jeff."

Shaking his head at the shameful racist remark, Scott stepped back from the window as he saw Jeff leaving the bedroom.

"I'm going over to the office to wrap things up. Try to behave."

As Jeff came outside, Scott arrived in front of the house. "Thought you'd like to talk before our meeting with Brad and the staff?"

"Just the man I wanted to see." Jeff clasped Scott's shoulder. "I'll need your backing for this one."

"I have your back."

"Update me, son."

The word son made Scott cringe. Even though he was thirty-six, he liked it, but it had a flip side. It brought him back to his father's accident on the farm. He would never get over the shock of seeing his father's body—the image now dreamlike—floating silently, falling from the barn roof onto the tractor below.

Scott shared the status of the employee strike over the tribal woman's sacrifice and the details of Vanessa Gold and her film crew's arrival. "We're at a near standstill at this point, Jeff. I took a ride up to the employees' huts today. Hundreds of our men are doing their mumbo jumbo and thrusting protest signs in the air, all in Indonesian or some dialect. Who knows what they said? My interpreter said there were two primary demands: to receive higher wages and to kill the woman."

Jeff paused in front of the management office trailer. "Looks like the sacrifice is the easier part, compared to dealing with pay issues with the new Indonesian employees from the more sophisticated cities. I'm surprised how savvy they are."

"Although, Jeff, we aren't paying most of the locals more than three squares, and they don't know the difference. All they care about is free meals, keeping the damn nature spirits happy, and sacrificing that woman. But you're right, the workers from the more modernized islands understand money, and want fair wages." Scott thrust his hands in his pockets. "It's going to really hit you in the profits."

"We should never have brought them in. We had a good thing going with the more remote tribes—three meals, no hunting or gathering. They're thrilled to work all day." Jeff opened the door to the corrugated metal trailer office.

Zell Baxter Global Mining maps were taped to the wall, and stacks of papers created a chaotic atmosphere in the little tin central command. A rough door cut out of the end wall led to a second trailer that served as their small communications room. US Marine plaques were strung proudly on the wall. Jeff adjusted the small confederate flag on his desk.

Brad and Scott's assistant, Jim, were waiting for them.

"Hey, Jeff, here's the mail, plus this week's magazines and duplicates of last week's, I picked up. Let's hope the locals don't run off with them this time." Brad dropped a bag on the floor.

"We need all troops on alert to keep an eye on our lady journalist. She arrives the day after tomorrow." Jeff picked up a magazine and tapped on Vanessa's face. "Don't be fooled by the smiling beauty. I hear she's no lady. She's a black widow, and I need everyone on high alert." Jeff pulled the cord to open the dusty Venetian blinds and bent to peer out.

The sight of Vanessa Gold's face on the magazine cover unnerved Scott. As chief of security, he realized he was the most vulnerable caught between loyalty to the company and himself. He had to find out how she got her hands on that film footage. And he needed to destroy it. Scott refocused. "We've got your back, Jeff."

"I know you do, son. Never a doubt about that." Jeff patted Scott on the back.

"Look, we have to make it look good with Lady Gold. If we'd resisted, it would have looked like we had something to hide." Jeff lit a cigarette and blew smoke at the world map. "We are in the most god-forsaken place in the world. How the hell did we deserve this attention?"

"She might just provide the solution for us. Vanessa Gold has turned worse situations around. Let's not make her the enemy quite yet." After hearing Delilah and Jeff's perspectives, Scott tried to keep his boss in check. Things could get out of hand quickly, and wherever *Turning Prism* went the press followed.

"The sacrifice thing with that tribeswoman is a lose-lose. Mass hysteria for the local tribal workers and a labor strike for the city folks. I know I can count on a fellow marine to keep close tabs on the infamous Ms. Gold and her team. We may not have had a choice about her coming, but we do have a choice about her staying," Jeff added.

Jeff's words alarmed Scott. "How's that?"

"Just create bigger bait for the almighty Vanessa Gold somewhere away from my mine site."

"Got it. Got anything in mind?" Scott liked the idea, but it didn't solve the sacrifice issue. And he needed some leverage over Vanessa Gold. He needed that twenty-year-old evidence destroyed.

Jeff picked up one of the new magazines. "How about the celebrated new Woman of the Year?" He dropped it on the desk, and a cloud of dust rose into the afternoon sunlight that had fought its way through the dirty open window.

"Fiona O'Farrell? She's great but how does that play in here?"

"America's sweetheart, just so happens to be playing in Jakarta, and we just happen to be sponsoring her first concert for her new foundation. Got the Indonesian Minister of Mines to convince her of the lucky date—the nineteenth."

"The day before the full moon, right? I'm not sure I get it." For the first time, Scott didn't trust Jeff's judgment.

"O'Farrell's offered to take in one of the local orphans to her music school. Good PR for us for one thing. We can get rid of one of these urchins that wander the site. And I'm working on a distraction that Vanessa Gold couldn't resist."

"But what's the plan for the distraction? Gold isn't going to bite on a piano concert just because the performer is a famous American and loves helping kids, not when she has a cross-cultural challenge in her sights." Scott shrugged his shoulders. "How do we get Gold to Jakarta? It's right at the time of the moon ceremony. If she's here to stop the sacrifice, what would distract her?"

"You leave the distraction part to me. Just keep Ms. Truth in News here until the nineteenth, then we get her out of here before the moon ceremony fiasco on the twentieth."

Did Jeff know that the sacrifice could happen at any time before the full moon? Scott would stay out of it until he knew exactly what Jeff was up to.

"We have everything at stake here, son! We're losing millions of dollars, a mountain full of gold, copper, and silver, and our jobs, frankly. This is war!"

Scott felt like he was back in the Marines. It excited him, but he wasn't up for another battle with PTSD. "Yes, sir. You got it. I'm on it."

Jeff sat behind his desk. "So *ideas*?"

Scott didn't want to be the brains behind this one. Not against Vanessa Gold.

"I'd like to hear what you have in mind first, Jeff."

"First, I suggest we put a ransom on the tribal woman's head, offer a reward for her capture and a bonus if she gets thrown overboard by the twentieth. Use a go-between. Then, we meet with the tribal leaders, let them know we're on it, enlist their cooperation. What kinds of things do they want, Scott?"

"Weapons and food. I know money doesn't work with the tribal locals as well as goods do, but cash works with the Indonesians from more developed places, like Jakarta."

"Scott, we're warding off mass hysteria and a labor strike. Other tribal leaders and workers at the mine are picketing. The mining company is losing millions. The issue isn't just cultural, it's now turned economic. Purely economic. What was originally a small tribal issue is now expected to be a worldwide public spectacle. We need to find that goddamn native woman and get Vanessa Gold to find a way to satisfy both sides or get rid of her." Jeff smashed his fist on the metal desk. "Not easy to recognize one tribal woman in a grass skirt when you can't tell one bare breast from another." He snickered at his own joke.

Offensive. The more he observed Jeff under pressure, the less Scott trusted him. You need a measured mouth in these circumstances. And then there's Delilah. Scott would have to manage these two when Vanessa or her film crew were around. "Jeff, it's right in front of your eyes. I should say right in your own backyard. Literally."

"What do you mean, son?" Jeff paced with hands on his hips.

Scott explained that the corkscrew end on Jeff's gardener's koteka identified him as a member of the accused woman's tribe. "It's a small remote tribe. He has to know her. I think we have a willing and unsuspecting helper."

CHAPTER 26

PROTESTING HERSELF

Lukeem

LUKEEM STAYED IN the cave for a cycle of light and dark. Abruce had not returned. Her urge to see her new world overcame her. With her flashlight in hand, Lukeem followed the labyrinth of interconnected caves and tunnels carved out of the mountain rock over time by the rushing water from above. The music of the dripping walls as the water found its way down to the sky spirits' valley reminded Lukeem of the sounds of her own tribal area. She pushed the thoughts away.

Peering through a gaping hole in the side of the tunnel, Lukeem heard the ceremony.

"Sorceress! Sacrifice her!"

She heard booming voices of chanting people speaking words she'd yet to learn. Repeating the words to herself, Lukeem crawled out on the rock ledge only a tall tree's height above the group. She was partway up the mountain above the sky spirits' homes.

A new chant arose. "More pay! More pay!"

Tribal men with the coverings of the sky spirits, some wearing their honored hard hats, were carrying designs in the shape of a flag on wooden sticks called signs. Abruce had told Lukeem about this— they were picketing, celebrating. Chanting, and buzzing with passion, they thrust the signs up and down with intensity while a sky spirit they called Scott paced back and forth in front of a large hut.

"Sacrifice her! More pay!"

Lukeem memorized the sounds.

A tall sky spirit came up the path in a land insect. Abruce had called the strange creature a *truck* when Lukeem had seen one near the food shack. The sky spirit stepped down to watch the ceremony. His posture told her he was a leader. He stood on top of his truck and spoke.

The gathering of dark-colored men stepped back, but they did not cower. Then they lurched forward in unison crushing each other to reach the feet of the white leader who towered above them.

The black-haired leader tried to signal with his hands, bellowing a command, but the followers screamed back at him. He spoke louder. "We'll find her! Be patient! The sorceress will be punished. A member of her tribe is our employee. He is helping us to find her. Go back to work!"

Lukeem listened carefully, trying to understand their passionate stories. She was happy to see that even women were allowed to join in the celebration.

Finding her way down the side of the cliff, Lukeem used the deep-rooted vines to lower herself to the ground. She was caught up in the energy and the sight of a woman celebrating.

The woman offered Lukeem a stick with a sign on it. She accepted it and blended into the screaming crowd. "Sacrifice her! Kill her!" Lukeem chimed in, eager to belong.

Dancing zealously, Lukeem pumped the sign in the air, purging her pent-up tension, shaking off the pain of her losses. Her feet lifted up sharply, and she imitated the traditional movements of her tribe that implored the sky spirits to return. "More pay, more pay!" She brought her stiff hand to her eyebrow and snapped it away.

The *others* saw her and repeated it until the entire crowd copied her gesture as her tribe had learned to do from the sky spirits of their ancestors. Lukeem moved and danced the steps of the ritual of her tribe—a dance only a man would be allowed to do. Freed by the new traditions of the *others*, she twisted the celebration stick in the air and felt thrilling energy pass through her.

A man with a short, thick koteka approached the center of the crowd with a long knife. The chants became more intense, growing as the mountains joined in, sending the calls back again, adding to the thunderous voices.

Lukeem jumped higher and spun around proudly with her celebration stick. She had never felt the joy of her body moving with such freedom.

A woman and her young child were shoved into the center of the group. The little girl, one who had seen no more than six rainy seasons, pushed against Lukeem, looked at her pleadingly, and took her hand. It was moist and hot. At the sight of the terror in the child's eyes, Lukeem's joy melted.

The white leader turned his back, sat down in the truck, and it moved down the steep hill toward the valley.

Sickened and shocked, Lukeem watched a man grab the child and pin her hand down on a large rock. The girl's screams were unbearable as he sliced through the tip of the child's small finger.

Lukeem abruptly pulled down her celebration stick.

The mother silenced her daughter.

How could the mother accept what was happening? The scene deeply confused Lukeem. The dark *others* are cruel beyond imagining, she thought. Gripping her stomach, Lukeem tried to keep a spasm from erupting as the child's screams were swallowed up in the crowd's fervor.

Fear choked Lukeem and brought her own sacrifice to mind. Her muscles tightened, and she forcefully peeled the stick from her own frightened grasp. She spotted a face in the crowd that looked like

Abruce; it was not her son. But the ache she felt for Abruce grew with the crowd's haunting voices, and the vine that had wrapped around her chest tightened.

Lukeem slumped to the ground, staring after the mother pulling her daughter away, unable to comprehend what the child could have done to deserve the torturous punishment. Why hadn't her mother protected her?

There was no memory of such anger and violence in Lukeem's tribe until the day of her own accusations. In her tribe, no child would ever be treated in such a way. Her tribespeople lived their days simply, searching for their food, loving their children. They only moved to find a comfortable place to gather leaves and ferns to build a cover for the night, or when there was a scarcity of food. Lukeem understood why the men had once brought back the skull of an *other* to display proudly on a stick in the center of their fire. The men seldom saw *others*, but she now knew the *others* must be evil. And yet the dark man at the top of the tram had been so kind and welcoming, and he was certainly an *other*, she thought. The mysteries felt like the webs of many spiders crisscrossing on the same tree.

She searched her language, but she had no words for such things, and the sight could find no place in her understanding. Perhaps she would never grasp the ways of the *others*.

A second truck crawled up the steep path. Inside the truck, Lukeem recognized the light-haired leader from the helicopter and a dark-haired sky spirit she'd never seen. In the back of the spirits' truck, she spotted Abruce. They had come for her, finally, she thought. The truck slowed. She waved her trembling hand.

Jumping from the truck, Abruce moved through the celebrating crowd, then appeared again. He pulled Lukeem by the hand and ran with her toward the mountain. "Ma, hurry! I will explain. We can take this path to reach the caves."

Lukeem couldn't find her voice. The young girl's screams echoed.

Lukeem's mind exploded with fear and confusion. A numbness spread through her body.

"Here is the opening. We have to hide you." Abruce wrapped his arm around her and guided her.

They entered the cave and wound their way to the depths of the mountain. For many moments, she was silent. Abruce led her, squeezing her hand to give her his strength. Her exhaustion was beyond her experience. She breathed in deeply to renew herself. "I need to sit."

Abruce stopped and settled them on a rock ledge. Like the tree stump, infested with insects, that had crumbled into dust under her feet, her illusion of the dark *others* was destroyed by the single cruel act she'd seen. There was much evil in the *others* and now the strangeness of the *white* ones. She had to turn to more hopeful things.

CHAPTER 27

PRIMITIVE THINKING

Vanessa

VANESSA SAT UP WITH an aching neck from sleeping against the cold window of the plane. A gauzy veil still clung to her from the hangover over a day before. The monotonous whine of the engine prevented her from thinking clearly. She hadn't slept. Crushing loneliness had crawled inside her since Mother Anne Marie's death. Vanessa realized that the holy woman was the only one who really knew her. The only one who shared Vanessa's history from start to finish.

"And still loved me," she whispered.

Untethered was the word that came to her.

She sipped a Bloody Mary and snacked on fish crackers, straining to keep the remaining darkest secret from exploding from her mouth. Her less than full confession to Canyon about her past had caused a dark heaviness in Vanessa's chest. She'd tried to force out the facts about her grandfather's death before crashing on the theatre chair in her LA home when her words had flowed. "There's more," she remembered calling to Canyon, but her brain had been swimming in Merlot. Vanessa had wanted to excavate the last of her lies with Canyon on the trip to Indonesia. She needed to feel a sense of peace, the elusive and foreign feeling that she had craved throughout her adult life. She wanted to get it over with, suffer the punishment, come clean, and have Canyon help break through to Vanessa's deep isolation. She hadn't always been the heroine Canyon thought she was. Now in the daylight, starting over with no momentum, Vanessa's courage withdrew deep inside. And Mother Anne Marie's death consumed her.

Canyon roused from her sleep on the reclined seat across the aisle. As she sat up, groaning and stretching, Vanessa handed her a Bloody Mary. "A touch of the dog that bit you?"

"God, I'm exhausted. Thanks." Canyon drank it down, lifted her sliding window shade, and squinted into the light. "This may sound crass, Van, but I'm glad you're so obscenely rich. I couldn't have faced anyone these past thirty-six interminable hours. This private plane is so luxurious. Do I look as terrible as I feel?" Canyon turned to her. "I still can't believe your mother is Fiona—"

"*Please*, Canyon. I can't get anything through my head either. We're about to land. And I'm already so miserable." Vanessa stared at her friend. "How can you wake up and just start talking?"

"You know me." Canyon nodded toward her empty Bloody Mary. "Sorry, but a woman who is famous for loving children, why would she abandon her only child?"

"I don't know." The memory of playing the piano with her mother made its usual flash through Vanessa's mind. She felt trapped as if the demons she'd wrestled in her nights for years had been unleashed on her days by telling Canyon the truth. No time for this, she chastised herself.

Fifteen minutes later, the plane landed. They thanked their pilot for such a smooth yet seemingly endless flight.

"I'll have the helicopter pilot transfer your things, and good luck. It was an honor to meet both of you." Descending the ramp that two native men had provided, their pilot Crysti waved goodbye.

Through the window, they watched a man wearing a Zell Baxter jacket transfer their belongings from the plane to the helicopter. Was he the pilot who'd sent the photos and intel, Vanessa wondered? He shook hands with Crysti, and she headed into the small rustic terminal building.

Vanessa and Canyon stood on the hot tarmac that sucked at their shoes.

The helicopter pilot approached.

Canyon nudged Vanessa's arm. "Did you say I'd find a caveman, Van? He's . . . he's more like—"

"Down, girl. Let's see who's who before you go off on a rendezvous."

"*Van*, I wasn't . . . I was just saying he's—"

He smiled. "We need to move quickly before the afternoon fog rolls in on the mountain. Makes it easier to land. Much better view too. Brad Wainwright, by the way. I know you're Vanessa Gold, and you must be Canyon Swenson."

"Canyon is our anthropologist. She's part of our original *Turning Prism* team."

"Yes. I saw the news, and I've read about you, Professor. Pleasure." Brad turned his attention back to Vanessa. "I brought Tony in two days ago. He's waiting at the mine site for you. Took him up to see Father Carey. Listen, I'll just check-in and be right back. Enjoy the view."

It was a relief to stretch after thirty-six hours in transit, Vanessa thought. LA to New York, New York to Sydney, and Sydney to Kubin Island Airport. She unfolded the small map Brad had given her and pointed out their location to Canyon. The island's airport was located just beyond the great barrier reef with a spectacular view of the Arafura Sea. In the distance, the Australian coastline appeared like a foggy strip of mountaintops on the horizon.

Vanessa and Canyon turned around. Above them loomed a trio of deep green, massive mountains topped with glaciers that glinted in the afternoon light. With their arms around each other, they admired the spectacular panorama of nature.

"Breathtaking, Van. I can't wait to see this from above on the heli-copter ride to the mine site. Imagine?"

Glancing over her shoulder, Vanessa saw Brad approaching. "Here comes your blonde bombshell, Canyon. Go easy now."

Canyon snapped her hand on Vanessa's forearm.

"Oh, never mind, Canyon, you're safe, relax, his name doesn't start with an F, my alphabet-soup-eating friend."

"Funny. Shush, he's coming."

"Ready?" Brad reached out with his muscled arm and offered to help them up into the helicopter.

Canyon blushed.

Releasing a muffled one-note laugh, Vanessa climbed the steps behind Canyon. She set her briefcase and cameras down on the floor beside her seat. She could always count on Canyon to give her respite from her sadness and her buzzing mind. Settling into the back seat next to Canyon, Vanessa stared at Brad's profile as he prepared for take-off. "So, let's cut to the quick." She leaned forward and peered over his shoulder. "Who else knows you took those photos of the failed sacrifice on the cliff and sent me the letter?"

Brad whipped his head around from the cockpit.

"I thought so. It *was* you." Vanessa studied Brad.

"You don't waste time, Ms. Gold." He stretched around in the squeaking, cracked leather seat to face Vanessa and smiled. "Well, I can't take full credit, not my idea, but when a certain famous woman suggested you, I knew you were the right one. Those photos were burning a hole in my duffel bag, but I didn't know who to trust with the whole story. I gave them to the head of security, Scott." Brad adjusted some controls. "But then I thought, I don't really know him, and he and the director are old Marine buddies, so I wrote the letter to you with the true details and sent a full set of copies."

"Does Zell Baxter Mining suspect you contacted me and sent the letter in addition to the security director?"

"I think the mine execs assume it was a missionary or one of the NGO's around here who like to stick their noses in cultural issues. They're the only ones nearby with helicopters and planes." Brad snapped his headset on and flipped some more switches, then faced her again. "I think my co-pilot Jim has thrown them off my scent, and he volunteered us to hunt the sorceress down."

"Can you trust him?" Vanessa watched Brad's face closely.

"He's an old school buddy from Wharton and an Air Force comrade, and he owes me. And he talks a lot, so we can feed him whatever word we want to spread around. Headsets by your seats if you want to talk. This thing's a rattle trap."

Canyon's eyes widened at the word Wharton, and she grinned at Vanessa.

Yes of course, Brad would be a smart, educated guy too. Vanessa shook her head and smiled as Canyon's thoughts transferred without words. Vanessa would pursue the whole "from Wharton to piloting in the jungle" storyline later. What had brought him here to this far-flung place?

The rotor started to turn; it would drown out their words with its accelerating swoop.

Vanessa adjusted her headset. She believed him—his eyes, his gestures, all good. "So, whose idea? Someone I would know?" She was intrigued to find out her ally's name.

"Not sure if you know her personally, but she is sure a fan of yours. Fiona O'Farrell, the pianist. Of all people. Funny, huh?"

Vanessa pulled at his seat back to lean in closer.

"Met her in the Jakarta airport. I've been tasked with finding an Irian Jaya child for her new music school in Jakarta. Have you read about that? It's all over the news here."

"Yes, I know all about it." Vanessa was enraged.

"She got talking about you, and she got me talking, and I told her about the situation." Brad shrugged, glancing over his shoulder at

Vanessa. "She was passionate about you helping Lukeem, and it all just came together."

"I am sure it did." Vanessa was speechless, reeling from the news of Fiona's shocking intrusion into her life. *Damn you, Fiona,* she thought. She had no desire to reunite with her, even if it was Mother Anne Marie's dying wish. The nun's loyalty and forgiveness were touching. Still, from her cloistered world, Mother Anne Marie had a limited view of Fiona, quite unlike the public persona of Vanessa's outrageous mother. It would have shocked and disillusioned the holy woman. *Fiona was not the dear old Irish best friend the nun had known,* she thought. *Vanessa couldn't forgive. I need to focus,* she told herself. *Just three days until the full moon.* She would honor Mother Anne Marie by saving Lukeem or in some other way. That's all she could do.

Without a word exchanged, Canyon reached across the aisle and squeezed Vanessa's forearm to affirm. Her look said, "Let's do this."

Vanessa submerged herself in the hypnotic fluttering as the helicopter made its noisy way up over the mountain peaks.

Negotiating a sudden turn, Brad tilted away from the side of a cliff. "Took a little detour to show you the place. Right there." Brad indicated a frightening drop off. "That's where I took the photos."

Vanessa imagined Lukeem drifting over the thousand-foot drop. How would she have felt? What would she think as the river grew larger and larger and she knew her body would be crushed on the rocks and swallowed up in the raging water? How would she feel knowing her own people had condemned her? What would be Lukeem's last thought?

Vanessa had experienced several near deaths, but they were sudden, no time to think, just react, it was over, and she was alive. The thought of the suspended time, the time to regret and feel your losses, made Vanessa cringe.

"Brad, I couldn't tell from the photos. Did you go back? Did you ever interact with Lukeem again? Your letter never said." Vanessa remained riveted on Brad's profile and his disembodied voice in her headset.

"Just that once when we dropped supplies up there. Lukeem was curious. Sweet woman. Jim let her sit in the helicopter. You should have seen her face all lit up."

"Sky spirits, after all." Vanessa imagined the woman's joy at meeting the lost sky spirits her tribe had worshiped and awaited their return for nearly half a century.

Canyon shared an insight. "Can you imagine, based on the dense jungle area she comes from, this woman had likely never seen a horizon? There are few peoples left like this who have no experience with perspective due to their closed jungle environments. No familiarity with open space or how everything appears smaller at a distance. So, imagine the sky spirits in a helicopter, and her first view from the edge of this cliff. She must have been spellbound."

"Yeah, she was glowing, fascinated. At the time, we didn't realize what it meant to her, Canyon, but we never had a woman look at us like that before." Brad laughed. "Jim wanted her to come with us. But she ran away. Wish I'd listened to him. None of this would have happened."

They rode in silence, taking in the dramatic scenery.

BRAD GLANCED AT the control panel and his watch. "OK, we're about ten minutes out. There's our valley." He pointed south and the glint of the sun on the corrugated roofs signaled the locale.

The familiar tension crawled up from Vanessa's gut into her throat as the helicopter descended into the lush mountain pass. It swooped over a razorback road and approached the mile-wide Quonset hut town nestled in the valley between three massive mountaintops. She was on. Vanessa tried to bury her sorrow, but it resisted and hung around her. That was a first. She couldn't excavate the clear-headed, laser-sharp self she'd always conjured up to start an assignment. She couldn't rise from beneath the oppressive sadness she was carrying—the devastating death of Mother Anne Marie, her soon-to-be-marriage to Tony in jeopardy, the lies, Fiona's manipulations—it was all too much.

She knew the drill. It was up to Vanessa to call the shots. She never really had a plan in mind until it began to unfold rapid-fire. Still, she understood that everyone around her needed to sense her confidence, trust her control, and have faith in her instincts, if the *Turning Prism* team were to pull things off.

To gather herself together, she called upon the tortured face of the native woman in the photos. Vanessa had faced down corporations and rescued political victims before, but this was a complicated situation when it came to both culpability and resolution: corporate greed and ignorance, cultural norms and flux.

There was no clear right or wrong, she thought. Restoring the delicate cultural balance was key to preventing a disaster well beyond the life of one tribal woman. There could easily be chaos, slaughter, genocide, perhaps. Bottom line, Vanessa had exposed Lukeem to the world, and she couldn't let the woman die.

Canyon sat up from her nap. "Look at that waterfall! It's absolutely electrified in the sunlight, and there's another one, two, three—this is amazing. Oh, and look at that river. Magnificent!" She leaned closer to the window.

The sound of Canyon's excited voice gave Vanessa some release from the intensity growing inside her. She had her secret weapon back, her stress buster, her best friend. There were so many times that Vanessa had missed Canyon's smart, quirky spirit over the years, especially in the heat of a dangerous mission, and Vanessa knew this was going to be one.

Brad pointed at the snaking river that wrapped in and out of the valleys at the base of the three mountains. "Ranu Lolo."

"Canyon, it's stunning, isn't it?" Vanessa scanned the dozens of near-naked natives in kotekas that bounced in rhythm with their running footsteps toward the helipad.

"Amazing, huh?" Brad pointed at the line of enthusiastic indigenous men with their heads tilted up, shading their eyes in anticipation. "Your welcoming committee."

Vanessa enjoyed the look on Canyon's face. "You're not acting like a social anthropologist, Canyon." She tried a much-needed laugh. It hung irreverently in the air—too soon after Mother Anne Marie's passing, she thought.

"It's one thing to hear about it or teach theory, but another to live it." Canyon put her hands to her head and laughed while taking in the exotic sight. "Hard to remember all my fieldwork after ten years of classroom teaching."

Vanessa admired how Canyon could let go in the moment to enjoy the spectacular view, indulge her charming naiveté, and then, in an instant, return to the serious task at hand. She'd once called Canyon's gift to the team, *a calming breath between two screams*. Vanessa acknowledged that she would never learn to come off red alert once she'd flipped the switch like Canyon could.

The helicopter hovered, and Canyon looked out at the crowd of men. "Notice they're wearing different sizes and styles of amber-colored penis gourds—some straight, some long and narrow, some thick and short. It reflects individuality and tribal identity amid the sameness."

Each man held his bow and arrows in his hand. Coarse woven nets in earth tones hung from their foreheads down their backs. A woven armband, a feather, or a string of small shells here or there completed their garb. Every individual sported his own style of nose bone in his own fashion. Some of the half-moon bones were worn curved upward like a second smile. Some were set downward frowning, and some of the natives preferred a straight rounded skewer that kept a constant line of balance on their faces, accentuating any tilt of the head.

With the perfect touchdown, Brad landed on the elevated dirt helipad. Surrounded by an endless chain of mountains off in the distance, the small mining town sat in a crater as though a meteor had landed and wiped out all the lush vegetation. The site was barren except for two young shade trees planted by a community pool.

Why did Vanessa want to cry for those other trees that had lost their lives to convenience? An indication of the culture of the mining company—easier to just wipe it all out, she thought. The heavy gathering clouds and ground fog seemed like a prelude to the enormity of the task facing her.

CHAPTER 28

SOFT LANDING

Vanessa

ONE LONE MAN stepped forward from the group. He drew the bone from his nose, licked it, and replaced it with one swift, well-rehearsed gesture. He flipped the crescent-shaped bone curve-down and created a second frown on his serious face.

Vanessa leaned over Canyon and studied the men on the ground below. "Is that the leader coming forward, Canyon?"

"He's too young, maybe. And they call the leader of the tribe, the 'honored one'." Canyon looked through the scratched window. "Oh, he can't be. He's wearing a different koteka than the others."

The young adult indigenous male dragged a set of steps up to the door. A yellow, rust, and brown woven net bag hung from his forehead and down his back, a simple shell necklace decorated his throat. His look was completed by a hollowed-out penis gourd strapped around his waist with a unique double twist at the end. He stepped onto the platform and pushed his fierce dark face up to the window.

Startled by his sudden movement, Vanessa pulled back.

Canyon didn't flinch.

"You're like Margaret freakin' Meade, Canyon."

"This is so beyond exotic." Canyon laughed and put her hand to her forehead and grinned. "I love it."

The native looked confused, then copied Canyon's gesture with his hand to his forehead. "How easily we can impact their cultural norms, huh?" Tugging on her blonde dreadlocks, Canyon tossed them back away from her face, a nervous habit Vanessa had seen a thousand times. She knew Canyon's gesture well. Her friend was onto something. Canyon drew out her copies of the photos. "He's from Lukeem's tribe." Canyon's finger pointed to the end of the twisted koteka that every man wore in the photos. "Each tribe has a distinct choice of sheaths. His tribe goes for corkscrew tips."

"You're back in the game, Canyon. You're right. He's the only one in the group with that style."

"Yes, but whose side is he on? That's what we need to find out." Canyon settled back into her seat.

Vanessa was relieved, but could Canyon deal with all the stress after her breakup and so many years away from the action? "Canyon, promise you'll stay out of the fray. Background only on this one?"

"I promise. Don't worry. I'll provide the insights and the words, but I have no interest in hanging from a cliff with arrows zinging by my head, and you shouldn't either, but I know warnings are wasted on you."

Leaning over Canyon toward the window again, Vanessa examined the young man's broad solemn face.

He looked confused, then he burst into a wide smile as he looked past Canyon at Vanessa and waved. Sparkling with kindness and openness, he exhibited no self-consciousness about staring directly into her eyes.

"Thin personal barriers, little social agenda or self-consciousness, and wears all his emotions on his sleeve. Well, not sleeve." Canyon provided more cultural context.

Waving back, Vanessa stretched over Canyon toward the window. "He seems to recognize me. How?"

The native raised his long bow, nodding his approval at Vanessa.

She felt the familiar process take hold. A machine gun barrage of questions filled her head. She began to take in details. Making internal checklists, processing on high alert, her own personal realities faded cooperatively into the background. She was relieved to feel the familiar lock-into-the-task-at-hand take place. The wavering fish was always the victim of the shark. That was something Vanessa understood intuitively. Every inch of her body had to say, I know what I'm doing. I'm right. She had to stand in the light confidently to cast a bigger shadow than the opposition, especially when she was in the crosshairs. Not a flinch. Trust was not an option, not for Brad, not for this young man, until she'd satisfied her instincts.

Brad popped-open the door and offered a muscular arm to help them down the wobbling wooden steps. Again, Canyon took hold, and Vanessa declined. Greeted by a wave of cheers from the natives, they were wrapped in the intense background chatter and unfamiliar warnings from the jungle wildlife.

Vanessa gratefully settled into the rich, chaotic nature sounds that replaced the incessant engine whine they had tolerated for two hours in transit from the coast below.

The same young male native approached Vanessa, bowed his head slightly, and looked up at her with what seemed to be a look of recognition. Stepping forward, he extended his rough, dark hand to greet her. The indigenous man was clearly pleased with himself for knowing her way of meeting hand-to-hand. Placing his hand over Vanessa's heart, he spoke. "Abruce."

Vanessa's instinct was to pull back at the intimacy of his gesture, but her eyes were fixed on the long, twisted, hollow gourd that was tied with a cord over the young aboriginal's privates, extending at least two feet out from his torso with a humorous double twist at the end. Her fingers brushed the bizarre projectile as she grasped his hand in greeting. When she glanced at his koteka, he pointed to it and smiled.

"Koteka."

Vanessa nodded and consciously stopped herself from smelling her hand marked with his curious scent.

"It's charred pig fat. The natives use it to keep warm on the mountaintops," Canyon explained as Brad unloaded some gear from the helicopter.

Returning Abruce's greeting, Vanessa said, "Van." She offered him a single syllable to make things easier for him, then gestured toward her companion. "Can-yon."

He looked at Vanessa with admiration, then turned to Canyon. Imitating her simplified, two-syllable name, he repeated, "Can-yon," and put his hand on Canyon's chest.

"Van, the intimacy of Abruce's tribal greeting must wreak havoc on the so-called civilized community when it comes to the American miners, especially the women." Canyon had done her homework. "The rest of the tribes in this area shake hands with a weak grip and then place their hands over their *own* hearts in greeting."

"Canyon, what would I do without you?"

As though on cue, the remaining men stepped forward. One by one, they shook hands with each of the three new arrivals, then placed their hands over their own hearts.

"Hmm? I've only seen Abruce shake hands American-style. Must be showing you some kind of tribal respect." Brad shook hands with Abruce. "Hey Buddy, how's it going?"

"OK, so I am an anthropologist. And I can keep my professional perspective, but I'm also a mid-westerner, not to say I'm a church-going prude at heart, but really!" Canyon stepped back as soon as Abruce removed his hand from her chest.

Vanessa repressed a laugh as some of the men moved in closer to examine Canyon with looks of fascination. They surrounded her with bobbing kotekas and pointed to her braided blonde hair.

The voices of the other natives created a babbling buzz around

Vanessa as the cool afternoon fog wisped in around them ankle-high, pushing the hot day skyward.

Abruce looked into Vanessa's eyes and spoke.

"What did he say?" Vanessa and Abruce both looked to Brad to share his words with them.

"I think he said, 'I wait for you.' I'm not great at his language. It's very rare. Abruce is the only one around here I know who wears this shape koteka and speaks like him. He's been teaching me some basics these past few years. He was a stowaway from the area I showed you on the flight in today. The former pilot landed in the circle up there, and later, when he unloaded at the mine site, this guy jumped out and ran. He works gardening for the mining director on the site now."

Abruce maintained his stare and spoke to Vanessa in his language as a group of local tribesmen gathered around. The slow turn of the idling helicopter propeller gave the scene an eerie sense of anticipation, swallowing Abruce's soft-spoken words.

"I missed what he said. Sorry." Brad ran his hands through his hair.

Looking over his shoulder at the other men, Abruce moved closer to Vanessa. Speaking in a low voice, he placed his hand on Vanessa's chest. "Hello, Van Gold. You are the special one. The color of a new leaf is in your eyes. I have your flat spirit here." He pulled out a magazine with her photo on the cover. "You come for Lukeem." He pointed out over the mountain.

Vanessa was shocked at his English, shocked that he knew her agenda, and dumbfounded at the sight of the magazine cover in the hands of a man living a stone-age existence. She could see that Brad shared her surprise.

"I had no idea. But now I know how the magazines from the mail room disappeared." Brad moved closer to ensure privacy. "Makes sense he can speak English after five years, but he's been holding back, for sure. Smart guy."

"So he believes I am a white goddess with powers?" Vanessa glanced at Brad. That gave her a slight sense of trust when it came to Abruce, but she had to get him alone to talk, she thought. She was impatient with the introductions, but Vanessa knew not to rush the niceties. That tendency to want to get to the point fast had bitten her before back in the early days before she'd learned to observe and be patient. Relationships and loyalty in these assignments were everything.

"Abruce is from one of the most remote tribes. His people are pretty much untouched. Father Carey says Abruce's people still believe we are the sky spirits. The other tribes near here have been disabused of our angelic status, having been exposed to us long enough to know the difference."

Canyon and Brad shared a laugh.

Moving closer, Abruce watched Brad's mouth as he spoke.

"Don't know where Abruce's head is after five years, but the way he looks at you, well, I would say he sees *you* that way, at least—a sky spirit. That'll help."

Vanessa watched a stream of sweat run down Brad's jaw. He wiped his forehead, unbuttoned his cuffs, and rolled up his long sleeves. "Hot in the midday, cold in the afternoon. Anyway, to the tribesmen who are rebelling against the pay inequities and government interference and restrictions, the Americans and the Indonesian Central Government are seen as the fallen angels." Brad pointed to the group of several dozen men. "The rest of these locals are from right around here. They don't work for the site, though. They just like to hang around and be fascinated, so to speak. They're friendly. No worries for your safety. The locals who are hired by the mine have to wear mining clothes. No kotekas allowed."

"Notice Abruce's broader chest? And he's shorter than the lowland natives." Vanessa turned to Canyon.

Chiming in with her research, Canyon explained. "The natives from the higher, remote regions have a greater lung capacity, developed from adapting to the thin air up here. And maybe his tribe's narrower waist is the result of his former diet—mostly plants and some meat when they can find it. Although that's changing here with three meals a day available."

"Speaking of thin air. The lower oxygen will slow you two down until you adjust," Brad said.

A handsome, well-built man wedged between Brad and Canyon and interrupted. "Good advice, Brad. You two should just lay low for a while and acclimate. You're a mile and a half above sea level at the top of the tram." He smoothed the back of his hair twice.

Vanessa saw it as a self-conscious or nervous gesture.

"Hate to interrupt your lecture, Brad." He tapped Brad on the back. "Scott West, Regional VP, Fallstaff Gardner Worldwide Security, nice to meet you, Ms. Gold. Finally."

Finally? Vanessa could feel the tension in his grasp. He examined her face as intensely as she did his. "And this is Canyon Swenson, our veteran anthropologist from the original *Turning Prism* team."

"Nice to meet you. I apologize, but I have some things to do before the welcoming dinner. I flew in two days ago from another assignment, and I need to check up on our team."

Vanessa read Scott. His words were friendly, but his body language was suspect—at odds with his demeanor. She registered him on the questionable side. Anyone who arrived just before one of her assignments was always suspect.

"As you know, we have an extremely volatile situation here. I'll grab the mail, Brad. Save you some steps. With all the action here now, we need to monitor things a little tighter." Scott stepped away, reached into the helicopter, rustled around the baggage for a few minutes, and pulled out two large satchels of mail. He stopped in front of Vanessa as he left. "Ms. Gold, I hope you'll listen before you judge."

Vanessa flashed her eyes in Canyon's direction. When had she ever just stampeded her way into a situation? Abruce imitated Vanessa by raising his eyebrows and rolling his eyes toward the departing Scott.

Vanessa found it endearing and a small signal of loyalty. Still, she was also sensitive to how every little introduction of even the smallest new gesture on the part of a white sky spirit had the power to change cultural behavior. The trick was to proactively create the right cultural changes.

"See you tonight at the mining director's house for dinner." Scott left down the mountain path, weighed down by the bags.

"Yeah, see you." Dismissing Scott, Brad deposited their luggage on the ground. "Sorry, I forgot to mention the dinner details. Six p.m. Here's a little map of the site. Not much to it." He glanced at his Rolex.

Vanessa scanned the map and looked down the long path from the mountainside helipad to the mining town below.

"It's four o'clock now. You'll have time for a shower and rest. The trip is tough, I know. Really good to finally meet you, Vanessa, and you, Canyon. We might as well be on a first name basis. This could get ugly, and I'm all in."

"Thank you so much." Vanessa wondered if she could trust Brad, but the credits were building in her mind—sending the letter, following her lead in skipping out on her bodyguards, his respect for the natives, learning the local languages, and his suspicion of Scott. Those were all pluses. The printed name on the side of his duffel struck Vanessa. 'Bradley Mitchell Wainwright, III.' No amount of sweat, leather, and flannel could disguise the scent of old money, she thought. She saw a runaway with a dark story in his sky blue eyes. An element of risk remained.

"Abruce and the other men will bring your luggage to your digs." Brad interrupted Vanessa's thoughts. "Tony's supposed to be here. I radioed in that you blew off your government security goons at the airport. He said he'd come. Are you OK here? Maybe I should stay until he arrives."

"We're fine." Vanessa gazed at the paths going down the mountain. "But the less fanfare and bodyguards around, the easier it is for me to get the lay of the land when I arrive somewhere. The bigger the offense, the bigger the defense, but thanks, Brad."

"Makes sense, and you should be safe. Oh, and here, your cameras. You'll need these." Brad seemed to speak to the natives in two different languages and climbed into the helicopter. "One more run for the day. I need to deliver this equipment to the storage warehouse and arrange transportation back to Jakarta for those government security goons. Hope they don't take it out on me. They know I was complicit in ditching them." He winked.

"They're used to it, I'm sure." Canyon stepped back from the helicopter.

Vanessa's positive assessment of Brad was taking root, and she moved him to the 'good guy, trust him' side of the ledger in her mind.

The prop spun, and he lifted off.

"He's an interesting guy. Linguist and gorgeous." Canyon followed his takeoff over her shoulder. "I read there are hundreds of distinct languages. Think about how hard that is when one tribe encounters another. But I think I could speak Brad's lingo."

Vanessa shook her head, half smiling. "I love how you can do that, even in the jungle. How can you still have raging hormones at forty when it's ninety-nine degrees?"

"Easy, clouds rolling in, and I'm still thirty-nine."

"Cute. Canyon, look, I need to get some alone time with Abruce before Tony gets here and everything moves forward, but let's get some quick photos first. You keep them busy, and while everyone is distracted, I'll vet Abruce, OK?" Vanessa turned to get her briefcase. "My briefcase is missing. Probably still on the helicopter." Vanessa reviewed her steps in her mind. She had left it beside her seat in the aisle in clear sight. Her mind went to Scott and the mailbags. "Damn, Canyon, Scott may be on the dark side of this."

"You sure? Brad might have it. Oh, why am I questioning you?" Canyon laughed. "Your instincts are always dead on."

As Vanessa took a picture of Abruce, she did not expect the other men would cower at the sight of the camera pointed at them.

Canyon filled her in. "The natives think it's a black magic box. They believe we're stealing their spirits and taking away their power. We have more than twenty thousand years between our cultures and unimaginable differences in experience. But if anyone can bridge that, you can, Van."

"So that's why you gave me this Polaroid."

"Yes, once stolen on your Nikon, you can instantly give their souls back with the Polaroid."

"Brilliant. I definitely don't want to upset the delicate balance." Vanessa took a few quick photos of the group with her Nikon. She immediately followed with a Polaroid shot of the group, ensuring the other men that she was leaving their souls behind. Taking another photo of Abruce, Vanessa handed him the photo by the edge, signaling not to touch it, and showed him how to wave it in the air to dry. "Photo," she said.

"*Foto.*" He moved the photograph in the breeze as she had gestured, staring at it as though he was expecting the magic to begin. The group gathered in tight around him. The plain piece of shiny paper held no interest until the shadows and colors began to spread over the square. The group was mesmerized, silently staring at the image that was appearing before their eyes, as the details clarified, the colors blended, and the shapes took form. Watching his amazed reaction as his image magically appeared on the paper was as equally fascinating for Vanessa. Then Vanessa took individual photographs of one man after the other with the Polaroid and handed them the blank wet squares.

"Ah!" one man said when his was the first image to become clear.

"Don't touch, wait." Vanessa held her hand up and modeled for the men by putting her free hand behind her back to prevent them from spoiling the wet image.

They all withdrew their empty hands, and tucked them behind their backs, while flapping the wet photo in their other hands.

It was a gesture Vanessa realized might become a permanent part of the culture. That was how impactful introducing a simple gesticulation could be.

"Ahh! Ahhh!" Each man leaped back at his apparition with one hand still behind his back. Then they clustered together again to look at each other's photos and jumped back at the sight of another man's image. Pulsing with their fascination, the group folded in and out with each other's revelations.

CHAPTER 29

TESTING TRUST

Vanessa

VANESSA STOOD NEXT to Abruce as he watched the outline on his Polaroid shot appear. The colors rose one after the other, the yellow, blue, red, joining together to create his image.

After touching his nose bone, Abruce put his hand to his shell necklace. Shifting the photo lower, he looked down to compare the shape of the miniature printed replica with his own long koteka. He looked behind his shoulder to see the thick greenery surrounding his image.

Vanessa could see some level of understanding was slowly invading his face. With a broad smile and a furrowed brow, he tilted his head, pointed to his chest, and then to the full-color image in the photo. With pride in his eyes, he stood taller.

"Van Gold, Abruce now lives in two spirits—one flat, one alive," he whispered and pointed to his chest. "One foto?" he asked and pointed back and forth between himself and Vanessa.

She handed the camera to Canyon and posed with Abruce. Waving the square in the air, he walked around some tall moss-covered rocks, and sitting by the edge of a drop-off, Abruce chewed on a plant he'd plucked from the ground on his way.

Vanessa followed him and lowered herself onto the hard rock

beside him. She took off her shoes. Not able to squat, Vanessa sat in a yoga position on the mossy ledge with her knees splayed and bottoms of her feet together. Holding onto her ankles she mimicked his posture as closely as possible.

He took in a deep breath. It was contagious. She copied him.

They sat together staring out at the deep valley. The majesty of the massive mountains, topped in the distance by blue-white glaciers, made Vanessa feel small. A tightening and a rapid thumping began in her chest. The memory pressed in. Her head resting on Mother Anne Marie's chest. The slowing, the skipping, the stopping—the unbearable stopping. Vanessa fell into the silence aching for the belonging she'd felt with her mentor. A dried leaf blew past her, dancing over the top of the lush groundcover, unable to light, the only brown in a field of green. Vanessa felt that way—dried up, empty inside, colorless.

Abruce faced Vanessa. He tilted his forehead and touched it to Vanessa's head. She was stunned, but stayed still. It was as though he could feel what she was feeling. She could smell his pungent sweat, the musty odor of the pig fat on his skin, and his earthy breath with some subtle hint of sweet herbs perhaps. Slowly separating from his oiled forehead, Vanessa refocused, needing to know if she could trust him and knowing she didn't have the luxury of time to build it.

Reaching over, she took the bow and arrows from his grip. It would be the ultimate trust test, wouldn't it—to take a man's weapons? Clear and simple. With no resistance, he released them, and Vanessa lowered his only possessions to the ground.

"Abruce." She looked into his eyes. "Who is Lukeem?" A bird cawed from the tree above as if to warn her. The wind picked up and wailed like a boiling kettle as it split around the outcropping behind them. A small creature scratched at the soil under the bushes nearby. She listened . . . waited.

He turned his head away and gazed down at the ground. "Ma."

"Lukeem is your *mother*?" Was that an English word? Vanessa watched his body language carefully. His head dropped slightly, and his shoulders rounded, indicating shame, she thought. His eyes fluttered, a tear spread out between three tightening lines at the corners, and his lips pressed together. Sadness or guilt? Then he opened his eyes and looked up to the left, signifying he was searching for his memories, recent events, connecting with his truth.

Vanessa was quiet, studying, interpreting. "Abruce, are you helping the bosses to find Lukeem?"

He turned toward her and blinked several times. Did it signal stress? A possible lie?

"Yes."

Vanessa held her breath. It was a critical moment that would change everything. "Will you help them to sacrifice Lukeem to river Ranu Lolo?"

"No sacrifice!" His wide-eyed glare revealed deep fear. Still, he remained locked onto Vanessa's eyes. "Abruce find Lukeem first. I protect her. I hide Ma in the caves." He pointed to the hillside on the other side of the town and looked straight into Vanessa's eyes.

She was stunned that Lukeem was at the site, but Vanessa believed he was telling the truth, and she sighed with relief. He was her only connection to Lukeem. Only Brad, his co-pilot, Jim, and Abruce knew what Lukeem looked like. The photos that were all over the news now would never lead anyone to Lukeem. She had no distinguishing markings or characteristics—at least for the Americans, she was like one of the thousands of natives living in sameness around the mine. The local indigenous population, who had torture and atrocities in mind for the sorceress, had no access to the photos—at least not yet. Vanessa still had time.

"Where is Lukeem now?" Vanessa watched every minute reaction to reinforce her trust for Abruce, to see if he would tell the truth. Even trust and truth were cultural norms open to interpretation. She'd learned that the hard way. The truth was a variable from culture to culture, especially between a sky spirit and a believer like Abruce. There was the danger he would tell her what he thought she wanted to hear, to please her, out of respect. In many cultures, Vanessa knew inferiors were almost incapable of telling the raw truth to someone of honor. It wouldn't be considered a lie. Goddess trumps truth, she thought. She would have to be very alert to that.

Abruce kept his gaze riveted on her eyes. "Ma, ride tram down to there, yesterday, yesterday." He pointed at the mining town a short distance below them.

"She is *here*?" The heat rose up in Vanessa's face.

"No, *there*." He pointed again to the rustic residences below.

Vanessa half-smiled at his literal use of here and there. She would have to be careful communicating in his second language. "I want to help Lukeem. Can you bring me to her tomorrow? You understand tomorrow? Lukeem rode the tram down yesterday, yesterday, meaning two times of sun and dark?"

He nodded and made two up and down motions with his finger, and pointed to the sun.

"*Today*, I met you, Abruce. *Tomorrow*, I meet Lukeem. Do you understand that?" Vanessa wanted to ensure she was communicating.

"She waits for tomorrow, one dark night, then new sun, and you meet Lukeem. OK?"

"Yes, OK." Vanessa confirmed.

Abruce removed his nose bone, stood up, reinserted it, and when she struggled to rise, he helped her up and shared a long, open, untenable gaze.

She was aware she couldn't hold his stare for as long as he could hold hers and was surprised that he wouldn't cast a humble downward gaze out of respect. His society was so unexposed that the rules might be different, she thought. They were at odds. Personal space was so culturally based. Americans demanded more space before awkwardness set in. She'd learned that in the Arab world, they met you nearly nose to nose and needed to take in the scent of your breath before they would feel comfortable with you. And maybe I have too much to hide, she thought. The only long gaze she had experienced was with Tony—highly sexual, a come-on, love-based.

Abruce remained connected to her. She cringed at the closeness. Had to disengage. She couldn't last any longer, but looking away would risk seeming untrustworthy to *Abruce*. Vanessa repeated, "I want to help Lukeem." Her breath and his intermingled. Breaking the silence helped her to continue to stay with his eyes. A look of happiness lit his face. Canyon was right. He *did* wear his inner emotions on his sleeve. She could count on that. It was a relief after years of needing to question and scrutinize the so-called "more civilized" people.

"Abruce, does anyone else know Lukeem is here?"

"No. Van Gold and Abruce."

"Good." She reconnected their gaze. "Abruce, only speak English with me now, OK? To keep Lukeem safe. Our secret. Speaking English is our secret. Do you know secret?"

"Yes, I keep secret for Mrs. Jenkinson, boss's wife. She has secret *foto* of one man. She puts her lips on the *foto* for love. When I see this, she says do not tell her mate, Mr. Jeff." Abruce kissed the photo of Vanessa and him. "One *foto* for Ma." He stored it in his head bag.

Another soft spot for the mining director. A cheating wife, she thought. Vanessa began to walk away, but Abruce stopped her with his bow. Her moment of fear passed quickly as he dropped to the ground and replaced her shoes on her feet.

Vanessa was moved. There was a certain freedom in being with Abruce she'd never felt with Tony. She thought of Canyon's words, "Thin personal barriers, little social agenda or self-consciousness, no judgment, wears it all on his sleeve." That was why Vanessa experienced no emotional burden from her past when she was with Abruce. There was trust. A kind of childlike trust.

Vanessa and Abruce took the path back down, skirting the

outcropping and rejoining the crowd of native men and Canyon. Vanessa could see the indigenous men hadn't grown weary of having the blonde white goddess in their midst. The fascinated natives stood around her smiling, anticipating.

"Are you good, Van? I am running out of ways to entertain here." Canyon took three small green rubber balls out of her small backpack and began to juggle with smooth precision.

Vanessa looked at her with surprise as Canyon completed an advanced juggling trick surrounded by the fascinated group of local natives. "Juggling? I didn't know you had that trick up your sleeve."

"Learned it from one of the clowns I dated." Canyon laughed.

"Oooh, Ahhh!" The amazed men called out. One native swiftly picked up his bow and shot a ball in midair with uncanny accuracy, interrupting Canyon's act. He smiled proudly.

"OK, time to go, Canyon. Oh, and our friend, he's Lukeem's son, and we can trust him."

CHAPTER 30

INAUSPICIOUS ARRIVAL

Vanessa

"SORRY, I'M LATE, TEAM!" Tony came up over the rise to the helipad. He waved and thrust his arms in the air.

Vanessa had missed his grounded love, but he brought her troubles with him too. For sure, Canyon had seen her stiffen. Standing close behind Vanessa, she whispered, "You'll find the right time to tell him everything. Like you did me."

Vanessa turned to find her luggage but Abruce had already hefted her bag on his shoulder. Bowing his head slightly at Vanessa, he adjusted his load. He walked gracefully under the weight, as the long, curled gourd he wore kept the tempo of his pace like a metronome. Another man had Canyon's bag balanced over his head and pointed his chin toward the narrow dirt path with a wide smile. Their strength was mesmerizing.

When this is over, I'll deal with my loss, Vanessa thought. I have to stay focused right now. This is for you, Mother Anne Marie. She'd just experienced the most painful loss of her life, and again, she couldn't share the full story with Tony.

Standing on the side of the path, Tony let the men carrying the luggage go ahead of him before continuing to stand in front of Vanessa and Canyon.

Vanessa pushed her mourning and vulnerability aside and accepted Tony's energetic embrace and kiss.

"You look exhausted, Van. Everything, OK?"

She kissed his cheek. "Yes, fine. No, actually, I missed you. Tony, the nun I told you about who was ill, Mother Anne Marie, she passed away. I was so close to her in my childhood. You remember, I talked about her. It's just bringing back my losses. And things are tense here." The wounded part of Vanessa wanted to be comforted. Still, the whole recent connection with Fiona made her want to move past the subject with Tony. She wanted to help Lukeem and forget her own problems.

"Oh, babe, I'm so sorry." Tony put his arms around her and took a deep breath, hinting that she should do the same. "Wish I'd met her. But I respect the cloistered commitment."

"I'll be OK."

"You always are, sweetheart. What worries me is you have no time to mourn."

The purity of the deep gaze she and Abruce had shared lingered, yet Vanessa couldn't make extended eye contact with Tony. That closeness would make her erupt with sadness. Despite their intimacy and love, there could never be honesty until there was truth. She foolishly wished they could start over with the innocence she'd experienced with Abruce—pure, no agenda, no lies. But concealing the truth was the key to her entire existence. Tony's love, their careers, and the lies kept her in lockstep with her pain, she thought. Why could she think of nothing but the negative side of things lately?

Vanessa drew back from Tony. "My briefcase is conveniently missing. I'm betting snatched by Scott. What did you learn from Father Carey?"

"Here we go, Van. The trouble starts. Scott was probably trying to do a little 'research' about your 'intentions'. As for the missionary, it's a brutal situation. I'll tell you what Father Carey said and get this gorgeous hippie anthropologist's take on it, but first, this." Tony grabbed Canyon and spun her around in a bear hug. "Ten years without our lucky charm. We've missed you, Canyon."

"I've missed you guys, too. But couldn't we have done a nice coffee at Starbucks instead?" Canyon laughed. "I suspect this will be our last laugh for the next few days, so we should enjoy it."

"*Tony*, what about the missionary? And we need to see the mine site in daylight."

"We'll get to that."

The fog was snaking around the mountain and was already knee-high. Vanessa felt impatient. The cackling and calls of the jungle's creatures were eerily quieting as the blanket of gray rose.

"This is the weird thing. This cloud bank sags down around the mountain about as low as this helipad nearly every day by noon, but a hundred feet down below, it could be blazing hot. Like two separate worlds: *cool and hot,* and *dark and light*."

"Like a hot fudge sundae." Canyon put a supportive arm around Vanessa.

"We need to get going." Vanessa picked up the pace down the path. "That full moon isn't waiting for anyone. We have three days to find Lukeem and make some yet undetermined cultural change take hold. Can you fill us in, Tony?"

"Alright, guys, let's drop off the luggage. I'll talk on the way."

"Wait. I'm surprised we've been given free reign here." Vanessa stopped, adjusting her camera straps over her shoulder. "That seems suspicious. Which could mean we're being watched, and Scott may be giving us all the rope we need to hang ourselves. Who else in Robin Hood's group of merry men secretly speaks English?"

Abruce and the man carrying their luggage had stopped after Tony stepped aside, waiting for them to follow. Vanessa thought about what Canyon had told her on the plane; in many of the island's cultures, a man is valued by the number of his pigs and wives. Vanessa observed the tribal men's faces to see if they showed any signs of comprehension, Vanessa announced, "I have a gift of three pigs for anyone who steps forward."

Abruce advanced one step forward, luggage still hoisted overhead.

"I will get those pigs for you later, Abruce. OK?"

He nodded.

Vanessa was reassured.

"These aren't the guys likely to speak English. Remember Brad had told us they're just local hunters who wandered in here to see the show," Canyon said.

"Just wanted to be paranoid." Vanessa patted Canyon's back.

"The Zell Baxter Mining execs have been that way with me for the past twenty-four hours—totally open, including Scott, the new security director. He said he would meet your helicopter. You mentioned he might have taken your briefcase? He actually aired the dirty laundry with me and took me up the main road yesterday. If you want to call it a road—that treacherous razorback path that follows the top of the mountain, there."

Vanessa followed Tony's pointer finger across the valley to a jagged, brown *Etch a Sketch* line that cut through the green along the high side of the mountain.

"Took me in a jeep up to the mid-station where the workers were picketing."

"Clever strategy." Why were they being so cooperative, Vanessa wondered? Brad had indicated the execs weren't to be trusted.

"Well, it was brutal, guys—massive tension, thunderous chanting. It's gonna blow sky high if they don't sacrifice Lukeem before the full moon. Sounds like a B-grade movie, I know, but the fear and anger are palpable. Can't say what they'll do. Not like a riot or protest in the west."

"Canyon, what do you think?" Vanessa tore her gaze from Tony to focus on her best friend.

"Very volatile and unpredictable. The cultural gap is too wide. A minor innocent thing misinterpreted can cause a calamity or a calming, and then something unfamiliar can be seen as threatening or amazing. Not to mention, there's a history of headhunting and cannibalism with multiple tribes in the area, and it still occurs. Thankfully, not in Lukeem's tribal traditions, but some of the mineworkers are from those tribes. To complicate things further, this is not one single culture. There are numbers of tribes with different variations on dialects and traditions—some peaceful, some enemies to each other." Canyon waved her hand around her, gesturing toward the mountains. "Can you even imagine the shock when tribes who haven't had contact with others meet after twenty thousand years of isolation in these vast jungle mountains?"

Vanessa listened to Canyon while keeping Abruce in sight to gauge his reactions.

"Lukeem's tribe isn't even involved here. They're too remote. Her tribe sees us as sky spirits, saviors. Local tribes see us as oppressors, right Canyon?" Tony talked as they continued down the path.

Canyon added, "And the Indonesians from other islands are far more sophisticated and westernized. They're onto the mining company's tricks and want higher pay."

"Stop. Listen to that." Alerted to the daylight chatter, Vanessa noticed it had turned on like a light switch when they dropped below the cloud bank. Once again, they heard the buzz and hums of insects, and the calls and cries of creatures that had stayed below in the valley to live in the sun. "Sorry, what were you saying, Canyon?"

"I was just saying that these local tribes have been contaminated and overwhelmed by western ways and things they've never seen before. It seems the more exposure to the Americans, the more violent the tribes are. With the new concept of possessions and jealousy, politics, and competition—it's the classic *haves and have-nots*." Canyon bent over to smile at a little boy who skirted the bushes beside her as they walked down the steep path. She handed him a Kit Kat bar from her purse.

Vanessa stopped to watch him peel the package open. His face showed both anticipation and suspicion. The first bite told all with his beaming smile.

A large striped lizard complained with a "Hehhh" when Canyon crossed its path.

"Canyon, be careful."

"Don't worry, Van. That lizard's a vegetarian."

"Funny. As long as *he* doesn't think I'm a carrot." Vanessa moved closer to Tony.

Tony put his arm around Vanessa's shoulder. "Not to mention, some of the local natives have guns now with only basic knowledge of how to use them. Sold to them by the American workers trying to make some extra cash. The local tribal miners get their pittance pay, and they trade the money for guns. Dollars and Indonesian Rupiah are just slips of paper that mean nothing to them until they can exchange them for a weapon that can threaten an enemy and kill prey from such a long range. Some tribal workers are happy to have three meals a day. That's the real compensation."

Vanessa stopped and turned to Tony. "Sounds like your meeting with Father Carey was very enlightening."

"Or frightening." Tony's comment didn't reassure Vanessa.

Abruce turned, signaling to take the left path as they approached, bouncing the luggage overhead.

"We know how they feel about women and sorceresses." Vanessa scanned the housing area of the makeshift mining town as they were coming to the halfway point.

Ripple-roofed Quonset huts were lined up against the far side of the valley. On the farthest end of the town, a stunning 'mansion,' made of several metal trailers, surrounded by lush gardens hugged the cliff that overlooked another drop-off. The center of the mining community was taken up by a cluster of metal buildings, a swimming pool, and tennis courts.

Along the edge of the town, against a high rock wall, was a long cafeteria facility. As they descended, Vanessa watched the tribesmen through the wide windows, sliding trays down the line, selecting early dinner offerings. Smiling native workers were exiting while stuffing food into their head sacks.

Tony broke in. "Listen, the way it's being portrayed by the American mining guys, it's all the fault of these so-called *primitives'* bizarre traditions, and the company is caught in the middle. I'm not thrilled with that tag, primitives. Not sure who the real primitives are around here if you get my drift. Yesterday, I heard the mining director, Jeff, stand up on a jeep and promise the picketing workers that the company would find the woman sorceress and fulfill the sacrifice."

Canyon followed the man who had hefted her luggage overhead. "At the very least, the local tribesmen, hired as miners will all leave their jobs and scatter. This concept of labor for pay is not yet fully ingrained. They can't understand which jobs are worth more or are more important in the hierarchy, so the pay doesn't make sense to them, and jealousy arises. They ask, why does the man who stands by and watches make more money than those who sweat, chiseling away at a cave wall?"

"A walk out would be financially disastrous for the company," Tony said. "At this point, it's all about the stockholders. That's when you know you're really in trouble."

"Is anyone else feeling lightheaded? Canyon, you weren't kidding about the thin air at this elevation." Vanessa took in several slow, deep breaths.

A young boy approached. He was wearing a miniature-size replica of the adult-size gourds his elders wore. "Abera." He extended his hand to Tony, and he shook it.

"He's so cute, huh?" Tony hunched down and shook Abera's hand,

and the boy put his right hand over his heart. Tony followed suit, placing his hand over his own.

A young girl appeared behind Abera.

"She's the first female we have seen."

"Bina." The little girl was shy, but stepped forward.

Vanessa repeated the gesture, shook hands with Abera, and introduced herself. Smiling, she touched Bina's cheek. Vanessa rummaged through her travel bag to find some little gift of friendship to break the ice. Squatting down, she presented two treasures—a bag of airline peanuts for each child and a pink, peek-through, plastic keychain with a picture of foreign students at Reed College housed inside.

Speaking soothingly to the frightened girl, Vanessa noticed that the tip of her ring finger was missing and newly healing. She reached out and took the girl's hand. "Look." Vanessa showed the child her own scarred hand.

Bina blinked, tilting her head, and touched the dents that ran across Vanessa's knuckles.

Opening the peanuts, Vanessa sampled one to intrigue her, then tapped a few into the child's hand.

Bina cautiously ate one and smiled, shook Vanessa's hand, and put her hand on her own heart. The warmth of the small hand in hers touched Vanessa, and Maureen's eyes came to mind. Green like her own. What was it about that child that she kept her re-emerging in Vanessa's mind? And likely in Tony's too, she thought.

Bina ate the peanuts, one by one, while staring with amazement through the little peephole at the tiny sky spirits living inside the little pink plastic viewer.

"We always learn so much from the children on an assignment. They're so honest and haven't fully internalized their parent's beliefs yet." Vanessa stood. "We should catch up with our porter service."

Vanessa's bags were already moving down the last yards of the path, held high on Abruce's shoulders. She marveled at his strength and agility. Despite his short stature, he was lean, muscular, and powerful. She wondered if he would be able to tell her his age. His life would not be so carefully calendared as hers. If Abruce was in his early twenties, Lukeem must be no more than forty, maybe?

Tony looked at the ground and hesitated. "When we were up there, I saw something that made me sick." His tone made them stop to listen. "I mean literally, for the first time on these shoots, I got sick to my stomach. I won't go into details, but they're starting to involve the little girls in appeasing the nature or ancestor spirits when anything goes wrong, just like Father Carey had warned us. Like this little girl's finger. It's an injury inflicted by one of the tribesmen who works at the mine. It was some kind of mini sacrifice. Oh, and we watched Abruce pull a woman out of the crowd and into the mountains. Who could that have been?" Tony stopped.

Vanessa kept an eye on Abruce as they spoke. He'd obviously heard his name—his body conveyed a state of alert. He put down the luggage and moved closer within earshot to stand protectively next to Vanessa.

"Abruce." Vanessa looked at him intensely. "Tony is my mate. You can trust him. You can speak English with him. But don't let anyone hear. OK?"

Abruce nodded.

"That woman with Abruce was Lukeem," Vanessa told Tony.

"What?" Tony passed on his incredulous look to Vanessa and Abruce. "She is down here? How? *Where*?"

"Abruce hide Ma in cave, over there." He pointed.

Vanessa realized the critical connection she'd so quickly developed with Abruce transcended their cultures. He trusted her.

Taking the lay of the land, she noted that the only escape routes were the treacherous roads down to the airport on the coast and the tram up to the mid-station and onward to the top of the mountain where the digging took place.

The late sun flashed off the tin roofs of the buildings and trailer residences as their group descended into the streets of the mining town. Dozens of smaller metal trailers, ten by twenty feet in rows of six, were set in a wheel around a large swimming pool, tennis courts, and a barbeque area. The din of children's voices squealing and the splashing in the pool echoed in the hardpack dirt streets. The town was barren, stripped like a meteor had hit in the middle of the lush jungle. Yet some of the residences had small patches of flowers and plants.

"Typical. It's simpler to just raze all that beauty when they needed to build, I guess." Tony pointed. "Van, look at this guy coming toward us."

"I need to get a shot of this. I know it's funny, but this is exactly the kind of thing that saddens me." Vanessa snapped some photos of the approaching native. The proud man drew a crowd who buzzed about his new look. He wore a yellow rubber flashlight in place of his koteka, fastened with rainbow grosgrain ribbon. An oversized blue plastic paperclip replaced his nose bone, and teabags dangled from his woven necklace. He jumped up and down, performing his enviable paraphernalia dance to get attention from the gaping crowd.

"We'd better get back so you two can get a little rest before dinner. This is only the tip of the iceberg." Tony guided them.

Vanessa looked back over her shoulder to see the group of natives tossing rocks in the air and dropping them, competing to see who could master the sky spirit woman's skill first. It seems they wanted to recapture the attention from their newly decorated, fancy friend who wore the flashlight as a koteka. The little boy, Abera, managed a few juggling cycles and got praise from the men. He grinned at Canyon, put the rocks in his net bag, and followed close behind her.

"Canyon, look what you started." Vanessa smiled. "And you have an adorable admirer."

Canyon demonstrated another juggling trick for Abera.

Vanessa patted Abera's shoulder.

"Yes, Van, anything new like that is either enthusiastically accepted or violently rejected. And there's no predicting which."

They walked past the truck, loaded with film equipment, that had carried the crew up the treacherous razorback mountain road from the main airport thousands of feet below on the coast.

"It is spectacular up here." Canyon admired the dramatic view.

A line of dark-skinned tribesmen in hard hats disembarked from the tram and walked in a weary line toward their temporary housing. Few of them entered their metal homes. Instead, they sat outside, began to make their evening fires, and gathered grasses for their beds. Several of the workers climbed the side of their trailers to reach a sleeping area on the roof.

"What's that about, Canyon?" Tony shaded his eyes and watched the roof-top lodgers.

"Their tribes must be tree-dwellers."

Some traditions are hard to break, Vanessa thought.

"Imagine transporting all this equipment and materials up here?" Canyon gestured toward all the buildings and facilities.

"One load at a time." Tony nodded. "I was informed that they're planning to build another tram on the other side of the mountain. That's where the incident occurred with the attempted sacrifice."

"Brad flew us over the spot. So treacherous." Vanessa would never forget the photograph of Lukeem suspended over the abyss.

Tony led Canyon and Vanessa toward their quarters.

Squatting as though on guard, Abera sat by the steps to Canyon's entrance, a miniature mirror image of Abruce, who kept an eye on Tony and Vanessa's door ten feet away.

"Abera, Abruce," Vanessa greeted them with a wave and a smile.

Opening the door to Canyon's half of the double connected trailer, Tony led her inside. "Well, here we are, your home away from home. Your own little cracker box guaranteed to swelter in the heat of the day and freeze in the chill of these primeval nights."

Vanessa followed Canyon inside. It had two twin beds, a small chest of drawers, closet, small shower, and a sink against one wall. "It's like a doll's house, Van. No, like our dorm room at Berkeley."

"Cozy. See you at dinner, Canyon. It feels so right to be together again—just the three of us." Vanessa hugged Canyon. "We're right next door if you need us."

"We love you like a sister, you know," Tony said tenderly as he turned to leave.

"Oh, Tony, thanks, buddy." Canyon hugged him.

His simple statement touched Vanessa, reminding her of what was at stake.

Tony added over his shoulder, "Have a rest and a shower, and we'll be by for you in a couple of hours. You're in for a real people-watching treat tonight. See you at six."

A few paces away, Tony pulled open the door to their half of the trailer for Vanessa. She glanced at her new protector, squatting with his black knees spread, adorned with his tan gourd with the corkscrew tip that perpetually pointed to the heavens. She had a strangely familiar feeling about Abruce as their gazes locked. He sat patiently, with seemingly unquestionable confidence that all would be well. More pressure on this sky spirit, she thought. "Tony, how can these gentle people have such violent traditions?"

"Good question. I know less than you do. I have to say I feel safer with them than some of the so-called civilized people we have dealt with over the years."

"So then, what makes it so easy to connect with these strangers, these exotic people? I can understand a child, but Abruce?"

Tony laughed and walked down the path. "Like Canyon explained, he has absolutely no social agenda. Assumes the best about his white goddess. No context to judge you. I'll be back shortly. Gotta check on the equipment and settle the team into their quarters. See you before six."

CHAPTER 31

INDECENT EXPOSURE

Vanessa

VANESSA UNDRESSED and turned on the shower. The water was rusty and cold. A cockroach the size of quarter perched on the showerhead and stared back. While waiting for the water to get warm, she wrapped the small white towel around her. It resurrected memories of the rough convent towels.

There was a knock at the door, and she opened it. "Tony?"

Scott stepped in and handed her the briefcase with shaking hands. "Your briefcase, Ms. Gold. You didn't know I would find it, did you?"

"Excuse me?" She tightened her grip on the towel. "Can you step outside for a minute? I am feeling a little vulnerable here."

"Sorry, no locked doors around here. Not used to women in the staff trailers." Scott stood staring for an uncomfortable moment, then stepped outside, letting the door slam.

After dressing quickly and turning off the water, Vanessa invited him in. "I didn't know my briefcase was lost," she answered with a slight edge of sarcasm. His heavy cologne masked a hint of sweat.

"Damn, I've got to hand it to you—you blew me away." His hand automatically reached for the back of his head in his habitual double-stroking gesture.

What is that? Vanessa thought.

"You win. You've got me where you want me." He dropped the briefcase on the bed.

"Really? I don't know what choked your chain, but that was easy."

"What do you want, Ms. Gold? I don't have many options here. I've got too much to lose." A sheen of sweat coated his forehead.

Why was *he* the nervous one? Confusing. "My reputation must have preceded me, Mr. West. Here's the truth, and it's simple. There's one agenda here. I want you to help me make sure the woman isn't captured and turned over by Zell Baxter to either her tribe, the local tribes, or the protestors. You do understand the local tribes want to torture her? And her tribe wants to sacrifice her. Security is your job, right?"

For the first time, Vanessa stopped to ask herself what precisely would she do for Lukeem once she prevented the sacrifice? She was used to not having the answers and still moving ahead, confidently folding in the facts and waiting for the answer to evolve. She would figure it out.

"Look, the Americans didn't dream up sacrificing women to the river spirit to break some crazy curse. It's Zell Baxter you should feel sorry for or aren't you that patriotic?"

"If they'd done a little research or cared about anything but Zell Baxter's gold doubloons, they wouldn't have used that sacred area as a landing pad. The tribal mineworkers wouldn't have walked out this afternoon."

"How do you know that?"

"Zell Baxter single-handedly resurrected a tradition that was dormant in that tribe since World War Two. You'd be surprised what I know. And there's the egregious, unlawful practice of paying workers with a few plates of food. And selling guns to tribespeople."

Vanessa was grateful Tony had briefed her on what he'd seen on his mine site tour. Her usual soft approach, building a bridge, was off the table after hearing from Tony that the company had publicly committed to the workers that they would kill Lukeem. Greed was going to trump decency and righteousness again, she thought.

"We'd be doing them a favor to end this curse thing. It's spreading to other tribes nearby."

So much about Scott's behavior was unnerving and confusing. "And, by the way, how did *they* hear about the woman who comes from a tribe a jungle away? I bet you're sorry they taught Bahasa Indonesia and English to the workers now, aren't you? Now their anger has a common language so they can share. Now, word can spread fast."

Scott tilted forward aggressively. "Am *I* sorry? Have you seen that tribe? Father Carey told me about all those crying babies with swollen bellies. The natives believe this stuff. Read up a bit, Ms. Gold. We'd be doing them a favor to complete the sacrifice. English and Bahasa Indonesia didn't spread this. *You* did. And if I hadn't seen those photos you so graciously released on the news on my way here, I wouldn't have noticed Abruce planted right there in Jenkinson's garden for me, twisted koteka and all." Scott crossed his arms in front of his chest.

He had something to hide, Vanessa thought.

"And he's agreed to find her for us. He wants it done for his people, Ms. Gold."

Vanessa fought to repress a reaction about Abruce. She couldn't let emotion get in the way, but her instincts on the young, indigenous man were strong. "Oh please, Mr. West, this is not about favors to the helpless local inhabitants. And it started out as a discriminatory pay issue. The sorceress was an add-on, so the native workers could focus on something they understood better. Zell Baxter is leveraging the situation."

"Fine, the company's losing millions." Scott acknowledged. "If she isn't turned over by their stupid moon ceremony . . . Look, Jeff wants me to—"

"Jeff? What *is* it that the mining director has over you, exactly?"

"Nothing like what you have over me."

What was *that* look? What was he covering up? "Is that your version of flirting, Mr. West?" She was baffled by the entire conversation.

"No, ma'am. You don't flirt with someone who holds your life in their hands." He held out a file with Edward's note to her.

"You opened my briefcase?" Vanessa dropped the file of papers as if they were on fire.

"Security." Scott was poised to escape. He retrieved the file, gave it back with trembling hands, and walked out the door. At the bottom of the steps, he looked back at her. "Did you ever think there might be more to this than you know? You're the exposé expert."

Searching her mind, Vanessa reviewed their exchange. Scott was the one who likely held *Vanessa's* fate in his hands, she thought, now that he'd seen the file about her grandfather's murder. Had he watched the VHS? Vanessa went with the flow of the conversation. Listening was always better when understanding was lacking. There was some odd familiarity in Scott's eyes Vanessa couldn't place. "Not even once have I doubted what's right here. If you know more, have the courage to share it." Vanessa closed the door behind him.

From outside the closed tin door, he asked. "Will you let me know when the wrath of the great Vanessa Gold will rain down on me?"

His reactions were puzzling. Vanessa wilted onto the narrow bed and gave herself time to speculate. She was incredulous and horrified that he knew about her grandfather's death. It came thundering in on her. Why had he chosen those articles? But he couldn't have ID'd me, she thought. I can't let this happen now. I can't be leveraged before I secure Lukeem. Why did she bring that video and the file? Did she really think being on the other side of the planet would help her share everything with Tony?

Within seconds, Vanessa pushed aside her paranoia. She calmed down, remembering that only she would know the significance of the aged evidence. She read the headline. "Red-haired Witness Sought for Questioning". No one could recognize her from those articles. Redhead. No, there was no possible connection to her. Then why was it so important to Scott? And what did she have over him? Did he see her TV segment calling for information on the murder?

The note on the file from Edward read: *Murder: Rabbi Moshe Cohen, April 30, 1970. Hey, Ms. Exposé, here's the research and the recording of your enigmatic 8mm film. No, I didn't watch it. Go get 'em, Vanessa. I'm ready for whoever is the next Exposé casualty.*

Vanessa opened the briefcase to replace the file. The cassette case had been opened. She dragged open the door to watch Scott leaving. You can learn an awful lot from a person's back as they walk away. Vanessa knew that from filming. The sunset drew most photographers, but the best shots, she'd learned, were often with the sunset at your back, focusing where the best light was being shed. Again she caught that gesture, the smoothing of the back of his hair. The confident, cocky posture Scott had exhibited upon arrival at the helicopter had shifted. Now his body language reflected a worried man—low strides with a slight drag, slumped shoulders, and nervous looks over his shoulder toward the Mining Director's office. Perplexing.

Tony came up to the door as she was closing it. He paused in front of Vanessa. "Checking out the enemy?" He flashed his eyes over his shoulder toward departing Scott. Behind Tony, young Abera squatted. "He's been following me around like a puppy."

The child's bond with Tony wouldn't help keep the 'children issue' in the background, Vanessa thought. "Strange guy with something big to hide, that Scott."

Vanessa retreated into the trailer and popped open her luggage. She pulled clothes out like a magician's scarves, searching for something to wear to dinner. She needed to keep moving to avoid facing the edge of sadness that had hovered over Tony lately. A long, blue, batik cotton skirt and a white blouse seemed right for Indonesian jungle dining. The small space was pressing in on her. The tension was palpable. "Tony, I'm going to check out something while you shower, OK?"

"Got it. See you soon, sweetheart. I'll meet you at the dinner. I have one more thing to discuss with the team."

At the sound of the sputtering shower, Vanessa looked in the mirror over the small dresser and ran her fingers through her hair. Her red roots screamed back a warning. A reminder that they would constantly grow back to haunt her. She stretched a wide black hairband on, flipped her dark hair out on either side and left the trailer.

She needed to clarify what Scott's suspicious behavior was all about. If he saw the video with the intro slide saying, "*Turning Prism*," he would surely have put two and two together. She and Scott seemed to share one skill—they were both keen observers.

The little hand-drawn map led her to the manager's residences two rows over from her own. Each trailer had a cardboard sign with a name on it above a mail slot by the door. She read three before she found Scott West. She knocked. The door was ajar and slid open. "Scott?" No answer. It was clear the little room was empty. She stepped in and closed the door behind her. There was no escape hatch, and it made her alert and nervous. The late sun cut a dust-speckled angle of light through the tiny window that drew her eyes to a chest under the bed. It stuck out just enough to see the open lock. It was quiet. Everyone's at the cafeteria, she thought. But where was Scott?

It was worth the risk. Everything was on the line. How much did he know about the murder? About her? Taking a chance, Vanessa dragged the chest out over the linoleum floor just far enough to prop open the lid halfway.

Flipping through a short stack of neatly folded military clothes and some souvenirs, she exposed a cheap, blue photo album. The first peel-back plastic sleeve held the x-ed-out US Marines dishonorable discharge papers in Scott's name. "Well, sir, you have a soft spot too."

Vanessa read the articles organized by aging tones of yellow from the lightest and most recent to the oldest. They told a story of a mercenary soldier who went from war to war, ending with Fallstaff Gardner Security, shooting up the ranks at the young age of thirty-six to Regional Director for Southeast Asia.

So why security director at Zell Baxter now?

She turned another page and read the headline, "Rabbi Moshe Cohen Murdered". There were several more articles on her grandfather's murder, the same ones Eddie had researched for her.

The musty scent assaulted Vanessa when she slid the fragile article out of the sleeve. It took a moment to sink in, then a high voltage punch to her gut froze her in place. These aren't copies of the articles, she finally absorbed. They're *originals*, caramel-colored evidence roughly torn out of the newspaper that had aged with the decades. Each headline on the three newspapers carried the same story accompanied by the unforgettable date that was seared into her memory, April 30, 1970.

Confusion rushed through her mind. Like a rapidly folding deck of cards, she ran through a hundred ideas, and her perplexed thoughts shuffled into line—fifteen years old on April 1 of 1970, and her grandfather's death April 30, 1970. She touched the top of her head where her red roots had begun to show. Was there a remote possibility that Scott was the boy who murdered her grandfather? He seemed afraid of her, but why? Her power to expose him, of course, but did he know she was the redheaded college girl who'd been filming that day?

She reassured herself again. There was no way he could know.

His dark hair and the unconscious habit of covering the back of his head cycled through her thoughts, and she pictured the back of a boy's head with the swastika carved skin-deep into his black hair. The bizarre possibility became clear. He was the murderer, and at the very least, he thought she was after him.

CHAPTER 32

RITUAL REVERSAL

Vanessa

VANESSA WALKED next door, intending to get Canyon for dinner a few minutes before six. She couldn't help but notice the unexpected lull between the exotic concert of the daytime and the nighttime sounds of nature that endlessly broadcasted over the surrounding mountains.

Hearing nothing but a whoosh of wind, she wandered down the path a bit, enjoying the silence. The squawks, caws, and the whirring of flying insects that had become a constant hum in the background had ceased. The sun and moon seemed to have a momentary stand-off in their tug of war over the volume control as the creatures of the day settled their voices down for the night, and the nocturnal talkers had not yet come alive. In that brief in-between at dusk, a gift of eerie quiet soothed Vanessa's nerves.

Since she'd arrived, Vanessa had been alert to every sound in the constant din, and she felt unusually agitated. How had she become oblivious to the sounds of her own world in LA—traffic, honking horns, sirens, partiers on the streets, the back-up beeping of trucks, and the constant whine of jets overhead? Filtered by familiarity over time, Vanessa had blocked them out.

Acclimation, then adaptation, she thought.

But here in this primordial environment, everything was new, and that aspect of the unfamiliar nudged her toward culture shock.

"*There* you are. I've been looking for you. Where's Tony?" Canyon caught up with her on the path. "What's wrong?" She moved around in front of Vanessa and blocked her way.

"Canyon, listen . . . Finally quiet."

"Yes, it's amazing. Like a switch was flipped. But you're not answering me. So, where's Tony?"

"Had to check on the team. He'll meet us at dinner."

"I'm at a loss. It's new territory having you two at odds over this children issue." She put her arm over Vanessa's shoulder. "You and Tony are my rocks. Shouldn't you think about telling him—"

"Canyon, honey, not now. There's something I need to tell you about that dangerous character Scott."

Tony approached them on the path, and Vanessa stopped her conversation short. She touched his arm and tried to find the right words to melt the tension between them.

He stepped aside. "Sorry you have to be involved with this, Canyon, but better you than some outsider." He rested his hand on Canyon's shoulder. "Look, let me just put it out there. We've been through too much to let our personal lives interfere with doing our jobs. No matter how tense this is between Van and me, I don't want a woman's torturous death on my conscience. I'm sure you don't either. As hard as it is, let's just leave this beehive alone until we get home."

"I agree." Vanessa thought better of starting a conversation. Bad time, wrong place. Turning to walk down the path, she felt both parts of her existence disintegrating—her life with Tony and her life's work, her safe places.

"Oh, and let's get the lay of the land first before we go to the mat with the head guy, Van."

Vanessa was stung by Tony's lack of faith in her judgment. Another first.

"Tony, you're actually questioning Van's instincts? Wow, things have changed." Canyon hooked her arms in Tony's and Vanessa's. "Come on, you two."

She walked them up to the quadruple wide trailer home disguised as a southern mansion.

Familiar old jazz tunes swelled from behind the door. Vanessa's favorite music usually calmed her, but a song came on that triggered her emotions. "What are you doing the rest of your life?" The lyrics made her pull inside herself to escape. She had no answer for her own life, but she could see Canyon was ready to play their usual game to provide some normalcy. This was an answer Vanessa knew.

"OK, Van, you're on. What's the song? Who sang it? Show us your stuff."

Vanessa was quiet.

"Come on, Van."

"Sarah Vaughn. 'What are you doing the rest of your life?' Lyrics, Alan and Marilyn Bergman. Music by Scott Legrand." Vanessa pulled the facts from her music vault.

"That's *all*? You're slipping, Van," Canyon said.

"OK." Vanessa whipped off the answer. "Grammy winner in nineteen seventy-three. Academy Award nominee for Best Original Song for the movie, *A Happy Ending*, released in nineteen sixty-nine." A happy ending, she thought. Of all the songs in the world. Vanessa sighed.

"You haven't lost it." Canyon rang the doorbell.

Jeff Jenkinsen greeted them and introduced his wife, Delilah. She looked up at Vanessa with her hands pressed together as though she would break out in a chorus of Hallelujah. "Come in, come in, oh my goodness, it's Delilah Jean but do call me Delilah, Ms. Gold."

Immediately recognizing Delilah's look and anticipating the ooze that was about to follow, Vanessa sang Canyon's praises, explaining her history with the original *Turning Prism* team. There was no avoiding it. It was sweet, but ironically, Delilah's kind of adoration always prevented any real connection to people. Vanessa succumbed with a forced smile.

The hosts were a proper southern couple. Jeff, tall, magnetic with more black hair than was likely at sixty-something. Delilah was weighted down with thick make-up and big hair, no more a blonde than Vanessa was brunette. She had to have been in diapers when her husband graduated college, Vanessa thought. The couple held themselves in perfect posture. Jeff's thinly veiled contempt for Vanessa was palpable. It was familiar. It was no secret that her methods of exposé were relentless when human rights were at stake. Vanessa always picked up on the tension in the air when she first entered a room on an assignment.

"How do you do?" Delilah gestured for them to enter. "I *cannot* believe that Ms. Vanessa Gold is in my home! I watch your show, *Exposé*, all the time—those darlin' little foster children you saved, and you were so wonderful on Oprah. And your documentaries!"

Vanessa's stomach tightened at the compliments; they were always hard for her.

"I believe you've met Scott West, our security director."

"Yes, we have." If Delilah only knew how *insecure* the security director had made Vanessa feel.

As usual, Tony stood off to the side when these fan reactions happened, giving Vanessa the limelight. It made her nervous that he wasn't shooting her his usual warm, crooked smile. Not negative, just not loving.

"Delilah Jean, we mustn't gush. But, yes, congratulations are in order, and thank you for coming to help us with our little problem," Jeff added.

Vanessa was stunned. Your little problem? She studied Jeff carefully, caught off guard by his good-ole-boy welcome. His body was on high alert, at odds with his saccharin smile. She could almost see his well-defined muscles twitching under his shirt. A disingenuous tone pushed through his words despite his obvious efforts at projecting sincerity. His eyes scanned Tony and Canyon, but he made no eye contact.

Diffusing the potential contentiousness with a charming welcome was an unexpected strategy. Clever. Vanessa thrived much better when she had an obvious enemy to confront. It kept her on alert. She was most in her element, reading people. Any emotional state was in her favor. But Jeff had things entirely under control, wrapped tight. That worried her. She had expected a more adversarial reaction, which confused her. What is your strategy, Jeff? Vanessa assessed him. Delilah is my best source to get at the truth, Vanessa thought. She's star-struck and maybe more than a bit naïve. She's a potential asset, but Jeff, he's a pro, she thought.

"You are a true American heroine, Ms. Gold, but we are being rude to keep you to ourselves. Please do come in and meet the others." Delilah led them through the house toward a set of open French doors.

Their host stopped at the threshold and waved her arm to welcome them into a spectacular lush garden, recreating the landscape of a fine southern mansion. Strings of tiny white lights adorned the trees. Trellises, fountains, and meandering walkways transformed time and space. Treetop-high mesh screens were draped naturally and invisibly around the entire area to keep the pests at bay.

An indigenous tribesman wearing a white jacket and black dress pants served Vanessa a mint julep and moved on among the guests. Jeff nodded at him, and the server removed his nose bone and put it in his pocket.

Delilah opened her eyes wide and gestured to a second servant who held a plate of grilled, skewered shrimp.

He touched the top of his penis gourd that flared out the front of his black slacks out in a socially unacceptable way and tucked it more securely under his belt.

Delilah's look made it clear she was frustrated with the tribal man's failure to comply with her Pygmalion makeover by wearing the koteka under his proper serving attire.

He awkwardly spoke to Vanessa. "Good evening, sir."

"Oh, I'm so sorry." Delilah tittered. "Sometimes they call me, 'sir,' too. They just don't seem to understand gender tags. Seems that's the only phrase they'll learn anyway." She fluttered her hands at the servers as if to shoo them away to avoid more embarrassment.

"This is culturally and morally wrong on so many levels." Canyon kept her side remarks low. "I'm impressed by the garden transformation, but really? The black slacks and dress shirt? And his koteka underneath? Looks like he has the biggest—"

Vanessa had to turn away to repress a laugh as Canyon stopped herself. "We know Jeff doesn't want a bridge built. He wants Lukeem dead."

"Yes. Show the guy no mercy, Van. It's the only thing that works with this kind of guy. Oh, here comes Delilah."

"Excuse me? I missed what you said?" Delilah swept in and shimmied her tight black dress down.

Canyon covered up. "Delilah, your garden is spectacular."

"Why, thank you, Ms. Swenson. I wanted it to be just like home. Well, the garden maybe, not the help. They're, well, not like our staff at home. But I couldn't bear to leave our garden. Took me five years to get it like this. I admit to doing a little smuggling to get some of these plants here from my hometown."

"Delilah Jean!" Jeff scolded.

Vanessa smirked, knowing Jeff would not want to share a single bit of their corrupt world with the queen of Exposé. But she was getting impatient with the small talk and looked up at the swelling moon illuminating the garden. There was so much to learn, and time was running out.

"And my flowers, well, y'all came just in the right season." Delilah gestured to the rows of plants. "Abruce, our gardener, has gathered these centerpieces."

Fifty feet away in the dimming light, Abruce cut more flowers from the rows of beautiful plantings. Vanessa wondered how he felt about doing what would be considered women's work in his culture. He had such a dignity about him. Was it his misplaced pride in working for the sky spirits? She was anxious to get through the night and finally meet Lukeem in the morning. Vanessa was aware that Delilah was watching her observe Abruce.

"Oh, I'm sorry, I don't make the outside help wear a uniform." Delilah shrugged and tucked her chin into her shoulder.

"Of course, I understand." It said so much to her that Delilah interpreted Vanessa's interest in Abruce in that way. The word naïve came to mind. But her husband, Jeff, he was another story.

Thousands of tiny lights came on automatically, creating a fairyland around a beautifully set table. Everything was decorated in tones of blue. Vanessa was aware that her favorite color was a known fact. Nearly every gift she'd ever received from admirers or sycophants was some shade of blue. It softened Vanessa's judgment of Delilah. She was so sincere, with more than a touch of innocence.

She nodded to Abruce when he approached with the armful of flowers. He smiled, set them down, and left for the other side of the garden.

Scott's stare was unnerving. Vanessa realized he was following her line of vision to Abruce. He leaned over to speak to her privately. "I've decided he's so critical to this situation, I'm going to keep him in lock-down after dinner until the search in the morning. For his own safety, of course."

"To protect both of them, of course. Makes sense." A sizzling wave of panic set in as she went along with Scott's plan. Better that her apprehension wasn't showing on the outside.

"The word is getting around that he is from Lukeem's tribe. That twisted koteka's a dead giveaway. That could work both ways, I suppose. He could be mobbed or be a hero for turning her in. But without him, we'd never find Lukeem. We'll find some leverage to inspire the guy. No one will recognize her from those photos. No koteka to distinguish *her*." Scott laughed. "Let's do this, Vanessa."

The nervousness and the enigmatic conversation she'd had with Scott just a few hours before seemed to have dissipated. She couldn't get a grip on him. Vanessa's head was buzzing. She didn't see that coming, and she wanted to warn Abruce, but leaving the group was not possible. She wasn't used to feeling so unfocused and so easily unnerved.

Tony was standing by a magnolia tree engaged in conversation with a woman she hadn't yet met. Vanessa couldn't get his attention. The distance between them was more than a garden. She missed that close connection they always had while they worked.

"Well, we should team-up. We both have the same goal after all." Scott's body position was almost flirtatious, she thought, too close, invading her personal space.

"Sounds good." She could also play their game of *who can seem more obliging*. It was the only path to follow if she wanted more information.

"I will meet you by the holding tank after breakfast. It's at the end of the path to my trailer, two over from yours. Can't miss it. It has an American flag over it. He'll be fine there overnight. See you at eight a.m., if you can handle that after your travels."

"Of course, I'll be there." *Holding tank*. The expression wasn't a term that comforted Vanessa.

"No need to bring the whole *Turning Prism* team thing. It will slow us down. Might alert everyone if we have those cameras around. Agreed?"

"Agreed. Tony will spend the morning picking up things at the airport, and the team will spend the day getting general footage at the mine site and doing interviews." She responded purely on intuition, not logic. Vanessa was suspicious of Scott's cooperation. He wanted to get her alone, but why? To outline the terms of his deal? To leverage her with the information he had on her? To silence her, forever? Was it possible he wanted to make up for his crime? At least for now, Lukeem was in hiding, but Vanessa knew she had to get to Abruce and Lukeem first. What then? She had no idea. She worked on instinct, and Vanessa had thousands of irate workers and a spider web of complex cultural norms between her and the answer.

CHAPTER 33

SURPRISE APPEARANCE

Vanessa

THE GUESTS SAT IN the garden at a table set for nine with the incessant sound of thousands of tree frogs croaking in choral unison, echoing off the dark mountains that loomed behind them.

"That non-stop sound reminds me of trying to have a conversation at happy hour in this popular LA bar I know." Tony started off the conversation by making everyone laugh.

Jeff stood and made the introductions. The group included Ibu Susanto, the woman Tony had been speaking to, an Indonesian anthropologist, and her husband, Munadi Susanto, an entomologist dealing with the Malaria problem. With Canyon, Brad and Scott West that made a total of nine.

When Jeff introduced Scott, he added, "a fellow Marine to boot," and patted him on the back. There was a strong bond there worth noting. Vanessa was volunteering for a trap. She knew that, but she'd planned to have Lukeem in hand long before the trap snared her.

What then?

"Please, *silahkan makan*. That's Indonesian for 'I invite you to eat'." Delilah gestured for service to begin. "Now, this is the traditional *Rijsttafel* dinner. Influenced by the Dutch when they invaded Indonesia. Anyway, it means 'rice table'." It was evident that Delilah wanted to show how special her arrangements were for Vanessa's arrival. She went on about the tradition and described each of the dozens of colorful dishes while looking adoringly at Vanessa.

Delilah's voice faded as Vanessa watched a woman come out from behind the shed in the garden. It was a bit far away to tell, but she looked like the woman in the photos, and she was bare-breasted, not wearing the white bra newly required for all indigenous women. It must be Lukeem. Dear God, she was within yards of their outdoor dining table. Vanessa took in a slow breath to calm herself and flashed a look at Canyon.

Canyon knew that look meant *create a distraction now*. She immediately took a bite of the ruddy-colored beef dish that Delilah had warned was "quite a hot one" to cause a distraction. Her eyes flew open. Quickly drinking her water to still her coughing spasm, Canyon finally sputtered out the words, "Delicious. Sorry, wrong pipe."

Tony stood and patted Canyon's back, knowing there was some reason for the interruption. He knew she could eat any pepper without flinching, no matter how hot.

"Careful. A few of them are a little spicy for the uninitiated. That one is called *rendang*. Try some rice—that cools it better than water, dear." Delilah seemed proud of her knowledge.

Vanessa caught the attention of Abruce and shifted her eyes and her chin in the direction of Lukeem and the shed. She couldn't afford to react or draw attention for more than a few seconds. It was clear Abruce had picked up on her signal. Vanessa returned to the conversation, mentally searching for strategies as she took her seat again.

Moving slowly from the area to avoid drawing attention, Abruce connected with Lukeem, hurried her inside the shed, and closed the door.

Vanessa had anticipated a search through the mountains to find Lukeem. But this up-close drama had never crossed her mind. She had to get Abruce to keep Lukeem under wraps, along with himself.

Jeff rose and put his hands on the table stiff-armed. "Look, let's put all these niceties aside and talk turkey. Ms. Gold, the reason I invited you here—"

"Yes, thank you for inviting me." Vanessa perfectly controlled her tone between a tinge of sincerity and a touch of mockery.

Jeff clenched his jaw, clearly not used to a female opponent.

Vanessa wanted to push his limits to break through the layer of bullshit he was smearing over the truth. Truth always pushes hard on an agitated mind. She knew that. With enough aggravation and Jeff's arrogance, he might give it up, explode it out. Vanessa needed to know about their intentions.

There were two conditions in which she knew the truth could be excavated. They were opposites; under extreme duress or in the safety of a lull with defenses down. For Jeff to give, it would take duress. Delilah was the crack in the door, most likely to make the slip that would let Vanessa really know what was going on behind the scenes. Jeff's wife would succumb to the lull.

"I should say we are glad to have you here with us because, frankly, we need your expertise." He held himself in check. "The situation is beyond tenuous, and we are between a rock and a hard place. We were hoping you could help us to find her and to figure out a way to stop the tribesmen from committing this atrocity. And save the woman, of course."

"I'm sure she knows we are innocent victims here. Don't *you*, Ms. Gold? After all, *we* didn't start this vile tradition," Delilah said.

"I have great compassion for the situation." Vanessa placed her hand on Delilah's arm.

"Delilah, I was speaking." Jeff put his hand on her other arm. "As I was saying, we are literally, between a rock and a hard place trying to find a way to save this one tribal woman while keeping the locals happy—which would also save the entire project." Jeff settled back in his chair. "I would be delighted if you, and your team of course, could figure out a way to stop this sacrifice and get my guys back to work. What is your strategy, Ms. Gold?"

"Jeffrey, be polite. Let Ms. Gold eat first." Delilah passed another spicy Indonesian delight.

Vanessa was relieved. She needed to buy time. The plan had not yet gelled in her mind. There were too many missing pieces, and Scott's plan to lock up Abruce, just when she was about to connect with Lukeem, was threatening her progress.

Seated next to Vanessa, Brad leaned in. The music in the background, the conversations at the table, and plates passing gave them just enough privacy to talk. "I have some intel for you. I overheard Jeff and Scott at the communications office just before dinner. Jeff says they might not have had a choice about you *coming*, but they do have a choice about you *staying*."

"What does that mean?"

"Well, I'm not sure. Jeff says he'll create bigger bait to lure the almighty Vanessa Gold from the mine site. Bigger than what brought you here."

"Like what?"

"Here's the strange thing. The diversion has something to do with Fiona O'Farrell or, as Jeff said, 'the celebrated Woman of the Year who happens to be in Jakarta this week.'"

Vanessa's hands began to shake. She found herself touching her headband which concealed the roots of her hair.

"Yeah, right?" Brad continued, "She just keeps showing up. What's with that? First the photos, now she might be some kind of target, or maybe she's involved somehow. Hard to believe though, she's America's sexy senior sweetheart."

"Was that all you heard?" Vanessa squeezed the silver mint julep goblet so tight that the condensation nearly made it pop out of her fingers. *What are you up to, Fiona?*

"Well, he mentioned she'd called him earlier this week before you arrived. They made some agreement. Said he'd give her whatever she wanted. I couldn't hear the rest. The fax went off. But I know he plans something to get you out of here before the full moon. Oh, and Jeff said to Scott, 'Leave the distraction to me. You just keep her busy for the next twenty-four hours. Then we'll get her out of here before that moon fiasco. That stupid woman's going over that cliff. We're losing millions. This is war.' His words, exactly."

Canyon turned to the sophisticated Javanese woman in formal batik dress with hair swept up classically in the traditional bouffant style. "Mrs. Susanto, as an anthropologist, what can you tell us about the situation here?"

Canyon focused the group's attention on her fellow anthropologist while Vanessa went to work, scanning the faces in the group, looking for a clue to identify her allies and enemies. She didn't need more information than the body language of the anthropologist and her entomologist husband to know they were on the payroll. They kept their heads lower than Jeff's, and they made no direct eye contact with him, while he kept them riveted in his sights. When they shared the company line and betrayed their professionalism, they looked at each other with an edge of shame visible on their faces.

Mrs. Susanto shifted in her chair. "According to the missionary in that area, she was disenfranchised by her tribe for desecrating the men's sacred place forbidden to women. Somehow, she escaped their punishment," the anthropologist said. "She is reported to have the ability to disappear."

"Literally?" Vanessa was confused but decided to bypass the absurdity.

"And the punishment is?" Canyon jumped in.

Canyon's ongoing questions allowed time for Vanessa's observations. Their duet. Vanessa missed their teamwork. None of the information Mrs. Susanto shared was new to Vanessa, but she never wanted to assume. The more perspectives, the better.

"Human sacrifice to the Ranu Lolo River, I'm afraid."

"Where is she now, Mrs. Susanto?" Vanessa asked.

"No one knows exactly."

Vanessa was relieved. She believed her. They didn't realize Lukeem was right under their noses. "These peoples seem so affable and gentle in nature. I've heard from a missionary that the punishment for women labeled as *sorceresses*, and are thought to have caused bad luck, is unthinkable public torture—being scorched with hot pokers or burned alive." Vanessa continued her probe.

"Yes, Ms. Gold, that is true," Mrs. Susanto said. "However, this woman is from a tribe deep in the mountains who adhere to the older tradition. They are good-natured and do not torture or burn their sacrificial victims."

"In that case, she's fortunate to simply be thrown off a cliff unless local tribesmen find her first," Vanessa said. "It seems that the closer the tribes are to the 'civilized Americans' the more uncivilized the behavior is. Interesting, isn't it?"

"And a charred woman's body was found a while back, remember, dear?" Delilah added. "Right after a man had an accident and fell from the tram and died, wasn't it?"

How did I get into this line of business? Vanessa wished she were filming something uplifting and inspirational. Tony was right. Maybe they would be better off changing to more positive subjects. She sighed. Wasn't it her own doing? Vanessa shook off her thoughts and focused.

"Yes, well it is difficult to understand these things through our own cultural filters," Mrs. Susanto said. "Not to justify the violence, but it does serve to give the men a reason for the tragedy that had befallen them. Sets things right, puts back the balance, appeases the nature spirits—from their perspective, that is."

"Yes, the miners up on the tram said the woman's screaming went on for days." Delilah chimed in again.

Jeff held his hand up to Delilah.

Canyon laser-focused on the anthropologist, knowing that she was not taking the conversation in Jeff's desired direction. "Would you agree, Mrs. Susanto, that the culture clashes, confusion, and unpredictable evolution of traditions are caused by the ignorance of the technologically advanced societies? Isn't their failure to research the local indigenous populations' traditions before they invade their turf irresponsible?"

Mrs. Susanto glanced at Jeff. "I suppose one could—"

"Certainly." Canyon's fork clanged against her porcelain plate as she set it down. "These changes in the natives' lives would not have happened if we had not brought the wealthiest and most technologically evolved people in the world to mine for copper and gold within the environs of tribes virtually living a Stone Age existence and without the benefit of experts to guide the cultural impact and change, is that right?"

"I suppose. I would certainly have wished to be involved sooner, Ms. Swenson."

Vanessa felt the absence of Tony's usual support in these types of conversations.

"Well, yes, the misunderstandings or misinterpretations are unavoidable at times." Mrs. Susanto attempted to backpedal her statement.

Red-faced, Jeff interrupted the anthropologist. "Look, lots of cultures do things like this to appease the gods. Our Hawaiians made sacrifices to the volcano gods."

"What about the tradition of severing portions of fingers from all of the females in a family when a man dies, Mrs. Susanto?" Canyon kept the pressure on.

"It has to do with acknowledging the power of the spirit of the deceased, and the fear of the unknown, of course." Mrs. Susanto set down her water. "The act pays homage to the dead, a supplication they hope will ensure kindness, or at least mitigate against revenge, in the future, on the part of the nature spirit."

Vanessa challenged her with a rhetorical question. "As an anthropologist, Mrs. Susanto, do you not find it perplexing that the male human species puts a woman on a pedestal, pursues her nurturing with a passion, has a protective instinct for her, depends on her to have his children and carry on his line, would even *die* for her—and yet they can commit such atrocities against her?"

"Yes, we have all three seen it in our careers together," Canyon added. "It seems it's pandemic—a worldwide story of abuse, rape, acid burnings, sex trafficking little girls—unthinkable atrocities against the very persons they adulate and desire in their own lives." Canyon perfectly quoted Vanessa's speech from the award ceremony that she'd read in the papers. Vanessa searched their faces to see how much news detail had reached the site.

"I'll never get that." Tony looked at Vanessa.

Vanessa knew he was referring to the circumstances that had brought Maureen into their lives. Vanessa felt vulnerable.

"That's another subject for much discussion," Mrs. Susanto answered.

"But it seems the dialogue needs to take place." Vanessa countered.

"I saw a little girl today who was missing part of a finger." Canyon pushed on before the anthropologist could answer. "Was that from a new or old tradition?"

Jeff became impatient, signaling to Mrs. Susanto to stop the discussion. "We don't need to bring up their business here. I'd like to know who the troublemakers were who shared the details about the photos that started this whole thing. Turned it into an international fiasco. Some no good, do-gooder NGO that never had to be responsible for a company and stockholders and a thousand employees who don't even speak English. *That's* who!"

Vanessa furtively glanced around the table; she noted that Brad's face was a mask of innocence, however, Scott seemed to be sweating. Was it from the heat of the evening or nerves about possibily being discovered as the sender of the photos, as Brad had mentioned.

Delilah attempted to pacify her husband. "We have to respect their traditions, and we have no control over their actions in any case, like you said, dear." She added. "Because we're the innocent victims here."

"Jeff, you are right," Vanessa interjected with an entirely different meaning in mind. "There are innocent victims here."

Delilah smiled. "You see, dear, I told you she would see it our way. After all, as you said, Jeff, it's a good trade—one primitive woman nobody's life for the good of everyone and the *entire* company."

Jeff's wife had spilled much more easily than Vanessa could ever have imagined. And the pressure made Jeff show his hand as well. As Tony had heard, the company had planned to assist in killing Lukeem.

"Delilah, why don't you serve dessert?" Jeff suggested. "It's getting time for everyone to go." Jeff stood and placed his hands on the table in front of him. "Ms. Gold, I would be delighted if you could figure out a way to stop this sacrifice and get my guys back to work. Bottom line."

"Especially when so many people's livelihoods, not to mention the entire project, depends on it, right dear?" Delilah looked at Jeff with a smile. Was she looking for his approval?

"Agreed. For the good of everyone," Jeff said.

"I wonder if the woman herself would agree as she tumbles into the abyss," Vanessa whispered to Brad.

Brad gave the slightest nod, indicating that he agreed.

"Well, this is a common phenomenon—wherever cultures blend, there are cultural confusions, mutations, and a breaking down, Ms. Gold," Mrs. Susanto said.

"Isn't it true that these peoples have never had a concept of possessions or emotions such as jealousy and seemed to hold little animosity even toward their enemy tribes once a balance is struck? It seems they are now being contaminated by the *have-and-have not* circumstances they find in working at the mine," Canyon said. "Wouldn't it make sense that they are becoming *more* belligerent in unexpected ways now that they see all of the fascinating and intriguing things the Americans have, but to which they have no access, even though they work just as hard in the same jobs?"

"Our government is sponsoring programs to support more civilized behavior among our peoples," Mrs. Susanto said.

"With all due respect, Mrs. Susanto, I saw the women wearing ill-fitting cotton bras *in public*, not exactly acceptable in sophisticated international society. I've also heard about banning the kotekas as an embarrassment to the outside civilized world," Vanessa continued her attack.

"Forcing people to wear certain clothes and taking away their traditions diminishes the beautiful diversity in our world, don't you think?" Canyon played off of Vanessa's words.

"We need to welcome them into the twenty-first century, Ms. Gold. The Stone Age is well over, my dear." Mrs. Susanto was clearly delighted with her own cleverness.

Tony interjected. "This simple, so-called Stone Age society has spawned a group of local rebels who are inciting sit-outs at the mine and fighting government troops quite successfully, I understand. This kind of minuteman stand doesn't seem very Stone Age to me at all. My own country was established by such means. And I saw the workers carrying placards, protesting salary rates, and the government programs written in *Bahasa Indonesia*—Unity in Diversity, Mrs. Susanto. And isn't your country's motto, Unity in Diversity?"

A nervous silence enveloped the group at the end of Tony's tirade.

Vanessa watched Canyon lean into Brad, who sat next to her, eating her coconut dessert, at her invitation. "You're so different from the mining execs. What brought you here, Brad?"

"It's the proverbial other end of the world that we all seek when things go terribly wrong."

"What could *you* be running from?" Canyon tilted her head.

"The truth, but that's for another time." Brad glanced at Canyon and patted her hand. "Be patient, I'll tell you."

"Well, ladies and gentlemen, it has been, shall we say, a truthful night. But the truth is—I have a very early roll call." Jeff folded his napkin and stood to leave.

Brad stood, saluted, and assisted with Canyon's chair. "I'll be ready at five o'clock to take you down to the Jakarta airport, Jeff. I can pick up the mail on that run, and the new communications equipment should have arrived. I've missed getting the sports. And Tony will join us since he has some supplies that he needs to pick up that missed his flight."

"Yes, we're all feeling a little cut off from civilization lately without television. But they're working on the satellite issue." Jeff stood behind Delilah's chair. "Oh, Brad?" Jeff raised his voice. "Did they figure out where all the limes went? I need some for my bar."

"No clue. Tea bags, limes, magazines, and flashlights. Nothing else is missing."

"When they kept to the trash picking, I didn't mind, but this is getting annoying." Jeff pulled back Delilah's chair.

"Well, thank ya'll for coming. Good night and welcome, Ms. Gold and company. This is the most exciting thing that's happened in years. Y'all coming here, I mean. Ya'll will be careful, won't you?" Delilah added.

Brad walked out with Vanessa and Canyon. Tony lingered behind.

"Canyon, I'd love to show you around a bit if we get some down time while you're here. You know, for your anthropological interest," Brad said. "Maybe I can show you the communications room and how I plan to get the news of your expedition to reach the farthest reaches of the universe." He winked.

"An undercover photographer *and* a saboteur? Now, I'm even more intrigued."

"Yes, I have always fancied myself a saboteur sipping a straight-up martini neat, with a beautiful woman in an exotic place. Looks like I got to play out my fantasy tonight." Brad winked again.

"Now you're flirting." Canyon lightly nudged him with her elbow.

"You're catching on fast, Ms. Swenson."

"And if I'm not mistaken, so are you, Brad."

"Canyon, no matter how tense things get, then there's you." Vanessa leaned over and whispered, "Get a room, girl . . . or should I say get a Quonset hut?"

They shared a much-needed laugh.

CHAPTER 34

CIVIL SAVAGE

Vanessa

THE SINGLE-BULB lights in front of each trailer lit the path back to their quarters. The volume of the night sounds had kicked up. "Tony, I'll be right in. I want to talk with Canyon for a minute."

"No problem, I'm heading back to meet up with the team. I'll be gone an hour or so. Good night, Canyon." Tony closed the door to their tin home away from home and left.

Vanessa stepped into Canyon's room.

"OK. What's going on, Van?"

"Canyon, Scott is holding Abruce in lockdown overnight. He wants me to help him find Lukeem tomorrow."

"What? What are you going to do?"

"I'm going to wait until after Tony leaves at dawn for Jakarta, and then I'll free Abruce. That's all." Vanessa saw Canyon's expected look. "Don't worry, I'll be careful. It's only fifty feet from here. I'll release him just before the sun rises, then come by to get you for breakfast. I'm supposed to be at the holding tank at eight a.m. to meet Scott for the search."

"You're not going to involve Tony?"

"You both need to be innocent if Scott or Jeff wants to get tough later. And I promised to protect you, Canyon."

"Your call. Be careful."

"I'm just going to release him. It'll be fine. Good night."

"I'm so happy we're doing something meaningful together again, although I'm scared out of my gourd." Canyon hugged her tightly.

"THAT KID, ABERA, is so damn cute." Tony closed the trailer door behind him. "With his tiny koteka. He's already looking at pig bones for his nose bone when he has his manhood ritual."

"Aren't you glad *you* don't have to wear a koteka?" Vanessa began to undress for bed.

"I hate that the kid's parents died of Malaria. He follows us around like a lost puppy."

"I'm so exhausted. The time change has me all turned around. Come snuggle in here for a minute. I'm not long for this world, Tony."

"Van, that's not a good expression for an assignment in such a remote jungle." Tony tucked in beside her on the twin bed for a good night kiss.

"True. So you leave first thing. And you'll be back in the afternoon?" She ran her hand down his side and moved closer. She knew the next twenty-four hours would be intense. "Maybe we shouldn't waste this precious time talking about contentious things." She kissed him.

"Well, that's one sure-fire way to stop an unwanted conversation, ma'am." He pulled her closer.

THE SHARDS OF sunlight flashed up the mountainside and lit up the valley, a kind of sunrise Vanessa had never seen from her cliffside oceanfront home.

Following the path from her trailer, she found the makeshift jail, a miniature Quonset hut with a chain link gate affixed to one open side. Abruce was huddled back in the shadows.

Removing his nose bone, he licked it and replaced it, leaving it in the down position as he moved close to Vanessa.

"Abruce! Oh, damn you, Scott! This is inhumane." There were only two things she understood from Abruce's softly spoken string of syllables—he'd done nothing wrong, and he needed to help Lukeem.

Abera tapped Vanessa's arm and pointed to the security officers coming their way.

"I'll get help." Vanessa promised Abruce using hand signals. She slid her hand in the slot between the bars and touched Abruce's fingers to reassure him.

He exchanged a few words with Abera. "Abera take you."

Following Abera, Vanessa took a path behind the holding tank. Avoiding the security guards, she returned to her trailer. The VHS player on the small nightstand was on pause. Who had been in her trailer? Frozen, on the screen, was the face of her grandfather. Pacing and thinking, Vanessa checked her red roots in the mirror and replaced her headband. Did she still have leverage with Scott? She needed to find out.

As always, Abera was squatting outside her trailer door when she exited. He reached out for her handshake, and Vanessa bent over so he could place his hand over her heart, a tradition she'd yet to adjust to. He followed her to Scott's trailer. The warped door was ajar again. Cautiously, she looked inside. No one was there, but she caught sight of a Maxwell House coffee can under the bed. Vanessa bent over and rescued it from the dusty floor. Curious, she opened it. An amber-colored, aged news clipping was tucked inside. Unfolding it, she read: "Hasidic Rabbi Moshe Cohen Slain—Antisemitic Gang Blamed".

Under the article, Vanessa pulled out a twisted lock of silver hair encrusted with rusty black. She dropped it as though she'd been stung. Acid rose up into her throat. It took her only a moment to put the picture together—his enigmatic words, "You win. You've got me where you want me," and his telltale habit of nervously smoothing his hair on the back of his head. She was right, *he isn't after me; he thinks I'm after him,* she realized. Vanessa envisioned the boy in the flannel shirt and wool cap trying to fast forward his face two decades. "Impossible!" At the bottom of the coffee can, was a photo of a boy with Scott's characteristic black hair in front of a row house with a young woman, most likely his mother, Vanessa thought. On the backside of the photo, she read the faded inscription: *April 1, 1970, Arrival in Brooklyn, Scottie, 15yrs. and Me.*

"*Scottie?*" Vanessa turned it over again and examined his face. *He had looked much younger than fifteen. I would have guessed thirteen. It was him.*

Stunned, Vanessa put the things back in place, stuffed the unspeakable evidence into her pocket, and ran out of Scott's trailer.

Abera sat on guard outside her door just as she had seen Abruce do. He led her on another path to the jail. They peered out through the underbrush and waited. Seeing no guard, Vanessa approached the holding tank.

Abera pulled at her hand, directed her to a nearby shed, and handed her a crowbar. Leveraging the tin sides of the cage open, she freed Abruce.

Thanking the young boy, Abruce placed his hand firmly over his heart and pointed to the underbrush signaling for Abera to hide.

"You! What are you doing there?" The security guard arrived with his firearm ready.

Abruce and Vanessa ran toward the thick brush, but Abera lay flat on the ground next to a group of vine-covered rocks.

"We can't just leave him here!" Vanessa tugged at Abruce's arm. She turned around and discovered Abera had inexplicably disappeared.

Pulling Vanessa by the hand, Abruce ran with her through the thick jungle underbrush with the sound of security guards' voices close behind. They reached the sheer mud and rock wall near the cafeteria. It was covered in vines with hardly any places to climb.

"What are we going to do?" Vanessa gazed up the rockface wall. "We're trapped! There's no time to climb, Abruce." Emotion welled in her throat.

Abruce lay down flat on the ground next to the wall and signaled for her to follow.

"What are you doing? They're coming! Get up! We have to get out of here!" She quickly glanced behind them, trying to gauge how close the guards were.

He reached out with his bow in his right hand and deftly lifted a section of vine. Shimmying on his back under the fissure, Abruce beckoned her with his left hand as it slid out of sight.

Following suit, Vanessa slid under the vines. She maneuvered under the rock only inches from her face. Standing up in a gap, Vanessa shifted around two fold-back turns that led to a large cave.

"That was amazing!" Her words echoed back, *amazing, amazing, amazing.* That's how Lukeem *disappears*, Vanessa thought. As her flashlight dimmed, she saw a crude unlit torch against the cave wall. "We need light, Abruce. Can you light this? Can you make a fire?"

He threw the torch down.

"What are you doing? We need that, Abruce. Please."

"Abruce have better light." Reaching inside a wide crevasse, Abruce pulled out two miner's hats with headlights and flicked them both on. He led her upward through a labyrinth of dripping passageways until they reached an opening.

The look of surprise had not yet left her face when he gestured for her to gaze out of the hole.

Flipping his nose bone, Abruce positioned it in an upward smile matching the direction of his proud mouth.

"That was brilliant."

"Abruce find the way." He pointed to himself, smiling.

The security guards' voices grew louder. "I saw a light up there!" a voice called.

"That's impossible. They couldn't climb so quickly," another voice answered.

Abruce guided Vanessa through the passageways. At another opening in the dirt wall, they heard the men's voices from outside. Crawling out onto a carved-out ledge, he stuck his shoulder out beside the waterfall's edge, inviting Vanessa to peer out at the security guards below.

"Now you're showing off."

MALE BONDING

Brad

"I'VE ARRANGED FOR Zell Baxter limos to take you and Tony back to the airstrip." Jeff said as the three of them descended the private plane at the Soekarno Hatta International airport in Jakarta.

"Thanks, Jeff." Brad glanced at Tony, nodding as they followed Jeff from the plane to the entrance of the airport. "Tony will pick up his things that just arrived here, and we'll meet back at the plane."

"And Brad, you'll head over to the concert hall to take care of that little matter we discussed, right?" Jeff glanced over his shoulder.

"Of course, I have an appointment with her."

A man ran up to Jeff as they entered the sliding doors and took him aside for a few intense words. Brad watched as Jeff handed the stranger a briefcase that he'd grabbed from behind his seat on the plane when they had disembarked.

Once outside at the pick-up section of arrivals, Brad got into the company limo and opened the window. "See you in an hour or so, Tony."

"Got it. I'll meet you back here with my equipment." Tony glanced at the signs. "Hopefully it arrived like the airline said."

"Baggage claim is that way." Brad pointed out the direction for Tony. "Driver, concert hall, please." The limo pulled away.

CHILDREN AND THEIR parents were streaming into the luxurious concert hall.

Waiting by the entrance door, Brad read the sign that announced the private event introducing the young Indonesian participants and their families to the World Peace Music Foundation.

He waited on the sidewalk listening to the sea of worldwide participants speaking different languages as they arrived with their children.

A limousine pulled up and parked next to the Zell Baxter car. The driver went around the side, opened the door, and Fiona O'Farrell emerged from the back seat.

Brad thought she had a certain familiarity, exuding an irresistible and nurturing warmth. "Dr. O'Farrell." Brad extended his hand as she walked toward him from the stretch limo.

"This means the world to me. Is the child in the car?" She laughed. "Excuse my manners. I'm so excited about this whole thing. Good to see you again, Bradley Mitchell Wainwright the third, correct? I see my idea regarding your photographs worked."

"Thanks to your brilliant suggestion, I secretly sent a letter and backup copy of the photos to Ms. Gold." Brad was surprised to feel a bit star-struck. "They were burning a hole in my duffel bag, so to speak. The *Turning Prism* team is at the mine site now, and you were right about Vanessa Gold being the right person to handle it. She is one impressive woman."

"My pleasure. When you told me about the photographs and the native woman's fate, I felt Vanessa Gold had the right reputation and power to do something about it." She looked toward the tinted glass windows of the limo. "Well, Mr. BMW, back to the child. So nice of you to arrange this. Is the child in the limo?"

"No, ma'am. We needed a little more time to select the candidate. The culture is quite different in the remote area we are dealing with, but we will have her here for your final concert in two days, guaranteed. As the company pilot, I will make sure."

"I like your attitude. You will make sure it is a little girl, won't you? It's important to have an even number of girls and boys."

"Of course, Dr. O'Farrell, I've been told to give you whatever you need."

"Really? Then there might be one other request. Since Vanessa Gold and her crew are at your site this week, I thought maybe she would like to personally deliver the girl and join in our celebration . . . It would certainly bring more press to the event for both of us considering her endless work with children. I am sure little ones are precious to her. Wouldn't you agree?"

"I'll be sure to pass on the message, but I believe she may still be filming on the twentieth. For cultural reasons, she needs to finish by the full moon."

"Of course, there is no way she could leave now. What was I thinking? I saw the awards dinner on TV on my quick trip back to the States. I was hoping things were resolved. I have an even better idea. There must be a lack of entertainment at your remote mountain site, would you agree, Brad?" She smiled.

"Yes, you could say there's a certain lack of 'culture' at the mine site, and I don't mean from the natives." Brad enjoyed his joke.

"Would you be able to arrange a live TV feed for my opening concert on the evening of the nineteenth? If that's within your power and enough time for you to arrange it—at my expense, of course?"

"For you, it can be done," he assured her. He was relieved the new communications equipment had arrived.

"Wonderful. Maybe this is a way for me to begin a connection with her," she said.

"Funny you two haven't met yet. Seems she has met every person of import on the Earth." Brad teased. "I guess she hasn't done a music exposé yet."

"You never know, Brad. I could be next." She teased. "I might have some deep dark secret around this children's foundation."

"Ha! I doubt there's anything more innocent or purer than what you're doing." Even at twenty years his senior, Brad found Fiona to be alluring. "It has been a real pleasure. Do you mind my saying you are the most charming and lovely person I have met since—"

"Since you met Vanessa Gold?" She took a guess at finishing his sentence and winked.

"Not what I was going to say . . . but now that you mention it, you two do have a certain similar magnetism, and a way of getting people to be open." He thought about it for a moment, then said, "You even resemble each other."

"I will take that as a compliment and as confirmation that the Irian Jaya girl and the live stream are in good hands." Fiona gently squeezed his arm. "My, what have you been lifting, young man?"

Brad felt a rush of heat cross his face.

BRAD AND TONY sat quietly in the plane on the return trip to the airport nearest the mining camp. Jeff had told Brad he was staying in Jakarta for another night to attend a business meeting. Brad looked over at Tony as he leveled the private jet out at forty-one thousand feet. "Well, Tony, did you get the things you needed?"

"All set."

"It'll be a rough ride back with all the headwinds," Brad said. "There are new magazines tied up back there with the mail. Why don't you grab a few and relax a little while it's smooth?"

The radio broke through the engine's drone. Brad hadn't been expecting any communication other than typical tower chatter.

"Boston Bird, come in Boston Bird."

Brad opened the mike for Tony to hear.

"It's one of Scott's assistants." Brad turned up the volume. "What's up John? Over."

"It's Abruce. They'd put him in that holding crate contraption until morning. Over."

"Damn! That thing makes me sick." Brad signaled for Tony to put on his headset.

"That's not the worst part. Security guards saw him drag Ms. Gold into the mountains. They're gone. Over."

"What does he mean, *gone*?" Tony's voice was agitated.

Brad put a hand of support on Tony's shoulder.

"John, explain, please. Over."

"I guess the security guards say they followed them but lost them at the sheer rock wall. They just disappeared. Over."

"Oh, God." Tony yelled. "Tell him to keep Canyon off that damn mountain!"

Brad relayed, "Keep Ms. Swenson company. Don't let her leave the job site. Over."

The speaker crackled, went silent, and then came on again. Brad added, "And ask Ms. Swenson to meet us at the communications hut, and we'll talk to her. Over."

"Got it. I'll let her know. I left a message for Scott to help find Ms. Gold too. And I called Jeff. He says we need to reach Abruce before the security guards do. Doesn't want things to go sour. I'll go tell Ms. Swenson right now. Over."

"Good. Thanks, John. We should be arriving at the mine site in two hours. We're making our approach to the airport. Over and out."

"Roger that."

"But we're going up by helicopter to look for Vanessa now, right after we land, aren't we?" Tony's voice leaked his panic.

"We'll have to wait until tomorrow morning. They could have gone a hundred ways. I think she'll be safe with Abruce—she's a *sky goddess*, after all." Brad exacted a turn and leveled out to land.

Brad glanced at Tony who stared down at the thick jungle mountains below, with a hollow, lost look in his eyes.

AFTER LANDING THE plane, Brad and Tony had quickly transferred all their gear from the plane to the helicopter. They were quiet again until Brad guided the helicopter over the mountains heading for the mine site. Tony stared at the blanket of jungle trees below.

"You doing alright? Damn, buddy, I'm sorry."

"Yeah, thanks." Tony stared at his hands.

"Hey, you might as well spill it. I don't shock easily." Brad shifted in his seat.

"Seems after twenty years we're unravelling. We've come to a stand-off. I want a family. Vanessa doesn't. To be fair, we've constructed a situation with our careers that doesn't exactly warrant having a child. You know, all the travel and the danger. I've reached a point where I don't see how this can work."

"There is something about this place. Nearly everyone who ends up here is running from something, usually themselves," Brad said.

"*You're* not! You seem so solid."

"Held together with the glue of guilt. But never mind me." Brad shut down the that line of conversation.

"I gave her an engagement ring on our tenth anniversary. Not exactly rushing it. Ten carats, ten years, romantic, right?" Tony told the story in a monotone.

Brad turned to Tony. "She turned you down, obviously."

"Not as bad as when I suggested we celebrate our fifteenth anniversary by having a baby. That went over real big."

"How did she dodge that one?"

Tony sighed. "She said, 'What would we do? Drag a baby all over the planet, exposing it to the most diabolical people in existence'?"

"So she changed her mind once her career took off?"

"We never really talked about it before we got together. Brad, we're talking seven sisters in an Italian Catholic family. Of course, I wanted kids. Wouldn't you just assume?"

Brad tilted the chopper to adjust to a sudden updraft. "You know the old cliché about assume."

"There was always another story. Vanessa was always so intent on getting the bad guy." Tony leaned forward in his seat, adjusting to the flight pattern. "Always so in control, so perfect."

"Obviously not." Brad sighed. "We do crazy things. Here you are desperate for a child, and I gave my little girl up to my parents and high-tailed-it out of town when she was a day old."

"Because you were a single guy? Where's the mother, Brad?" Tony leaned back against the seat.

"My wife? I killed her." A silence opened in the cockpit that seemed to overpower the noise of the rotors. "I was the drunk driver. She was a few days shy of delivering our first child. It's a long story, but not really."

"It was a tragic accident." Tony offered.

"No excuses. I spent one minute looking into my dead wife's face and our crying newborn in the hospital and I ran."

"God, Brad, I'm sorry. How long ago?"

"Over four years now."

"Do you think you'll ever . . . I mean, have you ever thought about going back for your baby girl?"

"After all this craziness, it's on my mind a lot lately."

"Canyon got anything to do with that?"

Brad thought Tony might be getting a little too personal, but it didn't matter. Hell, the whole conversation with a guy he hardly knew was strange. There was something about being in this remote place that changed the boundaries. "Actually, the truth? Yes. Ridiculous, right?" Brad laughed. "I've only known Canyon for two days."

"Not really. Just means you have good taste. She's solid. Big heart, big brain. I'll stop there since I'm like a brother to her, but it's obvious, she's the package."

"I've spent years meditating, being one with the universe, being OK with everything and everyone else, but I'd forgotten about myself. What *I* wanted." Tony told Brad about finding the VHS and the newspaper clippings of the rabbi's murder.

"Why would Vanessa hide something you would have obviously accepted in your line of work? And she was a college kid, right?"

"Vanessa witnessed the murder. She filmed it! She was twenty years old, and she filmed his murder and ran with the evidence," Tony said.

"Sounds familiar. The running part, I mean."

"You know, Brad, she was so intent on me becoming her cameraman after that spring break—she was much better than I was. She said, 'so we can right the world's wrongs,' but I was going into movies, entertainment."

"And she's stunningly gorgeous, so you agreed, right?" Brad smiled.

"Gorgeous, wrapped so tight, those green eyes. Never once put her eye to the camera lens again. She said she needed to see it from a different perspective to direct. I should have known something was funny." Tony shook his head. "I think about that day she'd returned to campus from her break in New York. I hadn't questioned her makeover. I'd been helplessly in love."

"Most of us only see what we want to see."

"Brad, she grew up in a cloistered convent. She might as well have been an orphan. Her mother was killed in a car accident. She was motherless, yet Vanessa won't have children. I don't get that."

"She leads a dangerous life. No question, a child of yours would have a tough life. It's damn hard to keep a secret. It makes you do crazy things. You really can't go far enough to escape it, can you?"

Tony ran his fingers through his hair and gripped his head. "That's why I went along with not having kids, at first."

"Hard to see it now, but maybe there's more to it. You'll understand it better when you talk to her. Maybe it's better not to make assumptions again." Brad tilted his head and shifted his eyes toward Tony.

"First, we have to find her." Tony rubbed his ring-less finger. "I feel like I just got diagnosed with some life-threatening illness."

"No, just a serious case of male bonding." Brad punched Tony's arm.

"Yeah, sad to say, seems like it might just be the only real bonding I've had in years."

"There's the helipad lights just ahead." Brad began his descent.

"I was already feeling so distant from Vanessa. Now she is off in the jungle with Abruce."

CHAPTER 36

SECRETS DISCLOSED

Canyon

CANYON SAT AT HER desk, hands poised over her computer keyboard. The screen was empty except for two words FADE IN. The first scene of the documentary outline eluded her. What would make a dramatic opening scene? She threw on a jacket and picked up her flashlight when a knock stopped her.

"Ms. Swenson? It's Scott's assistant, John," a voice called.

Canyon opened the door.

"Uh, Ms. Swenson, there's a problem."

"Yes? What happened, John?"

"Your boss Ms. Gold—she's gone. The security guards saw Abruce drag her off into the mountains. They're looking for her now."

"What do you mean he *dragged* her into the mountains?"

John cut her off. "Anyway, Ms. Gold must have been nearby when he escaped the holding tank, and he took her as a hostage."

"Hostage?" You don't know Vanessa, Canyon thought. "Where's Scott?"

"Not sure. I put a message in to him. He'll find her. Scott's a great tracker, has studied the maps of these mountains. Mr. Amorino and Brad asked me to stay with you until they get here. Another two hours. They'll meet you at the communications hut. Have you eaten?"

"No, I haven't eaten, John. Why don't you give me a minute, and I will meet you over at the dining hall."

"Yes, ma'am, that sounds good."

"See you shortly." She assured him with her sweetest, midwestern tone. Canyon crossed over to Vanessa's trailer. The VHS recorder had been left on pause. "I'll just release him quickly." Vanessa's words came back to Canyon. Pushing the reverse button she watched the opening frame with the date, followed by footage of the old man's death. Campus closing, spring of our senior year, Canyon thought, putting the timeframe together. *My name is Colleen Anne Cohen.* Canyon recalled Vanessa's confession. Vanessa's notes told the tale—the rabbi was her grandfather?

Canyon ran to Scott's trailer to see if he'd left yet and found the door open. She saw a security guard rush up to Scott who stood at the end of the row of trailers, fifty feet away. The excited guard relayed some news that Canyon couldn't hear, and Scott headed toward the mountain at a fast clip.

Checking over her shoulder, Canyon ensured no one was in sight. She entered the trailer. A crumpled news article was on the floor. She read the headline and then the underlined sentence in the article: *A young, red-haired, female tourist with a camera seen running from the crime scene is being sought as a witness for questioning.*

April 1970? Dear God, who is Scott? Does he know Vanessa is the redhead? Nestled next to an open chest near the bed, a photo album caught her eye and she began to flip pages. She scanned Scott's dishonorable discharge. Her mind swirled with confusion. Whatever Scott knew or whoever he was, Canyon knew he was dangerous. This is what Vanessa was trying to tell her.

Canyon closed the door, rushed through the town center, and entered the communication office. It was empty. Fumbling awkwardly with the microphone, pushing buttons, and praying, she finally heard Brad's voice.

"What is it, John? News?"

"Brad, it's Canyon."

Brad must have signaled for Tony to put on his headset because Canyon heard Tony's clipped voice. "What's going on down there? Have you seen Vanessa? I need the truth."

"Oh God, she's in the mountains with Abruce. Tony, there is no way he would do anything to her!" Canyon looked out the trailer window to see if anyone was approaching.

"Canyon, listen to me. Find Scott and stay put!" Tony insisted.

"Too late, he's gone. And Scott might be dangerous," she said. "Tony, there's more."

"What? Is she hurt?"

Canyon shook her head, frustration building. "Tony, it's complicated. I promised Vanessa I wouldn't tell—"

"Canyon, dammit, tell me. Vanessa is out there alone in the jungle with Abruce, security guards in pursuit, and now you tell me Scott is dangerous?"

"OK, OK, fine. I found a VHS paused in your room. She witnessed a murder in New York, our senior year. Remember that spring break she dyed her hair and came back to school a vegan?"

"Of course I remember, but what does that have to do with what's going on *now*? And I know about the murder. I watched the tape."

"Did you know that she was being sought by police as a witness to her grandfather's murder? He was a Hasidic rabbi in Brooklyn. His murder was the act of antisemitics."

"Are you crazy? You must have misunderstood her." Tony insisted. "Her parents were from Ireland."

"Not parents, just *a* parent." Again Canyon looked out the window of the communication hut, scanning for approaching guards. "Her mother was Irish, but her father was a Hasidic Jew from Brooklyn. There was no inheritance. She grew up in the convent, alone, with no family. Tony, her mother abandoned her, and she's very much alive."

"Canyon, I don't follow. What are you talking about?"

"Never mind that. I found evidence in Scott's trailer. He might be the murderer."

"Murderer?"

"Vanessa's grandfather," she yelled. "The rabbi, from Brooklyn!"

"Canyon, promise me, you'll stay put. Lock up until I figure out what the hell is going on," Tony said. "We're still two hours out."

"Don't worry." Her voice was lost in the poor crackling connection.

Turning off the mic, she rushed back to her trailer. She needed a cover up for when Tony came to find her. Piling towels and clothing under her covers, she used a technique she and Vanessa had cooked up in their college years that had worked to fool the dorm resident advisor when they'd slipped out at night. Canyon felt foolish but she needed to buy time. It would work.

She grabbed the oversized flashlight from the desk. Stepping down out of the trailer, Canyon spotted young Abera sitting guard for her—a small substitute for Abruce. She took his hand, and he led her down toward the river to search for Vanessa.

She had to have gone this way. There was no way she'd climbed that vine-covered stone wall, Canyon thought.

They wound their way down a switchback path to navigate the steep mountainside and entered a cave. She spoke to Abera, as they went in the direction of the river's rushing sound, knowing he would have no idea what she said. "This is my first solo."

CHAPTER 37

TRANSFORMING THE ROCK

Vanessa

VANESSA TRIED TO remain calm. The confusion over Scott began to edge her into a panic, a feeling so foreign to her. She grappled with the impossible ease with which she'd found her criminal. Scott was delivered to her in the planet's farthest reaches, farther away than she would ever have dreamed to search.

Or was *she* delivered to him?

She followed Abruce with blind trust. The branches stung her face as she ran through the brush like a runner, chest first through the finish line. Then crazed with thoughts of her past, arms flailing in front of her, Vanessa followed the bouncing circle of light from her hardhat that shone on the intertwined trees. Unaware of the painful stings of the vines and branches, she pushed on. Time was blurred. Pictures moved swiftly through her mind: the sepia-colored, tick-ticking of the old film played back as she ran to exhaustion.

A raging fire consumed her body from the desperate run. Vanessa panted, trying to replace her depleted oxygen to clear her woozy head.

Vanessa, let's go, dear; he's gone, your father is gone, Mother Superior had whispered, lifting the lid to the piano from Vanessa's immobilized young hands.

She pictured her grandmother's suffering face that day. *She hadn't meant to slam it down on my hands, Mother Anne Marie.* Mother's gentle voice interrupted. *Oh darlin', she's suffering too. She wasn't in her right mind.* Then Fiona's voice invaded Vanessa's thoughts. *Are you ready for the note, my Colleen? Here it is, listen—it's coming, my dear one.*

"*Mother?*" Vanessa called out to each phantom pleadingly as her memories unraveled. Her body calmed; its sounds blended into the emerging night noises of the mountain. Blasting into the clearing behind Abruce, Vanessa fell, and the sound of her pounding heart replaced the ticking of the old film in her ears.

A WOMAN APPEARED as though on cue for a dramatic moment in a play. She extended her arm, reaching down to help Vanessa up from the cold ground. They silently stood suspended for minutes, a profound counterpoint to the intensity of the escape. She looked at Vanessa with recognition and said one word, "Van."

Vanessa was stunned.

Abruce drew in deep breaths. Tenderly pressing his head to the woman's forehead, his heaving shoulders quieted, and he began to calm.

"Your mother? This is Lukeem?"

"Yes, she is Ma."

The woman separated from Abruce, put her hand firmly on the crook of his neck, and indicated they should follow. Then she turned around and reconnected to Abruce's forehead for another moment. They breathed deeply, in and out, hands on each other's hearts in concert—a serene and silent moment amid the chaos and intensity.

A tradition, an instinct? Vanessa wondered. If only a person from her driven American culture would stop to take such a comforting pause in times of chaos. Their natural openness immediately made

Vanessa feel like she'd already known Lukeem. They were likely close to the same age, but Vanessa followed her like a child, shining the hardhat light ahead as they entered a cave.

With her body casting a liquid figure on the undulating walls inside, Lukeem introduced herself. "Lukeem." She placed her hand over Vanessa's heart.

"Van."

Lukeem awkwardly wrapped her voice around the strange name again. "Van."

Sitting on a rock shelf, Lukeem took a photo from her head bag—a Polaroid of Vanessa—the one Vanessa had given Abruce when they'd arrived on the mountain.

"Van Gold." Removing her head nets, Lukeem plumped them next to her and signaled to Vanessa to come closer.

Compelled by Lukeem's warm dark eyes, incapable of resisting, Vanessa lowered her weary body to the ground. Too exhausted to think, she followed her most basic instincts. Resting her head on the woman's rough, woven sack, Vanessa's breathing calmed and she hummed her mother's famous song and fell asleep to the stranger's gentle stroking of her hair.

ABRUCE AWAKENED Vanessa. He signaled that they needed to keep going. The circles of Abruce and Vanessa's headlights led the threesome to a corridor of twists and turns in a series of caves until they came to the end of the interior channel. There appeared to be no exit to the underground hideout.

Vanessa turned to Abruce questioningly.

"How do we get out?"

"Ma will find the way."

Lukeem pressed herself against the wall in front of her, and Abruce followed. Again, they shuffled sideways and disappeared into a crevice in the rock wall.

Vanessa mimicked their movements, and her body slid into the narrow gap. She could see a line of light not far off to her side. Continuing to pulse her way, flattened along the narrow opening, Vanessa arrived at the escape hatch to the underground route.

Standing straight and proud by the exit, Abruce was waiting to greet her as Vanessa emerged into the light.

The sound of rushing water welcomed them as they came into a clearing. Walking back to the edge of the brush, Abruce dropped onto the ground pushing his feet ahead of him as the vines and bushes seemed to swallow him. His urging finger pointed toward the water crossing as his arm disappeared under the greenery.

Vanessa kept her eye on the waterfall, as instructed.

Moments later, an arm pushed up out of the water just below the frightening drop where a small tree treacherously clung to the rocks. Waving a victorious hand to Vanessa, Abruce stuck his head out through the edge of the wall of water, grinning.

"Abruce!" Vanessa was stunned at the complexity of the subterranean aspect of the mountain.

He signaled for her to cross the rocky bridge.

Taking a quick breath, Vanessa cautiously tap-danced over the stones, stopping only to wave to Abruce who still peeked out from the rushing water below.

Lukeem had once again seemed to evaporate into the jungle.

Appearing on the other side seconds after Vanessa, Abruce glistened in the late light. Flipping his fingers through his hair, he shook off the excess water that beaded over the oily surface of his body. Quickly, he readjusted his nose bone and indicated they were ready to push onward.

Vanessa noticed a change in the way he carried his shoulders, as though the burden of his accusations had been erased. He held himself lighter, walking like a young boy. The waterfall had cleansed him of the challenge of the muddy underground, but Vanessa's clothes were damp and dirty. She put both hands to her face to wipe away the perspiration. The lingering scent of pig fat from Abruce's guiding hand overwhelmed her. The familiar odor remained near enough to her nose that it became a constant reminder of her predicament. She looked down at her hands streaked with both rusty dry blood and bright red reminders of the wicked branches that had stung her face and hands in their escape.

Vanessa sat on a rock, wet, shivering, bedraggled, and wondering where Lukeem had gone.

"Where does Lukeem go, Abruce?"

He dropped his chin to his chest. "She looks for a gathering." Taking Vanessa's hand in his, Abruce slowly turned it over to view her palm. He stared at the contrast between the top of his dark hand and hers, pale and pink. The expression on his face changed.

Vanessa stared into his dark eyes, searching for answers.

Abruce stood up abruptly, signaled for her to stay, and ran off, leaving a confused Vanessa behind.

Her intuition rooted in reading people's eyes, bodies, and actions for decades, her well-honed weapon forged from a lifetime of ferreting out the truth, told her that the young man could be trusted. Did he feel wounded, confused, and betrayed from his lockup? Trusting he would return, she sat patiently, shivering, and listening. Every crack of a branch, every sound in the dense green made her head snap in that direction fearing Scott had arrived.

IT WAS GETTING DARK when Abruce returned, winded, his woven head bag bulging. He held a large gourd of black gelatinous ooze. Vigorously, he rubbed a string and stick back and forth like an earnest cellist, and a blackening singe on the threads of dried vine caught fire as his delicate breaths fed the fragile embers. When the fire raged with the added branches, he warmed a substance over the flames, and it softened and liquefied.

Vanessa felt the chilling discomfort of her soiled and wet clothes. They had not held up well under the harsh regiment of their escape over the rugged mountain.

Abruce approached her, speaking with words she couldn't understand, interspersed with English that bore the suspicious lilt of Delilah's southern accent. His eyes were filled with a look of deep concern. He gestured from the woven head bag to Vanessa, softly repeating his words.

What was he trying to convey?

"Abruce change y'all."

"I don't understand." She felt she would never stop shivering.

He imitated her chills, holding his arms across his chest just as she was doing, vibrating his entire body while pointing to the net bag. Plucking at her soaked blouse, he tried to communicate with his English. "American clo-thez make y'all sick. Better, like this." He pointed to his oily skin.

Vanessa understood his meaning—he'd seen too many of the local tribal mine workers who'd agreed to wear the shirts and pants of the Americans, grow sick, and die. Brad had explained that well-kept corporate secret. With no habit of laundering, the over-worn clothes were a source of bacteria and illness.

Coming closer, Abruce kneeled in front of Vanessa. Tearing off a piece of roasted pork from the partial carcass he'd brought back with him, he offered it to her. Vanessa hesitated, but her hunger overcame her. She ate greedily, peeling the meat from the charred leathered skin dotted with tiny, singed hairs.

Abruce handed her a gourd of musty water, and she drank for the first time since their escape. They ate through smiles. The simple, familiar act of eating suddenly seemed like such a blessing to her. It was something the indigenous tribal people did whenever they had a food source and it was something scheduled for her three times a day that she tried to resist to keep her figure.

Wiping his grease-covered hands on his thighs, Abruce removed his head bag, arranged the strands in his hair with the excess oil, and shifted closer to Vanessa. Nothing was wasted.

He had a look and manner unlike any way he'd ever approached her before. Slowly, his rough hands extended to her throat. She sat stone still. He tilted his head and stared at the line of buttons that held the covering across her chest.

Inexperienced with clothing, the top button of her blouse proved difficult for his fingers. Considering the buttons once more, he reluctantly pulled at the first one.

Associations with that one gesture and his tender hesitation flooded up involuntarily from her past—memories of the anticipation, the excitement, and Tony—all inappropriate to the enigmatic exchange between Abruce and Vanessa. She brought herself back to focus on the moment.

Finally giving up, he signaled that she should take off her wet clothes and put on the things he had brought her.

"Y'all, better be me." He alternated pointing from her to himself. He smiled when Vanessa nodded that she finally understood.

She took the head bag full of things and walked into the small cave. With the hard hat in her hand, Vanessa signaled him with the headlight to sit on the opposite side of the rocks.

Abruce followed, then guided her back out into the twilight to make use of the natural light. He gestured for her to undress with his clear eyes and a tug of her sleeve.

Vanessa held her breath. Her trust in Abruce was intuitive and deep after all they had been through together. Still, she was suddenly aware of the vast space and time that separated their lives and experience. Vanessa knew so little about his culture and ways that it seemed bizarre, even to a worldly person like herself.

Vanessa thought she understood that he wanted her to look like a tribal woman, to fit in—a stroke of genius that might just save them all. She gestured, twirling her finger in a spiral motion signaling him to face away from her. "Please turn around, Abruce."

He hesitated, and then spun around full circle to face her again.

She laughed at her failure to communicate her cultural norm of modesty.

Conflicting feelings came over her as he tried to help remove her wet clothes. Vanessa stretched them out to dry on the side of the cave. Finally, left exposed, wearing only bikini bottoms, she resisted her impulse to fold her arms around herself. She needed time to process the strange place in which her emotions hung, suspended between her culture and his, balanced precariously between her intellect and her instincts. She needed to distract herself and buy time to assess. Peeling open the package of leaves Abruce had given her, Vanessa ate the warm sweet paste inside.

Abruce removed the gourd from the fire. Inside the vessel was the steaming gelatinous fat he used to protect his own body, the source of the glistening effect on his skin. Vanessa was getting used to the all too familiar smoked bacon scent that permeated the mine site.

Taking a handful of the dripping fat, Abruce began at her shoulders, then covered Vanessa's back with a thick warm layer of charred camouflage.

The spread of warmth resurrected a deeply buried memory of a day at Coney Island. Her mother's hands had spread the oily protection over Vanessa's ivory skin. Her long elegant fingers touched her face tenderly. Her thumbs ran a swath of white shine across the fragile skin beneath her eyes.

Vanessa was pulled into an ebb and flow of emotions as he smoothed the transforming thick, blackened oil over her body. Her mind changed perspectives, searching the norms of his culture and hers, riding a series of crashing waves of clarity and confusion. She struggled to understand from his viewpoint and from hers. It was beyond conversation. Vanessa's years of balancing on the razor's edge, where clashing cultures met, made her postpone judgment. Having learned to cast off her own cultural veil, made her more comfortable in the confusing space between them. But she became unsettled when he reached her breasts.

Abruce stared at them with an enigmatic look, perhaps sadness, she thought. His eyes grew moist. He smeared the protection over her chest, and she pulled back slightly, her face raging with the heat of embarrassment born of her own world. Vanessa fought to keep her perception out of the equation. She resisted the emerging thoughts that fought to contaminate her well-honed intuition.

He continued matter-of-factly, as he had with every other part of her body.

Feeling more confident in her insight, she eased a little. But knowing his actions were innocent, and fully breaking out of her life-long enculturation, were two different things. She understood that the nourishing body parts had remained in the open, exposed to Abruce his entire life. Whereas in her own culture, breasts were paid homage with bizarre games of peek-a-boo—too absurd a role.

There was a tenderness that she'd longed for in the care he was giving her. It was nurturing, and the intimacy that rode the most delicate line between erotic and innocent, between her world and his, could not be denied nor defined. For all her worldliness, she'd never experienced anything remotely like the feeling she had at that moment—an act with no hidden agenda, no self-consciousness, an act of pure humanity. Vanessa took a deep, relaxing breath, and in that poignant moment, she opted for the freedom of non-judgment. She decided to trust.

Letting out her breath, Vanessa helped Abruce spread the grease and black soot over her arms and legs. Finally, they reached her face. Except for her soft green eyes, she imagined that she'd been rendered unrecognizable, and acceptable. At least from a distance, she wouldn't draw the attention of tribal people; she would fit in.

The layer of warmth felt good in the chilly mist of the mountain air. Vanessa removed the gold clip she'd used to keep her hair piled stylishly on her head. Her hair cascaded over her shoulders, and she slipped the clip into her woven sack.

Abruce deftly and patiently work the fat through her hair, separating it into a hundred twisted strands. He patted ashes into the red roots that accented her scalp—the only imperfection in his handiwork. Pulling each section forward from her crown to her forehead, Abruce completed the transformation. Who would have expected a salon treatment in the Irian Jaya jungle? Vanessa smiled.

She had no mirror and no need for one. In her revealed state, she felt a safety she'd never known in her perfect world. Vanessa felt surprisingly warm, and that was all she cared about at the moment.

Abruce tied a string of cowry shells around Vanessa's neck as she tied the crude grass and shredded plant skirt over her waist.

Although it provided little extra protection from the cold, Vanessa was relieved to be partially covered.

Reaching over his head, Abruce transferred one of his three net bags to her head to finish the job.

Letting a long breath escape slowly, Vanessa cleared the last of the tension silently built through her transformation. She'd willingly given up her damaged identity to her new world. She'd freely cast off the disguises of perfection she had constructed over the years—the perfect smile, the perfect words, the perfect posture—revealing her hidden self. The glint of her Rolex watch was the only remnant of her former life.

The space between our cultures is immeasurable, Vanessa thought, a young man living a rare Stone Age existence, a world-renowned modern '90s woman from LA. She imagined the headlines her culture would create if they saw this scene. Their lives were as different as any humans on earth could possibly be. Abruce crossing glaciers barefoot, hunting food with crude weapons, only smears of pig fat protecting his glistening, ebony flesh; Vanessa driving in the back seat of her limo through a city of lights, world fame, silk slacks, and fine dining. *Him* relaxed and smiling, *her* on high alert.

Her eyes fixed on the long, hollow gourd tied around his waist with twine, extending two feet from his torso, covering his privates. Canyon had provided the critical key—Abruce's distinguishing corkscrew twists at its end identified his tribe. As Vanessa grasped Abruce's extended hand, her fingers brushed the bizarre projectile, an experience no longer beyond her comfort zone.

When they reached an expansive view at the cliff's edge, Abruce signaled for Vanessa to sit. The cool fog wisped in around them, pushing the hot day skyward. As they watched the shards of sun slice down the cliff and disappear in a blink, darkness settled in.

Perched on the precipice together, Vanessa didn't feel like a world-renowned, intercultural investigative reporter, but more like an unschooled, in-over-her-head American on a foreign assignment beyond her understanding. She'd never experienced any feeling like being with Abruce. They were *being* together with no social agenda, no time-watching, no judgment—nothing to interfere with the peace she felt while overlooking the vast view. She laughed to think that she was sitting with a young man, naked—his tribal women's norm—and he'd made no notice.

Amidst caws, cackles, hisses, the whining wind splitting around the rocky outcropping, and canopy branches snapping above from unseen creatures, Vanessa and Abruce took in the natural spectacle. The waterfall shared its thundering voice off in the darkness as they shared a fragile, palpable moment of connection. She was afraid to breathe, afraid to break the spell.

He touched her hair. She fingered his shell necklace—all intimate yet somehow not invasive. No conversation ensued. She would never be able to convey the feeling she experienced the moment her walls came down. The two of them were simply communing, being more human than she'd ever been before, more human than she'd known she *could* be.

Sitting inches apart on the edge of the earth, the space between them was as distant as the moon that hung nearly full against a jungle blackout sky, yet as close as the breaths they drew, she thought. There were no lights of modern man to interfere as darkness dropped over them, and the majesty was unveiled. She couldn't bear to leave the magnificent overlook.

Forty-years old, she'd never seen stars like those until that day, Vanessa thought. Not in LA, where fireflies gave off no more glimmer than the splatter of dim dots in the sky, where ambient city lights swallowed any hope of "star-light, star-bright".

To Abruce, it was a common sight, these spectacular stars against a black sky. Not like the illuminants emanating from bridges, streetcars, and buildings, twinkling only with the excitement of Vanessa's sprawling city life.

Not until she was suspended ten thousand feet up on a mountain ledge did she see real stars. Mother Nature had no competition in the primeval place; only a sprinkle of man-made campfires flickered on her organza gown of green across the valley.

Amidst the jungle sounds, looking skyward with childlike amazement, Vanessa and Abruce watched the brilliant cutouts in the inky sky gather into tribes of twinkling constellations. In the darkest of darkness, after the sun had slipped behind the craggy mountains, billions of stars shone down on them. No wonder his tribe saw nature as their powerful spirits, she thought. For the first time, Vanessa felt at one with the natural world, as nature blinked open her electrifying eyes.

It was a rare and genuine moment of connection—beyond Abruce's nakedness, her color, his ways, her thoughts—being a *part of* not *apart from* nature.

Abruce hung his head. Vanessa couldn't read the pain reflected in his face. He put his head in his hands, shoulders heaving up and down. "No mate. Ma wants Abruce to have mate."

Lamenting his lack of connection, Abruce cried with heartfelt emotion, the streams of tears trailing down his glistening face. Squinting more tears onto his slick chest with his sorrow flowing.

Vanessa inched forward. She put her hands on his forearms, touched her forehead to his, and held tight to comfort him. Looking deep into his unembarrassed eyes, she wiped his tears.

He answered her searching eyes with a long string of unfathomable words, connecting with her at a level of communication beyond spoken language. The intimacy exposed a blossom of openness in her well-protected heart, rendering her feeling comfortable in the nakedness of her own emotional vulnerability for the first time she could remember.

ABRUCE BUILT A FIRE. Then they sat beside each other in silence, waiting for Lukeem.

Once again, she appeared out of the darkening mist. How had she found them time and again? She whispered to Abruce, and he translated.

"Ma says you need power of sky spirits."

Taking a finger full of the ashen disguise from Abruce's head bag, Lukeem squatted down and wiped a wide, even darker stripe under Vanessa's eyes with her two thumbs. She repeated the face painting on Abruce.

Vanessa wondered at the tradition's meaning. Was it empowerment for whatever was ahead? She was so far out of her element, yet she was more at ease than she'd ever been.

Drawing a Sports Illustrated magazine out of her bag, in the flickering light, Lukeem pointed to the cover photo of an NFL player with two streaks of black grease under his eyes.

Letting out a long breath, Vanessa laughed. More missing magazines, she thought. Vanessa spied Lukeem's stash in her open head bag—magazines and limes. Selecting another publication, Lukeem handed it to Vanessa. Her face was on the cover.

Choosing another, Lukeem held it up. Fiona O'Farrell, Woman of the Year. She smiled and touched each face. Her gesture sent a wave of chills down Vanessa's arms. "What would I do if you didn't speak some English, Abruce?" It was a blessing, she thought.

"Missionary teaches English, Mrs. Jenkinsen talk, Abruce listen. I learn English y'all."

Vanessa's head was spinning with the number of cultural differences. What misinterpretations was she making since she'd arrived?

"Lukeem says wait, not good." Struggling with the words, Abruce tried to convey his mother's intent as Lukeem stepped behind a thicket nearby.

"What's wrong?" A rush of concern moved through Vanessa, and her calm dissipated with his furrowed brow. Did she offend in some way?

"Ma says careful, a man follows us. We go to mating ceremony now. Sorry, you, not good." Abruce apologized, drawing an imaginary line with his finger from her head to her feet.

Lukeem stepped out from behind the greenery wearing Vanessa' slacks and blouse she had taken from Abruce's bag. The clothes hung perfectly on her lean body. Imitating Vanessa's sophisticated upright and controlled gait, Lukeem strutted back and forth. Then, in contrast, she walked with flayed feet, testing the earth, heel-toe, heel-toe, making Vanessa's usual disconnect with the earth very clear.

Imitating Lukeem, like Eliza Doolittle, Vanessa took part in the reverse Pygmalion lesson. It gave her a much-needed moment of comic relief. They repeated the practice before the blazing fire until Lukeem and Abruce nodded to affirm Vanessa had it. Safe in her new Stone Age state, Vanessa followed Abruce and his mother.

They walked through the jungle path—three identical tribe members in a row.

CHAPTER 38

BROKEN PATTERNS

Tony

"TONY, SORRY WE HAVE to wait until morning for the search. I hope you understand. There is nothing useful we can do at night. They could have gone in a hundred directions." Brad turned off the engine, and the pulse of the rotors slowed. "We'll be up there first thing, I promise. Meet me here at dawn. And John told Canyon you'd meet her at her trailer. No need to go to the communications office."

"Got it. Thanks, Brad." Tony walked back to their trailer. He was frustrated by Brad's words but knew he was right. Stopping next door to find Canyon, he knocked. No answer. The unlocked door creaked open. "*Canyon*?" Tony sighed with relief to see her safely tucked into bed. "Canyon, it's me, Tony." Something made him uncomfortable. It was too early for night-owl Canyon to be in bed.

Leaning over, he nudged her. They needed to talk. No, *he* needed to talk. His hand collapsed into the piles of clothes she used to create the illusion that she was safely tucked in for the night. She was gone. Where the hell was she?

Muttering, he returned to his own trailer. Pacing back and forth in the small tin space, Tony knew his only choice was to get some sleep to prepare for what he knew would be a harrowing next day.

He eyed the video player next to the other twin bed, sat down, and pushed *play*. The specs and lint gave way to the click-clicking of scenes in the old Jewish section of Brooklyn. The video brought Tony to his feet. What more could he learn from watching this again?

The soundless scene was haunting—the glimpse of the scissors in the boy's hand, the boy cutting the lock of hair away, the helpless gesture as the old man silently pleaded with the boy, the shaking of the wrinkled hands in a pattern that eerily matched the passing of the frames one by one. Still the camera moved in and out of focus, wobbling, as it searched for the body. What were you thinking, Van? Why hadn't she helped the old man? Why hadn't she come forward to the police? This wasn't the passionate Vanessa he knew. Tony wanted to shut the recording off, but his life's work and his desire to understand the woman he'd loved for twenty years spurred him on.

The eye of the voyeur lingered with fascination just seconds too long before the camera's line of sight dropped low, continuing the story from a bizarre oblique angle, capturing the rocking motion of the old man's shoe. As Tony watched Vanessa's haunt—he began to understand the worst moment in his love's life, her torture that kept her from living in the present with him. It was the key to the mysterious part of Van he had rocked and soothed but could neither erase nor quite comprehend. He imagined the old film hiding in their home and Vanessa's mind for two decades.

"Who are you, Vanessa?" Tony's voice was hoarse as he whispered in shock, watching the final scenes of the young boy panicking and running away with the swastika on the back of his head.

Now Tony understood—in those few lingering seconds of filming, the true motive of the perpetrator had transformed from Vanessa's passionately sought-after, award-winning footage on culture into her lifetime guilt. Tony understood Vanessa's inner torture for the first time. The way she'd stopped his filming just before its violent endpoint—her signature style that had become world-renowned. He considered Van's complexity. The times Vanessa yelled, "Cut, Tony, that's enough!" in conflict with his almost insane push to capture any atrocity, to expose any wrong, now made sense.

He'd seen enough to know Vanessa could have stopped the boy. She could have prevented the mistake that had held her captive for all her adult years. "My God, Vanessa," Tony whispered.

Tony's emotions waffled between compassion for his lover and deep hurt. Or was it anger that sat burning in his gut? She'd kept her secrets from him, hadn't trusted him—broadcasting the search for the boy every April 30th for all these years.

Was there anything real between them?

AWAKING FROM HIS restless night, still fully dressed, Tony splashed water on his face and ran both hands through his hair.

The situation's reality crashed in around him, and he found himself standing at the door, still in a daze and half asleep. He didn't allow his thoughts to go too far. Stay in the moment, just stay in the moment, or you won't be any good to them, he counseled himself. He took one last look in the mirror and encouraged himself, she'll be OK.

Leaving the trailer, Tony rushed out to meet Brad and begin the search, muttering, "Those two women *never* listen."

Brad tossed a duffel bag behind the seat. He too had on the same flannel shirt he had worn the day before. That must be because of Canyon, Tony thought. He had found Brad last night and informed him of Canyon's ploy in her trailer. Neither of them had been happy with her stunt.

"OK, Tony, let's find them." Brad kicked on the engine. "Only God knows where they are, but let's just go. I have a few ideas." They took off at a slant in the helicopter.

"I have a bigger question," Tony said.

"What's that?"

"Who are we going to look for first, Canyon, Scott, or Abruce and Vanessa?"

"I'd say Vanessa. Do you have any idea what made her go off with him, Tony?"

Tony reviewed the horrid old film in his mind. "Pretty sure twenty-some years of torture did it. There's a lot I don't know, Brad." As they climbed in altitude, Tony related more of Vanessa's past to Brad and the details of the story of the boy who had killed the rabbi. "It seems the woman I have spent the last twenty years with is suddenly someone else. But now that I think of it, she always has been."

"Like I said, nearly everyone up here is someone else, Tony."

"My Irish redhead, the Queen of Truth in News, is half Hasidic Jew and a witness on the lamb! She watched her own grandfather die. This has got to be the punchline to some outrageous cosmic joke."

Scanning the ground, they spoke above the engine noise.

"She doesn't know who did it?" Brad turned to Tony for an answer.

"No. At least, I don't think so. But I'm not sure of anything anymore. Scott plays into this somehow."

"Tony, you don't think Abruce is capable of hurting Vanessa?"

"That's something I've been struggling with. In my gut, I don't feel he is. The culture is still foreign to me. Let's face it. I don't think anyone can bridge this culture gap."

"I've never seen a violent impulse from Abruce since I first met him," Brad said. "OK, Tony, knowing Vanessa, where would she be headed?"

Tony put his face in one hand for a second. "Where the drama is—she would try to find the woman before the sacrifice."

"Let's check it out. I'll take the long route along the other side of the mountain and follow the river." Brad dropped the helicopter at a sharp angle and slid sideways toward the mountain's north side. "Tony, I'm supposed to be a dropout. You know . . . no responsibilities, only peace and quiet."

Tony shared his complaint. "Yeah, I knew I'd signed up for this supporting role the minute she said, 'I love you'. For this woman of mine, I thought I could do that." Tony sighed. "She has a strong hold on me. Honestly, lately, I sometimes wish she didn't."

Brad smiled and shook his head at Tony. "I get that."

They continued the search in silence, crisscrossing over the mountainside. Tony's anxiety led to reviewing scenes of Vanessa and himself over the twenty years they had been together. He loved her, but there was a bitter edge to the blurred memories.

"You OK, buddy? Don't know how much longer I can watch you grind through whatever memories you're excavating that put that look on your face."

"Brad, has it helped?" Tony looked out the window, avoiding eye-contact. "I mean, being a dropout—up here all alone, isolated?"

"Not really. That's why I had to send those photographs and the truth to Vanessa to redeem myself somehow. I guess we all want different things in life. It's ironic."

"No offense, Brad, but if I had a little daughter somewhere like you do, I wouldn't be here, that's for sure," Tony said. "I'm desperate for a daughter, and her future mother is wandering around a wild mountain saving some Stone Age woman from a human sacrifice. Who could even make that up? Before we left the States, Vanessa mentioned getting married after we had a conflict over starting a family. I think she was just stalling the kid thing." Tony watched Brad slip into the silence of his own thoughts, and the flutter of the rotors overhead drew him into more memories of his past too.

Tilting the helicopter, Brad followed the river that curved around the other side of one of the three mountains that formed the mine site valley for a few more minutes. "Tony! Look down. On the edge of the river at three o'clock."

CHAPTER 39

INSTANT COMMITMENT

Vanessa

ABRUCE AND VANESSA followed Lukeem with difficulty. She had a sudden purposefulness that gave her an energy level that seemed impossible after a long day of moving through the jungle. Vanessa had relived her pain with this stranger, and instinctively trusted her. There was clearly something only the native woman could see that gave her a mysterious single-mindedness and determination. Lukeem's feet moved over the rough terrain like a young warrior.

After traveling through the thick jungle for what felt like hours, Vanessa heard faint chanting off in the distance. Following the swelling sounds, they positioned themselves by a thick bush and then dropped down to observe a group of natives engaged in a ceremony. "Abruce, what's happening?"

"Big moon. Four times between rainy seasons. Everyone coming together in many places. These people speak our way, but not our tribe." He made a gesture with fingers flayed, then he folded them in joining both hands. "Finding mates. Ma find Abruce a mate in other tribes, speak same but different."

"So no one here knows you and Lukeem?"

Abruce scanned the faces. "Not our tribe."

This was what Lukeem was searching for when she left us for hours at a time, Vanessa thought—a moon ceremony for Abruce to find a mate from outside his tribe who could speak his language. Of course, what woman in his tribe would want a mate who was the son of a sorceress. Vanessa's attention was riveted on the fascinating scene in front of her. It was an advantage that Vanessa could blend in disguised as a tribal woman. The appearance of a woman sky spirit at this event would surely have interrupted Lukeem's plan.

The men were singing on one side of a large, blazing fire. And the women sat on the other side, sharing looks of amusement, shyness, and attraction for the crooning men. One man came forward and began to sing his heart out to his chosen woman. A stuttering chant, with more rhythm than tune. She turned her back, snubbing him. He continued singing. She rebuffed him again with a quick flirtatious glance over her shoulder. He sang more yearning verses. The nubile young woman turned her body slightly toward him, urged forcefully by another older female. She handed him a small package. The man considered the gift for a few moments, then he smiled. A clear victory, an instant decision.

"What does it mean, Abruce?"

"She now his mate." A look crossed Abruce's face. Disappointment? Sadness? What was it?

Vanessa was amazed at the pattern of courtship. The same emotions were happening worldwide every day, but the rituals in each culture were so different. In her world, Vanessa thought, they were complex in comparison. She watched as the prolonged courtship of her own culture was minimized into a few brief moments in the tribal cere-mony. Fueled by the chemistry and passion of an instinct trusted, the mating ritual collapsed to meet the uncompromising demands of the imminent full moon.

Tony, I'm sorry. I could never be spontaneous like that, she thought.

One after another, for an interminable time, the singers wooed their prospective mates. Deliveries of intentions marked by arrogance, heartfelt aching, or shyness were answered with pride, coyness, and confidence as the men and women played out their individuality in the courtship ceremony.

Vanessa recalled the pages of Father Carey's orientation book. No description could ever have captured the feelings she was having now, witnessing the emotions of the most intimate moments of a person's life exposed for the entire community to share. Their excitement and passion were palpable. She watched Abruce's sad face, fascinated by his openness in crying silently in front of her. How old are you, my friend? Vanessa wondered as she considered his personal life. Vanessa looked directly into his watery eyes. "I see you as a real person. I know you are sad that you tend flowers and plants, as only a woman in your culture would do. I know you feel guilty about deserting your mother." Vanessa understood he wouldn't fully comprehend her words.

"Ma sees my eyes. I see you."

Vanessa wondered at his words—were they simple or profound?

They continued to observe the ceremony. Coy women brought more small gifts to the men whom they found attractive. Men were accepted or rejected after performing their best skill: shooting arrows, jumping, feats of strength, and singing with gusto.

Observing his mother, Abruce seemed nervous.

Vanessa realized the significance. "Abruce, your tribe will be looking for Lukeem. And the local mining tribes too. We have to get her out of here," Vanessa gestured to complement her words.

He nodded.

Lukeem pointed to Abruce, enmeshing her lean fingers, and folding her hands together, signifying a union. Lukeem spoke in her tribal language with a tone of sincerity.

"Ma wants Abruce to have mate. Abruce wants too."

Vanessa's eyes flickered with concentration. Lukeem nodded, insisting that they stay.

"Boss never let Abruce to go mating ceremony."

"Quickly, Abruce." Vanessa removed the bag from his head, examined the contents and pulled out a colorful Cassowary bird feather he'd found that day. She handed him three limes and stuck the feather in his hair.

"Which one do you like, that one?"

They reviewed the remaining candidates for his match. The process made Vanessa uncomfortable. Selecting his mate as though he were choosing the perfect apple in a supermarket.

Abruce smiled, pointing to a woman who stood shyly on the outskirts of the group. She had a half-moon pink area of missing pigment on her breast and a sweet countenance.

Lukeem spoke and touched Abruce's face.

He translated for Vanessa. "Ma says, this woman different too. Like Ma. White moon on chest may be message from sky spirits."

Vanessa took his signature nose bone from his face, slid her gold hairclip in its place, added her Rolex to his shell necklace, and pushed him out into the clearing.

Abruce approached the woman and smiled.

She turned a coy shoulder.

He began to juggle with precision as he had learned from Canyon on the first day they'd arrived. Who would have thought his new juggling skill would be the key to his love life?

Vanessa bit her lip to repress both a laugh and her tears as the group went silent with amazement.

All of the women gathered around Abruce, clearly entranced. "Ooooooo!" Several women offered gifts to him, wearing smug smiles, pushing the blemished woman aside. Did they feel that the woman with the moon-shaped missing pigment marring her looks couldn't compete with them?

Moving through the group, Abruce faced the original woman of his choice. She smiled, then snaked her arms around her chest. To hide her shameful difference, perhaps?

Lit by the glowing fire, he stepped closer, juggling in front of her.

The group's chants went quiet. The prospective mate hesitantly handed him a simple woven armband, and he accepted. Placing her hand over her heart, she shared her name. "Noat."

Vanessa twisted the woven ring on her finger that Tony had given her at the mining site. Why couldn't she be as spontaneous with a man she'd been with since she was a teen?

Closing her eyes and nodding her head, Lukeem began to hum, and a lightning insect appeared. Reaching out to Abruce's new mate, Lukeem raised the young woman's hand and summoned the creature to land on Noat's finger.

The tribe quieted. "Ahhh!" They seemed astounded by the magic as the iridescent flying insect lit on Noat's index finger.

Vanessa shook her head. How little it takes to change the crowd's perception.

They surrounded Noat and began chanting and jumping up and down in a circular dance of acceptance.

"Yes!" Vanessa cheered Abruce's victory, her voice echoing across the village gathering.

CHAPTER 40

REVERSING PERSPECTIVE

Vanessa

SQUATTING ON THE edge of the ceremonial fire, Vanessa was shocked to see Scott leap off the rocks and run toward them.

"Vanessa! Stop! Dammit!" Scott yelled, "Wait!"

The security guards and a group of angry *others* arrived, along with Lukeem's tribesmen. They threw stones and water into the fire, raising a camouflage of flying embers and a cloud of smoke for a distraction. The people at the mating ceremony scattered in all directions.

Vanessa lost sight of Scott in the mayhem. Shots from the security guards flew by them along with arrows from the natives.

Abruce looked back at Vanessa and his mother. He reluctantly ran from his confused, newly betrothed young woman to join them. His face revealed his emotions as he seemed to call out words that ached with regret and promises over his shoulder to Noat. His tone spoke to Vanessa beyond his foreign words.

Reaching toward Abruce with her arms held high, Noat called his name and took a few steps.

"Abruce, go back for her." Vanessa waved him back to Noat.

Lukeem turned to submit to the tribe.

Vanessa understood she wanted to complete the sacrifice for the good of her tribe and to restore Abruce's place with his people.

Abruce motioned Noat to come to him. Grasping her hand, he ran toward his mother. "No, Ma, no."

"No, Lukeem, the suffering is not your fault." Vanessa's scream was hoarse from the smoke in the air. "Abruce *tell* her. The animals leaving was not her doing. The sky spirits have returned." Vanessa understood the guilt Lukeem must have with the memory of the suffering village in her heart. The photos of children with bloated bellies that Father Carey had shared with Tony were scenes Vanessa would never forget. "Please, Lukeem, go! Please, run! Don't do this. We'll find a way." Vanessa begged and pulled at Lukeem's arm with the sounds of the security guards closing in. How could she explain to Lukeem that modern technology had caused the food source to disappear? "Abruce, tell her it's not her fault."

Lukeem hesitated behind a massive tree. She listened to her son's pleading words, studied his loving face, and reluctantly agreed. They escaped into the dense greenery on the opposite edge of the encampment. The moon was a sliver shy of full. "We only have one more night until the full moon ceremony. We need to get Lukeem out of here!" Vanessa warned Abruce, pointing at the moon.

Loud voices exploded as a group of tribal hunters sighted them.

Lukeem entered a passage of trees that dead-ended at a waterfall. As the voices got closer, Vanessa knew they had no escape route.

Abruce spotted something and ran to the brush. He pulled out three segments of a metal mining shoot that must have been leftover from the early years of contruction. Abruce snapped them together and pushed the long semicircular section up onto the rock ledge at the waterfall's edge. He signaled to Vanessa to sit. With faith, Vanessa squatted on the makeshift boat holding onto Lukeem, who had her arms wrapped around Abruce's frightened new mate.

Abruce shoved off directly into the powerful crashing water. Like a treacherous luge ride, he jumped on the end of the tube behind Vanessa, and they passed into the thundering cave. Driving through the water into a tubular cavern half-full of rushing water, they twisted and turned, the clatter of their metal make-shift boat against the stone walls echoed through the cave.

Holding her head bag with kindling and clothing over her head, Vanessa struggled to keep it dry. Abruce, Lukeem, and Noat tucked in their arms to avoid the shards of rock that scraped at the sides of their half-moon raft until the four of them were dumped into a cave pool. Vanessa managed to keep the kindling dry.

Hidden among the rocks along the pool's edge, Abruce deftly made a fire, rotating a string around a stick he had in his head bag.

When the fire flared, Lukeem boiled a potion for Vanessa and Noat.

Vanessa sniffed and sipped the brew cautiously. "The tea bags! Constant Comment." She watched Noat experience the sweet beverage foreign to her. Innocently, Lukeem showed Vanessa the box of teabags. Then she signaled for her to rest.

"I'm fine. You rest, Lukeem." Vanessa motioned for Lukeem to sleep. "Abruce, can you translate?"

Lukeem shook her head slowly, looked into Vanessa's eyes with a compelling kindness, and placed her hand firmly on her shoulder. Her eyes closed, and after a moment of quiet, a gentle, calming energy flowed through Vanessa.

While tapping her fingers on her knee, Lukeem began to hum.

What was happening? A chill traveled down Vanessa's spine, and she gave way to the exhaustion coursing through her. She drifted off as Lukeem squatted beside her humming Fiona's song, "Rise to Be You". Had Lukeem memorized the melody from Vanessa's constant murmurs on their treacherous escape together? Over her shoulder Vanessa watched Abruce wrap his arms around Noat, rocking her to the rhythm of Lukeem's humming.

AWAKENING, VANESSA felt the pressure of the full moon's timing. "Lukeem, please, we have to go! We should go back to the mining site. Tell her, Abruce." Vanessa insisted again, looking from Abruce to Lukeem. She needed Canyon and Tony's support.

They left the protection of the cave. Vanessa wanted to find the tram to descend the mountain.

After a few hundred yards pushing through the denseness in the dim, pre-dawn light, a loud male voice broke the morning silence. Lukeem's eyes opened wide with recognition at the sound. A second voice responded.

"Kralu." Lukeem signaled to Vanessa. There was no question. She wanted Vanessa to take cover, but where? Used to taking control in most situations, Vanessa had relinquished herself to the woman for the entire previous day. After running like a deer in several directions for a few hesitant steps, Vanessa froze.

Lukeem tried to separate from Vanessa, then grabbed her by the arm, and pulled her off the path into the tall brush. Vanessa felt the burn as the first arrow brushed along her arm.

"Oh my God!" Vanessa rubbed her hand over the near hit on her left arm. It jolted her into flight and awakened her to the need to be responsible for her own escape and not depend on Lukeem.

The tribesmen's words were foreign, but the tone was universal.

Vanessa knew why the two men were after Lukeem. Abruce pushed them ahead, and they ran, stumbling, and shifting in different directions to confuse their trackers.

Lukeem, we need another of your secret caves, a secret entrance to somewhere safe, Vanessa thought, praying for a miracle.

The voices behind them were violent and determined. It was amazing that they had not yet been caught.

They climbed up the side of a huge rock with only seconds to spare as the men passed directly underneath them.

No wonder, Vanessa thought, observing the withered natives below her. They were weak and slow from the lack of food. She tried to calm her breathing, but her exhaustion gave their location away. The men drew their bows pointing up toward Vanessa and Lukeem, demanding that they drop down off their perch.

Vanessa focused, assessing her options. Then she saw the more fearful enemy. On the opposite side of the clearing, an agitated group of men tended a roaring fire, chanting words that Vanessa knew held their fates. They raised the red-hot metal rods up over their heads, pumping their arms, stabbing them to the sky, as the pace of their chants accelerated. The innocent threaded rods, meant only to hold the soil back in the mining tunnels, were clearly to be repurposed for some torturous ritual.

The crowd was growing. Women and children's faces glowed, fascinated with the tools of torture that became deadlier, reddening ever brighter in the fire. How could this ritual have become such a spectacle for a community of people? Shivers rushed through Vanessa's body. How different the mining tribes were from Lukeem and Abruce's tribe.

The stones crumbled under their heels as Vanessa and Lukeem slid helplessly down the side of the elevated rock wall and were delivered to the ground at the bare feet of the men.

Looking up from the ground at Lukeem's wiry tribesmen, Vanessa was saddened by the sight of their powerful kotekas fastened to their wrinkled waists. Her compassion was only fleeting when she saw the looks of hatred on their faces as they spoke to Lukeem. One of the men roughly took Vanessa and Lukeem by the arm, and the rest of the tribesmen kept their arrows cocked and pointed at them.

Abruce yelled at the man.

Was that his father, Kralu, Vanessa wondered? She struggled to escape the mob. The second group of men approached with gruesome, chalky painted faces, intensely arguing with Lukeem's tribesmen.

They moved quickly, shoving Vanessa and Lukeem down the path.

It was clear the rituals in each of the tribe's traditions were in conflict. One required the long-suffering of the victim but with the possibility for survival, forever haunted by the torturous memory and the unbearable scars, and the other, certain death from a slow drift to the rocks and rushing water of the Ranu Lolo river far below.

The argument ensued, each group's honored one intent on winning the prize, as Abruce translated.

Holding onto Lukeem, Vanessa moved toward the precipice, assisting in the choice of their demise. Would they sacrifice her, as well?

The earth dropped off immeasurably. A smooth surface where a waterfall had once thundered was the obvious place they'd planned to use for their fateful fall.

Focusing, Vanessa sought an escape route. To their left, a high rock wall was topped with trees like decorations on a model train town. To their right, a small path led away from the treacherous drop. While the old men screamed and argued uselessly in words the other tribal group couldn't understand, Vanessa considered her final moments. Tony, I'm so sorry. Dear God, please help me. She prayed for the first time since she had knelt with Mother Superior in her last hour. A sound interrupted her prayers, and a figure swept down from above, knocking over several of the weak and distracted men. The arguing and chanting stopped.

Over her shoulder, Vanessa saw him as Lukeem's tribesmen all dropped to the ground at the sight of Scott.

"Abruce, help!" Vanessa screamed, and in a panic, pulled Lukeem down the path away from Scott. Her call for help echoed in the abyss, fading farther and farther away.

Scott's heavy footsteps were close behind them.

"Vanessa! Stop, dammit!" Scott shouted.

Struggling, Vanessa carried Lukeem, thrusting her ahead to escape the hateful man who had murdered her grandfather. Vanessa felt the arrow slide by her left ear, past her head. From the bizarre close perspective of her left eye, it appeared to emerge from her own skull before it embedded in Lukeem's shoulder.

Weakened, Lukeem ran on despite the hit, and they broke into another clearing.

The open space made them an easy target. Vanessa pulled Lukeem away and ran along the edge of the sheer rock walls. She tried not to look down at the impossibly distant river.

Scott roared toward them.

"No, Scott!" Vanessa screamed. Then it was over.

His strong hand closed around Vanessa's arm just above the elbow. Dragging her forward a few steps, away from the edge of the cliffs, Scott caught up to the exhausted Lukeem. He threw Vanessa down to the ground and straddled her between his legs to free both his hands. Quickly, he broke the long arrow off in Lukeem's shoulder, leaving only a short stub. Then he pulled Vanessa to her feet and swiftly supported Lukeem, featherlike, under his other arm. Running in a random pattern across the open space, he deftly dodged the arrows shot by the weak warriors.

Vanessa pulled against him, but he was too powerful to stop.

"Don't fight me!"

She shuddered at the thought of him participating in the ritual, throwing the loving woman into the river. Vanessa pulled at him violently again.

"Stop resisting. Do you want to die, right here? They'll torture you both." Scott's husky voice threatened. "Vanessa!" He growled as one of the arrows grazed his calf. He reached around stopping only for an instant to pull out the long thin arrow that had superficially embedded in his flesh. He looked around to get his bearings.

Lukeem pointed.

Scott shoved Vanessa toward the thick bushes, which opened into a slightly smaller clearing.

Another magnificent waterfall thundered and hissed before them.

The system of caves and falls had ceased to surprise Vanessa. She felt helpless watching Scott drag Lukeem toward the turbulent water.

Vanessa held her breath as he strong-armed her into a space beside the booming wall of water. Stunned by the reality of her imminent death, Vanessa called out, "Tony, I'm sorry." The water pounded down beside her. "*Mother*!"

CHAPTER 41

TURNING PRISM

Vanessa

INSTEAD OF DEATH, Vanessa found herself in the cave she'd prayed for only moments before.

Scott burst through the water and lay Lukeem down.

Abruce and Noat followed.

Adjusting to the darkness and choking from the spray of thunderous water, Vanessa and Scott stared at each other from across the cave, breathing heavily in unison.

They sat motionless, poised to react.

Vanessa's anger, tempered by her fear of the evil man, kept her immobilized. In the presence of Scott, she took on the filters of her own culture, and her embarrassment over her nakedness immediately rose up red in her face. "I'm feeling extremely vulnerable here." Taking her wet clothes from her head bag, she turned around to put on her blouse.

Their attention shifted toward Lukeem as she sat up and reached out for Vanessa's hand.

"Lukeem, dear." Vanessa moved closer to offer comfort. She was shocked when Lukeem also took hold of Scott's trembling hand.

Slowly, Lukeem began to speak, bringing their hands together.

Vanessa drew hers away abruptly, but Lukeem insisted with her eyes in such a way that it melted Vanessa's resistance and she took Scott's hand. As their fingers touched, Lukeem spoke in her language and nodded as though encouraging them to talk.

"Ma says, your eyes meet," Abruce explained, as he set a flashlight on a ledge and lit a fire.

Vanessa took the net bag from her head and pulled out the lock of encrusted silver hair as the rage built up inside her. "I know who you are, you Aryan racist! Why did you kill him? How could you murder an innocent old man?"

Intervening, Lukeem placed one hand on each of their hearts. Reaching out, she placed each of their hands on the chest of their enemy.

Vanessa felt the rapid beating of Scott's heart.

"Why?" Vanessa gazed into Scott's face for clues.

He spoke as though from his childhood self. "My father died. My mom and I moved to my uncle's place in Brooklyn. I'd never been anywhere. The gang at school . . ." Scott unconsciously rubbed the back of his head as she'd seen him do so many times. "They held me down and shaved that Swastika in my hair. Made me promise to get a lock of hair from a rabbi. They said it was tradition and wouldn't hurt him. I didn't know Jews. I didn't know anything. Then it all went wrong. I went to pick up the book for him, and I saw my chance, but he fell after I cut it, and I fell too." Scott stared off into the dark end of the cave.

Vanessa knew that Scott wasn't staring at the stone and vines in the cavern. He was looking back into his past.

"When I saw those scissors in his shoulder . . . the blood was everywhere." Scott's truth was glowing from his eyes, rushing scarlet to his face. "I saw a girl, a redheaded girl. She was filming it. Just standing there filming it like it wasn't real! I called, 'Wait! Wait! Help!' But she ran. And I ran home, hid under the porch, looking through the lattice where I'd spent every day after school alone. Then the newspaper came. I read the headlines, and I fled. I had to go—I was afraid they'd get my mother. I couldn't let them know where I lived. Couldn't let them get her." Nearly breathless from his reveal, he finished his confession. "I never belonged there in the city."

Vanessa imagined the innocent child hiding behind the lattice and touched his fingers with hers, scarred from her own pain.

"I just wanted the lock of hair. I never meant to hurt the old man." Scott kept his gaze on the ground between them. "They made me. Said they would get my mother, and I wanted to belong." His voice was dull, like he was in a trance.

Vanessa reached out. Smoothing the hair on the back of his head, she caressed his child's face.

"That redheaded girl, I screamed for her to help, but she kept filming. She gave you that film, didn't she? How did she know who I was? Maybe if you destroy the redhead's film, my suffering will end." Scott puffed out a long sigh. "I don't know. I've imprisoned myself, anyway, never letting anyone get near."

"You don't *know*?" She took the woven bag off her head, revealing the red roots washed partially clean of the disguise of ashes and oil by the rushing water.

Scott pulled back abruptly. "You? It was you? You kept filming. Didn't do anything! It was all about a goddamn story for you, wasn't it, even way back then?"

Lukeem took Scott's hand, and he calmed.

"Yes." Vanessa confessed. "I did. I kept filming."

"Why? Why? A man was dying." Scott stared into her eyes.

"I don't *know* why. It didn't seem real. You fell behind the hedge, the bus, the traffic. I was caught up in the story for my senior film school competition." Vanessa dragged in a breath. "My father told me not to go there after they disowned him for marrying my mother, but I went. I thought maybe things had changed. There wouldn't be such hatred. And he wasn't just an old man—that would have been bad enough. He was my *grandfather*. I had only met him once eight years before. I didn't know. I should have helped you. I *wish* I had helped you, believe me!"

Looking at her with shock, Scott ran his hand through his hair and sighed deeply.

Vanessa's eyes grew wide with sudden realization when she thought of the final flickering scene of the old evidence film. It had been there all along, obscured by her own guilt and hatred, and her need to see it solely as *his* crime.

It was Scott's look—a look of *horror*, not hatred.

CHAPTER 42

CONFLICTING CULTURES

Vanessa

VANESSA GAZED DOWN at her right hand. Scott reached for it and examined the scarred ridges on her knuckles.

A wave of trembles showered over Vanessa, and her stomach quivered with nausea as she recounted the past. "My grandmother. She closed the piano on my hand in a fit of anger when my father died. It was an accident, I'm sure. It had to be her rage blinding her, having lost her son. Scott, I'm so sorry. I was forbidden to go to their neighborhood. I couldn't enter their world. It's so different looking back at forty. After that, I had to hide behind my changed name. I lost my family, lost myself forever, left the convent, and deserted the one woman who'd loved me like a mother."

"I understand mistakes and loss." Scott reached out to Vanessa and held her. "Nothing is lost forever." His voice was soft.

Scott and Vanessa drew back from each other.

Words failed them.

Lukeem had forged a connection between them at the deepest level, unlike anything Vanessa understood was possible. Did he experience the purging too?

"Scott, it feels as if I've . . . I don't know, it's as if I've been purged of the guilt and the hatred I've carried for twenty years." She was sitting across from the one person she'd focused on her entire adult life, the stranger who'd driven her passions and haunted her nights.

He opened his mouth, then hesitated. "I feel like my whole past—the suffering, isolation, and loneliness—was somehow purified by that profound confession. I never dreamed I would ever have a shared empathy with that redhead. It's impossible it was you, Vanessa Gold. Maybe Lukeem *is* some kind of sorceress. I mean, it's like she cast a spell . . . a good spell. How did you keep all that pain in?" Scott looked off into the corner of the cave where Lukeem sat, and he nodded. "Thank you."

Abruce, who'd been silent, sitting in the shadows with Noat, shared his mother's words. "Ma says, you come together, here." He put a finger to his eye.

"I'm sorry about your grandfather, truly, Vanessa. I lost my mother over the whole thing."

Vanessa finally engaged Scott's eyes. "In a way, so did I. Scott, I played a role in your loss. Can you forgive me?"

"You shouldn't look at it that way, Vanessa. It's childhood damage. We should cut ourselves a break, you know?"

They were jolted from their intimate connection by invading the chants that grew louder.

Lukeem tried to rise. Healing their hearts seemed to have drained her even more. Abruce took a thick oily green substance from his bag and spread it around the wound where the arrowhead had pierced Lukeem's shoulder. He did the same for Scott's injured leg.

Pointing outside to where the chants were intensifying, Lukeem looked at Vanessa pleadingly and spoke.

Abruce translated her words. "Ma says she makes trade. Her sacrifice for me. I belong to tribe again and have mate. She says we need tribe. She wants me to complete the sacrifice." Abruce brought his mother's forehead to his. "No Ma!"

Scott helped Lukeem to sit with her back to the cave wall. "She wants to go, Vanessa. You've seen the village, her family, her people, and their rejection of her only son."

"No, Scott. Not alive. We can't!" Vanessa begged him. "I can't, Lukeem." She leaned down close to Lukeem. "I can't let you go!"

"Maybe she has the right to be the hero in her ending," Scott said.

"Lukeem, not Ranu Lolo, please? We can save you. We'll find a way." Vanessa took off her shamrock necklace, put it around Lukeem's neck, and kissed her cheek.

Struggling to stand, Lukeem looked into Vanessa's eyes with a motherly, loving look that shattered the final fragments of Vanessa's hardened shell, breaking through to her heart. Taking a crude woven ring from her thumb, Lukeem placed it in Vanessa's hand. She looked deep into Vanessa's eyes again, engaging her in a place so unfamiliar, that newly felt place of profound vulnerability. Tilting her head, Lukeem brought Vanessa and Scott's foreheads together and moved their hands to each other's hearts.

Vanessa felt their rapid heartbeats blend in concert; her ache roared back—the ache for Fiona buried deep inside since her father's death. Breaking open, the demons of disappointment escaped Vanessa's heart, the remaining decades of inhibited emotions flowed out. "No, I'll go instead, *please*?" Vanessa cried. "I can do it."

She kissed Lukeem's cheek and rushed toward the watery exit of the cave.

Diving to grab Vanessa around her waist, Scott stopped her. She broke into sobs. "I deserve it," she screamed.

"It doesn't work that way. She won't have peace. They won't accept it." Scott pulled Vanessa back to her senses.

Lukeem gestured for Vanessa to remove her head bag.

With the bag in her lap, Vanessa retrieved her wrinkled slacks and handed them to Lukeem.

Removing her grass skirt, Lukeem put them on, then pointed to Vanessa's blue wilted blouse.

Vanessa didn't hesitate to remove the garment, leaving herself protected only by the ash color of her oily disguise. Lukeem would want to wear Vanessa's clothes for the occasion of the sacrifice. Vanessa knew this from Canyon's discussions of the culture and the look in Lukeem's eyes—it was an honor from the sky spirits. How could Lukeem still believe in us, Vanessa wondered? She helped Lukeem button the blouse—any last request could not be denied.

Dressed in Vanessa's damp clothes, Lukeem ran her tired fingers over the soft fabric of the soiled sky blue blouse, smiling and pointing to the cliff outside.

Vanessa's mind blurred in search of a way to avoid Lukeem's intent to sacrifice herself. "We shouldn't have come here." Vanessa cried out, "*None* of us should have come here."

"Or maybe we were meant to come here." Scott added more salve to Lukeem's wound, which was already beginning to heal from the treatment. "Lukeem said the sacrifice was her final purpose, restoring her son's place in his tribe." Scott picked Lukeem up in his arms, but the suffering in Vanessa's eyes must have changed his mind. He hestitated and then lay Lukeem down in Vanessa's arms. Squatting down behind them, he rocked the two women.

Watching Lukeem's black foot swaying in front of her, back and forth like a metronome, Vanessa was thrust back to her grandfather's death. Back to the rocking of his black-soled foot. Vanessa squeezed her eyes shut, then opened them and focused on her mother's shamrock necklace. Finally, Lukeem let Vanessa comfort her.

Vanessa shuddered, releasing a painful sound. "No! I will *not* let Abruce lose his mother to a sacrifice."

Scott crouched in front of Lukeem and Vanessa. "Wait, you said it at Jeff's dinner. If one change in a cultural norm could cause all this chaos, another might reverse it." Scott shook his head. "You know whatever it was you said. You must find a way to bridge the cultures. It's what you do, Vanessa. The whole reason you came here is *now*!"

The cacophony of the chanting, muffled by the curtain of water, grew louder and closer, echoes reaching deep inside the cave.

Vanessa had to pull herself together. She kissed Lukeem's head and at that moment, the idea formed. She called Abruce closer and whispered to him.

He shook his head no.

Vanessa had to convince him. She had to convince them both that her strategy to satisfy the tribal tradition was the right thing. It pained her.

Abruce nodded and ran off through the cave. She had a decision. There had to be a sacrifice. There was too much at stake. The sacrifice would be enough, and it could change everything, Vanessa thought. And the presence of Scott, a sky spirit, could keep Lukeem's tribe at a distance.

Vanessa could not let Lukeem suffer any torture before the sacrifice if the mine site tribes arrived. They had to hurry.

"What did you tell Abruce, Vanessa?" Scott wiped his brow and glanced in the direction of the chanting crowd. "Where did he go off to?"

"Scott, trust me, take Noat with you, and please keep the tribe at a distance."

THEY LEFT THE CAVE to complete the sacrifice.

Kralu and his tribesmen approached fast, bows drawn.

Holding up his arms, Scott herded the dozens of agitated men back from the rock ledge at a distance from where the sacrifice would take place. "Stay back!"

They acquiesced to the sky spirit, humbling themselves on the ground.

With the sorceress's limp body held over his head, Abruce emerged from the cave entrance beside the waterfall and ceremoniously walked behind Scott and Vanessa to the brink of the abyss.

Scott kept his arms held high to prevent the gathering crowd of excited tribesmen from advancing closer.

The chanting stopped.

Holding onto Scott with her face pressed into his back, Vanessa began to hum to distract herself.

Abruce, please, have the courage to do this. She closed her eyes, hoping he would follow the plan.

"Lukeem gives her life for our tribe." Abruce's words, nearly lost in the crashing sounds of the waterfall, were repeated by the closest tribesmen, then carried on in waves until the entire group chanted her intent.

Vanessa held her breath; she was proud of Abruce for his courage.

He approached the edge of the cliff. "The sky spirits have honored Lukeem with their clothes."

Kralu came forward and called out to his mate, "Lukeem! Your sacrifice to please the river spirit."

Was that to garner some credit for her sacrifice? Vanessa turned, peeking around Scott's shoulder to observe Kralu.

He dropped his head, and a silence fell over the group. Only the rush and thunder of the waterfall could be heard, as Kralu straightened his slumped body, took aim, and shot an arrow. It came treacherously close to Abruce and embedded in the chest of the sorceress.

"Ranu Lolo! Ranu Lolo!" the group chanted louder and louder, calling for the sacrifice.

Deep regret and feigned agreement fought for expression on Abruce's face as he released the sorceress's body into the abyss.

Vanessa held on to Scott as they watched the body soundlessly drift down, down to the rocks and the raging river below.

CHAPTER 43

FATEFUL FALL

Tony

"THERE SHE IS. It's Canyon." Tony strained his neck to keep her in his sight as Brad angled the helicopter to descend.

"You sure?"

"Yes, what other native has blonde dreadlocks? It's her. Oh, and there's the boy Abera too." Tony felt relief surge through him.

"Where?"

"There, by the riverside. Just before the bend." Tony pointed to a spot just a hundred yards upstream from them. "What the hell is she doing down there with him?"

"Better question—how the hell did she get down there with him? There's a perfect rock outcropping to land on." Brad redirected the helicopter. "See it, just above them? And there's a path down to the riverside."

Below them, Tony saw Canyon waving. "She was supposed to stay put."

"I've only known Canyon a couple of days," Brad said. "Still, I know her well enough to guess she wouldn't sit in her room patiently waiting for you while her best friend went off into the jungle. Canyon is loyal if nothing else, right?"

Tony had to agree with Brad.

Brad skillfully landed on the river's edge. Tony and Brad leaped from the helicopter and made their way over the rocky bank of the river toward Canyon.

"Tony, Brad, thank God you're here!" Canyon rushed up to the bank and threw her arms around Tony. "Where's Vanessa? Did you find her? What's happened?"

"Not yet, Canyon. We were going up there to check out the cliff area where they planned the sacrifice." Tony glanced up at the ledge high above them. "What the hell are you doing down here?"

"I followed Abera. He seemed to know where he was going. It didn't seem possible Vanessa could climb that sheer mountain wall." Canyon patted Abera on his shoulder. "You wouldn't believe the cave system in this mountain. Abera showed me the tunnels that lead down to the river. I thought I could find Vanessa down on this side of the mountain. Now what?"

"Damn, guys, check this out." Brad shaded his eyes and pointed to the top of the cliff.

Tony followed Brad's line of sight and, in the distance far above them, they could barely make out a figure holding a body overhead. The native man thrust the body out over the abyss.

"Oh my God, Tony. They must have found Lukeem." Canyon grabbed onto Brad's arm.

The body floated down, drifting in toward the rock wall. Bouncing down, it became clear the body was clothed. It wasn't Lukeem.

"*Vanessa?*" Tony recognized her signature blue top. His heart dropped. Frozen in place, he watched the tragic ending to the woman he loved, his powerful Vanessa, drifting helplessly down toward the whitewater rapids of the Ranu Lolo. Tony's legs gave out. "*Vanessa!*"

Canyon fell to her knees and screamed as the body splashed down and was swallowed up by the fast-moving water a hundred yards upstream. She scrambled to her feet and followed Abera, who waded bravely into the water ahead of her.

Tony steadied himself and followed quickly.

"Guys, it's treacherous in that river. It's too late after that fall." Brad yelled as he ran alongside on the riverbank, tracking their progress.

"Abera has her!" Tony caught sight of the boy navigating the river, grasping Vanessa's blouse. They bobbed in and out of view from the rapids. "Vanessa, my Vanessa." Rushing down to the river's edge, he forged out over the shallows to retrieve her.

When Abera washed by, Tony grabbed for him, but the child's hand slipped from his grasp.

The boy clung determinedly to the floating body with a fistful of fabric, grasping at the slick rocks along the riverbank.

Tony swam toward Abera to assist him.

Following them in the water, Canyon fought to catch up.

"Hang on, Abera. I've got you." Just as the boy lost his footing on the slippery underwater rocks, Tony grasped him by the arm. They drifted hand in hand down the treacherous rapids, sputtering and struggling to stay above the surging water. The body was swept along, dragging them behind. Dear God, don't let Abera drown too. Tony gripped Abera's hand tighter. Canyon caught up to them.

With a sudden surge of the river, Tony and Canyon were safely swept into a quiet river pool, along with Abera, who still held onto the body that drifted face down.

Wrapping his arm around Abera, Tony pulled the boy through the water to the muddy bank, with the blouse on the floating body still locked in the boy's fist. With one arm around Abera, Tony grabbed the familiar blue blouse with his other hand and struggled up the riverbank to safety, assisted by Canyon.

Encumbered by a wave of crushing sorrow, Tony fell over her soaking remains, his chest heaving, gasping for air.

Safely on the riverbank, Tony turned the body over. "Oh my God." He backed away, revealing a head bag filled with stones and Vanessa's clothes stuffed with grasses and twigs—a replica of the woman he loved. Gripping his head, Tony yelled, "Son of a bitch! Who the hell would do this?"

In a rage, wavering between relief and fury, Tony unwound the shamrock necklace from around the fabricated model's neck and tore the stuffing from the clothes. Pulling the wet blouse to his face, Tony released a tortured scream.

Crying at the sight of the substitute victim, Canyon collapsed into Brad's arms. "It's a fake. It's not her."

"It's alright. It's alright, Canyon." Brad kissed her drenched hair.

"Tony, come on. Let's go find Vanessa. She's alive, buddy. She's got to be *alive*." Brad put his jacket around Abera and helped Tony to his feet. After a few shuffling steps, Tony turned around to rescue the remnants of Vanessa's clothes—her favorite blue blouse and black jeans.

Tony was numb. He couldn't feel his body. His heart was banging in his chest. With his arm around Canyon, the wet and weary group dragged themselves back to the helicopter.

Brad climbed into the pilot's seat, followed by Tony, who was still spinning from the swing of his emotions—from terror and distress to anger and relief.

Brad's radio crackled. "Come in, Brad. It's Scott."

"Scott, what the fuck happened? Where's—"

"Vanessa is fine for now. She saved Lukeem by having Abruce throw a dummy over the cliff—Vanessa's clothes stuffed with sticks and stones."

"We saw it, believe me!"

"Oh shit, Brad, that must have been terrible. Sorry," Scott said. "Was Tony there?"

"Unfortunately. And Canyon. Brutal. They're in shock. We're all in shock.What about Abruce, Scott?"

"Abruce is being cheered by his tribe for completing the sacrifice, but Vanessa says get up here right away and bring the clothes. The second step to her strategy's coming up soon. There's some ritual start-ing. Vanessa needs the clothes to carry it out. Their beliefs are surreal. They would have thrown Lukeem overboard to please the river spirit. Land the chopper on the southside of the waterfall. We'll meet you there and get this damn thing over with. Oh, damn, Brad, the mine site tribes just arrived, and they're heating up. I've gotta go."

"Brad, tell Scott I know who he is." Tony's anger was boiling over.

Brad ignored Tony as the sound of the props, and the engine kept his words from reaching Scott. "Got it, Scott. Be there in fifteen."

CHAPTER 44

CHANGING CHANTS

Vanessa

THE GASPS OF CLEAR disappointment came from the mine site tribespeople in the crowd who held their glowing metal rods ready to inflict Lukeem's punishment if her tribe did not make the sacrifice.

Canyon had been right. Once the sacrifice had been made, their passions would be satisfied, and they would drift off to return to their tribal area to celebrate the demon's demise. Their chanting could be heard fading off into the jungle toward the tram platform.

Sounds of relief rose from the voices of the honored victim's family at the fulfillment of the rightful sacrifice—the death of the sorceress. Lukeem's tribe chanted, "Abruce, Abruce."

Signaling for silence, the honored one invited his tribe to peer over the edge of the cliff. They joined Scott and Vanessa, staring down the mountainside.

Vanessa studied their faces. Were they awaiting some sign of satisfaction in the moving waters of the Ranu Lolo?

The honored one shuffled to the edge and peered down. On the riverbank below, the sky spirits' magical bird began to rise, approaching them, growing larger and larger. The honored one spoke. Abruce translated for her. "With sorceress sacrifice, spell no longer."

The weakened tribesmen pounded their bows and arrows on the

ground and leaped up and down, celebrating their relief. The crowd of Lukeem's tribesmen left the Long View and headed to the ceremonial circle to complete the celebration—a tradition Canyon had described would happen after any sacrifice was made.

BACK IN THE CAVE behind the waterfall, Scott stood guard. With the music of the trickling and gurgling water as their backdrop, Vanessa congratulated Abruce and Lukeem for their courage in creating a new tradition. Human sacrifice wasn't in keeping with the culture of the tribe, as Canyon had said. Lukeem was pleased with the symbolic sacrifice. She'd agreed her tribe was kind and affable when left to their own ways. Only a few of the elders in Lukeem's tribe had any memory of a sacrifice. Hopefully, the tribe would be ready to relinquish the violent tradition to a non-violent, symbolic ritual to satisfy the river spirit should trouble befall them again.

Abruce translated, explaining that, in the end, he and his mother both understood it was for the good of all. The spell would be broken, the tribe and the river spirit Ranu Lolo would be satisfied, miners would get back to work. Lukeem, Abruce, and Noat would be accepted again, reunited with their tribe.

"Ma says, we no more sacrifice women." Abruce stood proud next to Noat.

Lukeem pressed her forehead first to Vanessa's, then Abruce's and Noat's as if to seal the agreement.

"Tell Lukeem, thank you for being so strong."

They were grateful and satisfied with their new perspective. Now to bring the clothing from the sacrificial replica and dress Lukeem for the finale. And to ensure these sacrifices never happened again, Vanessa would enlist the sky spirits for step two of her cross-cultural strategy. She left the cave and joined Scott at the cliff.

"Good work, Vanessa." Scott put his arm around her shoulder, and they stared down at the river together. The Zell Baxter helicopter was only a short distance away.

A growing frenzy behind them, with a purpose of its own, finally drew their attention. "Lukeem's tribe is starting their celebration in the men's ceremonial circle. Better tell them to hurry. Scott, did you radio to tell the team what we did? Or should we wait until they get up here?"

"I just told them that we're safe and get up here pronto."

"Make sure they bring my clothes, please. I'm running out of inter-cultural tolerance here." She looked down, and her black and white streaked skin. Vanessa was still bare-breasted; the trek through the jungle and the heat of the day had wreaked havoc on Abruce's transformation. As the disguise melted, so had Vanessa's comfort level at being exposed. But she was determined to complete the plan, and her native guise might still be necessary to succeed. Vanessa was fascinated that her self-consciousness flared when she was with Scott. She folded in on herself on instinct, trembling. Still, that mortified feeling faded into the background of her awareness when she was with Lukeem, Abruce, or their tribespeople.

Vanessa edged closer to the sounds of celebration, peering through trees to the ceremonial circle. It struck her then; the tribal mine workers did not hold the white sky spirits in high regard. They held no illusion that white skin and clothing signified kindness and good intentions. Vanessa understood now that her native guise had provided her anonymity in the jungle. But when it came to Lukeem's tribe, her clothes and fair skin would empower her. As Scott approached, Vanessa blended the ash oil across her chest to even the color and waited for her clothes to arrive.

"Weird, I've almost stopped noticing." Scott glanced over at Vanessa. "Well, maybe not quite."

She punched his arm and signaled him to give her his shirt.

The drone of the helicopter was growing in the distance. Facing Tony now would be daunting. Finally, confessing her lies and explaining her trickery—the extreme risk she took sacrificing a bag of clothes filled with sticks and stones in place of Lukeem.

Seeing the honored one wearing leather combat boots across the way in the ceremonial circle, Vanessa rushed through the underbrush to observe him. His face glowed with the anticipation of the ritual as the excited crowd of tribesmen pressed in closer to watch.

The tribal women clustered around the barren circle's edge in the thicket of vines and plants.

The rhythm of the men's rapid breathing was palpable. Seeming to rise in unison, the men's voices created a commanding energy around them. The tone of the chanting changed abruptly.

Standing among the women at the edge of the ceremonial circle, Vanessa spotted the glowing, red hot metal rods moving through the gathering, scattering Lukeem's tribespeople. Dear God, the mine site tribesmen had returned with fury on their faces. There was no question as they thrust ahead through the celebration; they were moving toward her. The women surrounding Vanessa ran as the inflamed tribesmen took her by the arms, dragged her toward the fire, and tied her to a nearby tree.

"*Mea culpa, mea culpa.*" Vanessa closed her eyes, and repeated the Latin phrases from her childhood, praying for forgiveness. "Through my fault, through my fault. Bless me, Father, for I have sinned." She struggled against the twine, calling out the words of her Catholic confessional, imagining the kindly priest leaning in close to listen. She listed her sins for her confessor: "I abandoned the holy woman who lovingly mothered me. I punished the damaged birth mother who abandoned me. I took no action to save an old man who only wanted to love me. I denied my lover his dreams. I never honored him with my truth. I've had hate in my heart."

A sweaty, strong hand grasped her leg.

CHAPTER 45

CEREMONIAL SWITCH

Tony

HOVERING NEAR THE drop off that overlooked the valley where the Ranu Lolo flowed, Brad negotiated the wind currents attempting to land near the waterfall.

From the front seat of the helicopter, Tony had a view of a gathering off in the distance. A large crowd of natives, wearing corkscrew kotekas, jumped and chanted in a dirt circle carved out of the jungle green. "Lukeem's tribe," Tony called out to everyone on the helicopter.

No native turned to follow the engine's whine and the swirling propellors. The waterfall's thunder and the tribal chants must have swallowed the sound of their approach.

"Tony, be careful. These tribesmen need to burn off their anger and fear after fulfilling the sacrifice of one of their tribeswomen." Canyon shivered in the back seat holding Abera. "Are you sure it's Lukeem's tribe?"

He also needed an outlet for his anger, he thought. His body still held the terror. His breath sped up, and his heart pounded whenever he relived those suspended seconds, watching the image of Vanessa, his love, launched off the precipice, floating down to the wild river.

"Tony, what's happening now? I can't see from back here," Canyon said.

"Not sure. A ritual. There's a huge fire. Celebration of the sacrifice, probably."

Before Brad could settle the helicopter onto the spongy surface outside the waterfall, Tony jumped to the ground searching for Vanessa. Flying ashes from a fire fifty yards away, fed by dozens of men and boys, burned Tony's eyes, and blurred his vision. Deafening chants and the jumping of the frenetic crowd prevented him from getting close. On his right, Tony spotted Scott by the edge of the waterfall.

With Vanessa's clothes in hand, Tony ran to Scott and grabbed him by the throat. "You bastard."

"Hey buddy, you've got it all wrong. Calm down, man." Trying to explain, Scott fought off Tony, and pulled him around the edge of the falling water and into the cave.

In a dark corner of the cave, Vanessa sat rocking herself, as Lukeem spread a green oozing sap over her scorched thigh.

"Van, Honey! Van?" Tony squatted in front of her. "Darling? Look at me! Look at me!" He saw the life come back into her haunted eyes, and her tears flowed, seeming to signal that he'd reached her. "Van, I'm here. I'm here." He turned to Lukeem. "Thank you." He took Vanessa in his arms. "Who did this to you?" He kissed her cheek and wiped the black soot from his lips. "You don't understand. I'm sorry, Van. Scott murdered your grandfather. He's the one. Did he do this to you?"

"No, Tony—"

Tony hated to deliver the terrible news. "Canyon found evidence in Scott's trailer." He swiped his finger down Vanessa's ash-covered, oiled arm. "I don't understand. You're alright, babe. You're alright?" Tony soothed her, rocking her in his arms. He glared at Scott. "What the hell did you do, Scott?"

"What did *I* do? I goddamn saved her from those torturing natives with the hot metal rods. They tied her to a tree trunk." Scott stepped closer. "I used my sky spirit status and enlisted Lukeem's tribe. They were hyped up from the sacrifice and drove the crazies off just before you arrived."

"Tony, no! We *both* did it." Vanessa said.

"What? You two were in on your grandfather's murder?"

"No, no, Tony, I meant the sacrifice." Vanessa met his eyes. "We faked the sacrifice together."

"Vanessa, what happened to you? Scott is the murderer. Your grandfather's murderer." Tony threw up his hands in confusion. "I don't even know who you are!"

"Tony, it wasn't a murder." Her voice was weak. "And you know who I am—just not who I used to be." Vanessa sat, looking at the wound on her leg.

Lukeem brought water in a round leaf, and Vanessa drank.

"We need to finish the ritual, Tony. Please give Lukeem the clothes." Vanessa stood on shaky legs.

Lukeem dressed again in the damp and torn blouse and slacks, removing her grass skirt.

"Scott, where's Abruce?"

"He went to the circle with Noat, as planned. He's waiting to meet the helicopter."

"Tony, honey, I'm going to ask you to trust me. I know that is a big ask after all that's happened. This is critical. Can you carry Lukeem to the helicopter? Scott's leg is injured. We all need to go. Tony, please help me get Lukeem onto the helicopter, will you? She'll be fine; she's just weak." Vanessa looked deep into Tony's eyes. "Scott and I have forgiven each other. I need you to do that for me too. You have a lot to forgive. More than you know."

"You've *forgiven* him?"

"There's more we need to talk about, Tony, but not now." Vanessa pleaded. "We need to get Lukeem to Abruce and Noat. And Scott's leg is injured. He needs help."

Carrying Lukeem to the safety of the helicopter, Tony handed her up to Brad and called out to Canyon. "Vanessa's OK, Canyon. She's traumatized, but Scott and Lukeem's tribe saved her."

"Brad, you need to get them over the crowd and land to the north, upwind of the fire," Scott said.

Tony helped Vanessa up the dropdown steps.

"It won't be easy, but what has been?" Brad prepared for takeoff.

As Vanessa reached her hand out and beckoned Scott aboard, Tony stared at her confused.

Limping into the back seat, Scott comforted Canyon, who sat with her head in her hands, Abera curled up beside her.

Vanessa turned around and looked at Canyon. "Thank God, you're still wearing it. Can you put your necklace around Lukeem's neck when we land?"

"Sure." Canyon said. "Why?"

"You'll see." Vanessa turned back to Tony. "Do you have the one from the dummy?"

Tony leaned back and pulled the second shamrock necklace from his pocket. She put it on.

Tony sat next to Vanessa and held onto her with his face buried in her neck. "Vanessa, when I saw that body falling, crashing against the cliff, and I thought—"

Immediately lifting the helicopter above the crowd, Brad skillfully guided it next to the scene of the ritual. The swoosh of the rotors swept the fire's ashes skyward like gray snow, blinding the crowd, dispersing them in fear, fanning the inferno. It pushed the flames down, only to have them roar up dangerously in response, singeing the underside of the helicopter. Brad settled it upwind of the blaze and cut the engine.

Tony kissed Vanessa's forehead. "Darling, you're OK. Let's do this." He helped her down the steps to the ground. Covering his eyes with his shirtsleeve, he leaped over the prone men who'd dropped to the ground at his arrival.

As Brad, Scott, and Canyon joined him and Vanessa, the honored one and his fellow tribesmen returned to the circle.

With Noat beside him, Abruce proudly carried his lifeless mother down the helicopter steps to the center of the sacred circle and lay her down. She remained still. "Lukeem sacrifice herself to Ranu Lolo, but sky spirits protect her body from rocks and raging river. They return her body undamaged. To honor her, nature spirits command we have no more sacrifices." Abruce repeated the words in his language.

Vanessa leaned closer to Tony and whispered to him, "I'm grateful that Abruce remembered the words we'd planned."

"No more sacrifice." The honored one pounded his bow and arrows into the ground, and Abruce translated.

Tony watched the event unfolding. Vanessa took hold of Noat and quickly entered the circle. Bows were drawn, as once again a woman desecrated the men's circle. Lifting the shining shamrock necklace on his mother's chest, Abruce held up the matching one on Vanessa's neck for the tribe to admire—signifying that the sky spirit approved of the presence of Lukeem. The tribe members nodded to Vanessa.

Vanessa walked to the edge of the circle, took two ancestral skulls in her hands, handed one to Noat, and they started a new circle of honor around Lukeem's body.

Following Vanessa's actions, Tony brought another ancestor's skull to continue the new ceremony.

Abruce stood silently by his father. Staring with a pained face at his mother's body, he turned to his elders with strength in his eyes. "The sky spirits first showed themselves only to my mother, Lukeem." Abruce lowered himself to one knee and placed a skull above Lukeem's head.

Scott and Brad followed the pattern, each moving an ancestor's skull to encircle Lukeem. Kneeling on the ground, Canyon bowed over Lukeem, who remained limp and silent, her eyes closed. With her back to the tribesmen, Tony watched as Canyon removed the silver shamrock necklace that Vanessa had asked she put around Lukeem's neck in the helicopter.

At the sight of the woman sky spirit's homage, one by one, Lukeem's tribesmen, in turn, added the skulls of their ancestors to complete the circle. Lowering their heads, they nodded respectfully to the sky spirits as they passed them.

Vanessa put her hand to her forehead. Tony knew she was in disbelief because she'd found the bridge—a symbolic sacrifice.

All of the natives followed suit, imitating Vanessa's gesture. Putting her hand over her heart, they copied her again, resuming their traditional greeting.

What a woman he had, Tony thought. And maybe for the first time ever, she was truly the person he thought she was.

Vanessa threw her arms up and announced to the gathering. "If one mistake or change can cause a cultural tragedy, can't another change cause a new cultural norm?" Vanessa's body language and the tone of her voice carried her powerful message to the tribesmen as Abruce continued to translate.

Reaching out to Abruce who'd left his father's side to stand in front of her, Vanessa pulled his forehead to hers.

Tony watched their shared tears fall on the ash-covered ground between them. They placed their hands on each other's hearts. Tony could only imagine the love that Vanessa felt for Lukeem flowing through her son.

Abruce fixed on Vanessa's eyes. "Thanks, y'all, Van Gold."

Vanessa bent over and touched Lukeem's face. She had told Tony that touching Lukeem was the signal they had planned that would change everything.

Solemnly, Lukeem rose to the gasps of her fellow tribesman. She stood with her arms raised in triumph.

Tony watched Canyon furtively hand the necklace back to Vanessa. Canyon said, "You will need this, my friend. You *are* so damn amazing, staging that whole thing. This necklace has been around, and you know where it belongs, right?"

"Oh Canyon, I can only hope." Vanessa smiled. "Wearing these necklaces was your idea, remember?"

"That was unreal, Van, and brilliant." Tony kissed her cheek. "You just saved a lot of lives and a lot of jobs."

"And I'm not finished yet, Tony. Both she and Abruce deserve to be reinstated in their tribe." Vanessa stepped forward and pressed her forehead to Lukeem's. "Lukeem, Lukeem, Lukeem." Rumbling through the gathering, their chants changed tone to express their wonder and esteem.

Kralu moved to her side and spoke hesitantly. Abruce translated his father's words of apology and admiration for Lukeem and gratitude to the river spirit.

The honored one spoke. "The sacrifice has been made. The sky spirits have returned." He wiped his brow.

Removing his leather boots, the honored one urged Abruce to wear them as Kralu handed his son his own bow and arrows.

CHAPTER 46

ONE STEP

Vanessa

GLANCING AT VANESSA for his cue, Abruce raised his arms and announced to the tribe, "Father, the sky spirits showed their faces to Ma."

Kralu nodded, and Abruce led the tribal dance.

The tribesmen jumped up and down, thumping their bows on the ground, a ring of men entwined, and a new tradition ensued. Saluting, marching in step, the natives lifted their legs, left-right, left-right, just as the sky spirits had done decades ago when that fateful mistake was made. They each fell to the ground, lay prone in silence, then rose, and reached their arms to the sky as Lukeem had done.

Vanessa was overjoyed at inventing the symbolic sacrifice.

Although its meaning was unknown to the tribe, Vanessa wiped her brow again with relief and smiled, followed by Tony, Brad, Canyon, Scott, Abruce, and Noat. A subtle substitute for a soldier's salute. Vanessa had inadvertently created another new cultural norm. Yes, whew indeed, she thought.

"Let's go, Canyon. We'll add one more step forward and finish the plan while the window is open for change." Vanessa tugged Canyon toward the edge of the ceremonial circle where the tribeswomen were gathered. "Time for the women to celebrate."

"I'm in. And Vanessa, I wouldn't have missed this. You made me come alive again . . . like Lukeem."

"Canyon, could we ever have imagined this would be the outcome?"

"If the whole experience hadn't been so terrorizing, the scene of the ceremonial dance would've been humorous."

Taking Lukeem's arm, they both joined the tribeswomen, swaying and chanting with their feet buried in the dense vines on the outskirts of the ceremonial circle.

Lukeem entered the clearing, taking one of the tribal women with her. The women around her vocalized their shock. "Oooo."

"The sky spirits desire us to celebrate." Lukeem smiled, stepping over the remaining chain of ancestors' skulls.

Just enough to challenge tribal rule, Vanessa thought.

Canyon followed, encouraging two more women.

The chanting went silent, as the men observed the entire line of women joining in the new tradition—women, appallingly, dancing within the men's ceremonial circle with arms stretched to the sky.

The men held their silence. The crackling and spitting of the raging fire was the only sound.

Vanessa exchanged a worried look with Canyon, who moved next to Lukeem in support.

Picking up Vanessa's signal, Tony grabbed Scott and Brad and crossed the bones into the circle. Taking Noat's hand, they delivered her to Abruce who stood stone still in the center of the tribesmen's celebration.

The men folded away in fear, or was it respect, for the sky spirits? Vanessa would never be sure.

Starting to sway, Vanessa chanted her mother's famed piano piece, "Rise to Be You". Canyon echoed the tune. When Lukeem joined in, the other women tried to follow along. The thought of her mother's tune hummed by Stone Age tribesman in the remote jungles perhaps for years to come was ironic yet gratifying, even joyful for Vanessa.

It was a gift to Mother Anne Marie. *Play your mother's song for me.* If Vanessa could only have seen her face glow as she told the story to the nun who'd inspired her.

There was a silence among the men that threatened Vanessa's intention. In those few seconds of silence, she questioned what she'd done. Hadn't she criticized the mining company for deeply impacting the local culture? What would be the unforeseen consequences of her own interference?

Then the tribesmen approved, and on cue from the honored one, began to clap in a steady rhythm.

The flutter of the helicopter engine starting drew the men's attention. Tony and Scott lifted their arms to invite the tribespeople to come closer to the sky spirits' bird.

The tune was contagious. The men broke out in the new chant, facing the circle of their tribeswomen who didn't dare to go beyond that single step into the revered space.

Brad waved to the team and Vanessa, Canyon, Tony, Scott, Noat, and Abera boarded. Abruce climbed the steps last, turned, and spoke to the tribe calling out in his language. Once on board, he sat next to Noat, who looked amazed.

"Abruce, what did you say to them?" Vanessa leaned forward from the back seat to hear his answer as Brad took off.

"Abruce say to tribe, like sky spirits say long time before, 'We will return'."

LOOKING INTO TONY'S eyes, Vanessa touched his face lovingly. She started to speak but he stopped her with a finger on her lips.

"Don't talk, babe. Just let me hold you. That was the closest yet, too damn close. I can't keep risking the chance of losing you. What you did was amazing, but, really, Van . . ."

"I know. Only this time I truly couldn't have done it without you." She gazed in his eyes.

"Van, when I saw what I thought was you falling . . . I can't stop thinking about it. Whatever it is you haven't told me, it's gone too far into your soul—you need help."

"You *are* my help. You're my angel of forgiveness. You always were. I just needed to forgive myself first." Tony's silence sent a wave of fatigue and nausea through Vanessa. Could he ever forgive her?

Canyon reached over the seat and squeezed Vanessa's hand with an understanding that didn't need words.

"We'll be at the site shortly. Hey, guys, I feel I have to share something. I was going to make it a fun surprise, but after this crazy stressful day, I'm not sure if it's good or bad."

"Brad, go ahead, tell us. We could use a distraction." Vanessa tucked a blanket around herself, and Tony held her close."

"Well, once we clean up and breathe a bit, we'll all appreciate it. I've arranged for a live broadcast of Fiona O'Farrell's concert in Jakarta. The opening of her worldwide residential music program for kids."

"How did you ever manage to make that happen? Great work, Brad. Love her music. Don't you, babe?"

Vanessa and Canyon exchanged glances. They rode in silence. The only sounds were the wind and the rotors.

CHAPTER 47

TRAP DOOR

Vanessa

"DELILAH, YOU ARE lovely to host this evening's concert broadcast in your home."

"Oh, Vanessa, Brad has done everything to set it up. And after what you've done, the strike is over now that the woman was sacrificed. Jeff is grateful. We're all so grateful." Delilah smiled. "I know it's tragic, but as I said, one woman's life for the good of—"

"Yes, well, you're so welcome." It took everything for Vanessa to be civil, but she didn't want Delilah's ignorance to ruin the evening. Too exhausting to deal with, Vanessa thought. How long would it take before the rumors of the rising, sacrificial sorceress would reach the mine site? So far, the local tribesmen only knew that Lukeem had been sacrificed.

Only Lukeem's tribe had witnessed her illusion of rising up from the dead. Only they had absorbed the sky spirit's command against future sacrifices.

Vanessa turned her attention to the program. "Is everything all set, Brad? I can't believe you arranged this concert." It was suspicious, the whole thing, she thought. Was this Jeff's strategy, a bizarre coincidence, or Fiona's doing? Or was Vanessa just being paranoid?

"All good." Brad gave a thumbs up. "The new equipment is cooking, and the interview before the concert is about to start. Everyone will be here soon." Brad adjusted the screen, then turned back to Vanessa. "I hope you get to Jakarta in time to meet Fiona O'Farrell. She's quite something. Do you like her music?"

Vanessa nearly choked. She held back a groan over the insanity of it all. "Yes, I've heard it a time or two."

"Tony, how's our hero, or I should say our hero and heroine?" Brad asked.

"Emotionally and physically exhausted, but we're all fine. For some reason, Vanessa, or maybe I should call her *Colleen*, is very nervous about this concert."

"OK, fine, I deserve a dig or two, Tony. You've earned the right." Posturing a good mood, Vanessa held her final secret, rumbling inside her.

"Funny, Brad, Vanessa was never a piano enthusiast, more into antique stringed instruments. But I guess I have a lot to learn about this new woman I'm soon to marry." Tony held up his woven tribal ring and pulled her close.

"Happy for you, buddy." Brad shook Tony's hand and gave him a brisk pat on the back.

"And to you too, Vanessa. He's a great guy."

"How brave am I to marry a complete stranger?" Tony kissed Vanessa's cheek.

Was there an edge of anger in his tone, or was it her own insecurity? "Well, you'll soon get to know me better." Vanessa shivered at her truthful words. It was the wrong time with the concert about to start. Or maybe it was the perfect time for the final disclosure. Would it ever be the right time? It wasn't so much telling Tony, but wouldn't sharing it publicly shatter their world? The entire team's reputation for the truth would wither into a joke at every press gathering for decades to come. *Ms. Truth in News?*

Taking Tony aside, Vanessa started her confession. "This has been a week of revelations, to say the least." She inhaled, preparing herself. "But there's more—"

Sipping his beer, Tony nearly choked. "*More*? So I finally get the truth from the horse's mouth. Well, that's not very complimentary. I should say my fiancé. Maybe."

"We can't joke our way out of this one, Tony. I know I've disgraced you with my lies and pretenses. I can only deeply ask for your forgiveness." Vanessa glanced across the room, looking for Canyon, but she wasn't there. But if her dear friend had accepted her truth and forgiven her, wouldn't her lover of twenty years? Maybe that was too much to expect. She would accept the consequences either way. In Canyon's forgiveness, Vanessa thought, she had found her strength.

Calling on the spirit of Mother Anne Marie, Vanessa continued. With the sounds of the group's chatter around them, she delivered an abbreviated version of her life story, the truth, and nothing but the truth, except when it came to Fiona. She just couldn't say it out loud. Fiona O'Farrell was her mother, the face that graced every tabloid. She would tell Tony after the concert when they were alone. It didn't feel right to dump that on him when they were about to watch the concert with the group. He deserved to know, but not now.

Tony was silent, studying her eyes. "Babe, I want to be furious. At another time, I might have wanted to punish you, make you feel as wretched as I do—being kept on the outside, in the dark our entire time together." He cradled her cheek with one hand. "And yes, depriving me of the family I wanted, to keep your lies a secret. That hurts, Van. In a deep place. I just can't—"

"Can't what, Tony?" Had he changed his mind? "Tony?" Was he ending things? Vanessa's intuitions were failing her. She had no clue where her truths would lead them.

"I keep seeing your body falling off that cliff, banging against the rugged stone wall. Those suspended, aching moments when I *believed* it was you, being sacrificed, dying before my eyes . . . And then when

I knew it wasn't you, I feared your possible torture by those incited, crazed tribesmen."

She could see his emotions take over. His hands on her shoulders trembled, liquid formed along the edges of his eyes. Attempting to repress his emotions, a brief sound escaped Tony like the moan of a wounded animal.

He gripped her shoulders too tight. Tony's words were thick with emotion. "Van, the pain I felt, believing I'd lost you to the most torturous death. When I grasped your favorite blouse to save you from that damn wild river, and Abera nearly drowning to try the same, then finding out that it wasn't you. It was . . ."

The seconds of Tony's silence created a void that Vanessa couldn't fill. She was at a loss for what to say. No please, Tony, she thought.

"That moment put a context around our lives going forward forever. Do you understand?"

"I think I do, but—" Vanessa tried to keep eye contact with Tony like she'd learned to do from Lukeem and Abruce. She didn't want to lose her precious connection with him.

Was it hurt or anger that rushed across his reddened face? What was he looking for in her eyes? He crushed her in his arms. "That fucking moment, Van. That's when I understood the depth of my love for you."

"Oh, God." Vanessa embraced him. She couldn't get close enough. "I am so deeply sorry, Tony. I can't imagine you experiencing that." She cried into his neck, and she couldn't hold it back. "Honey, I need to depend on that context once more. I have one more thing to confess, the last of my revelations. I promise. I know the timing of all of this is just ridiculous."

"*What*? You're serious? What *more*?"

Brad called from the far side of the living room while fiddling with the TV monitor. "Hey Tony, Vanessa, I hope it was OK to have this broadcast party as a private event. It's just after all we've been through."

They were both silent.

To Vanessa it appeared Brad was oblivious to his interruption at the poignant moment.

"Of course, we're recording the concert. We'll replay it for the entire site tomorrow. Jeff is conveniently in Jakarta at the event." Delilah sounded annoyed that she wasn't also there. "So we're calling our own shots. He'll call in and give us the inside story of the concert. He went to deliver Bina to the school to attend the concert. What a blessing for a child so recently orphaned. A chance for a new life. That Dr. O'Farrell is one incredible woman."

"Here they are now." Tony pulled away from Vanessa. He crossed the room to greet Canyon and Scott as they entered and accepted a cocktail from the server's tray.

The disconnect threatened her at first. Then she realized Tony was taking the attention away from her so she would have time to pull herself together.

The clean but bedraggled group took their seats.

Vanessa wiped her face with the edge of her shawl, took a calming breath, sat next to Scott, leaned in, and tapped his arm. "I hear you have some news about your mother."

"Yes, thanks for the help. Your investigators were amazing. I'm headed out to meet her next week in Wisconsin. It seems I have a sister, well, a step-sister."

"Oh, Scott. See, things can change. But, truthfully, my original motives in investigating you weren't to help find your family."

"I know, but it all worked out for the good."

Hearing her uncharacteristic hopeful words, Canyon snapped her head around and looked at Vanessa incredulously. "Yes, Van, things *can* change for the good. Isn't that what you do for a living, bring hope to oppressed people? Why not for your own future?"

Tony joined them and took his seat next to Vanessa and Scott. "Sorry about the choking part, Scott."

"No worries, Tony, I get it. I've been trying to do that to myself my whole adult life."

"Where's Abruce?" Vanessa went outside to the usual spot where Abruce sat on the cold ground on guard, waiting with Noat, who sat with her arms around Abera.

Motioning Noat to follow him, Abruce lifted Abera into his arms. "He is our boy now."

"Oh, Abruce." Again she was touched by a commitment made so easily in their culture. Vanessa nodded, brought them into the living room, and whispered, "Come, meet my mother."

Abruce looked confused but followed.

Vanessa sat them next to Tony as the concert began.

Who felt more awkward, she wondered, Abruce and Noat and young Abera, treated as honored guests, sitting on chairs, or Delilah hosting three near-naked natives in her home—one bare-breasted and two wearing nothing but kotekas? Vanessa loved the outcome of her intercultural feat. As crazy as it was, sacrificing a substitute for Lukeem had worked. There would be no arguments from their host, Delilah, when it came to the so-called famous cultural bridge-builder, Ms. Vanessa Gold.

Vanessa silenced a laugh and shook her head.

There were so many times over the past days that Vanessa doubted that she could live up to her reputation in this extreme assignment. Lukeem's lessons were at the core of all that had happened. How could a woman living a Stone Age existence teach so much about life to a modern woman with so much experience? How could a so-called primitive young man have bridged the vast cultural gap between them, opening Vanessa to herself? It was difficult for Vanessa to think about never seeing her mentor and her son again.

Why not? Couldn't they make an annual, sentimental journey on the anniversary of Lukeem's resurrection? And couldn't Vanessa carry all that she'd learned about openness and freedom, forgiveness, and the healing aspect of being in nature into her hectic LA life? It was possible she would never fit into that world again.

Who would Vanessa *be* now that she had a mother and would perhaps *be* a mother? The most profound experiences and memories of her life would always reside in this remote place, she thought. Who else could say that? Vanessa would never look at stars in the same way again.

Within seconds, Abruce and Noat slithered down and squatted in the aisle with Abera.

Tony snapped a few photos.

It was a scene that no one would have imagined when they set out on this assignment, Vanessa thought. Near-naked natives watching a concert played by Vanessa's secret mother in one of the most remote places on Earth. A cocktail party story Tony would tell in the future, or, perhaps, a bedtime story. Vanessa gathered herself to address the group. In Canyon's encouraging eyes, Vanessa found the strength. "Everyone, can I have your attention?" Vanessa raised her voice and moved in front of the large screen.

Canyon looked at Tony in anticipation of the announcement.

On cue, the screen cleared, Vanessa stepped aside. The interviewer began with a shot of Fiona O'Farrell sitting poised at her piano with dozens of little children sitting in a horseshoe of chairs around her on the stage.

Shaking off a wave of chills, Vanessa continued, "I would like to introduce you to Dr. Fiona Anne O'Farrell—my mother."

"Your *what*?" Tony looked at Canyon as if to see if he was the last to know.

Vanessa's announcement was buried in the deafening applause on the screen, volume conveniently turned up by Brad, who winked at her. Had Canyon shared the secret with Brad?

Loyal Canyon shushed everyone as the program began. "It's starting."

Mr. Munadi, the government program coordinator, took the time to introduce himself and Fiona. The crowd was pulsing with excitement in the full concert hall. In the background was the low hum of the security guards and audience whispering in preparation for the important event. The elevated sparkle of young voices tittering excitedly with their parents could be heard through Brad's speakers.

Gracing the stage was a magnificent piano painted with the colorful faces of dozens of smiling children with a range of skin tones. They represented the forty cultures of the world that would eventually participate in Fiona O'Farrell's passionate decade-long dream team, Mr. Munadi explained. He outlined the international program, and announced that the final child, from Irian Jaya had arrived. "Our thanks to Zell Baxter for bringing her in on their jet today. Dr. O'Farrell, we are ready to begin. Your ending is our beginning."

Bina tugged at her new school uniform and appeared dazed in the spotlights.

"Music is a bridge," Fiona said. She held out her arms to Bina, who hesitantly moved closer to the piano.

Fiona began to play.

Vanessa sat, slid her hand under Tony's tense arm, and tilted her head to lean against his shoulder. She was too ashamed to look him in the eyes after her final reveal.

Reading Tony's nervousness, Vanessa kept her eyes on the screen, but whispered, "We'll talk, I promise. I'm sorry for the surprise—"

"*Nothing* surprises me anymore, Van. Remember, I watched two women rise from the dead in one day."

She nudged him with her elbow. "Are you sure? *Nothing*?"

"Well, maybe imagining Fiona O'Farrell as my mother-in-law is a tad unexpected."

Vanessa was grateful to sense a hint of their usual banter returning. "I love you." The phrase seemed to fall short of what she truly wanted to express to the man who had stood by her through all her deceptions. "And all the love you ever felt from me was the most real part of me, Tony."

The concert began, and the emotional music that came from the hands of the genius on stage took on a life of its own. The cameras scanned the audience as the inspiring sounds seemed to cast a spell on each listener. Eyes closed, smiles rose, and bodies swayed to the mesmerizing sounds. Piece after piece, the camera's lens captured the connection between her inspired fingers and the pure excitement on the children's faces, the pride in the parent's smiles, and the audience members' enjoyment. When she stopped, the electrified crowd spontaneously rose to their feet in a roar.

Mr. Munadi introduced the Minister of Culture and Tourism, who spoke glowingly of Fiona's new school program, bid farewell, and a happy belated birthday to its benefactor.

A new awareness came over Vanessa. Here, in a country far from the local tabloids, the rumors, and sullied reputation, her mother was a hero. She had sacrificed everything to help children experience the power of music, to bridge their cultures, and have a chance for a good life.

"As you know, Dr. O'Farrell will cease her public performances for the next decade to dedicate herself completely to teaching and her children's music foundation. The children you see here, and many others worldwide will have the joy of attending her program, including a special student from one of the farthest reaches of our country. Bina comes from the island of Irian Jaya and is sponsored by Zell Baxter Mining Company in honor of Ms. Vanessa Gold."

Vanessa was caught off guard. Zell Baxter honoring *her*? She took a deep breath and prayed that the sky spirits at the mine would take advantage of the new start. They needed training and support, she thought.

"Bina will be a part of this special night to begin her new life here in Jakarta. And for her final farewell selection for this evening, as is traditional, Dr. O'Farrell will play for us her first Grammy and most beloved award-winning piece, 'Rise to Be You'."

The irony of the song title made Vanessa shake her head and sigh.

The crowd shared nods and smiles and broke into a frenzy of appreciation again. With an elegant sweep of her inviting hand, Fiona smiled and welcomed the little dark-skinned girl from among her classmates to join her at the piano.

The petite waif of a girl awkwardly crossed the stage in her uniform, looking down with pain at her first pair of shoes. Bina lifted her feet and placed them down with great concentration. Her footsteps echoed in the hall's high ceiling.

Fiona delayed the concert. Lifting Bina onto her lap, she removed her shoes and socks and rubbed her tiny feet tenderly until the child smiled. The camera panned the audience members who waited patiently, holding their breaths, soundless—some smiling, some stunned, and some tearing at the touching moment.

Vanessa's eyes filled under Tony's scrutiny as she watched Bina on the screen. "When I was a little girl, I always wanted to play barefoot, but my mother—"

Vanessa stopped, holding back the impending flow of tears.

"Damn, Vanessa, Fiona O'Farrell, queen of the tabloids is your *mother*? Why didn't I see that?" Tony stared at the screen. "How did I miss that resemblance?"

"Shhh!" Canyon pleaded with Tony to be quiet as the music began again.

The camera lens opened wide and zoomed in close to display Fiona's flowing red hair and the face of the American icon. She played to the delight of everyone, and a standing ovation welcomed the well-loved song. The applause began in anticipation of the last note, a note in memory of her long-lost daughter, as Mr. Munadi had announced, "A note that, forever since, had been omitted."

The audience, filled with her admirers from around the world, took in breaths of anticipation, some putting their hands over their hearts or grasping the hands of their loved one. They listened, waiting to hear the well-known, historic, missing note for the first time.

The sound of an explosion rocked the hall as the red and gold blast spread across the screen, swallowing the final note in the deafening sounds. The screen changed to gray buzzing chaos. Vanessa's mind filled with questions as she stared at the gray noise of the screen, trying to comprehend what happened.

Tony grabbed Vanessa. "*Look* at me! Don't assume the worst." He fixed on Vanessa's eyes.

"She wanted me to come. I was going to go to Jakarta. I waited too long. I'm too late for everything now. Tony, she *begged* me!" Vanessa screamed and buried her face in her hands.

"Stay calm. She's OK. I am sure, she's OK." Tony reassured her.

"I'll get the chopper ready," Brad said. "John, is the satellite out or just the feed?"

"We've lost it all, Brad!" the assistant answered.

THE SOUND OF THE private jet's engine droned on with no competition from the passengers inside. The helicopter trip to the small airport had been silent. Now, a few hours out from Jakarta, the plane's radio began to crackle. They had contact. "We are asking for an update on the explosion at the concert hall." Brad turned up the volume. "Any news on Fiona O'Farrell?"

Vanessa numbly stared out of the plane window, steeling herself for the loss.

"Keep the faith, honey." Tony squeezed her moist hand.

"Got it. OK, so the good news is—no bodies were found. No audience members were seriously hurt that they know of, but the children and your mother have disappeared."

"*Disappeared?*" Vanessa's voice was drenched with fear.

Brad called over his shoulder, "You realize they are still in chaos. He'll keep us up to date. We are still two hours out."

Tony pulled her closer. "Van, honey, I suspect that's very good news. It couldn't have been much of an explosion if no one was hurt. Over a thousand people were in attendance. Seems like it wasn't near your mother."

"Maybe it looked worse on our screen than it was." Canyon tried to comfort her friend.

Vanessa unraveled the silver chain, watching the shamrock pendant spin and spin like a hypnotic prayer as they flew on.

CHAPTER 48

LESSONS LEARNED

Vanessa

VANESSA WAS SILENT as they were swept through airport security. The Zell Baxter limousine picked them up at the airport door. Brad asked the driver if he had heard any more news about the explosion.

"Not yet, but the government thinks they know who's behind this. Some disgruntled political group. Had nothing to do with the concert or Dr. O'Farrell. They were after some of the government officials who attended."

"Where is Fiona now?" Tony inquired.

"At the city hospital."

"But I thought no one was hurt?" Vanessa sat forward.

"Apparently, Fiona and the children have been found," the driver said. "Dr. O'Farrell has been taken to the hospital."

"Do we know the extent of her injuries?" Brad probed. "What about the children?"

"No. But it's reported she had the presence of mind to grab the little Irian Jaya girl and gathered all of the children into the underside of the stage through the stage trap door."

"Trap door? Explain, please." Vanessa continued her questioning.

"An exit for theatrical productions. The children are fine—not sure about Dr. O'Farrell's injuries. Apparently, she didn't know if it was safe to come out. Fiona didn't know who to trust. She kept the children silent and eventually escaped with them from the building. They were found later in the new music school," the driver said.

Canyon reached into the seat in front of her and squeezed Vanessa's shoulder. "See, I told you!"

Tony hugged Vanessa. "Like mother, like daughter, always saving the kids."

"Head to the hospital immediately." Scott ordered the driver. "Assuming it's a minor injury, please notify them not to let her leave before we get there."

WHEN THEY ARRIVED at the hospital, they rushed through the emergency entrance.

"Dr. O'Farrell?" Tony paused at the admissions desk.

The nurse on duty checked her list. "Sorry, she is under guard. No visitors, sir."

"Who's in charge?" Tony put his arm around Vanessa.

"What's all this?" A security guard came around the corner. "Oh, Ms. Gold, good evening. I am sorry. Dr. O'Farrell is under protection until we verify and apprehend the people responsible for tonight's explosion at the concert hall. Only family, no exceptions, please, you understand. I am responsible for her safety."

Vanessa stepped closer to the guard. Before she could speak, he laid down the law.

"I know you are a powerful woman, but I must follow the rules. Sorry, no visitors—family only."

"Yes, I understand." Canyon assisted. "Would you kindly tell Dr. O'Farrell that her daughter, Colleen, is here to see her and also Mr. Amorino, her daughter's fiancé?"

The guard looked at Canyon. "Oh, yes, I will tell her." He turned to inspect Canyon again in confusion as he headed down the hall. The guard entered the hospital room and returned with the answer. "Dr. O'Farrell would like to see you, Mr. Amorino, and her daughter." He looked toward Canyon. He put his hand out to push open the door, then blocked Vanessa's entrance. "Ms. Gold, please, this is not news. This is Dr. O'Farrell's safety and privacy. Don't we owe her at least that much after what she has been through in my country?"

"I *am* her daughter!" Vanessa said.

"With all due respect, I have heard that you will do whatever it takes to get what you want, Ms. Gold. Dr. O'Farrell has no daughter to my knowledge except her child who disappeared long ago."

"Ask her, will you please just ask her what I look like? Ask her if I have blonde dreadlocks?"

The confused guard entered the room, came out immediately, and opened the door for Vanessa.

"You owe her safety and *privacy*, as you said, sir." Vanessa smiled with a warmth that she hoped would engage his loyalty. "We wouldn't want our private information in tomorrow's newspapers, would we? For her privacy and safety."

"I understand, Ms. Gold." He had a shocked look on his face. "I will respect your relationship with Dr. O'Farrell."

"Tony, can I go first, alone? Just a few minutes."

"Of course, darling, of course. I'll wait here."

Vanessa entered the dim room, fingering the silver chain and shamrock in her pocket.

Only a slice of sunlight from the window lit the dim room. Fiona rotated her crystal rosary beads between her fingers in bed with her eyes closed.

"Are you awake? It's . . . it's Vanessa." She went a few steps closer. Shouldn't she want to interrogate her mother? How had Fiona come to have her concert in Jakarta at that precise time? It couldn't be just a coincidence. And the explosion? Vanessa looked into her mother's eyes. Something had changed. Where had Vanessa's perpetual anger toward this woman gone? Where was her resentment that had sat in her stomach for decades? "Are you OK?"

"Dear God, you came." Fiona gasped, releasing an anguished sound. "Darling, Colleen. Oh please, sweetheart, may I call you Colleen just this once?" The exhaustion and weakness from the trauma of the explosion were evident in her mother's breathy, labored voice. "I know you have changed your name. I'm so sorry for everything." Fiona extended her bandaged hand. "Did you read my letter?"

"Oh God, your *hand*."

"It's just a minor injury. It will heal."

"What happened?"

"It was burned from the explosion when a flaming piece of the curtain landed on the piano."

The extended silence in the room shook Vanessa. Did she make a mistake assuming there could be healing after all these years?

"My hand will heal, but will *we*?"

It was as if Fiona had read Vanessa's mind. "I . . . hope so, Fiona."

"I'm so sorry that I was a despicable mother—the drugs, my shameful behavior. I don't know if I can ever explain. I don't know if I understand it myself. Not a public persona any child would want for a mother."

Vanessa sat on the edge of the bed. She searched for the anger that had sat on her chest like an anvil her entire adult life. The lightness inside her was unfamiliar. "Are you alright, really?"

"The doctor ran some tests. Just the smoke and the explosion. My lungs will be OK, and my hearing is temporarily affected, but I'll be fine, dear one."

How long had it been since Vanessa had heard that phrase with the edge of Irish inflection, calling her *dear one*? She moved closer and put the shamrock necklace around her mother's neck.

"I'm so sorry. Let me try to explain, please." Her mother sat up.

Why *didn't* Vanessa want to interrogate her mother? Why *didn't* the questions rumble inside her as they always had? "Let's not go there. Can we start from here and move forward?"

Fiona's hand clasped the sentimental treasure. "I love you, dear one. I've been so shameful." She stared out the hospital window.

"There's no need to be." Vanessa didn't want to hear it. Did it matter now?

"No. Please, I need to say this. There's not a single thing I've done right in my life except having you. Well, and hopefully, this children's foundation. I'm so sorry. Can you ever possibly . . ."

The image of Abruce and Lukeem surged through Vanessa. "Shh. Mother, I learned something recently from a native woman in the jungle. A ritual." Vanessa leaned down and pressed her forehead to her mother's. Lifting Fiona's uninjured hand, Vanessa placed it on her chest. She then reciprocated, placing her own hand on her mother's chest, to complete Lukeem's tribal tradition. The rapid rhythm of her mother's heart was all she needed to feel. "I forgive you. And you? Will you forgive me?"

"Oh darlin', your forgiveness is so unexpected, truly, but what is there for me to pardon? You've done nothing but good." Fiona pulled back and studied Vanessa's eyes.

Vanessa's throat thickened with emotion, preventing her from speaking. Looking into her mother's eyes, hearing that familiar touch of an Irish accent, made images flow through Vanessa's mind—like the flickering of the 8mm films from her childhood. They all spoke of love. The memories freed her words. "My lack of courage in reaching out to you all these years; my distancing from Mother Anne Marie to avoid you. For punishing you." The words needed to come out. "I love you, mother. I need you. And I adore what you are doing to change your life." It was like an out-of-body experience—surreal to feel the freedom of non-judgment. The reality of how much Vanessa needed to release the pressures of her own life began to sink in. "Honestly, I need to do the same for different reasons."

"Then I thank the wise woman for her *primitive* ritual." Fiona repeated the gesture, pressing her forehead to Vanessa's, her red hair flowing beside Vanessa's dark locks. Grasping Vanessa's shamrock that hung from her neck, Fiona kissed it. "And I thank my lucky stars."

Stroking her mother's fingers, Vanessa fantasized about sitting at her piano as young Colleen, waiting to play the last note of the senti-mental song. Vanessa felt her finger twitch, heard the final note, and her mother's tender loving voice with her lilting Irish accent. *Beautiful, my dear one.*

"To our future changes, Mom. We have a lot to work out. We're going to argue, the truth will hurt, but for Mother Anne Marie, we'll reveal our truths without judgment."

"Vanessa." Fiona touched Vanessa's lips. "You called me, *Mom.*"

The door to the hospital room opened slowly, and Tony entered. He walked hesitantly toward the two women as if he were uncertain that he was welcome.

Vanessa met him at the door, took Tony by the arm, and, smiling, rested her head against his shoulder. "Mom, this is Tony Amorino, my best friend, lover, life partner, my everything, I guess." Before he could respond, Vanessa added, "And fiancé, if he'll still have me?"

She looked at Tony questioningly.

"Such a tease, your daughter. I asked on bended knee, and she answered me a mere decade later."

"So you are the one who has been taking care of my baby all these years." Fiona opened her arms.

Tony walked to her bed, and Fiona hugged him, then held his face with one hand. "Thank you. I'm grateful since I failed for the most part in that department. If you should ever have a child, I promise to be a dedicated, well-behaved grandmother."

"Ma'am, I'm afraid that ship has sailed for us." He turned to pull

Vanessa closer. "And we're pretty much committed to our work on behalf of other people's children. In fact, like *you* now, Fiona—if I can call you that."

Vanessa smiled, but didn't respond. She thought of Abruce and Lukeem and the intimacy they shared, the sacrifice they were willing to make for each other, and the forgiveness they so easily offered each other after years of separation and change. Vanessa regretted denying Tony the life he wanted with her. And admittedly, beneath all of her fears and secrets, Vanessa had wanted that life too.

"Mom, I have a photo I want to share with you." Vanessa took out the picture of Maureen, the child from their foster system documentary—the one who'd stolen Tony's heart and charmed Vanessa months before. That private moment she'd planned with Tony to discuss the decision had never presented itself.

And wasn't this about family? She didn't want to spring it on Tony. But after he'd announced he was willing to compromise for Vanessa's sake, give up everything he'd wanted for her, Vanessa couldn't hold it in any longer. He so deserved to have the child he ached for, and she needed to stop running from herself.

"We might take a practice run, mother. There was a child named Maureen we met through our work with the foster care system. Tony and I both seemed to bond with her. So, I thought maybe we should explore the . . . well, we'll see. I confess, Tony and I need to discuss it. But I submitted an inquiry to adopt on our behalf. Is that OK, honey?" She touched his face and studied his eyes, hoping for a positive response.

"But what about your career? *Exposé*?"

"I have a new concept called *Confessions*. Imagine how many people like me are out there suffering."

Tony released a quick laugh and took Vanessa into his arms.

"I'll take that response as a resounding yes."

"Will you need a cameraman?" Tony winked.

The nurse stepped in. "I hate to disturb you, but would anyone like some good news? You're being released today, Dr. O'Farrell."

"Bless you. I'm so grateful."

"Oh, mother, that's so wonderful." Hesitating, she imagined her mother playing in the music room, resurrecting the love and trust they'd once shared. Before she could ask Tony, he nodded. In so many ways, he truly did know the real Vanessa. "You'll come home and recover with us in LA, won't you?"

"You can join Vanessa on her flight back. We need to bring some music into our home." Tony winked. "Although I understand my soon-to-be-wife has a hidden talent to share."

"I'd be honored, Tony." Fiona kissed the scars on Vanessa's hand.

"Wait, mother, I need to know one thing."

"What is it?"

Should she ask? Did Vanessa really want to know if her mother had anything to do with the explosion? Such a drastic strategy to reconnect with her estranged daughter. Sick, even. No, Fiona was flawed, but she would never purposely put a child at risk. Or was anyone ever really at risk? Wasn't it slightly suspicious that no one was hurt? The random piece of curtain that burned her mother's hand? And right before the full moon? Vanessa's investigative instincts were driving her. Or were they old habits that no longer had a place in Vanessa's new world?

Everything was in such a good place now. Vanessa thought of Lukeem's lessons in forgiveness. But she'd already committed to having her mother stay in her own home. Could Vanessa handle the truth? It would all come out in the exposé. Maybe just wait. No. That meant starting Vanessa's new life out with another lie. She had to be able to trust her mother. Didn't she?

"Colleen, sorry, Vanessa, your silence is unnerving, I confess." Fiona reached out for her. "Seems we both have so many truths to expose, my daughter. But there's time for that. I'll tell you everything. I promise."

Her mother's suggestion to delay sharing the truth momentarily raised that sick, churning feeling—Vanessa's instinctual, suspicious reaction whenever she heard something that had that questionable air. She couldn't even conjure the chaos she would face in the limelight. But something was different, she realized. Wasn't it all in the turning prism? Didn't it all depend on how you turned the lens? Hadn't Scott's perspective changed how Vanessa now viewed her grandfather's death? Was she anyone to judge?

CHAPTER 49

FINAL EXPOSÉ

Vanessa

"I NEED TO TALK TO Edward." Vanessa huddled into Tony's arms in the back seat of the helicopter. "Wait, did he contact you while you were searching for me in the mountains?"

"No, but sweetheart, you don't have to do this great reveal now! You need to let yourself adjust to all of this. You need *time*, Van. *We* need time to—"

"To get to know each other?" Hers was a story she couldn't fathom herself, she thought.

Releasing a short laugh, Tony shook his head. "Unreal."

Unravelling her history would be a challenge. The lies and truths had enmeshed so tightly into the woven fabric of her life over the years. Even Vanessa couldn't always distinguish fact from fiction. Vanessa would have to retell her entire story, resurrect her true memories to share with him, with everyone.

"Tony, who am I now?"

He tilted his head and paused.

Would Vanessa forever hold her breath whenever Tony hesitated? Would she ever forgive herself, even if he forgave her?

"Whoever you want to be."

His answer left her floating in an expanse, like the view outside the window. As they flew over the razorback road along the crest of the vast panorama of mountains, the whole experience seemed surreal. How had an American mining company found its way into this remote and treacherous jungle world? How had that one fateful, mistaken supply drop in World War II changed the lives of an entire population that might otherwise have been left untouched for centuries? And how in the world had it all led Vanessa to connect to Scott and reconnect with her mother again? She sighed. "You're right, Tony, there is no rush for a great reveal. I know it could destroy all of us. How do I come clean without hurting the people I love the most?"

"That's not my concern, darling."

"*What*?" Vanessa anticipated the worst again. She put her face in her hands, imagining the trauma she'd caused Tony. Would she ever trust that he could still love her?

"There's only one thing that could devastate my life. I realized that one thing when I saw your substitute-self tumbling down that cliff. I told you, it put everything in context."

"What is the *one* thing?"

"It's missing out on the life we deserve together. What did you think I meant?"

"I . . . thank you. I'm so grateful for your forgiveness, Tony. And while our careers are being devastated, we will have a family and each other."

"Vanessa, being married, having a child doesn't mean giving up your good work. I'll be damned if I will take responsibility for that. Your dreams matter too. We just need a redirect, a rewrite of our script, that's all. Something you do so well for so many." Tony wrapped his arm around Vanessa and kissed her forehead. "Let's bring the lens in tight here, Van. Focus on returning to the site to gather up our things. Then we should take a little time to digest all this change— your mother and possibilities with Maureen and your new concept, *Confessions*. I think it will be a hit. You know what they say, do what you know. It's huge. You'll have the entire flight home to reconnect and resolve things with your mother."

"As soon as we hit LA, the press will be all over this." Vanessa looked forward to the relief she would experience, yet she felt crushed by the notion. "I can handle it, right?"

"Yes. And for now, let's give *us* some breathing room. And you're tougher than your past, Vanessa."

"God, I've destroyed everyone's reputation, Tony. But I'm ready to own that and accept the consequences. Make amends."

Canyon twisted around and chimed in from the front seat next to Brad. "Van, you won't *destroy* mine. Look what you brought into my life." She nodded toward Brad. "Come to think of it, maybe I should stay here for a while. A little follow-up research. I know an American mining company that needs a little cross-cultural training." Canyon flipped her braids over her shoulder.

Her best friend's signature flirtatious move had always made Vanessa smile. "And then there's you, Canyon. You're never afraid to take a risk and you always know what you want." Vanessa patted her shoulder.

"But this is the first time I might get what I *need*."

"I'll vote for that. And I know a pilot who can give you a ride home." Brad took Canyon's hand.

"Wait, what about his name starting with the letter F?" Vanessa couldn't resist.

"What's that about?" Brad turned to Canyon.

"It's a long story. The stars say the man I was to fall in love with was supposed to have a name that started with an F. So I guess we have a problem."

"Fall in love?" Brad went silent. "Wait." His head whipped to Canyon. "My grandfather nicknamed me Flash as a kid—for Flash Gordon. Does that qualify?"

"Works for me, Flash." Canyon stroked Brad's hair.

Vanessa took in a slow, deep breath. The warmth of Canyon's happy moment was a respite from her burning thoughts, and her friend's bravery and spontaneity in pursuing what she wanted, as always, was inspiring to Vanessa. "I hate to intrude, but Brad, I need to talk to my assistant, Eddie. Can you do that for me?"

"No problem, I'll connect you." He stretched around and handed her the headphones. "It'll take time to link through to the States."

Vanessa couldn't miss the look on Tony's face. "Tony, I'm sorry. I just need to get things started. If we want to redesign our life, I need to get it all out in the open, let the press do what they do, be brave, then move on . . . with you, my mother, and maybe Maureen. But I want us to take our life back. There's a dresser back home that needs a family photo." She put on the headphones.

"EDDIE, HOW ARE YOU, my dear friend?" Vanessa began.

"*Dear friend*? So sweet. What happened to my sassy boss over there in the jungle? Oh, my Lord, Vanessa. I've been waiting for this call. Not a word leaked on the news since you arrived there. Not like you. Wait, first things first. You're safe, right?"

"We're all fine."

"And you saved her, right? Tell me you saved that poor woman."

"We did."

"Fantastic, you rock!"

Vanessa could almost feel Eddie's frenetic tension change to elation through the line.

"Are you sending the footage ahead? Did you build one of your incredible cultural bridges? Oh, this is my favorite part of the job. What happened to you over there, Ms. Truth in News?"

"It's a very long story." Vanessa almost relished initiating her own public confession. It made her laugh. "We'll be delayed a week." She squeezed Tony's hand. "Tony and I are stopping in Bali for a respite first. We need a break. Then Eddie, schedule all four, please."

"Slam dunk. The Quad Squad? This is big—in what order?"

"Oprah, Diane, Barbara, and Larry—that sequence should follow their airtime schedules. And please make me an appointment with—"

"I know, your hairdresser. You must be a mess, Ms. Jungle."

"Tell her I want to come clean—she'll know what I mean."

"You sound different, Ms. Truth in News. Come on, share. I've been dying. Are you sending the footage ahead for a documentary? Will we have an *Exposé* episode out of this too? Some primitive, savage American? Who is he?"

"Not he, *she*. And there is no film, Edward."

"What? No gut-wrenching exposé?"

Vanessa looked at Tony.

He sighed, and huffed a short laugh.

She palmed Tony's cheek and mouthed, "Are you sure?"

He nodded his approval.

"Oh, there's plenty of that. And gut-wrenching for sure. The juiciest, most shocking exposé yet, Eddie. Better yet, the culprit agreed to appear live on *Exposé*."

"You go, girl!"

"Oh, and there will be a willing special guest, too. The woman's mother."

"So *give*! Who is the evil, unsuspecting villainess we'll crush like a bug? Who's your next scandalous star of *Exposé*?"

"I am."

The End